By Jean Rabe

DRAGONS OF A NEW AGE

The Dawning of a New Age

The Day of the Tempest

The Eve of the Maelstrom

BRIDGES OF TIME

The Silver Stair

THE DHAMON SAGA

Downfall

Betrayal

Redemption

(July 2002)

BETRAYAL

The Dhamon Saga • Volume Two

Jean Rabe

BETRAYAL

©2001 Wizards of the Coast, Inc.

Distributed in the United States by St. Martin's Press. Distributed in Canada by Fenn Ltd.

Distributed to the hobby, toy, and comic trade in the United States and Canada by regional distributors.

Distributed worldwide by Wizards of the Coast, Inc. and regional distributors.

DRAGONLANCE and the Wizards of the Coast logo are registered trademarks owned by Wizards of the Coast, Inc.

All Wizards of the Coast characters, character names, and the distinctive likenesses thereof are trademarks owned by Wizards of the Coast, Inc.

Made in the U.S.A.

Cover art by Jerry Vander Stelt
First Printing: June 2001
Library of Congress Catalog Card Number: 00-103752

9 8 7 6 5 4 3 2 1

ISBN: 0-7869-1860-8
620-WTC21860

U.S., CANADA,
ASIA, PACIFIC, & LATIN AMERICA
Wizards of the Coast, Inc.
P.O. Box 707
Renton, WA 98057-0707
+1-800-324-6496

EUROPEAN HEADQUARTERS
Wizards of the Coast, Belgium
P.B. 2031
2600 Berchem
Belgium
+32-70-23-32-77

Visit our web site at **www.wizards.com/dragonlance**

Dedication

For the Milwaukee Summer Revelers

Kevin and Keith, who started it all,

Dave, who happily came along for the ride,

Rick, who oh-so-aptly took over at the helm,

and Steve, who has discovered a fondness for second place.

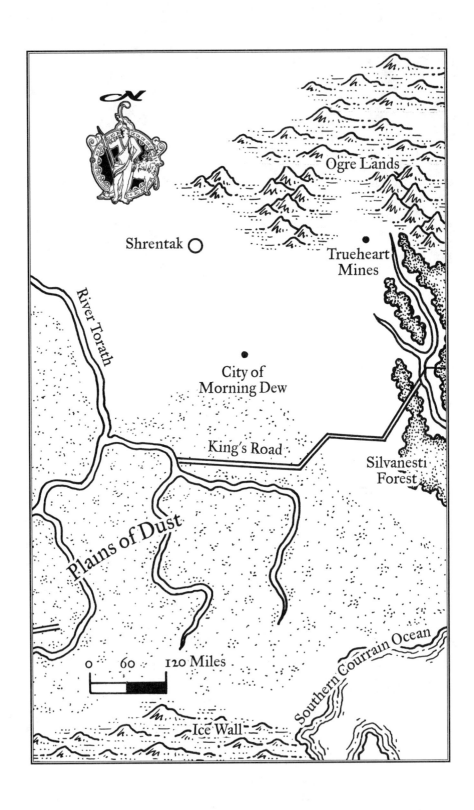

Ogre Lands

Shrentak ○

Trueheart
Mines

River Torath

•
City of
Morning Dew

King's Road

Silvanesti
Forest

Plains of Dust

Southern Courrain Ocean

0   60   120 Miles

Ice Wall

CHAPTER ONE
NURA'S CHOICE

nside the cave the darkness was an impenetrable blanket that cloaked the creature sleeping within. Only its breath gave it away—this raspy and uneven, echoing hauntingly against the stone walls and escaping as a breeze to tease the coppery curls of the child who stood just beyond the entrance.

She was no more than five or six, cherubic and clothed in a diaphanous dress that at first glance appeared to be fashioned of pale flower petals, but on closer inspection seemed instead to shimmer as if it were made of magic. The fingers of her left hand were clenched about the haft of a glaive, an axe-bladed pole-arm more than twice her height that looked far too unwieldy for her to manage. The fingers of her right hand playfully stroked the giant fern leaves that helped to conceal the cave mouth. The green of the ferns was intense, brightened by a fiery late afternoon sun and made slick with humidity. Droplets of water beaded and gleamed like diamonds.

"Mumummmm-ummm," she sang when she spotted a furry caterpillar, striped orange and golden-brown, standing out starkly against a diamond-dotted frond. She stared at it for several long moments, then gently picked it up and held it before her wide, blue eyes. "Soft," she pronounced. "Very pretty." The thing slowly wriggled, and in response she laughed in a voice that was not at all childlike. She popped the caterpillar into her mouth and swallowed it, just as she stepped inside the cave and was swallowed by the darkness.

"Master?" she whispered, as she instinctively padded forward, her bare feet slapping against the stone. It was an enormous cave, whose depths she couldn't guess, no matter if dozens of torches had been merrily burning. It was one of several the creature had in this part of Krynn, all connected through underground tunnels that the child was occasionally permitted to wander. This particular cave was the most familiar to her.

Though well shielded from the sun, the interior was stifling, the air damp and close and filled with the strong, sweet-sour stench of decay. The child inhaled deeply, holding and relishing the scent, then almost reluctantly releasing it.

"Master?"

A pause, then again she repeated the word, no longer a question now, as she effortlessly tossed the glaive to the floor, its blade clanging against the stone. In response, twin globes of dull yellow appeared in the middle of the blackness. They were eyes, larger than wagon wheels and cut through by murky catlike slits. Though there was a thick film on them, they gave off a faint light, eerie and just enough to illuminate the creature's massive snout and the child who was dwarfed by it. The girl stood on her toes and reverently stretched a hand up to graze the edge of the creature's jaw.

"You summoned me, O Very Old One?" Her voice was husky now and had an edge to it, a sultry woman's voice.

The creature's raspy breath was broken by a rumbling of words so sonorous and loud they caused a tremor to ripple through the ground. "Nura Bint-Drax," it said, each syllable excruciatingly drawn out and returning as an echo. "Nura. My very young servant."

"Your chosen one." The child smiled and shifted back and forth on the balls of her feet, spread her arms wide. She turned her head this way and that so the hot breeze of the creature's fetid breath could wash over her. "Your very loyal servant."

There were no more words for a time. The creature silently regarded the child, and the child basked in the creature's presence. Then the great eyes blinked, and the child haltingly stepped back, thin arms falling to her sides, shoulders squaring, unblemished face fixed forward, standing like a soldier at attention.

The rumbling started again. The words came so ponderously slow that the child had to concentrate to understand.

"Yes, Master. I have made a selection, a most suitable one. You will be quite pleased."

She felt the next question as much as heard it, the tremors shivering through the stone floor and tickling the bottoms of her feet.

"His name is Dhamon Grimwulf, Master. A human."

There was another silence, this one seemingly interminable, as Nura's legs and arms tingled from remaining straight and motionless for so long. She breathed shallowly and somehow managed not to blink. Finally, the creature's breath quickened and it raised its head, tucking its jaw into its neck and tilting it so as to look sharply down upon the child, eyes narrowing disapprovingly.

"A human," the creature stated, the two words uttered with such contempt and power that when the

3

ground shook this time Nura had to struggle to keep her balance.

The child bravely thrust out her chin. "Yes, Master. Dhamon is a human, but he is the one, I believe."

The creature growled, as bits of rock and dust fell from overhead like the beginning of rain. "You are certain, Nura Bint-Drax? You have no doubts?"

"He is the one." She tipped her head, and a corner of her mouth turned slightly upward. "I have been testing him, O Very Old One."

"I know." The ground vibrated softly this time, as though the creature was purring. It opened its eyes wide again, giving light to the cave interior. "Tell me of this. . . ."

"Dhamon Grimwulf." Nura's head angled back as far as she could manage, her wide child's eyes meeting the creature's steady gaze. "He was a Knight of Takhisis, Master, a commander of men. Once he rode a great blue dragon into battle, but he turned from the Dark Knights, anointed by the powerful goodness of an aging Solamnic, further touched by Goldmoon, who made him her champion. This is proof he can be swayed."

Nura paused, picking through the complex rumbling that followed. "Yes, Master. Dhamon Grimwulf was that man, the one who led a band of mortals to the Window to the Stars to confront the five dragon overlords. He was victorious that day, though not a single dragon died. Victorious because he took a stand and lived. A pity he did not recognize what he had achieved."

The rumbling intensified, and Nura put all her effort into keeping her balance and deciphering the words. When the ground quieted, the child waved her hands in front of her face and shook her head. "No, O Very Old One, he is Goldmoon's champion no longer. He no longer struggles against the overlords. Now he has no cares beyond his own pleasure. There are very few who call him friend."

4

"A fallen hero," the creature stated.

"Yes, Master."

"A common thief." There was a near-painful skritching sound, of something sharp being scraped across the stone, then a throaty growl that encouraged her to continue.

"Master, I believe Dhamon Grimwulf's spirit and honor died when he decided the dragon overlords were unstoppable. His beliefs in a better world and in himself as a catalyst to achieve that are buried deep in his heart. Hope does not exist for him."

The creature canted its head and gave a nod.

"Dhamon has been battered by life . . . or rather by a living death that seems to pursue him and instead claim the lives of close friends and charges. To be close to Dhamon Grimwulf is to risk corruption and death, it seems."

She moved closer to the creature, as it lowered its great head so she could tease the barbels that hung from its chin. "A young green dragon slew his men in the Qualinesti Forest," Nura added. "Then Dhamon killed his own second-in-command in the throes of drunken self-defense. Though there are many things that have gone wrong in his life, I think that act was the final blow that turned him completely inward. He has lost confidence in himself and in Krynn. Yes, he is a fallen hero, Master. But he is the one."

The creature closed its eyes, and the cave was plunged into darkness. Vibrations raced through the stone, intense and echoing. The child clamped her hands over her ears and stepped away. The creature rested its head on the floor, and eventually the vibrations slowed, before ceasing, to be replaced by the raspy uneven breath of its slumber. When it awoke several hours later, the child was patiently sitting nearby. The eerie light of the creature's eyes showed Nura's own eyes sparkling with anticipation.

"More," the creature stated.

"Regarding Dhamon Grimwulf?"

"Yes. More. You must do more so that I can be certain."

Nura digested the words and put a meaning to them. "You wish me to test him further, Master?"

There was a harsh grating sound that the child understood as affirmative.

"Indeed I shall test him more," Nura said, the excitement thick in her voice. "I shall test him to the very limits of his existence. If he dies, I shall have been proved wrong, and I shall search for another. If he does not die, and if he can be thoroughly broken, swayed to our side, made useful . . . ." She let the words hang in the foul air. "If this Dhamon Grimwulf can survive my tests . . ."

". . . then indeed he is the one," the creature finished. It turned its head, eyes looking past Nura and to a wall of mist that was forming before the cave mouth.

The child wheeled to see what it was the creature was observing in its magical vision. Forming across the face of the mist were trees and ferns and gently-swaying lianas, the varieties indicating the scene was far from this cave. It was night in the image, but there was the faintest hint of a flickering light.

"It must be a torch," the child said. A moment later her keen eyes recognized the torch-bearer, and she softly laughed. "That human woman with the red hair," she stated, "and the dark man who follows her . . . they are of no consequence to us."

The creature snarled almost imperceptibly.

"As you wish, O Very Old One. I will attend to them. I live to serve you."

CHAPTER TWO
FIONA'S IRE

"D" amn Dhamon Grimwulf, damn him to the Abyss!" the Solamnic Knight Fiona cursed as she plunged deeper into the swamp. "If I hadn't trusted him and his ogre friend, we'd be out of this ghastly place by now. We must be miles from Shrentak. Damn him!"

She was threading her way through a tangle of vines and working to skirt a moss-choked pond. The guttering torch she carried chased shadows up trees. Chittering insects swarmed around her as she held the torch close in a futile effort to chase them away—but that only made her hotter. Despite it being well past sunset, the swamp was steamy with the brutal heat of a particularly hot summer. The heat was suffocating and had caused her to abandon her precious plate mail. Sweat plastered her long red hair against her face and glued her tattered leggings and tabard to her skin. She shrugged out of the shredded remains of her cloak and tossed it aside, a gesture which did nothing to cool her off. Her feet were so sweaty inside her leather boots that they slipped with each step, creating painful blisters.

She breathed deep, trying to clear her lungs. Instead the heat and the moisture dug in, taking root in her chest and making her mouth and throat feel sticky. Her head pounded.

"Fiona, wait!"

She barely heard the words, and hadn't realized that Rig Mer-Krel had shouted her name three times. She paused, allowing him to catch up.

"Fiona, this is madness! We shouldn't be traveling in the swamp at night. That torch is a beacon to whatever's hungry and lying out there waiting for us. Might as well be ringing the cook's bell in the galley—one sea barbarian and one Solamnic Knight served up to order. Young and lean, downright tasty!"

She scowled and turned to face her comrade. Rig's dark skin was slick with sweat, and his vest and pants were so wet they looked as if they were painted on him. His expression remained stern only for a moment longer, his eyes softening as they caught hers.

"Fiona, we—"

"It's cooler at night," she said stubbornly. "I want to keep going."

He opened his mouth to argue with her, then stopped himself. He knew from the set of her jaw that the words would be wasted.

"Besides," she continued, "I'm not tired. Not much, anyway. I want to make some progress toward Shrentak."

That last word sent a shiver down the mariner's spine. The ruined city of Shrentak was the lair of Sable, the massive black dragon overlord who had turned this once-temperate land into a fetid swamp and claimed it and every creature in it as her own.

"As long as Solamnic Knights are being held in Sable's dungeons, I don't want to waste time," Fiona said. She frowned, brushing away gnats that had landed and become glued to the sweat on her face. "Perhaps my brother is there too, in Shrentak—alive, or dead, as you saw in the vision."

"I want to free them as much as you do, Fiona. Going after the knights—and whoever else is prisoner there— that was as much my idea as yours."

"Damn Dhamon Grimwulf."

He reached a finger up to nudge a dampened curl away from her eyes and noticed that she was holding back tears.

"I believed him, Rig. Trusted him. He and Maldred, that . . . that . . ."

"Ogre. I know," he said, tracing her lower lip with his thumb. "I guess some part of me believed them, too. Or at least wanted to."

Weeks ago Fiona had sought out Dhamon Grimwulf, despite knowing that the once honorable hero had fallen in with thieves and worse. She needed to raise a ransom to free her brother from Sable's clutches, and she hit upon Dhamon as the possible means to do so. After all, the Solamnic Council had refused to help. Dhamon had involved her in a certain errand for Donnag, the ogre-chieftain of Blöde. The errand, which involved killing some trolls in the mountains, yielded a chest full of coins and gems for her to use as a ransom.

Dhamon, his friend Maldred, and forty ogre guards were assigned to escort the ransom. Rather, that's what they said were doing. In truth, Dhamon and his friends were headed to Sable's silver mines, where many of Donnag's ogres were being worked to death as slaves. The chest of coins and gems was just a ruse to get her and Rig to come along and help. The ogre-chieftain had been impressed with her and the mariner's skills and wanted to add their sword arms to the mission. It wasn't until they reached the clearing outside the silver mine that she realized she'd been duped.

"Tricked," she hissed now at Rig, recalling it all so clearly.

She would have left Dhamon and the others right then and there, and that night she ought to have stormed off to Shrentak. But she abhorred slavery, so she had decided to help free the ogres first.

"I was lied to by Dhamon, people I had faith in."

They had battled spawn and draconians to free the ogres, along with a smattering of humans and dwarves also held as slaves. In the aftermath of the fight, a strange child with copper-colored hair appeared and cast a spell that trapped her and Rig and wrapped itself around Maldred and changed him. "Revealing him," the waif had said in an eerie voice. "Chasing away the spell that paints a beautiful human form over his ugly ogre body. Revealing the son of Donnag—my mistress's enemy!"

When the transformation was complete, Maldred stood more than nine feet tall, an ogre more awesome and physically imposing than any of the ogres with them. His human-sized clothes fell in tatters, barely covering his massive body. Fiona stared. Maldred, the human-looking Maldred, had made her feel things for him, trust him, made her doubt her love for Rig.

"Lies," she repeated now bitterly to Rig. "It was all lies. The ransom was never mine to keep. Maldred was never human. Dhamon was never trustworthy. Lies. Lies. All of it. . . ."

Her cruel work done, the child had melted away into mists of the swamp, taking Rig's magical glaive with her. Dhamon and Maldred announced they would escort the freed slaves back to Donnag, inviting Fiona and Rig to come with them. It would be safer. Instead, the Solamnic marched off into the swamp, Rig following. Maldred and Dhamon had called out to them for a time, until their voices grew distant and the animal and insect noises finally drowned them out.

"Damn Dhamon Grimwulf." Fiona whirled to resume her trek. "And Maldred, too. Damn the lying lot of them."

"I never did like Dhamon," Rig muttered as he fell in step behind her. He added softly, after they had traveled only a short distance, "I would like to get my glaive back."

The ground was marshy, thick with mud and rotting plants. It pulled at their heels with each step. Walking was hard work, but the harsh conditions only made Fiona more determined.

A sudden gust of wind whipped out of nowhere and extinguished her torch. The inky blackness of Sable's swamp reached out and covered them from all directions. The air stilled. The leafy canopy high above them was so dense no hint of starlight filtered down. Everything was blackest black.

"Fiona?"

"Shhh."

"Fiona, I can't see anything."

"I know."

"I don't hear anything either."

"I know. That's the problem."

The insects had stopped buzzing. The silence was unnerving. The silence, the heat, the darkness, and the dampness of the place. A prickly sensation ran down the Solamnic's spine, a feeling that suggested someone or something was watching them. Something that could see without any problem in this cavelike blackness.

Rig had never considered himself a man to scare easily. He had a respectable fear of the dragons and of strong storms at sea. He didn't fear much else. Now, though, he felt a horrible, constricting fear. He considered grabbing Fiona and retreating and wondered if he could even manage to retrace his steps and find his way back to the clearing with the silver mine.

He wondered if they might yet catch up with Dhamon and Maldred. Rig knew Fiona had to be frightened, too. He hated the notion of rejoining Maldred and Dhamon, but it would be the prudent thing to do. It was suicide to stand here practically helpless in the dark.

The insects resumed their constant drone, and the irritating noise made them both breathe a little easier.

"Can't see a damn thing, Fiona," Rig grumbled. "Not even the hand in front of my face. Maybe we should go back to the clearing. Get some torches. Maybe there's some lanterns in the mine. Maybe some food. We left too fast, without collecting something to eat."

"No. No. No."

"Fine." Rig let out a deep breath, the wind whistling through his clenched teeth.

"There has to be a clearing somewhere ahead where we'll be able to see." She dropped the useless torch and flailed about with her hand until she found Rig and laced her fingers with his.

They pressed on like blind people, brushing by the thick trunk of a shaggybark, slogging through a stagnant pool of water, wincing as thorn bushes scratched their legs. They walked through an enormous spiderweb and had to stop for several minutes to pull off the gummy mass.

"Just a little farther," Fiona whispered, determined to put more miles between herself and the silver mines. "Farther . . . away from Dhamon and Maldred."

A great cat snarled in the distance. Closer, something hissed. Directly overhead, a branch rustled, though there was no breeze in the swamp. A stench hung in the air, perhaps a large animal rotting nearby. There was the strong, pungent odor of dead plants decaying in the loamy marsh. The hot air and overall oppressive scent of this great bog nearly caused Fiona to gag.

"A little farther, Rig. Just a little . . . ."

"So hot," he said. The mariner was listening to a bird with an odd, throaty call, to frogs croaking noisily, to something making a rhythmic clacking sound. He wished for a breeze, another lone gust of wind, anything to stir up the air.

Fiona's pace slowed, her body admitting a fatigue her mind railed against. They stumbled over logs and fallen vines and blindly groped their way through clumps of willow- birches. A break in the canopy above painted their world in shifting grays.

Not starlight, Rig could tell, for the bit of sky was lightening, heading toward dawn. It was a welcome, if brief, change, however. They passed beyond the break, plunging again into utter darkness. Suddenly the mariner tensed. He gently squeezed Fiona's hand.

"What?" she asked.

"I hear something."

"Maldred? Dhamon?"

He shook his head, then realized she couldn't even see him. "I don't think so. Doesn't sound like boots. Hear it?" His voice was so soft she had to strain to catch it. "I think . . ."

He dropped her hand and took a few steps away from her, drew his sword and swung hard in a wide arc, the blade whistling in the air and glancing off . . . something. Wood? A tree? The mariner desperately needed to see!

There was more rustling, to the side this time, followed by a snarl that trailed off into a loud hiss. Rig spun and swung again, connecting with something softer. His unseen foe howled, the rustling plants hinting that the thing was trying to circle around behind them. What were they up against?

"Fiona! Stay put!" he shouted. "I don't want to strike you by mistake."

Rig heard the hiss of the Solamnic's sword being drawn, and he concentrated on the soft sounds in front of him, the leaves being brushed aside. He pivoted on the balls of his feet, following the sound and thrusting forward. Nothing! He pulled back and stabbed farther to his right. Another howl, and this time Rig knew he'd seriously wounded the creature, as acidic blood sprayed out, sizzling against the foliage and splashing against his arm.

"Ow!" Rig shouted. "Fiona! It's a damnable draconian. Stay put!"

Fiona heard noises in another direction, and she shifted her weight from foot to foot, listening intently. "Two draconians, Rig," she corrected. "You stay put, too!"

"Not draconiansss," a voice to her right hissed. "We are ssspawn."

"Draconians, spawn, what's the difference?" Rig spat. "You're monsters."

Fiona whirled, tripping over an exposed root and flying forward. But her fingers held tight to her sword, which was extended and somehow grazed spawn flesh. There were more sloshing footsteps, a series of hissing growls. There were more than two of them, she instantly realized.

How many?

She scrambled to her feet, swinging wildly to keep the creatures back, or, better yet, to hurt them. She grazed something again, an angry snarl vouching that it was a spawn and not the mariner. At the same time, she felt sharp claws dig into her back. Fiona bit down on her lip to keep from crying out.

"Woman is clumsssy," one cackled.

"Man clumsssy, too," another added.

"At least I'm not ugly," Rig countered. He wanted Fiona to hear his voice so she'd know where he was. "And you're about as ugly as anything gets."

Though he couldn't see them, he knew what they looked like: hulking manlike creatures with claws and wings, covered in glossy black scales.

There was movement directly in front of him now. Lunging forward, he felt his sword sink deep into muscular flesh. He rammed the weapon in up to the hilt and found himself drenched with stinging acid. He knew that black spawn exploded in a burst of acid as they died, and he wondered if the burning acid would leave scars.

"One down, Fiona!" he announced. How many more to go? Without pause, he blindly swung again and again, striking another and slaying it, too.

How many of them? his mind screamed.

There was another sound directly in front of him again, and he jabbed the sword forward, guessing he struck one in the chest. It, too, burst into acid. At the same time, a spawn behind him stepped in and bit down hard on his shoulder, clawing at his arms and trying to pin him down. Another was batting at his sword, trying to knock it from his grip.

"Ssspawn kill man. Man should not kill ssspawn," the creature behind him hissed. "Man should not kill my sisssters." The creature bit him again. This time it clamped down and did not let go.

Rig managed to thrust the blade forward, somehow in the darkness finding another spawn. The sword lodged firmly in the thing, and he dropped to his knees, his weight pulling the sword loose while also tearing himself free from the jaws of the creature behind him. Struggling to rise, he swept the blade in a forward arc and again was rewarded with a howl and a painful shower of acid. Behind him, he heard one creature crashing away through the foliage.

Rig flailed about. No more spawn, no trees, only vines that sought to entangle him. He turned again and barely

15

caught himself from stumbling over a broken tree limb. Leading with the sword and edging forward, he made his way past the limb and through a swath of branches and mud.

"Rig? Rig!" Fiona was panting, thoroughly spent and in agony from the burning acid unleashed by the spawn she'd killed. "They're gone. Dead or gone." Fiona sheathed her sword and felt around until she found a tree to lean against. "Rig?"

"I'm here," came the exhausted reply. "Wherever here is. Keep talking so I can find you."

It took several minutes, before they found themselves at the base of the same tree. Rig boosted her up, urging that it was safer than resting on the ground. Climbing was torture, straining wounds and already overtaxed muscles. Somehow they made it to thick, low limbs, ones they could straddle with their backs propped against the trunk. They emptied one of their water skins trying to wash away the acid. Nearly all the other water was shared down their throats.

"You know, there might be snakes—or worse—in this tree," Fiona said.

"Only thing worse than a snake is Dhamon Grimwulf," came Rig's hoarse reply.

"Right. Damn him. If I hadn't trusted him, hoped that he could help me . . . ."

"Fiona, with luck we'll never see him again."

"Yes, but maybe we shouldn't have parted company with them quite so quick," Fiona mused, her voice a cracked whisper. "I shouldn't have let my anger guide me. Maybe we should've got some food first. Found some extra water skins. Maybe. . . . Oh, I don't know."

Rig knew she couldn't see his shrug. He rested one hand on the pommel of his sword. The other arm he looped about a branch to help steady himself. He closed his eyes, and despite his aches and his pain-wracked shoulder where the spawn had bitten him, within a few heartbeats he was soundly asleep.

"You were right, Rig. At least we shouldn't have left the clearing without taking a few torches with us," Fiona said after a while. "Shouldn't have trusted Dhamon." She paused when she heard the mariner gently snoring. "Should have never doubted you," she added softly. "I really do love you, Rig."

They woke well into the morning, still sore from the fight, wounds festering. Fiona insisted they move again before Rig could even attempt to find breakfast. The mariner decided he could wait a few hours to eat. Before he knew it the day had melted away. As the light began to fade, they sought another tree to pass the night. Fiona was eyeing a dying shaggybark with wide limbs when Rig pointed through a gap in a veil of willow leaves.

"There's a light over there. Low to the ground and wide, like it's a campfire. Smells like something's cooking over it, too. We should take a closer look." His stomach growled. He hadn't eaten in well more than forty-eight hours.

"Hope we didn't get turned around in the dark," Fiona said. "Solamnus knows, we could very well be lost. Hope it's not Dhamon and Maldred's campfire." A small part of her hoped that it was. She'd rehearsed several times in her mind a tirade she would unleash on them.

She took a deep breath and brushed aside the leaves and edged a few steps closer to the fire.

Chapter Three
Glittering Promises

T he inn fire crackled softly behind Dhamon Grimwulf, tinging the air with the sharp smoky scent of too-green birch and the more welcome fragrance of slowly roasting pig. Both scents were more pleasurable than the other odors present: ogre sweat and the unidentifiable smell of food and drink that had been spilled who knew how long ago and never wiped up.

"Dhamon, it's much too hot today to have a fire going like that." The grumbling came from Maldred, a giant of a man with a shock of sun-lightened hair that spilled low over his brow. Beads of sweat liberally dotted his bronzed skin. He sighed, shook his head, and pulled his chair a few inches closer to the table—and thereby a few inches farther away from the flames. "Hot," he repeated, the word sounding like a curse. "I ought to tell the proprietor to douse this fire. It's just too damned hot."

"Aye, my friend, this end of summer is a particularly spiteful beast. But I fancy having some of that pig for dinner, and so I'll tolerate a little extra heat. Besides, the

firelight's being more than a little useful." Dhamon gestured to a map it illuminated. The parchment was
stretched across the top of a weathered table, four empty
mugs holding the corners and keeping it in place. "You're
the one who said we needed a place where we could
stretch out this supposed treasure map and get a better
look at it. You picked this hole. And this table."

Maldred grumbled an unintelligible reply. A moment
later he added, "You're the one who needed someplace to
rest—after this afternoon's bout with the scale on your leg."

Dhamon kept his eyes on the parchment. "Finding the
pirate treasure you say this map leads to will help my
pockets, but it isn't going to do anything to help my problem with the scale." Dhamon's words were barely above a
whisper, meant for himself rather than for his companion.
"I've no hope of a cure. Ever."

The big man replied anyway, keeping his voice low so the
other patrons couldn't hear. "I think you might be wrong,
my friend. I think, if my memory of folklore serves me, the
treasure at the end of this map will solve everything."

Dhamon's eyebrows rose, then he lifted his gaze to take
in their surroundings.

They were in the far corner of a squalid tavern, a long
day's travel from Blöten, the capital of the ogre lands. They
were as far away as they could get from the dirt-streaked
window through which strolling ogres glanced. There
were ogres inside the tavern, too, a quartet of them a few
tables away, all drinking and gambling and occasionally
looking hostilely in Dhamon and Maldred's direction.
Dhamon knew there would be more ogres soon when the
sun set in an hour or so, signaling for any race a traditional
time for drinks and fellowship.

"We're out of place here," Maldred said. "Haven't seen
a human walk by the window. Bet there isn't one in this
entire town. There were more humans in Blöten."

"We're out of place?" Dhamon repeated with a laugh. "No, my friend. I'm out of place here. These are your people—though they wouldn't know it from the looks of you. They can't see beneath that magical shell you've painted. No matter, we'll be away from this tavern and town soon enough. A few more days and we'll be blessedly out of ogre country. Forever." He stabbed a finger at the map. "Now, about this treasure. The map looks different than when we saw it at your father's. Don't you think?"

Maldred leaned over the parchment and gave a nod. "Different. But there's something about it. . . ."

It was old, the ink faded so badly in places most of the words couldn't be discerned. Even some of the features the firelight caught were so pale from age that Maldred and Dhamon had to guess whether the blotches were meant to indicate forests or lakes.

Maldred's finger hovered above a swatch the color of dried blood. "The valley," he breathed. "I had forgotten about the valley." He shook his head, drops of sweat falling on the map. "The Screaming Valley it's called, one of the few things about the land that didn't change after the Cataclysm."

Dhamon's expression told him to continue.

"You'll see it for yourself soon enough, my friend, when we get deep into the Plains of Dust. I've never been to the valley, but I knew someone who had stepped into the place. Said he couldn't go all the way through it. Said it was driving him mad."

"But we will, make it through—if that's the fastest way to the treasure. Besides, I don't have much faith in ogre tales. Any tales for that matter." There was a quiet strength in Dhamon's words. "I think it would take too long to go around the valley, if the treasure's down here, like you think." He pointed to a spot by a river. "A straight line to the treasure is the way we'll go.

21

"No matter where we travel, the land'll look different than what this old map shows. I've never set foot in the Plains of Dust, but I know it—and every place in Krynn—has changed since this was drawn. The Cataclysm. The Chaos War. Even this Screaming Valley of yours has to have changed."

"Perhaps."

Dhamon glanced at his friend, noting the big man's eyes were locked on the center of the map. "You were to the Plains before, weren't you, Mal? A few years back? I remember you telling me something about howling spires and . . ."

Maldred didn't answer, raising a finger to silence Dhamon, then lowering it to the map. A heartbeat later he was running his fingertips across the surface of the parchment, his eyes flitting now from edge to edge, then settling on a river that emptied into a sea to the south. His skin tingled slightly as his index finger passed over faint marks and smudges that at one time might have been labels for towns or important geographic features.

"There's magic in this," Maldred stated finally, after several minutes had passed.

"Aye, you cast . . . ."

The big man shook his head. "No. This magic is nothing I did to the parchment. The map itself seems to carry an enchantment. Very old magic. Strong. I get a hint of Red Robe sorcery." The summer's heat and the fire all but forgotten, Maldred allowed himself to be consumed for another several minutes by the ancient map, turning his body so he didn't obstruct the firelight. The soft glow from the few lanterns that hung about weren't enough to properly illuminate the map.

Dhamon cleared his throat to get his friend's attention and nodded in the direction of a pair of ogres who entered the inn and selected a table only a few yards away.

"I think I can access the map's magic," Maldred said, ignoring the new patrons.

"Maybe you should do it someplace else," Dhamon suggested. The pair of ogres were watching him, noses wrinkling and eyes narrowing to show their contempt for humans.

"No." Maldred was oblivious to the ogres, entranced by the possibilities of the map. "I want to see what this is about. I'll wager my father didn't know that not only did he have a treasure map, but he had a very magical one." He placed his palm over a symbol at the bottom that served as a compass. It was faded, like everything else, but the North and South arrows were the clearest of anything on the map.

Dhamon worried that his friend's sweaty hand might smudge what they could read. He looked at the pair of ogres, who were becoming increasingly curious about what Maldred was doing. "Don't you think . . . ?"

Maldred dismissed Dhamon's words with a gesture. He closed his eyes, and his lips formed silent words that helped his enchantment. "The key," he murmured softly between strings of arcane words. "What is the key to this wondrous map? The key . . . there."

Suddenly the map took on its own light, pale and yellow-gold, instantly drawing the attention of Dhamon and the two nearest ogres. The latter leaned closer but kept their seats.

"The key," Maldred repeated, his voice no longer a whisper. "Show us the pirate port of ages past, the port from before the time of the Cataclysm, from the time when the Plains of Dust were filled with freebooters and glittering promises of gold and more and . . . ah!"

An image formed on the map and above it, transparent but rendered with incredible detail. The tabletop looked like a sea, bright blue and shifting, the whorls in the wood

23

becoming frothy waves. The ale mugs shimmered, looking now like ships, one three-masted with billowing ghost-white sails fluttering in a breeze that seemed to surround the table and cut the heat of the fire and the summer. There was a cry, soft and sharp, of a gull, and in response the map's features became sharper and more focused. Names sprang up all over, of towns and woods, flowing script marking trails and rivers. The colors became intense and hypnotic and held Dhamon and Maldred's attention as firmly as any vise.

"The pirate port. The spot where they kept their stolen treasures," Maldred said, smiling when a spot on the map grew brighter still. It was a clamshell-shaped mark a few inches up from where the river spilled into the sea. "The pirate port as it was ages past," he stated, "and about as it is now. The port as it rests at this very moment."

The parchment glittered and the waves disappeared, the breeze vanished instantly to be replaced by the heat of the tavern, the snap of the sails replaced by the crackling of the fire behind them. The map's features were still distinct, but they were different from what it had displayed a heartbeat ago. The sea at the southern edge of the map was gone, in its place a glacier. The Plains of Dust were different, too, the river gone, though the shell-shaped mark indicating the pirate port was still there. The port looked to be in the middle of a dry stretch of land.

"It's buried," Maldred said. "The port's buried by earth and time. Can't tell how deep the pirate's treasure is. No matter. We'll find it. There has to be treasure."

In response the air sparkled like a shining diamond above the shell-shaped mark.

"Definitely treasure." He moved his free hand across the surface, brushing away the image of the land. "Now show us the sage, map. The Sage of the Plains."

Dhamon opened his mouth to say "What?" but the word didn't come out. Awe of the magic constricted his throat.

A circle glowed, shiny black and with an inner light. It was miles north and west of where Maldred's pirate port was. The circle gleamed and grew tall to represent a tower, stones black and reflecting unseen stars.

"The tower of the Sage of the Plains," Maldred began, his voice cracking. "I remembered my folklore correctly. Grim Kedar, that old ogre friend of mine, told me of a human woman who was said to be able to cure any ill and find a remedy to any problem. A healer. Grim wanted to meet her. We'll meet her for him."

Dhamon snorted. "Cure any ill. Remedy any problem."

"Your scale is both an ill and a very definite problem, Dhamon. It might cost you your life. I wonder if she might be the answer."

Dhamon shook his head. "You're looking at a map centuries old, Mal. Humans don't live so long. You know that. Though I appreciate your gesture, and though I very much desire to be free of this thing, I . . . what's this?"

"The Sage of the Plains today."

The map changed, as Maldred brushed his hand across the surface once more. It showed the land as it looked now—no sea, a glacier at its southern border again, the river the pirates had sailed gone. The image of the tower remained, though it was no longer glossy, and stars were not reflected along its edges.

Maldred cupped his hand near the tower image, and a figure appeared hovering above his palm. It was a woman, in black robes, features too small to tell much else about her.

"The Sage of the Plains," he announced.

The image nodded to him, then disappeared. The map shimmered. They stared at it silently for several moments.

Dhamon finally spoke. "So this sage who you think can cure ills, and who you think might have lived through all these centuries, do you think she can . . ." he searched for the words. "Cure me?" A moment later he drew his lips into a thin line, his eyes still fixed on the wavering image of the tower. "No. Such a person couldn't exist. Not then. Not now. And it's wrong to give me such hope."

Maldred, too, had his gaze still fixed on the parchment. "She existed then. Grim Kedar's tales are true. She exists now. I know it. Dhamon, it's why I selected my father's map of the Plains of Dust. Though in truth I didn't know it capable of magic. I remembered Grim's tales. I remembered the sage. I remembered the tales of the pirate port and their horde of booty."

"The pirate treasure," Dhamon coaxed. "You want it. I want it."

Maldred nodded, the gesture lost on Dhamon. "We need it. Grim said the Sage of the Plains could work wonders but that her every feat was costly—the wealth of a prince she could demand for her magic. There ought to be plenty in that pirate hold to satisfy her."

"If she's still alive," Dhamon whispered. "If she ever existed." He dropped his hand to his thigh, feeling the dragon scale beneath the fabric of his trousers.

"Worth our trying," Maldred said. "She ought to cure you for such ancient wealth. Perhaps magical wealth."

"Aye, worth it," Dhamon replied. "And if the sage is nothing but an old ogre's tale, we'll still have some pirate loot."

"Loot." The word was in the human tongue, though it came from an ogre who'd moved up silently and who was now leaning over the map. "Want loot. Want map." He grinned, showing a row of broken, yellowed teeth. A second ogre joined him.

"Map," the other fellow stated. "Want it." He jabbered in Ogrish, as Maldred rose and rolled up the map, directing him in Ogrish to keep back.

Dhamon drew his sword, which bought Maldred time to replace the map in the tube and stuff it in a deep pocket.

"The map's ours," Dhamon stated.

Maldred punctuated the statement by slamming his fist into the nearest ogre's face. The two humans fled the tavern.

"So much for your roast pig dinner," Maldred said as they rushed down the narrow dirt street.

Dhamon shrugged. "I wasn't that hungry. Besides, I didn't care much for that town. There's got to be one on the way out of this damnable country that has a few humans in it. Preferably the female variety."

Chapter Four
Hidden Treasures

hat say you and I start a fire, honey? One that'll make this hot summer day seem like it's the dead o' winter."

Dhamon Grimwulf didn't reply. He stared at the woman, dark eyes catching her watery blue ones and holding them. Faint lines like birds' feet edged away from her eyes, the lashes thick with kohl, the lids colored a deep shade of purple and reminding him a little of Rikali, a half-elf he used to keep company with and who was more skillful and garish in painting her much younger face. Finally he looked away, and the woman blinked and shook her head as if to rouse herself from a bad dream.

"An odd one, you are. You know, you could be a little friendlier, sweetheart. C'mon, give Elsbeth a big smile so she can see your teeth. I like a man what has all his teeth." The woman leaned over to gently kiss the tip of Dhamon Grimwulf's nose, coloring it red from the paste she had applied to her lips. She pouted when his stoic expression didn't waver.

29

"You haven't cracked even the teeniest grin, honey. How 'bout just a little one?" she cooed. "You'll make me think I've lost my charm. Everyone who spends time with Elsbeth smiles."

Dhamon remained impassive.

She made a soft huffing sound then, angling her breath up with her lower lip and causing the collection of curls that hung over her forehead to flutter and resettle. "Well, I suppose I could be cheery for the both of us. Wait! I know what this calls for. A touch more Passion of Palanthas. That'll get your blood stirring." She sauntered to a tray perched on a narrow wardrobe, ample hips swinging. Plucking up a crystal-blue vial, she generously dabbed some of the perfumed oil on her neck and behind her ears, let a little trickle run down the **V** of her dress, then turned to study Dhamon Grimwulf.

Dhamon sat on the edge of a sagging bed that smelled of mildew and stale ale. The entire room smelled of old wood and sweat and of various fragrances of inexpensive perfume, including now the potent, musky Passion of Palanthas. All the odors were warring for his attention, and the spiced rum he'd been drinking made his head swim. There was a basin of water on a small table a few feet away, and for a moment he considered dipping his face to clear his senses and cool himself—it was so hot today. But that would entail rising up from the bed, and the rum had numbed his legs and turned the rest of his body into lead.

Above the basin a large yellowed mirror hung on the wall. In its crooked glass he could see himself. His cheekbones were high and hollow, giving his face a slightly gaunt appearance. Shadows clung beneath his dark eyes, and a thin, crescent-shaped scar ran from just below his right eye and disappeared into an ill-trimmed beard as night-black as the tangled mass of hair that fell to his broad shoulders. Despite his disheveled state, he looked young and formidable. Through the gap in his black leather tunic his chest looked lean and muscular and tanned from the sun.

"C'mon, sweetheart. Smile for pretty Elsbeth."

Dhamon sighed, and in an effort to shut her up offered her a lopsided, put-on grin. She twittered, wriggled out of her clothes, and gave him a wink. She spun like a dancer so he could admire her long, blonde hair gleaming in the light of the setting sun that spilled through the second-story window. Finished with her display, she made an exaggerated show of stalking toward him, catlike, placing her hands on his shoulders and pushing him on his back, reaching for his legs and swinging them around so he was laying stretched out on the bed. She tugged off his boots, wrinkled her nose, and waved her hand to chase away an odor that he knew couldn't have been nearly as offensive as the other smells in this too-close room.

"You ought to go buy a bath, and then find you some new boots," she said, waggling a finger at him. "These boots have more holes in them than a slice of Karthay cheese." She playfully ran her long fingernails across the bottoms of his feet and scowled when he didn't react. "Sweetheart, you're gonna have to relax or you're not gonna enjoy yourself." She slid down next to him and toyed with the lacings on his tunic.

"Elsbeth, I think you've lost your touch." This from an overly thin, long-legged girl who was lying on the other side of Dhamon, her inky hair cut so short it looked like a cap on her head. She was dark-skinned, an Ergothian by her accent, and her small fingers traced invisible patterns on Dhamon's cheek. "I think maybe you're a mite too old for him, Els. I think he prefers younger women, ones with not so much flesh hanging on them."

Elsbeth made a spitting sound and with a sigh feigning hurt feelings tossed her blonde hair over her shoulder. "Satin, there's just more o' me to love. And you know I just turned twenty."

The long-legged girl laughed, the sound musical, like crystal wind chimes. "Twenty? Els, who are you kidding? Maybe twenty in dog-years. You said goodbye to thirty quite a few months ago."

The two women playfully pawed at each other over Dhamon's chest, laughing and taking turns grabbing at his tunic. Finally, they managed to tug the garment off and drop it on the floor.

"Lots of muscles," Satin said appreciatively, her fingers drifting down to trace a jagged scar on Dhamon's stomach. "You might want a man with all his teeth, Els. Me? I'll always take a man with muscles. Even if he is a little skinny." She leaned close to Dhamon and whispered something into his ear. He actually smiled then, though it was fleeting, his face returning to its imperturbable mask.

Elsbeth was studying the scar on Dhamon's cheek. "What'd you say your name was, honey? I'm not so good at names."

"Age does that to you," Satin cut in. "Ruins your memory."

"Dhamon Grimwulf," came a deep voice from across the room. "His name, ladies, is Dhamon Evran Grimwulf. Dragon-fighter, spawn-slayer, treasure-hunter extraordinaire. You'll find no more handsome rogue in all of Krynn. Except, of course, for me."

The speaker was a man even more muscular than Dhamon. He was nearly seven feet tall and stretched out on the other bed, a larger one that was threatening to collapse under his considerable weight—and the weight of the three scarcely clad women clinging to him. Their pale skin stood out starkly against his sweaty, sun-bronzed form, and two of them waved in unison to Dhamon, who had lifted his head to regard the others. The third woman was busy twining her fingers in the big man's chestnut hair and feathering his angular face with kisses.

"And you, sir, are . . . ?" Elsbeth asked, following Dhamon's glance across the room. "I don't believe I caught your name either."

The big man didn't answer her, pulling the sheet over himself and his companions.

"That's Maldred," Dhamon finally said. His voice was thick from the rum, his tongue felt clumsy in his mouth. "Maldred, crown prince of all of Blöten. He isn't in the least better looking than me. In fact, he's really blue and . . ."

"Hey," Maldred shot back, his face poking out from under the covers. "Watch your tongue, my friend. Dhamon, don't you have something better to do than talk? Coming here was your idea, after all."

All the women giggled.

"I don't mind if he talks, O Crown Prince of Blöten," Elsbeth said, her voice all silky now and her fingers brushing at the knots in Dhamon's hair. "You and he can do whatever you please. Talk or . . ."

The crown prince wasn't listening to her. He had disappeared again, thoroughly losing himself in the arms of his three ladies, the sheet ballooning and billowing like a full sail.

Elsbeth returned her attention to Dhamon, making a face when she saw that Satin was draped around him and that Dhamon's fingers were moving slowly across the Ergothian's smooth features.

"I know an Ergothian," Dhamon was telling her. "A former pirate." He hiccoughed and scrunched his nose when he smelled his own sour breath. "Name's Rig Mer-Krel. Ever hear of him?"

33

"No." Satin cocked her head and tugged at his short beard and tried futilely to snuggle into an even closer embrace with him. "Ergoth's a big place, O mighty dragonslayer."

"Spawn-slayer," Dhamon corrected. "I've never killed a dragon." Well, there was that sea dragon Brine, he thought, but he had had considerable help with that feat.

"Never heard of your Rig Mer-Krel," she continued.

"Good," Dhamon said. "You wouldn't like Rig anyway. A braggart and a fool. I never cared much for him."

"I like you," she returned, managing to insinuate a hand under his neck. "Now how about you take these off?" She tugged at his pants with her other hand.

He shook his head and hiccoughed again.

Elsbeth gave Satin a smug look and leaned over Dhamon. "Then how about taking them off for me, sweetheart? Maybe you do appreciate a woman with a few years on her, one what ain't so bony. Experience is better'n youth, you know. Like fine wine, I improve with age."

"And then turn to nasty vinegar," Satin whispered so softly only Dhamon heard.

"No." Dhamon shook his head stubbornly and made a move to rise from the bed. Elsbeth held him down. "I think I'll keep my trousers on, thank you."

Elsbeth made a throaty sound, which was quickly echoed by Satin.

"You are the odd one," Satin breathed. "You keep him put," she said to Elsbeth, "and I'll go get our spawn-slayer something to loosen his inhibitions. He was liking that spiced rum, right? Maybe the crown prince and our sisters over there would like another drink, too."

The sultry Ergothian crawled out of bed, grabbing Dhamon's tunic and slipping it on. Satin glanced at the bed across the room, then turned to wink at Elsbeth before she glided out the door.

Elsbeth brushed at the bit of red paste she'd gotten on Dhamon. "You'd be a real looker, Mister Dhamon Evran Grimwulf, if you cleaned yourself up a bit. All fancy with that nice sword . . ." She turned so she could see the scabbarded blade hanging from the bed post. The sword's crosspiece was fashioned in the likeness of a falcon's beak. "Bet it's valuable."

She stretched an arm down to a satchel that had been shoved partway under the bed. "This, too. Heard it chink when you dropped it. Like there're lots o' coins in it."

"Not coins," Dhamon said flatly. "Gems. There are quite a lot of them."

"We've quite a gem here, too," came a high-pitched voice from across the room. The speaker was hidden by the sheet. "The crown prince—and what he's wearin'. He's got himself a big diamond hangin' around his neck."

"The Sorrow of Lahue," Dhamon breathed, recalling that it was named for the Woods of Lahue in Lorrinar where it was found, that it was priceless, and that he'd taken the gem from the ogre-chieftain Donnag and offhandedly tossed it to Maldred three months or so ago.

Elsbeth sat back, keeping her hands firmly on his chest. "So you are a mighty treasure-hunter indeed, Dhamon Grimwulf. Your friend, too. Hidden treasures under my bed. And gem necklaces!"

Dhamon shrugged, the unexpected motion knocking Elsbeth off him and onto the floor.

"Of all the lousy . . ." she stopped herself and smiled, then scampered to rejoin him, throwing a leg across him and sitting on his chest to keep him in place. "I've got some treasures, too, O mighty spawn-slayer. What say we exchange some?"

Dhamon stared up at the woman. "Maybe we'll give you ladies a few gems before we leave." Softer, he added, "Maybe use them to get out of this gods-forsaken country."

"You'll give us gems?"

"Aye. We'll give you some gems." But not the best of the lot, he added to himself. The rum hadn't addled his senses that much. "You can have my damned sword, too, for all I care. Pawn it someplace and buy yourself some better perfume. That blade's done me little good."

She eagerly rained kisses on Dhamon's forehead and cheeks, spreading the red paste. "Honey, we don't get many folks passing through like you and the crown prince over there. Trappers, thieves, mostly ogres and their half-breed brothers. None o' them with more than a few coins in their pockets. None o' them with so many fine gems." She rocked back on her haunches and fixed her eyes at a spot on his chin, then dropped her gaze to a thick gold chain that hung around his neck. "So what brought you and the crown prince into—"

"We're on our way out of Blöde," Dhamon told her. "We're done with ogre lands. We're thieves, dear Elsbeth, like most everyone else who passes through here. But I wouldn't want to give away too many trade secrets." He laughed hollowly, draping his hand over his brow. His head was aching, the effects of going too long without a fresh splash of rum. The heat of this summer day was fierce. That, and the heat of Elspeth's body rubbing up against him made breathing seem difficult. He wanted another drink.

"Handsome thieves." She toyed with a thin gold hoop that hung from his ear, then grinned wide and snuggled closer. "Now, about those pants."

"No," Dhamon's answer was curt. He held her stare until he was certain she was more than a little uncomfortable. "When it's dark," he added after a few moments. "Then I'll lose the trousers."

"A thief and a proper gentlemen," she cooed, eyes again drifting to the gold chain around his neck. "So who'd you steal all o' those gems from anyway, honey?"

Dhamon laughed. "Those I earned," he said.

"Earned? Wanna tell me about it?"

Dhamon shook his head.

"Then how 'bout you tell us in exchange for something to drink?" Satin stood above the pair, a long-necked ceramic jug in each hand. "Spiced rum, right?" She moved so quietly that Dhamon hadn't even heard her return.

He sat up in the bed and reached for what looked to be the larger of the two jugs, thumbed the cork off it and drank copiously, letting the potent liquor slide down his throat. It burned for a moment, then turned into a pleasant warmth that spread to his head and chased the aches and pains away. He took another long swallow and offered the jug to Elsbeth.

"Oh, no, honey," she cooed. "I'll have some after."

"There might not be any left after," Dhamon shot back. He took another deep pull and held the jug beneath his nose. The scent of the spiced liquor was preferable to Passion of Palanthas and whatever sickly sweet fragrance Satin had managed to sprinkle on herself.

Satin thrust the second jug toward the other bed. Maldred's arm shot out from beneath the sheet to grab the neck of it. He mumbled a "thanks" as he pulled it beneath the covers.

"Yes, after, Mister Grimwulf," Elsbeth purred. "I'll share some after you tell us the tale of those gems. And after it's dark." Once more she playfully tugged on his pants.

Satin joined them, climbing over Dhamon and sliding down along his other side. "If your tale's a good one, dear, I'll fetch us another jug of rum. Or two."

Dhamon's dark eyes gleamed. He wasn't much for bragging or storytelling, but it was still light outside and there was plenty of time. He ran his thumb around the lip of the jug, downed nearly half of it in another deep swallow, and began.

"Mal and I had to run an errand for Blöde's ruler, an ugly-cuss ogre named Donnag. Our job was to rescue some slaves from a silver mine for his lordship and to haul the freed slaves back to Blöten. Cheery place, Blöten."

"It was the black dragon Sable's silver mine," Maldred pitched in from beneath his sheet. "The mine was guarded by spawn." There was a pause. "But as I said, Dhamon is good at slaying spawn. He's just not good at dealing with the folks of Blöten. Dhamon, go on. Tell them all about our trip to the ogre city. . . ."

CHAPTER FIVE
REMEMBERING BLÖTEN

Dhamon, Maldred, and the freed slaves from the silver mines stood before a crumbling wall that was fifty feet high in places, the taller portions being the most intact. In some sections the wall had completely collapsed, the gaps alternately filled with boulders piled high and mortared in place, and with timbers driven deep into the rocky ground and held together with bands of rusted iron and thick rope. Spears were jabbed into the tops of the wall, the points angled crazily to ward off intruders.

Atop a particularly weathered barbicon stood a trio of well-armored ogres. They were stoop-shouldered and wart-riddled, their gray hides covered with boils and scabs. The largest had a broken tooth that protruded at an odd angle from his bottom jaw. He growled something and thumped his spiked club against his shield, then growled again and pointed at Dhamon and Maldred. He raised his club threateningly and spat. The guard was suspicious. He knew Maldred but wasn't familiar with the blue-skinned ogre mage in this mundane human form.

Maldred answered the guard in the same guttural tongue. He practically shouted, as he reached his hand to the pommel of his sword. The other he dropped to the coin purse at his belt, and after a moment's hesitation he untied the coin purse and heaved it up to the guard. The ogre narrowed his bug eyes, set down the club, and thrust a doughy finger in the purse to stir its contents. Apparently satisfied with the toll—or bribe—he growled to his companions, who opened the gate.

Inside, ogres milled about on the main street. From nine to eleven feet tall, they varied greatly in appearance, though most had broad-faces set with large, thick noses—some of which were decorated with silver and steel hoops and animal bones. Their skin tended to range from a pale brown, the shade of Dhamon's boots, to a rich mahogany. There were some that were a sickly looking green-gray, and a pair strolling arm-in-arm across the street were the color of ashes.

"Rikali might still be here," Maldred said to Dhamon as they entered the city. "After all, you told her you were going to come back for her. The healer Grim Kedar would know if she's around, and his place is not far." The big thief gestured toward the southeast section of the ogre city.

Dhamon shook his head. "Mal, If Riki was smart, she wouldn't have waited for me. If she did bother to wait . . ."

He paused as he worked a kink out of his neck. "Well, then she isn't very smart, and that's her own damn fault for not moving on. I hope she's happy here. Me? I'll be gone. We intend to be in and out of this place in a couple of hours, right?"

Down a side street Dhamon noted a dozen ogres loading big canvas sacks on wagons. The workers wore tattered clothes and ragged animal skins, and they wore sandals or had bare feet. Every one of them looked filthy, every bit as bad as the freed slaves who continued to shuffle along behind him and Maldred.

"I don't want to be here," one of the few freed humans whispered fearfully. Dhamon's keen hearing picked up the conversation, and he mentally agreed with the fellow.

"It's better than the mines," the dwarf at his side returned. "Anything is better than that hellhole. I don't see anyone in chains here." The human and the dwarf continued their muted conversation. The ground they trod on was damp, as if there had been a lot of rain recently, an unusual occurrence for these normally arid mountain lands. The sky overhead was thickly overcast, threatening rain and casting a gloomy pallor over an already gloomy place.

"This is a lovely city," Dhamon wryly mused.

"Indeed," Maldred said, and meant it.

Within the hour—after a brief stop to buy a few jugs of the heady ogre ale Dhamon had acquired a taste for—they were seated at a massive dining room table in Donnag's manse. The freed slaves had been taken away somewhere by Donnag's guards, and Maldred was assured they would be well cared for.

"We are pleased you aided in the return of our people, Dhamon Grimwulf. Most pleased." The ogre-chieftain sat in a chair that could have passed for a throne, though the padded arms were worn, frayed especially where his clawlike fingers caught at the threads. "You have our deepest gratitude."

Maldred glanced at his father, then turned his attention to the sumptuous repast in front of him and dug in. Dhamon kept his attention on Donnag, not having much of an appetite for eating in an ogre manse. He was glad the ogre ruler had dismissed his guards in order to talk to Dhamon and Maldred, his son, in private.

"You owe me far more than your thanks, your lord-ship," Dhamon said, an obvious edge to his voice. The rings that pierced Donnag's lower lip jiggled, and his eyes widened imperiously.

"In fact, you owe me considerably, you bloated excuse for a—"

"This is an outrage!" Donnag stood. A rush of color came over his florid face, and he raised his voice. "Our thanks—"

"Isn't good enough." Dhamon rose too, and out of the corner of his eye he noticed Maldred had set down the fork and was looking back and forth between the two.

The chieftain growled. He clapped his hands, and a human serving girl who'd been hovering in an alcove brought out a large leather satchel. Empty. Dhamon's eyes narrowed.

"We anticipated that my son's friend might want some-thing more tangible," Donnag said, his tongue working as if the words were distasteful in his mouth. "I will summon my guards who will escort you to our treasure chamber, and you may fill that bag as you desire. Then, Dhamon, you may leave."

Dhamon shook his head. "I'll take that—filled with your finest gems—as payment for freeing the slaves. But you will still owe me." His fingers gripped the edge of the table, knuckles turning white.

Maldred tried to catch his friend's gaze, but Dhamon's eyes were locked onto Donnag's.

"I don't understand," the chieftain angrily sputtered. He turned to the serving girl. "Guards! Get them now." Softer, he said, "I had hoped we wouldn't need the guards. I had hoped this time the three of us could con-verse civilly."

"No," Dhamon interjected. "No guards." He turned to the girl and gave her a withering look. "You stay here for the moment."

The girl froze like a statue. "Impudent man," said Donnag. "Though you are a mere human, we have been more than generous with you. We have treated you better than we have ever treated others of your kind. That sword you carry . . ."

"Wyrmsbane. Redeemer," Dhamon hissed.

". . . the sword that once belonged to Tanis Half-Elven. We gave it to you."

"Sold it to me," Dhamon corrected. "For a veritable fortune."

Donnag's eyes were thin slits. "A most valuable sword, human."

"A worthless sword. I bet Tanis never owned this thing. Never touched it. Never saw it. Never knew this accursed thing existed. You cheated me."

Before Donnag could say anything else, Dhamon sprang back from the table, knocking over his chair, drew Wyrmsbane, and sprinted toward the ogre chieftain.

"Guar—" was all Donnag managed before Dhamon's fist slammed hard into his stomach, knocking the ogre back into his chair.

"It's not worthless," Donnag gasped, trying futilely to rise. "Believe me, it's not. In fact—"

"It's a piece of cow dung," Dhamon spat. "Just like you. Its magic doesn't work, Donnag."

The ogre sadly shook his head and settled back into the chair, trying to recover his dignity. He looked around for his son but could not see past Dhamon to Maldred, who was watching everything stonily, giving no hint of his emotions.

"Magic works different now than when that blade was forged. Perhaps now—"

"I think you knew all along this thing was useless."

The chieftain lifted a shaky hand in a gesture of argument, and in response Dhamon rammed his knee into the ogre's gut and leveled the sword at his throat. Behind the pair, Maldred slowly rose and warily backed away from the table.

"Dhamon . . ." the big man warned.

"Useless! Though I suppose this sword might prove useful for ending your petty life."

Dhamon glanced at the elven runes that ran along the blade's length, flaring up as if the sword knew it was being discussed, glowing faintly blue. He couldn't read them, however. What did he know or care of their meaning? All he knew was that Wrymsbane, the true sword of Tanis Half-Elven, was elf-forged and was said to have many other owners and names through the decades. It was reputed to be a sister sword to Wyrmslayer, Dhamon also knew, the blade the elf hero Kith-Kanan wielded in the Second Dragon War.

Legend said the blade had been bequeathed by Silvanesti weaponsmiths to the kingdom of Thorbardin. From there it went to Ergoth, where it fell into Tanis Half-Elven's hands. It was said to be buried with the great Hero of the Lance. Donnag claimed he came by it through a grave-robbing thief.

"I really should kill you," Dhamon stated. "I'd be doing this country a favor."

"Maldred, son," Donnag gasped. "Stop him."

Dhamon tensed, expecting his friend to do something to protect his father.

Maldred stood, watching stonily.

"Leave us," Dhamon ordered the serving girl, who was standing petrified against the wall. "Say nothing to anyone. Understand?" His eyes were ice, and the girl ran quickly from the room, dropping a tray filled with wine glasses. Dhamon paused, listening for her retreating footsteps, making sure no others were approaching.

"You're worthless, Donnag," he continued ferociously. "Just like this sword is worthless! The only difference is this sword doesn't breathe and steal good air from people more deserving of life than you. The sword of Tanis Half-Elven? Ha! I very much doubt it. This thing should be melted and poured down your throat." Dhamon's face was red, anger deeply etching his features, his eyes so dark and wide they looked to Donnag like bottomless pits.

The ogre chieftain tried to say something, but Dhamon's free hand shot up and gripped his throat. The ogre paled, his normally pasty complexion looking deathly white now.

"I'll grant you this sword kept me safe from the spawn's breath—their acid didn't burn me. I'll grant you that."

"Dhamon . . ." Maldred warned, padding a few steps closer.

"But Tanis's sword was said to find things for its wielder. Locate treasure and artifacts. Now, that would really be something valuable."

Donnag's eyes were pleading with him. Dhamon's fingers dug deeper into his throat and his knee pressed harder. "I'll also warrant you that the blade seemed to select the Sorrow of Lahue from all the baubles in your horde when I asked it for something worth my while."

"Dhamon . . ." Maldred was just behind him now.

"It didn't find what I truly wanted—a cure for the damned scale on my leg. Visions of the swamp, it gave me. Strange shadowy visions. It teased me, Donnag. Taunted me like a spiteful vixen. Worthless!"

Maldred stepped to the side of Donnag's chair, glancing briefly at his father before catching Dhamon's livid stare. "He is my father, Dhamon," the ogre in human disguise said softly. "I've no great love for him, else I'd be living here instead of traveling with you. But if you kill him, running this country falls to me. That's something I would not shirk, but I'd prefer it didn't happen for a long while."

45

Dhamon's jaw was working as he relaxed—slightly—
his grip on Donnag's throat. "I should run you through
with this worthless thing, your worthless lordship." He
smelled something then, and it brought a faint smile to his
lips. The ogre chieftain had soiled his regal garments.

"I'd leave this accursed sword here, but you'd only find
some other fool to sell it to. I don't want you to profit from
it a second time."

Donnag gasped for breath. "Wh-wh-what do you . . ."

"What do I want?" Dhamon dropped his hand from
Donnag's throat. The ogre gulped in air. Dhamon paused.
"I want . . . I want . . . ? I want never to see you again!" he
said angrily. "To never find myself in your lovely city
again. For that matter, to never set foot in this wretched
country again. And . . ." A true smile appeared on his face,
as he spotted the dropped empty satchel. "And I want two
satchels filled with your most exquisite gems. One for me
and one for your son. I'll fill my pockets, too. And I'll
drape chains and bangles around my wrists and arms.
That's not all. I want something more."

"Wh-wh-what more?"

Dhamon shrugged, thinking. Donnag looked helplessly
at his son, who made a show of looking unconcerned
about his fate.

"A wagonload of treasure. Two wagonloads, Donnag.
Ten! I want ten times what I paid you for this damn sword!"

Donnag was breathing hard, rubbing at his throat. "I
could give you what you want, but all of it will be stolen
from you before you leave these mountains. You and my
son are not the only thieves in this country. There are brigands on every trail. Though the two of you are formidable,
their numbers will win out."

"Their numbers or his assassins," Maldred whispered.

Dhamon slammed his fist on the arm of Donnag's chair,
the wood splintering from the impact. "I want—"

"There's something better we can offer."

"Ha! Another of Tanis's swords? Ha, ha!"

"We have treasure maps," Donnag said quickly. "There's a couple in particular I'm thinking of. They are pieces of parchment easily concealed. If you are robbed, so what? Give them the gems. You will have rare maps to guide you to greater riches. No one the wiser. Let me show you my true gratitude. I will give you gems and wagons, but best of all, I will give you rare treasure maps!"

"Any map you have will be as phony as this sword." Dhamon waved the tip in front of the ogre's eyes.

Donnag shook his head, the rings on his bottom lip nervously jangling. "No, no, we—"

"Let's see these maps." This from Maldred. "I can tell if they're genuine, Dhamon," he assured his friend. "I remember years ago he bragged to me about his collection of ancient treasure maps. There might be some truth to his words."

"Yes." Donnag nodded. "Let me show them to you!" His eyes were dull, as if Dhamon had forever chased away any trace of the fire and dignity they once held. "They're below. In our treasure chamber with all the gems and stuff. I'll summon—"

"No one!" Dhamon shouted. "You'll escort us to your treasure chamber all by yourself. I don't want any guards. No serving girls. No bearers. Just you. And I don't want you out of our sight for even a heartbeat. No tricks."

Donnag showed them three maps, all so old and brittle their edges had flaked away and the rest of them threatened to crumble to dust.

"This one is of the Teeth of Chaos, the islands north of the Estwilde and Nordmaar. I don't fancy traveling that far," Maldred said disapprovingly. "And it's vague of what we'll find."

Dhamon nodded in agreement. "But this one, it's of the Elian Wilds, the island east of the red overlord's land. Again, a far distance, but not as far, and I'm in no mood to stay around here. It hints at magical items, and that's worth a lot now."

Maldred was scrutinizing the third, a smaller map, older even than the other two, the ink so faded it was practically indiscernible. "This one isn't so far as either of those. We wouldn't need to find a sailing ship. And it certainly looks genuine."

Dhamon joined him, looking over his shoulder while keeping an eye on Donnag, who was nervously waiting on the stairway. "Aye, this indeed looks intriguing, my big friend."

"The land has changed, but this has to be of the Plains of Dust," Maldred said. "Due south of here. Through the Black's swamp. Bah, the map is practically falling apart. Let's fix it up so it's a little sturdier." He started his magic, humming, a throaty tune that rose and fell as his fingers flickered over the map. His eyes glowed pale green, the color intensifying and moving down his arms to his fingers, then covering the map.

"Son! What are you . . ."

"I'm giving the parchment a little fixing-up, father. It just takes a little of my power away, so little I'll never miss it." The glow dissipated as Maldred's shoulders rounded and he shook his head. "Magic is so difficult," he breathed heavily. "Seems harder now than even a few months ago. Good thing I have my masking enchantment down to an art. Looking human is the one spell that's still easy for me."

A moment later and he seemed his old self again, briskly rolling up the parchment and putting it in a small bone tube. He thrust this into a deep pocket of his trousers.

"Dhamon, you and I will take a much better and closer look at this map later when we're away from here. See if we can make out some of the writing." He nodded to his father. "We'll leave the other two maps. Don't sell them to anyone. Dhamon and I may want them later. We'll be back if this one doesn't work out."

"I still want those two satchels full of gems," Dhamon said. He was already filling his pockets to capacity, draping a thick gold chain around his neck and a bracelet around his wrist.

Donnag glowered at him. "Done," he said.

"Then," Dhamon continued, "I want you to escort us out of town. I don't want to give you a moment away from us to summon your generals or cadre of assassins. You'd better not have any of your minions follow us. Do you understand?"

A grudging nod.

Dhamon didn't even let the chieftain change clothes.

Of course, the tale he related to the women didn't include the fact that Maldred was an ogre mage disguised as a human thanks to a long-lasting spell he had mastered, or that Maldred was Donnag's son. Of course, he left out where the treasure map led. Too, he made no mention of the scale on his leg. Dhamon simply said that the sword did not function as promised and that he garnered two satchels of gems and a treasure map for Donnag for his trouble and for freeing the slaves.

"So we're through with Blöten," Maldred finished. "At least for the time being." The big man had tossed off the sheet, his body slick with sweat, his movements awkward from the alcohol. His three companions were still fawning over him. One of them took a big gulp of the spiced rum, then kissed Maldred and released the drink into his mouth. He cheerfully nudged her for another swallow. "Anyway, we wouldn't be safe there at the moment." He laughed loudly.

"Aye!" Dhamon laughed too, upending his jug. He steadied himself by leaning back against the rickety head-board, then he passed the empty jug to Elsbeth. "I s'warned you there might be none left if you waited."

"You're drunk."

"Aye, ma'am."

She frowned, then quickly brightened. "It's getting dark outside. I'll fetch another bottle. Maybe with a few more sips, you'll be wanting to . . ." She let the words hang as she slipped from his side, giving him a quick peck on the cheek before rushing out the door.

"So that's why you're in a hurry to get out of Blöde," Satin said. "Because of how you threatened the ogre chieftain's life?"

"Aye again," Dhamon said. "There's a s'warrant on me, no doubt through this whole damned country now—from Donnag, and from some Legion of Steel Knights we crossed earlier. And s'while every man's got to die some-time. I'd prefer it not to be in this filthy land. 'Specially not at the hand of Donnag's men. 'Sides, I s'think I hate these mountains. Time for a s'change of scenery."

"You are an odd but brave one." Satin cuddled close.

"So warm," he said. He ran a finger along her arm, deciding that her skin felt like her name—satin. "Warm," he repeated.

"It's the rum that makes you hot. This summer's not so bad. Really," she purred. "We've been through worse. I can make you hotter, and I know that you won't mind one little bit."

Her fingers drifted to his trousers, but she frowned as once again he batted them away.

"Hey, it's s'not dark yet," he said. "It's not. . . ." He watched Elsbeth return, two more jugs in hand. Maldred climbed out of bed to grab one, quick to return to his women.

"Ale," Elsbeth said, noting the sour expression on Maldred's face. "No more spiced rum. You drank the last of it. Sorry."

Dhamon accepted his jug without comment, however, and took a deep pull. Like the women's perfume, the ale was cheap and had a bothersome odor, but it was strong enough. His vision had blurred just enough so the crows' feet around Elsbeth's eyes had disappeared. She didn't look quite so plump now. She looked softer, prettier. Dhamon took another long swallow, then passed the bottle over to Satin. He reached out and grabbed Elsbeth's hair, pulling her face close, then kissing her. Passion of Palanthas wasn't as annoying any more, and the fragrance seemed to complement whatever Satin had on.

The girls were murmuring to him, unfastening his pants and tugging at them. It wasn't dark enough, he registered. There was faint light spilling in through the window, and someone had lit a candle, probably one of Maldred's companions. It should be dark, he told himself, but the alcohol and the perfume were heady, his tongue was too thick to protest and his fingers were too busy entwining themselves in the women's hair.

He heard a loud thump and a groan, a rustling of sheets, and he knew this was coming from Maldred's side of the room. No doubt the big man had fallen out of bed. Dhamon opened his eyes and canted his head, and through a gap in Elsbeth's curls, he saw Maldred laying on his stomach on the floor, the ale jug just beyond his limp fingers.

Dhamon would have chuckled, had his mouth not been alternately covered by Satin and then Elsbeth's lips, and then his mouth opened for another long swallow of the cheap ale. He would have clapped his hands in amusement had it not been for the fact he noticed the three women struggling to pull Maldred back on the bed, face down, and one of them tying the big man's hands to the bedpost.

"Hey!" Dhamon craned his neck. They were tying Maldred's feet, too, and now the big man's three companions were getting dressed.

"Somethin's not right." Dhamon tried to say more, but the words were lost somewhere between his mind and his tongue. He tried to push Elsbeth off him, but she felt terribly heavy. His fingers were thick and clumsy and difficult to untangle from her hair. He felt like a rock, unable to budge, riveted in place by the hefty blonde.

"You just lay back, honey," Elsbeth cooed.

"Have some more to drink," Satin said. She tipped his head back and poured more ale down his throat. The ale was strong, too strong, and the more he imbibed the more he tasted something not right about it.

"N-no," Dhamon sputtered, trying to spit it out.

"Honey, you should've been asleep some time ago. We put enough powder in these jugs to knock out a small army. One jug o' that spiced rum should've been more than enough for the both o' you. Seems like the two of you've got the constitutions o' bull elephants. Satin . . ."

The slender Ergothian upended the jug again, but Dhamon managed to grind his teeth together, and most of the ale splashed outside his mouth. His head alternately felt heavy, then light. He tried again to shove Elsbeth and Satin away, this time with some success. He rolled with Elsbeth, falling to the floor on top of her and becoming entangled in the sheet and his pants. He tried to rise, but his arms and legs felt numb.

Elsbeth managed to crawl out from under him and push him onto his back. Satin peered over the edge of the bed.

"Satin, look at his leg! There's a . . ."

"I see it, Els. A very strange scar it is. We'll take a closer look at it later. Here grab the jug. Do it!"

His eyes closed, Dhamon concentrated. Move! he told himself. Move, you sorry excuse for a man! He finally struggled to get free of the sheet and to tug his pants up, rolling farther away from Elsbeth. The drugged alcohol had so dulled his senses, however, that he forgot about the three wenches on the other side of the room. Several pairs of hands now grabbed at him, keeping him down. A moment later he heard someone shuffling toward him. With considerable effort he cocked his head and spied Elsbeth towering over him, empty jug in her hand. The jug was coming down fast and hard, soundly striking his forehead and sending him into oblivion.

He awoke minutes later—or at least he thought it was minutes later. Little time must have passed because the room appeared to be no darker than before, and his head hurt terribly from where Elsbeth had hit him. Satin was wearing his tunic, belted with the curtain cord to keep it from falling off her slight frame. Elsbeth was dressed, too, and busy pawing through his satchel, oohing and ahhing at the gems and jewelry. He could see that the three other women had already gathered up Maldred's possessions. Each had a long-bladed knife strapped to her waist.

Satin padded over and pulled Dhamon's sword off the bedpost. "Worthless, huh?" She unsheathed it and ran a thumb over the edge, jerking when she cut herself slightly, thrusting the thumb into her mouth and greedily sucking at it. "Might be worthless to you, but I'll wager it'll fetch a pretty steel piece somewhere. You see, we're headed out of Blöde, too—now that we have more than enough wealth to do it. All thanks to you."

Elsbeth had fastened her backpack and was leaning over Dhamon. She had a long-bladed knife on her waist, too. The knives were all the same, the handles wrapped with brown snakeskin and a symbol sewn on them, marking them members of some thieves' guild.

"You're not the only thieves in this pitiful town," Elsbeth said, "and we're obviously far better at stealing than you are. Than you were." She turned the knife and brought the handle down hard on his breastbone. She hit him a few more times, then drew the blade across his stomach until a thin line of red formed. "Since the drug hasn't completely taken you out," she said, "I'll bet you can feel that. At least I hope so." She slapped him hard across the face, then took a step back to admire her work before she slapped him again and again and again.

Dhamon tried to struggle with the ropes that held him to the bed, but all he managed to do was feebly move his arms. The ropes were tight, knotted as well as any sailor could have done. He was certain he could've gotten out of them if he had all his strength and wits—the drugged alcohol had sapped him of both. He lolled his head to the side, watching Satin move over to inspect Maldred, who was on his back, out cold.

She glanced back at Dhamon. "When you mentioned you've a price on your head, I considered finding a way to collect it, but I'm a thief, not a bounty hunter."

"So what're we gonna do with them?" one of the others asked her.

"No witnesses, girls," Satin told them. "You know that we never leave witnesses."

Elsbeth made a tsk-tsking sound. "Too bad, Mister Dhamon Evran Grimwulf, I kind o' fancied you. I would've liked to play a bit longer. But Satin's right. Leaving witnesses is an unhealthy thing to do." She reached behind Dhamon's neck and unfastened his gold chain, then hung it around her own neck. His gold bracelet quickly followed. "We just can't afford to leave anyone behind to tell o' our deeds. You understand, don't you?"

Two of the women had strapped on Dhamon and Maldred's backpacks and were climbing out the window.

Another was hefting Maldred's greatsword, trying to figure out how best to carry it.

Satin was wearing the Sorrow of Lahue and had purposely turned so Dhamon could see it hanging low on her, almost to her waist, the platinum chain catching the candlelight and sparkling like miniature stars. She tucked the rose-colored diamond beneath the tunic and smiled slyly.

"This large fellow here . . . Maldred, you called him. He's mine," Satin said. She held Wyrmsbane high over the big man's back, angling the tip down over the center of his spine, still watching Dhamon. "I'll kill him with your worthless sword. It'll be quick. Maybe he won't even feel anything."

"Then I guess you're left to me, Dhamon Grimwulf." Elsbeth drew her long knife and stepped closer.

Dhamon could no longer see either woman. His vision blurred. All he saw was a twisting mass of gray and black. There was one point of light, perhaps the burning candle. Everything else was gray swirls.

"I have to admit though, honey, I sure would've liked to have spent the night with you. And it would've been nice for you to get something in exchange for all this treasure you're handing over to us."

"Me first, Els," Satin purred.

The slender Ergothian winked at her companion, brought the blade high above Maldred's back, then, startled, spun away from the bed as the door was kicked open. The door struck the wall so hard the mirror fell and shattered on the floor.

"What in the name of . . ." Elsbeth turned, knife held in front of her, eyes narrowing at the woman who stood in what was left of the door frame.

55

The lantern light that spilled in through the hallway revealed a slight half-elf in a voluminous sea-green dress, a wild mane of silver-white hair fanning away from her face. She had wavy-bladed daggers in each hand and a sneer on her petal-pink lips.

"Not 'what in the name of,' " the half-elf corrected. "Who. Who in the name of. My name's Rikali Lockwood, and I truly don't mind if you kill those two worms you've got all trussed up. Riddin' the world of them would be doing us all a great big favor. You can do it nice and slow and painful for all I care. But while you're doing it, I want a share of the wealth you're takin'. It'd only be fair. I want in on your little operation."

Chapter Six
Family

T he three thieves stared at the half-elf.

"You heard me. I want in on your little thievin' gang," Rikali continued, eyes darting between Elsbeth and Satin and the one who finally had stopped struggling with Maldred's sword. She dropped it with a loud clang and reached for the long knife on her belt.

"Pigs, but there's no reason to be unfriendly. I just wanna cut a deal with you ladies." The last word was drawn out and spat on the floor. "As I see it, you've got a great scam runnin' here. Men come up here lookin' for a good time, and maybe you give them just what they're lookin' for. Then you rob them blind, kill them. I bribed the innkeep downstairs, an' he said you rented all the rooms up here today, so there'd be no one comin' by to disturb you. No one to interfere. No one 'cept me, that is."

Satin glanced over her shoulder, noting Maldred was still unconscious from the drugged ale. "Listen, elf . . ."

"Half-elf." Rikali tossed her hair so they could see the gentle points of her ears.

"Whatever. I don't know where you came from, woman, but . . . ."

"I came from Blöten. A truly wonderful city." The sarcasm was thick in her voice. "Dhamon Grimwulf left me stranded there. Said he'd be comin' back for me." She paused, huffing and glaring at Dhamon. "Should've known he wouldn't."

Dhamon tried to budge his ropes, but his arms weren't working right. All his fingers seemed able to do was twitch feebly. He couldn't see Rikali, but he could scarcely believe she was talking about joining these women. Did he hear her say to go ahead and kill him and Mal? He opened his mouth to call to her. Only drool came out.

"I saw him in Blöten better'n a week ago, maybe two, him and Mal. They were walkin' down the main street as big as you please with a column of grubby-lookin' ogres behind them. Right to Donnag's palace they went. Then right back out of the city. Didn't bother to look around for me—and here I was runnin' down a side street tryin' to catch up to them."

Satin smiled. "So you followed them here," she said.

"Pigs, but I did! But only 'cause I figure they owe me. Owe me big! And only so I could collect and give them a big piece of my mind. Straight to the Abyss with the both of them!" Rikali spat again, this time in Dhamon's direction. "So I'd even kill them for you—if you don't want to get your hands dirty and you'll let me in your little gang. For a fair share, of course. I figure whatever coin they got, some of it should be mine anyway. Like I said, they owe me."

"Sorry," Elsbeth shook her head. "We're a close-knit family, elf."

"Half-elf," Rikali corrected again.

"We don't need six in our family. The shares are too small as it is."

The half-elf quickly counted. "I only see three of you."

Elsbeth chuckled. "Cat and Keesha left a few minutes ago—with the 'coin' you're so interested in."

"I want what's due me!" Rikali raised her voice and tightened her grip on the daggers. "I've not come all this way for nothin'!"

"All right, I'll give you what's due you," Elsbeth said. "I'll give you this!" She darted forward, swinging her long knife as she came, then stopped with a shriek as her bare feet made contact with the mirror shards.

The half-elf had no such problem and advanced toward Elsbeth, boots crunching on the glass, daggers jabbing. Behind her a young man suddenly appeared in the doorway. He'd been waiting in the hall. Decked out in dyed green leather, he swung an oaken quarterstaff. Satin stepped up to meet him.

"Pigs!" the half-elf shouted at Elsbeth. "Women're supposed to be smarter than men, and here you are walkin' on broken glass! Dumb and fat, you are. I guess Dhamon lost his taste in women when he lost me."

When Elsbeth spun away, the half-elf slashed with her left dagger, the blade sinking into the surprised thief's side.

"Satin!" Elsbeth cried. "I'm hit! Bleeding! Help me!"

"Help yourself!" the Ergothian called back. "I've got my own worries." Agile as a dancer, she had ducked beneath the swing of the young man's quarterstaff. "So you're fast, pup," she muttered, "but not as fast as me." She thrust her knife forward. He jumped back. In the same motion, he brought his staff down, knocking her knife away. "Damn!" she cursed, as she dropped to the floor and rolled toward Maldred's bed, arm reaching to find the knife.

The third woman had managed to pick up Maldred's greatsword again and was holding it out in front of her like a lance, keeping the young man at a distance.

59

"You got no right to intrude," she hissed at him. "No right!"

Satin groped about under the bed, trying to find the knife. "Can't reach!" She gave up and jumped to her feet and in three strides was at the window, then climbing out of it. "Elsbeth! Leave them! Gertie! Lose the big sword and run! We've got more riches than we expected! Let's get out!" she shouted. "Elsbeth!" She dropped out of sight.

"Satin? Satin! No!" Elsbeth looked worried now, as she continued to spar with Rikali.

"Two on two," the half-elf sneered. "Varek and I are the better two, for certain, so you and your friend Gertie over there better drop your weapons and give up while you've still got the chance."

Elsbeth vehemently shook her head, taking a step back toward the window. "The odds are in our favor, half-elf," she corrected.

"Think again. Don't say I didn't hand you a chance to save your wrinkled neck." The half-elf darted in.

"I'll slice through your neck!" Elsbeth returned. The older woman dropped to a crouch, effortlessly parrying Riki's blades, forcing the half-elf back a few steps. While Riki kept her eyes on the long knife Elsbeth was holding, Elsbeth reached up to her hair and tugged free a wicked-looking hairpin. She held this hidden in her hand until Riki stepped close, then extended her arm, as if to ward off a blow, instead stabbing with the hairpin. The long needle sank into the half-elf's forearm.

"Pigs!" Riki shouted, glancing down at her arm and the needle in it, blossoming with blood. "Damn, woman, that hurts. And my dress. This is a new dress! New! Now the sleeve's gonna be stained for good!" She swung her twin daggers wildly, the tips catching Elsbeth's clothes and snagging them but unable to catch the flesh beneath.

"Riki . . ." Dhamon had managed to regain his voice, though the word came out almost unintelligibly.

The half-elf glanced over at the bed, saw Dhamon staring at her with a glazed look. She rolled her upper lip back in a snarl, though the expression was lost on him. The distraction cost her. Elsbeth stepped in once more, this time lowering her head, charging forward and smashing her head against Riki's face and momentarily stunning the half- elf. At the same time, the thief drove her knife forward, the blade slicing into Rikali's skirt and grazing her hip.

"Pigs, again! My dress!" Riki cried. "You foul woman! You're a dead woman now, you hear? Dead! Dead! Dead!"

Dhamon shook his head, still trying to shed the effects of the drugged ale. Pain danced behind his eyes. "Riki." He blinked, discovering his vision still blurred, but he could make out a few shapes and colors. He could still smell Elsbeth's Passion of Palanthas. "Riki." The word was stronger.

Concentrating, he bunched the muscles in his arms and pulled on the ropes. The hemp dug painfully into his wrists. He worked at it as Rikali and Elsbeth continued their fight. The ropes were slick with his blood. He knew that the half-elf was good with her blades, and for a moment he wondered if he should wait until she won and cut him loose. He vaguely remembered her saying something about letting the women kill him and Maldred and decided waiting wasn't a prudent idea.

He pulled harder and found some sensation returning to his legs. He tried to draw his knees up to stretch the ropes tied to his ankles. The bedposts groaned in protest, and he felt the wood, rather than the ropes, start to give.

Across the room, the wench named Gertie was effortlessly wielding Maldred's greatsword. She edged forward with it, while ducking under the swing of the young man's

61

staff. She forced him back, until he was cornered against the wall.

"Who are you?" she hissed. "Who are you to interfere in our business? You've no right, you insolent pup!" She ran at him then, thrusting the sword forward. Her target moved, but not fast enough. The tip of the greatsword managed to slice his side, cut deep into his tunic, and plunge through to the plaster wall, pinning him like a bug.

"You're strong!" the young man blurted. "Stronger than you should be!" He glanced at the blade. It was so far into the wall it must be protruding well out into the hallway on the other side.

"Strong?" She released the sword's pommel, grinning malevolently at his predicament. "You haven't seen strong."

She danced back and forth in front of him, easily avoiding the blows from his staff and watching him amusedly while he struggled to pull free. He couldn't afford to drop the staff and use both hands to tug out the greatsword, and his leather tunic refused to rip.

"Your clothes are well-made, boy," Gertie taunted. "You'll look good, buried in them." She skittered over to Dhamon's bed, reached for her knife, and raised it above his throat. "Before you die, boy, you can watch your fellows go first. You and the half-elf can watch."

"No!" The word sprang from Maldred's lips. The big man's eyes were open. He was struggling to shake off the drugged ale and had managed to turn his head toward Dhamon. He balled his fists and tugged on the ropes, but his efforts were too feeble. "Leave him be!"

"Yeah, Gertie, leave him be!" Elsbeth shouted as she slashed again at Rikali. "That one's mine to kill!"

"Sorry," Gertie replied with a smile. "He's mine now."

"No! Please!" This from Riki, who managed to slip away from the distracted Elsbeth and darted like a flash toward

Dhamon. The half-elf swung her knife, cracking Gertie's blade on the pommel and sending it away just as the tip had reached Dhamon's throat. The blade drew only a thin line of blood before clanging to the floor a few feet away.

"You'll not kill Dhamon!" Rikali spat. The half-elf swung again in a wide arc, and Gertie scampered back, laughing.

"Thought you said he owed you, half-elf," Gertie tittered as she glanced about for an unbroken weapon in easy reach. "Thought you said he owed you, that you didn't care if he was dead."

"He owes me, all right!" the half-elf sneered. She returned her attention to Elsbeth, narrowly dodging a swipe of the big woman's blade. "He's gonna owe me more for savin' his damn life!"

"Stay put!" Elsbeth cursed at the half-elf. She stomped her foot in anger, the heel cracking the wood of the floor. "You just stay put so I can kill you and be done with this! I've let this tussle go on too long!"

Riki dropped her gaze to the broken floor panel, then raised her eyes to meet Elsbeth's. The thief's eyes glimmered darkly like night, the pupils no longer blue. "What are you?" the half-elf breathed.

"Your death," Elsbeth stated. She stabbed forward just as Riki jumped back.

Gertie had moved to the end of Maldred's bed, one hand on the bedpost. In a heartbeat she'd pulled the post off the bed. A corner of the bed fell to the floor, and the still-drousy Maldred groaned. The thief wielded the post like a club, advancing on the young man still pinned to the wall. "Elsbeth thinks we need to end this, pup. I suppose she's right."

"Who are you?" Rikali shouted again. "The two of you ain't no—"

Her words were cut off with a loud crash. Maldred had finally shaken off enough of the effects of the drug and had pulled so hard at his bonds that he'd managed to shatter the rest of the bed. The big man fumbled to escape the ropes.

Gertie glanced over her shoulder and scowled. "Elsbeth! Let's be done with the game and be after Satin!" She hauled back on her makeshift club, dropped beneath the swing of the pinned man's staff and hit him soundly in the chest. The bedpost was old and cracked from the blow, and she cursed and discarded it.

"Beating the life out of you is going to take too long," Gertie sneered. She raised her empty hands. As the youth brought his staff down again, she caught it, the wood smacking hard against her open palms. "Blessed!" she shouted in surprise, as her fingers folded tightly around the wood. "That stung! You're a strapping pup!"

They struggled with the staff for a moment. She pulled him free of the wall, his tunic ripping. He fell on top of her, the staff still between them. They continued to wrestle over it for a moment, then she rolled, pinning him.

"Stop struggling, pup! I'll kill you quick! I swear! You're human and not worth selling."

"You shouldn't be so strong," the young man gasped.

Nearby, Maldred had managed to free his wrists and ankles of the ropes and was struggling to sit on the broken bed. "This . . . is . . . not . . . right . . . at . . . all," the big man said. "Something is not right about them." He tried to get up, but his legs were too heavy and refused to move. It was all he could do to lift his arms.

"Somethin's not right?" the half-elf parroted from across the room. "Whatever gave you that idea, Mal? They drive swords through plaster walls, rip posts off beds. They're as strong as bulls! Somethin's not right, indeed! Mal, I ought to—ow!"

Elsbeth had managed to cut the half-elf again, and Rikali was forced to put all her effort now into parrying Elsbeth's blows.

"Dhamon! Dhamon!" Maldred called across the room to his friend. "Move!"

Dhamon pawed awkwardly at his ropes, all the while watching the fight between Rikali and Elsbeth. The older woman had the half-elf against the wall and drove her fist forward. Rikali moved her head just in time, and Elsbeth's fist instead struck the thick plaster wall, knocking a hole in it.

The half-elf's mouth dropped open, and she stared in shock as the woman easily pulled her arm free and blew at the plaster dust coating her knuckles.

"I . . . I . . . I don't know what you are," Rikali stammered, "but you ain't no common thief."

"Not common for certain," Elsbeth retorted as her knife cut through a sleeve and deep into the half-elf's upper arm. "Maybe Gertie's right. Maybe I should stop playing with you and end this farce! But I don't want to hurt you too badly. You're not human and could be worth good coin."

"Pigs! Pigs on you!" Rikali's arm was numb, and she cursed again when her dagger slipped from her fingers. Her dress sleeve was dark with blood. "You cut me good that time, you lousy . . . lousy . . . whatever you are! " The half-elf darted left, then spun forward and right. The move took Elsbeth by surprise, and she retreated.

Rikali raced to the end of Dhamon's bed, turned, and brought her remaining dagger down hard on the rope that bound one of Dhamon's ankles. Two more quick moves and she'd cut it enough for him to break free. She hurried to the far side of the bed and hacked at the rope binding the other ankle. Broken glass from the mirror covered the floor here, but Elsbeth was no longer slow to follow.

The big woman charged across the room, crying out as the glass cut into the bottoms of her feet. The half-elf barely turned to meet her in time, bringing up the dagger to block Elsbeth's knife.

Elsbeth stepped closer and jabbed at her, swung her around and forced her toward the window.

Dhamon broke away from the bed, smashing the headboard. It took him three attempts to sit up. The room was spinning, but he was able to get a good look at the half-elf now.

He noticed how different she looked. She used to wear overly tight clothes. Now she wore an ample dress that fell to her ankles. Her face used to be painted—lips, eyes, cheeks, eyelashes thick with kohl—all of it in sharp contrast to her pale skin. Now she wasn't wearing any makeup, and her face had a softness, almost a fragility to it, like a ceramic doll. Her hair was the same, a mass of silvery-white curls that fanned away, but there was less of it, falling only to her shoulders.

"C'mon," he told himself. "Get up." His feet were suddenly on the floor, and he was standing. The dark blurs came into focus. He could make out the window and a glow, tiny, which he recognized as a candle. Lantern light spilled through the open door.

Dhamon heard a woman gasp. Rikali?

"I could use some help here, Dhamon, Mal!" came the reply. "I didn't know women could fight so well!"

Neither did I, Dhamon thought. Though his head was still muddled, he saw that Elsbeth was still fighting Rikali. Gertie was struggling on the floor with the young man. Maldred had made it to his knees and was twirling his fingers in the air. Casting a spell, Dhamon knew.

Dhamon reached behind him, to the broken bedpost where he'd hung Wyrmsbane, finding nothing. A part of him remembered that the Ergothian named Satin had taken the sword, and that she was no longer here. He swore softly as he tugged free a board of wood to use as a weapon.

Dhamon shuffled forward and raised his makeshift club, bringing it down with as much strength as he could summon and soundly clipping Elsbeth's shoulder. Unfazed, the whore continued to press the half-elf toward the window.

"Help Varek!" Riki shouted. "That bitch is gonna kill Varek! Dhamon!"

"Varek?" Dhamon glanced down at the floor. Gertie had her hands around the young man's throat. His face was red, and his eyes were bulging wide. Dhamon swayed back and forth on his feet as he took a step toward the pair. He raised the makeshift club and watched the room spin around him.

Several feet away Maldred continued his spell. In his half-drugged state, the enchantment came slowly for him, but he refused to give up. He concentrated on his fingers, which were becoming warmer—comfortably warmer at first, then almost painfully so.

"I don't want to hurt you, woman," Maldred said, trying to get Gertie's attention, "but I can't let you just kill that young man."

She ignored him.

"I'm warning you . . ." Maldred continued, aiming his fingers at the woman.

She dug her nails harder into the young man's throat.

"That's it." Maldred released his enchantment. Streaks of fire flashed toward her, striking her in the chest and stomach.

She didn't react, so he sent another fiery volley. This got her attention, and she released her grip, stumbled to her feet, starting toward Maldred. Her scant clothes were smoking, the skin beneath charred from the magical assault.

"I'd give up if I were you," Maldred said. The young man she'd been throttling gasped for air and rubbed his throat. "Stay where you are. Woman, don't you listen?"

He shook his head and spread his hands wide, mouthing a string of words in Ogrish. A sheet of flame shot from his hands. It struck the thief at waist level, and in an instant she was engulfed, writhing and screaming in a deep, harsh voice that sent chill waves down Maldred's back.

Maldred forced himself to his feet just in time, as she fell forward onto his broken bed, still writhing, the fire spreading to the sheets. In a few steps Maldred was at Varek's side, extending a hand and helping him up. At the same time, he steadied Dhamon.

"Room's burning," Maldred said.

"Aye, we better get out of here," Dhamon's words were still slurred, his tongue thick, but his head was a little clearer, and when he shook it, he was happy to note the room was now stable.

"Riki?" The word cracked from the young man's mouth. "Where's Riki?"

Dhamon and Maldred glanced about. There was no sign of the half-elf. Elsbeth was gone as well.

"Must've already cleared out," Dhamon said. "She knows when to run."

Maldred shook his head. "I don't think so." He pointed to the window, where the curtains fluttered, their edges tinged with blood. There was more blood on the sill. "I saw them near the window." Oblivious to the spreading flames, the big man snatched up his trousers and struggled into them as he stumbled toward the window and stuck his head out.

"Nothing," he said after a moment. "No sign of them."

"The wenches had this well planned," Dhamon said. "They drugged us, robbed us, and were going to kill us."

"Riki saved you." This came from the young man. "You two'd be dead if she hadn't come here. We must

find her."

Dhamon glanced at the stranger but didn't reply. He had the looks of a woodsman, dressed in a green leather tunic and thigh-high boots, with leggings that were a darker shade of green. His hair was thin and blond, falling straight to his jawline, and his eyes were an odd color, a gray the shade of ashes.

"Gotta get out of here," Maldred said, pushing himself away from the window, nudging Dhamon and the woodsman toward the door. The fire had spread to the remains of the bed frames and had started to lap up the wall. "Gotta get out now. Then we'll worry about Riki." He grabbed his boots and tunic in one hand, then with the other tugged until his sword came loose from the wall.

"Riki," the young man persisted. "We have to find my wife." He edged by the two surprised men and started down the stairs.

"Wife?" Dhamon asked to the stranger's back. There was no answer, and he put away the thought for the moment. "Maybe she went after the big wench," he suggested to Maldred. "Out the window, but more likely out this door. Those women . . . there was something not right about them."

"Riki wouldn't have climbed out a window in her condition," the young man said over his shoulder, "and she wouldn't have chased after any of those women."

"She was wounded," Maldred agreed. "I don't think she went anywhere on her own." The big man coughed as the smoke started to billow out of the room. He brushed by Dhamon and took the stairs two at a time. "We'll find her."

The stairway opened into a large room in which a dozen ogres were sitting, drinking from massive wooden mugs and tossing brightly painted shells and rocks in the center of a pair of big round tables. All of them stopped to stare at the wounded trio, pointing and mumbling in their guttural tongue when they saw smoke seep down the stairwell.

Behind the bar was a spindly middle-aged human with a greasy shock of salt-and-pepper hair that fell over one eye. He was polishing a glass with a dirty rag and trying hard not to look toward the stairway. He hadn't noticed the smoke.

"Did a half-elf come down here?" the young man asked the bartender. When the man didn't answer, he stretched over the counter and laid his quarterstaff across it. "I said, did a half-elf come down here?"

The man polished faster and gave the stranger a puzzled look. "Half-elf?"

"How about a fat wench? One of the ladies who paid you to ignore what they were doin' upstairs."

The man shrugged and tossed the rag over his shoulder. "Don't know what you're talking about. Haven't seen anyone."

Varek grabbed the bartender's chin, and in surprise he dropped the glass. Dhamon spun to keep an eye on the ogres, half of whom were keeping their seats, intently watching the barkeep as if he were the nightly entertainment.

Varek tugged the little man's head forward and twisted his chin until it pointed toward the stairway. Dark gray smoke was gathering at the top, thick tendrils creeping down. The scent of burning wood was beginning to overpower the other smells of the place—filth, sweat, and spilled ale.

"Fire!" the man shouted. "My place's on fire!"

Varek held him fast. "You'll burn with it if you don't tell me about the half-elf."

"I didn't see anything!" There was fear in the man's eyes but also the look of truth. Varek squeezed his chin hard before releasing him and rushing outside.

The barkeep ducked behind the counter, his hands a blur as he grabbed a few valuables and a coin box.

"Whole place is going to burn fast," Dhamon observed. He was coughing, too, and making his way toward the door. He paused when he saw Maldred wasn't moving.

The big man had his sword out, eyes locked onto the face of the largest ogre. Most of the other ogres were shuffling toward the door, grabbing up their shells and coins, a few toting their ale mugs along. All of them were cursing.

"The human women," Maldred said in Ogrish, leveling the greatsword in front of him. "Did you see them? Did you see a half-elf?"

The largest ogre shook his head and took a step toward the door. Maldred shifted his position to put himself between the ogre and the way out.

Smoke hung like a cloud now below the ceiling of the big room. There were spots of orange here and there, hinting that the fire had spread across the floor. Over by the stairs, a plank of the ceiling groaned, blackened, and fell to the floor.

"The women," Maldred repeated.

The ogre growled and stepped forward, dropping his shells and extending clawlike hands.

"Mal . . ." This came from Dhamon. "Mal, let's get out of here. Riki's a survivor."

Maldred ignored his friend and released one of his hands from the sword's pommel. He pointed an index finger at the large ogre and mumbled a string of words shot through with Ogrish. There was a musical quality to them, and when he finished, the ogre shouted in surprise. A ball of flame had appeared in the air a hair's breadth from Maldred's finger. It spun and crackled and followed his gesture, moving slowly toward the ogre.

The smoke cloud was growing thicker. Dhamon backed toward the door, calling for his friend to join him. The building creaked in protest around them, and the flames snapped and popped louder. There were "thunks" coming from above, signaling beams falling. From outside, came shouts: "Fire!" "Thatcher's place is burning!" "Riki!" The latter was frenetically repeated.

"Mal . . ." Dhamon urged.

Tears were running from Maldred's eyes because of the smoke. He coughed and gestured, making the ball of flame grow larger.

"The women." This time the words were accompanied with a snarl. "You have to know something." Still the ogre said nothing. Maldred pointed to the floor, and the ball of fire dropped, breaking as if it were a globe of water. Flames spread across the floor in a line between Maldred and the ogre.

The ogre howled, and Dhamon cursed. "Mal! This place is going to fall down around us."

"The half-elf!" Maldred shouted above the angry snaps and pops of the fire.

"They'd have taken her to sell!" the ogre shouted. "At the spawn village. That's what they do with elves. Sell them in Polagnar."

Maldred spun away, following Dhamon out the door. The large ogre was behind them, leaping over the line of fire and barreling past them.

The moon was full, making it easy to see the ramshackle town in the foothills. The place consisted of roughly two dozen buildings, all of them wooden and most of them looking as if they might topple before the year was out. A few were businesses—a stable, something that passed for a foodstore, another a seamstress and bootery, a closed-down weaponsmith and blacksmith. There was one tavern at the end of the dusty street. The tavern they'd just left was merrily burning. The remainder of the buildings were either homes and flophouses or abandoned.

There was a loud groan as the building, thoroughly engulfed, collapsed in on itself. There were loud shouts as flames leaped to the adjacent bootery. The barkeep was trying to rally his former patrons to go after Maldred. Nearby, Varek called for Riki.

"He did it!" the barkeep was hollering and pointing Maldred's way. "He set it to burning. Kill him!"

"I've no weapon," Dhamon said at Maldred's shoulder. "There's too many of them."

Maldred grunted. "The summer's made this place like prime kindling. We don't need weapons." He pointed at a building across from the burning inn, from the looks of it something that passed for a general store. Flames licked the columns that supported a shingled overhang. Another gesture from Maldred and flames were sparking on the roof of the stable.

"He'll burn down the town!" the barkeep shouted. The man was gasping for breath and waving his arms. "Kill him! Kill him and his friends!"

"Kill the humans!" a barrel-chested ogre shouted.

"See to your town!" Maldred shouted back, "or I will burn all of it!"

He backed up, Dhamon still at his side. Varek, still shouting for Riki, joined them.

"My wife," the young man said. His eyes were daggers. "I've got to find her. She's—"

"Not here," Maldred finished. "But I know where she is. C'mon!"

They hurried from the town, not slowing until the crackling of flames and the shouts of the ogres were memories.

"Where is she?" Varek shot at Maldred when he stopped to catch his breath. "Where's my Riki?"

73

"My Riki? Just who are you?" Dhamon interrupted.

The young man sputtered, red-faced. "Varek. Varek Lockwood. Riki's my wife, and I mean to find her. She insisted on coming here to find you and—"

"She's in a place called Polagnar," Maldred said, reaching into the pocket of his trousers and pulling out a bone scroll tube. "Or, rather, she's heading there."

Dhamon breathed a deep sigh of relief when he saw the tube. "The thieves got our gems, but they didn't get everything."

Maldred grinned. "No. They didn't get our map." He uncurled it and addressed the parchment. "Polagnar." A section of the map glowed, and a green smudge brightened. Images of trees and parrots appeared and swirled around the spot, then were displaced by the visage of a broken-toothed spawn with gleaming black eyes. Maldred noted the position on the map, and traced an invisible line from it to where they were now.

"Rikali's being taken to this village called Polagnar. If we move quickly, we might catch up to her and Elsbeth before they get there." Maldred replaced the scroll, then put the tube back in his pocket.

"Fine." Dhamon shook his head. "Let Varek here go after his wife. It's well out of our way. There's the Screaming Valley to consider, Mal. The sage I need to find." Dhamon's eyes were unblinking, his jaw firm. "We're not going into the swamp after Riki. She'd understand."

Varek cut Dhamon a withering glare and gripped his quarterstaff tight. "Ungrateful," he snorted. He set off down the road at a jog, heading in the direction of Polagnar, using the moonlight to guide him.

"Wife," Dhamon muttered sarcastically. "I'll just bet they're husband and wife. He's dreaming. Riki would no more marry that boy than—"

"We're going with him, Dhamon," Maldred cut in. "To Polagnar. We're going to find Riki. Maybe she is his wife. Maybe she isn't. But she's family to us."

"No. No, we're not. We're going straight south." Dhamon shook his head again. "Mal, I—"

The big man growled and whirled on his friend, hand shooting out and grabbing a hank of Dhamon's hair and pulling him close.

"What are you thinking?" The words were spat out forcefully and with a trace of venom. "Not go after Riki? She saved our lives by coming to that ogre town. Saved your life when that wench was going to slit your throat. You owe her. We owe her."

Dhamon's jaw worked and his hands knotted into tight fists, but he said nothing.

"We'll get through the Screaming Valley and find the treasure. Then we'll find the sage," Maldred continued, "but not until we find Riki." He released Dhamon and tromped after Varek, not looking to see if his friend was following.

CHAPTER SEVEN
SCALES

T he marshy ground grabbed at Dhamon's boot heels as he slogged through a thickening cypress grove. Varek and Maldred were a few yards ahead of him, talking. In the younger man's voice was a decided urgency. Occasionally Maldred turned and said something to Dhamon, though Dhamon didn't answer—he was paying less attention to his companions' words than to the persistent soft chitter of the cloud of insects that surrounded them. Dhamon was thinking about the mysterious healer to whom the enchanted map pointed.

"The pirate treasure first," he said to himself, "if it exists." Use as much of it—all of it if necessary—to buy the sorceress's cure. "If she exists," he added, though he hadn't meant to speak aloud.

"What did you say, Dhamon?" This from Maldred, who had stopped at the edge of a sodden clearing.

"I said I'll take first watch," Dhamon returned. "Sun's setting. I don't fancy walking through this bog in the dark. Especially since we've got no torches."

Faint stars began appearing by the time Varek and Maldred were asleep. Dhamon sat with his back to a spindly shaggybark. He could hear Maldred snoring, a chorus of crickets, and from a tall moss-draped poplar a parrot softly scolded them for intruding in its territory.

For the briefest of moments Dhamon considered stealing the enchanted map from his large friend and getting down to the business of finding the treasure and then the sorceress—maybe they would both prove hollow fantasies. "Let Maldred and Varek find Riki," he softly mused. "They don't need my help with that task. I don't need to waste time . . . by all the vanished gods, please not now!"

His right leg had begun to throb, gently at first. Within the passing of a few moments, the pain grew intense and his body feverish. He shakily stood and stumbled away from the marshy clearing, following the path of a small stream to the east for nearly a mile until his chest grew so tight and his legs so numb he could no longer walk. He stumbled down a low rise and into the night-cooled water, then struggled to pull himself up on the muddy bank. He pressed his hands against his thigh, feeling, through the worn fabric of his trousers, the scale as hard as steel.

"Damn this thing!" he softly cursed, "and damn me!" Icy cold waves pulsed outward from the scale now, as if Dhamon had been plunged into a frigid sea. His teeth chattered, and he curled into a ball, though he gained no warmth from the position.

The sensation persisted until he felt he could endure no more and until he nearly passed out, then began to dissipate, slowly, and after interminable moments he felt warm again. He gulped the late summer air into his lungs and labored to stand, the slippery mud pulling him down. His questing fingers found a vine, and he tugged himself to his feet.

For an instant he considered returning to Maldred and Varek, though he loathed the notion of looking helpless in front of them. Suddenly he felt warmer still. Jolts of heat stabbed into his leg where the scale was embedded, regular and pulsing like the erratic beat of a heart not his own. The heat intensified, and he clenched his fists, fingernails digging deep into his palms, in an effort to deny the agony. He felt blood on his hands but no pain. The wounds he inflicted on himself were insignificant compared to what the scale was doing to him.

"No," he breathed. "Stop this." He continued to stagger east along the stream, chanting the words, as if they might chase away the pain. After several more steps he crumpled, slipping on a oily patch of sawgrass and falling on his back, sliding down the sloping bank headfirst until his heel caught on a root. His hair hung in the water.

The heat again mounted, and the jolts quickened until he was gasping for air. His limbs trembled. He was unable to control them, and his arms flopped about as he prayed for unconsciousness, death, anything to relieve the pain. He rolled until his face was in the water, and he retched, emptying his stomach of the little food he'd consumed today. Then he summoned what strength he had, raised his head, and slammed it down against a rock, cutting himself and adding a dull ache to his miseries. He raised his head again, felt the root tug free, and felt himself sliding all the rest of the way down the bank, spinning until he was laying on his back immersed in the stream.

It was shallow in this spot, the water only lapping over his shoulders and rising halfway up on his face. Some part of him registered that it was pleasantly cool, but it did nothing to cut the all-consuming heat. By now Dhamon was trembling all over. He cursed himself for losing control to the pain, and he cursed the Dark

Knight and the dragon who put him in this vulnerable and tortured state.

His mind propelled him back to a forested glade in Solamnia. He was kneeling over a Dark Knight he had mortally wounded, holding the man's hand and trying to offer what comfort he could in the last moments of the man's life. The man beckoned him closer, loosed the armor from his chest and showed Dhamon a large blood-red scale embedded in the flesh beneath. With fumbling fingers, the knight managed to pry the scale free, and before Dhamon realized what was happening, the knight had placed it against Dhamon's thigh.

The scale molded itself around his leg, feeling like a brand thrust against his unprotected skin. It was the most painful sensation Dhamon had experienced in his young life. Worse than the pain was the dishonor: Malys, the red dragon overlord whose scale it was, used the scale to possess and control him. Months went by before a mysterious shadow dragon, along with a silver dragon called Silvara, worked ancient magic to break the overlord's control. The scale turned black in the process and shortly thereafter it had begun to ache periodically.

At first, the pain was infrequent, fleeting, and tolerable. Certainly it was preferable to being controlled by a dragon. Gradually the spasms grew worse and lasted longer. He had sought a cure numerous times from mystics and sages, from old men who peddled bottles filled with all manner of stinking concoctions. He had sought Tanis's sword, because it was said to find lost and elusive things for its wielder. Dhamon had told it to find him a cure. Instead it cursed him with unfathomable visions.

"Should kill myself," Dhamon hissed between clenched teeth. "Kill myself and be done with all of this. Not hope like some fool that Mal's healer exists." He'd toyed with the idea of suicide several times, but he either could not find the courage or he found a reason to hope things would change, found some notion to cling to—like Mal's mysterious healer in the Plains of Dust.

"If she exists."

He'd even begun to believe that perhaps the spasms were finally over. It had been nearly four weeks since the last episode. A part of him knew better, though, and tonight was the worst yet. In the past the pain had persisted until he passed out. This time it seemed he was not to be granted that mercy.

In the back of his mind images flashed of the great red called Malys, the shadow dragon, and the silver. He saw other images, too, bronze and blue scales and wings, and he wondered if his mind was imagining it all or if dragons of those hues were passing by overhead right now. The scale gave him the ability to sense if dragons were nearby.

He lay in torment in the stream for nearly an hour, tears running from his eyes, chest heaving, sucking in the fetid air of the place, images of bronze and blue and black dragons clouding his thoughts. When the waves of fire and ice finally became irregular and diminished in intensity, he crawled out of the stream and up the bank, finding flat, higher ground. He threw himself on his back and stared up at the myriad of stars that he could see through a gap in the foliage. He did his best to blot out the pounding in his head. When the warm air finished drying him, he climbed to his feet, fingers fumbling with the fastenings of his trousers.

Dhamon tugged down his pants and hunched over to study his leg. The large black scale on his right thigh faintly reflected the starlight and illuminated several scales the size of steel pieces that had sprouted around its edges. He counted the small ones—eleven—two more than he had a few weeks ago.

81

"What is happening to me?" he breathed. Mal knew about the one, large scale that had once belonged to the red overlord. Palin Majere, Feril, and a host of others knew about the scale, too. No one knew about the growing number of smaller ones. He'd managed to keep this unfortunate development all to himself.

He pondered returning to the camp and stealing Maldred's knife. He was as stealthy as any thief. The half-elf had taught him well. He could leave Maldred and Varek, slip away, end his life with a slash of the knife, end this misery.

"I should," he told himself. He tossed his aching head back to again study the stars. He didn't recognize the constellations. It had been weeks between this and the last episode, he reminded himself, weeks of freedom in which he and Maldred had indulged in pleasures in various ogre towns. He had honestly enjoyed the time with his friend.

"I should," he repeated.

But then the scale wins. He'd never been one to completely give up on himself. Krynn? Yes. He gave up on the world long months ago when he decided the overlords could not be bested. His friends? He gave up on most of the ones who hadn't died in his company. Palin Majere could do nothing about the scale. Feril left him. Fiona and Rig—the latter seemed always at odds with him—had given up on him and he on them. He had given up on most of them—but not Maldred.

"I should, but not yet. Not just yet." There was the healer the map pointed to. She was his last hope. There was the pirate horde, which came first. "Then the healer."

Oh, and there was the half-elf to rescue. Dhamon wasn't in the mood to rescue anyone except himself. If they did not come to this village Polagnar within a day or two, he'd do his best to talk Maldred into giving up on Riki and just pursuing the pirate treasure. Let Varek worry about his wife. Dhamon had the scale to worry over. He knew he was living solely for himself, but damn the consequences, and damn anyone who got in his way.

"Damn me," he said.

Exhausted from his ordeal, he returned to the spindly shaggybark. Nobody was awake. Nobody had noticed that he had been gone. He grabbed a flask of ale. A faint rosy light was intruding in the sky overhead, suggesting that dawn was only an hour or so away. He propped his back against the trunk and took a long pull from the flask. The ale helped to numb the throbbing in his head, which usually continued for up to a few hours after an episode. Enough ale numbed just about anything, he had learned. He drank nearly all of it, then replaced the cork and waited for his companions to wake up.

Chapter Eight
Thorns of the Mangrove

aldred was examining a veritable wall of close-packed bushes, trees and flower-covered vines that stretched to the north and south as far as they could see. It rose more than a hundred feet toward the sky.

His enchanted map had led him here, when he asked it again to reveal Polagnar. He looked for the shortest route, and now he wondered if that was a mistake.

"Does your map say how far it is around this . . . this . . ." Varek couldn't find words to describe the barrier formed by the tight weave of plants. "Is there another way to Polagnar?" When Maldred didn't supply an answer, the young man looked to Dhamon. "It's been three days since they took my Riki. Is there a faster way?"

Dhamon breathed deep. The scents here were intense and for a change pleasant—far different from the fetid odor of decaying plants and brackish ponds that had been more his experience lately. The light filtering down revealed water spreading away from the wall's roots. He

85

carefully stepped forward, discovering that the ground sloped sharply downward past the water's edge and the water actually went up to his thighs. He tugged at the tightly knit branches in front of him.

"Mangrove," Maldred pronounced, inhaling deep.

"Aye. It certainly is a mangrove, my large friend. And a strange and threatening one, if you ask me. Perhaps it's time we gave up on Riki and—"

Maldred shot Dhamon a withering glance.

"What's a mangrove?" Varek stared at the water.

"Something unpleasant," Maldred answered.

"Still, I don't know what—" Varek continued.

"A mangrove is this," Dhamon said irritatedly, waving his hand at the plants, then the water. "It's all of this. And it's a bad sign to run into a mangrove, a sign that we shouldn't be here."

Varek looked to the south. "Then we'll simply head around this mangrove to find my Riki and—"

"I'm certain," Maldred cut in, "those thieves wouldn't have bothered to take Riki around the mangrove. That would take far too much time. I'm equally certain Dhamon doesn't have the patience to take the long way either."

He consulted the enchanted map, noting again the location of the spawn village. He carefully replaced the map in the bone tube and thrust it in the waistband of his trousers, then stepped forward and joined Dhamon. Tugging at the smallest branches, with considerable effort he forged a path and slipped inside the living green wall.

"Wonderful," Dhamon mused, as he went after his large friend. Varek followed at their heels.

They continued to press forward, squeezing between spindly trunks and closing their eyes when fingerlike branches scratched at their faces. They came upon thick sections of sharp thorns, and Dhamon maneuvered himself past Maldred, plucking a knife from his friend's belt as he went. He used the knife to cut away some of the branches. As he watched, the foliage instantly repaired itself and grew even thicker behind them.

"Mal, you've usually got some magic handy," Dhamon suggested. "Why not use it and make this easier?"

The big thief gave a snort. "My magic's more for earth and fire, Dhamon. Everything here's too wet to burn."

At times they slogged through water that flowed up to their armpits. Maldred held the map above his head so it wouldn't get soaked. Just enough sunlight bled through the weave of branches to reveal tiny glints of silver fish that schooled around them curiously. At one point the fish darted away as something larger slipped through the water in pursuit, a thick green snake that had two sets of short legs near its tail.

"Did you see . . . ?" Varek whispered.

"Yes," Dhamon returned.

"Snakes don't have—"

"Apparently here they do."

In one place they had to double back, after coming up against a block of branches as solid as any dwarven-built construction. Not a leaf or twig would budge. Eventually they worked themselves around to a section of younger trees, the trunks of which Dhamon and Maldred could bend over so they could continue on their way. The water was deep here, rising to Varek's chin, and they sloshed through it for more than an hour. Each of them fell at least once, tripping over hidden rocks and logs, tangling their feet in roots. Dhamon noticed more and more fish here, a little larger than before, and the bigger ones were feeding on the silver fingerlings. Maldred insisted they keep going, that they were making progress.

They spent a few more hours twisting their way through the dense wall of vegetation. The morning passed into the afternoon before the trunks thinned and

the worst of the wall was behind them. Stretching ahead
of them, the sun shone down on an immense water-
filled clearing, easily a few miles across, encircled by
the plant weave.

Dhamon groaned at the thought of making his way
through the similar vegetation wall on the other side.

"Under other circumstances I could enjoy this," Maldred observed. He was slowly turning in an open expanse
of water that came to just below his knees. "I feel a nice
breeze, and I smell the mangrove blooms. I could get
drunk on them."

The other two looked at him as though he were crazy.
A grinning Maldred pointed to a pair of trees, the roots of
which started well up on their trunks, looking almost like
branches and angling into the water. Veils of dark red
flowers hung from their highest branches and spiraled
down, scenting the air with something sweet and unfa-
miliar and overpowering.

"I don't care about any strange-looking trees or flowers,"
Varek said. "I want to find Riki."

"Aye," Dhamon agreed. The sooner they had the half-
elf, the sooner he and Mal would be able to go after the
pirate's treasure. He caught Maldred's gaze. "Riki first,"
reminded Maldred, reading his thoughts. "We're getting
close. Then this healer of yours."

"Let's move." Varek headed away from them, striking
out to the west, careful to skirt what looked like a wide,
deep patch of water where larger fish swam near the surface. He turned and motioned for Dhamon and Maldred
to follow. "All this saltwater," he said, waggling his fingers just above the surface. The sunlight sent shimmering
flecks of gold across its surface and illuminated the
myriad of fish that swam everywhere. "Strange, isn't it?
By my reckoning we're too far south from the coast for
there to be saltwater here."

"By my reckoning," Dhamon snapped, "I suspect we're well into Sable's realm. And I'm certain the black dragon can create saltwater marshes wherever she wants."

"It's for food," Maldred said, barely loud enough for them to hear. He was sloshing steadily through the water "Her spawn fish in these places for her. Spawn like fish, and so does Sable."

Varek cocked his head. "Just how would you know that?"

"I know lots of things," Maldred said flatly. He was looking to the trees that ringed the place. "I know there should be some animals here too. Birds or something. Something other than these fish. There were snakes dripping from the branches everywhere else. Lots of lizards in the wall. Don't see anything now. Odd."

"Aye," Dhamon agreed. "There should be animals. Perhaps something scared them away."

"Something." Maldred peered at the distant foliage more closely. He caught a glimpse of bone-white through the rustling leaves. It was to the southwest, shaded by cottonwood branches and willow leaves, and it piqued his curiosity. He slogged closer for a better look.

"I think there's a statue over there. A big one. I want to get a closer look. It's on our way."

He gestured toward it, and Dhamon headed in that direction.

The water deepened to their thighs as Maldred and Dhamon passed through a veil of willow leaves. A few more steps, another leafy veil, and the water was past their waists again.

"Dhamon . . . it's not a statue."

"I see it, Mal. It's dragon skulls. Lots of them." Dhamon closed his fingers about the handle of his knife and edged closer to the thing. At the same time the scale on his leg began to grow warm, and he saw an image in the back of his mind, yellow eyes surrounded by blackness.

A dragon. His head began pounding, and the blackness of the dragon's visage became more distinct, scales as shiny as beads and sparkling like inky stars, the pupils coming into sharp focus. The great eyes blinked.

"A dragon's coming, Mal. A black one," he whispered so softly that Maldred couldn't hear him.

"Dhamon, Maldred, what is it? What's over here?" Varek was coming up behind them, brushing aside the first veil of willow leaves, gasping loudly at the sight of the skulls.

The three of them gaped at the mass of dragon skulls, which were arranged in a pyramid-shaped tower. The construct was wider at the base, which was comprised of the largest skulls. It rose nearly fifty feet, bone-white but covered in places with green and gray moss to add to the hellish image. The skulls' eyes softly glowed, as if candles were burning inside them, their colors hinting at the dragons they were in life: red, blue, black, green, white, copper, bronze, silver, brass, even gold. Most of the skulls had horns intact, and the one that crowned the top had some patches of silver scales affixed to it. A boa constrictor poured itself out the mouth of one skull near the top and slowly slithered and circled down the column.

With some effort, Dhamon thrust the image of the black dragon out of his mind and edged closer to the tower.

"Dhamon, don't," Maldred cautioned.

"Let's get out of here," Varek suggested. "This has nothing to do with finding my wife."

"Aye, we need to get out of here," Dhamon said. "A dragon's nearby. But I want to take a good look at this thing first. It's a chance not given many mortals."

The lowest skulls were massive, perhaps coming from dragons that were well more than a hundred feet long in life. Dhamon cautiously moved his foot forward until he felt another ring of skulls under the water's surface and wedged well into the mud. There had to be at least three dozen of the massive skulls in the totem. He stooped over to get a look inside of one, then looked into another and another. He moved as if hypnotized.

"Brains," he whispered in awe. "The brains are intact inside the skulls. I think there are brains inside all of them!"

"It's a dragon totem, for certain," Maldred said. There was a tinge of awe in his voice too. "Nobody's ever seen one and lived to talk about it. I heard about them from Grim Kedar's tales. This has got to be one of Sable's totems. Souvenirs from the dragons she killed in the Dragon Purge. There's much magical power in the collection. I can sense that without even touching it. Like insects dancing all over my skin." He paused. "I've no intention of trying to find out what it can do."

Varek cleared his throat. "Good. Now, let's get out of here. Dhamon says there's a dragon nearby, though how he can tell . . ."

Dhamon had turned away from the totem now and was pointing to a few glimmering specks in the sky. So graceful in their flight, at first they looked like gulls. Within a few seconds they became larger and more distinct and brought a snarl to his angular face. "Sivaks. Three of them."

There has to be a dragon nearby, too, he added to himself. The vision of a black dragon still haunted the recesses of his mind, and the scale on his leg was warming.

The three companions tensed as the draconians dropped from the sky, claws outstretched and muscular bodies angled like arrows. Dhamon waded forward almost eagerly, leaping and slashing at the lead one. Blood and silvery scales flew, and he swept the knife in a wide arc again and again, biting deep into the creature's leg. It retreated into the sky.

Its two companions dived at him, teeth bared, claws shining like polished steel in the late afternoon sun. The first dropped beneath Dhamon's swing, managing to skim the water and slash at his side as it glided past. Its wings beat hard, sending a spray of water in its wake and carrying it swiftly toward the advancing Maldred.

Maldred swept his greatsword at the creature and cleaved its left arm. The stump spurted blood in an arc that stung his face, blinding him. Unseeing, he continued to swing hard as he spun, miraculously landing another blow and slaying the creature. Maldred furiously wiped and pawed at his face with his sleeve, blinking to clear his vision

The other draconian clawed at Dhamon. "I need a sword!" Dhamon shouted as he shifted the grip on the knife. "This damn pig-sticker is useless."

"Mine'll do!" Maldred said as he charged forward. In the next instant, Dhamon dropped in a crouch beneath the thing's claws as Maldred swung and connected, slicing off a piece of the draconian's wing. It careened into the water. Varek shouldered his staff and headed toward the floundering creature.

"Dhamon, one's dropping!"

The last one now streaked toward them, claws outstretched, wings pulled close to its body.

"Foolish thing should get out of here while it's still alive. Foolish thing should . . . together now!"

Dhamon and Maldred struck it simultaneously, the latter's greatsword cutting deep into the creature's thigh. Dhamon drove his knife into the sivak's chest and tugged it free. He watched the draconian fall backward, sending a shower of water and blood away from its corpse.

Before Dhamon could catch his breath, the image of the black dragon swelled in his mind and paralyzed him for an instant. He sensed that the dragon was close, diving, streaking like a bolt of midnight through the lush green canopy of the swamp. Dhamon backed away, toward the nearest wall of plants. He looked up, searching the sky, expecting to see the dragon descending on the clearing.

"Nothing," he whispered. "Where is the dragon?" Suddenly he felt something brush against his leg. He dropped his gaze to see what appeared to be his own corpse floating on its back in the shallow water. There were gaping wounds on his abdomen and thigh. He stared at it incredulously, then quickly realized what it was—the sivak he'd killed. There were corpses of Maldred and Varek, too—the draconians in death imitating the forms of their slayers.

"Dhamon! By my breath, look! Look!"

Dhamon twisted, spotting Varek. The young man's mouth was open wide and his face was the color of bleached parchment. His trembling fingers released his quarterstaff. "By the blessed memory of Steel Brightblade, look at that!"

Dhamon had been expecting the black dragon to fly over the clearing, waiting for its shadow to block out the sun, perhaps accompanied by a flurry of sivaks. Instead, the creature rose slowly, ponderously, magnificently, from the deep part of the marsh.

The dragon was hideous and beautiful. Its wet scales glimmered like a star-filled sky, and its bright yellow eyes glowed like twin suns. Its head was horse-shaped, with a combination of sharp and smooth angles everywhere and a jagged ridge that ran from between its eyes to the tip of its wide nostrils. Its mouth opened, revealing stark white teeth that were so straight and perfect they looked sculpted. An incredible wash of fetid air escaped.

The three humans stood mesmerized, terrified.

A long black tongue snaked out to tease the barabels that hung from the bottom of the dragon's jaw, then retreated into the recesses of its cavelike mouth. Its serpentine neck cleared the surface of the marsh. It shook its head, spraying water everywhere. Its wings cleared the water, batlike and massive, beating against the marsh and then the air as it rose until it hovered just above the surface. Its body looked thin compared to the rest of it, its legs oddly long and thick for its form. Its dangling claws brushed the water. Its tail swished back and forth, stirring waves, then it inhaled sharply.

"Sable!" Varek shouted. "We're dead. All of us."

"Duck!" Dhamon and Maldred shouted practically in unison. All three dropped beneath the water's surface, just as the beast breathed, a fan-shaped gout of crystal-clear acid racing toward them. With the acid came the strong stench of sulfur belched by the beast's furnace stomach.

"It's not Sable," Dhamon gasped, as, after long moments, he surfaced and started running toward the plant wall. "It's a big one, but it's not anywhere near big enough to be a dragon overlord. Move, Mal! Varek!"

The creature was a hundred feet from nose to tail tip. A fairly young dragon, but one nonetheless formidable in size. Her jet-black claws clacked together menacingly, as her head swiveled and she caught Dhamon's eyes. He watched the dragon's eyes narrow to needlelike slits.

"Spread out!" he called. "Spread out!"

They were the same words spoken months ago by his friend and second-in-command Gauderic. He and Gauderic had led a force of elves and humans deep into the Qualinesti forest in search of a hateful young green dragon. They found a green dragon—though quite a bit larger than the one they'd been searching for. Dhamon recalled the incident too clearly. The men had panicked. Gauderic had shouted for them to run. "Spread out!" Guaderic had cried.

Dhamon had countermanded the order. As the ranking officer, he ordered them instead to plow forward and face the creature together, as a combined force. Yet when he felt the dragonfear, Dhamon ran from that battle, feeling the scale on his leg burning, his mind filled with frightening images of the green dragon, all the sensations overwhelming him and rendering him useless.

He and Gauderic were the only two to survive that day. He had fled, and the dragon had left Gauderic alive to tell the day's deeds—until Dhamon killed Gauderic in a drunken tavern brawl.

"Spread out!" Dhamon shouted again, as the dragon suddenly switched its attention to Varek.

Dhamon angled away from the wall of plants and backed toward the tower of dragon skulls. Out of the corner of his eye he saw Varek reach the treeline, pausing and glancing Dhamon's way.

"Run! Varek, run!"

Terror was etched deep on the young man's face, as he was caught by the powerful aura of fear exuded by the dragon. His feet were rooted to the spot.

Maldred was nowhere to be seen.

The dragon turned and buffeted Dhamon with its wings, sending a gust of water and wind his way. He wove and stumbled, fighting to stay on his feet, scrambling all the way to the tower of bones and leaning against it for support. He heard the dragon inhale again, and in that moment he stabbed his knife into one of the skull's eyesockets, puncturing the brain inside.

The dragon roared defiantly, a noise so loud it was agonizing to human ears. As the sound died the dragon roared louder still.

No? Dhamon wondered. Did the dragon scream the word no?

The beast roared again, buffeting the marsh, bending small trees with the force of the wind it had created and sending water everywhere. Again and again it roared.

Dhamon locked his arm around a bony horn and plunged his knife into another socket.

"Dhamon!" Suddenly Maldred was slogging toward him, leading with his greatsword, his eyes nervously darting around.

"Dragon!" Dhamon shouted, his voice barely able to be heard above the beating of the creature's wings. "Leave us or I'll destroy more!"

There was a great commotion, a horrible, sloshing sound, as the dragon crept closer, catlike, its eyes opening wide.

"Come no closer!" Dhamon held the blade in front of another socket.

"What are you doing?" Maldred said in a hush.

"You said this tower was magical," Dhamon shot back. "I'm betting the dragon doesn't want it destroyed—by my knife or its acid breath." To the dragon, he repeated, "No closer!"

Incredibly, the dragon paused, lips turned up in a feral sneer, acid spilling out into the marsh water, hissing and raising a curl of steam.

"I am listening, human," the dragon said after a lengthy silence. Its voice was gruff and grating, the words drawn out.

Maldred took a turn, leveling his greatsword at an eye socket. "We want safe passage from here, dragon," he stated. "If you promise . . ."

The black's eyes narrowed.

"Safe passage," Maldred repeated. "Out of this salt marsh and well beyond it." He edged the sword tip in.

"Given," the dragon replied.

"Don't trust the dragon," Dhamon warned.

"We don't have much choice, do we?"

 The dragon made a noise that sounded like a cackle, but it was loud and unnerving, sending shivers down their backs.

"Sable has other totems," came the reply. "Destroying this will not diminish her strength."

"Well, then . . ." Dhamon cleared his throat and thrust the blade deep into a socket. The pale blue glow that had emanated from the skull died when he pierced the brain. "Safe passage," he said sternly. "Or I'll wager I can put out quite a few more of these lights before you can kill me."

"Done."

Dhamon stared at the black dragon, watching as it turned and rose from the water, beating its wings and gliding across the marsh surface, then rising as it banked west and cleared the plant wall.

"Now, let's get out of here," Maldred said, backing away from the totem and toward where Varek waited, "before it comes back. Let's find Riki and get out of this damn swamp."

Dhamon lingered for a moment, sensing in his mind the dragon retreating, feeling the warmth of the scale on his leg diminish but sensing also that the dragon was still nearby. Perhaps it was keeping its part of the bargain and was waiting to see if they would leave the tower alone. Was the tower that important to the overlord?

"Dhamon . . . joining us?" Maldred was standing impatiently at the weave.

Dhamon followed his companions through the thick wall of wood that surrounded the saltwater marsh.

CHAPTER NINE
THE TEARS OF
KIRI-JOLITH

T he ground was a slick swath of mud, and the trunks of the trees were varying shades of charcoal. Even the sky overhead, adding to the gloom, was dark and oppressive and threatened rain. An involuntary shiver ran down Dhamon's back when he paused to take a good look at everything.

"Mal . . ." Dhamon pointed to what, judging by its form, likely once had been a willow-birch.

It was not covered with normal bark. Instead, it was completely clad in scales, smooth and supple like the skin of a snake. Dhamon reached out and tentatively touched it. Indeed, it felt like scales and was cool despite the oppressive heat. There was a thin coat of moisture on it from the humidity. Even the branches were covered with the snakeskin, and what few leaves grew were also in the shape of scales, as black as a starless sky. The dark roots, protruding from the mud here and there, were all angular, straight, and disturbing looking.

"Bones," Dhamon whispered. What he could see of the roots looked eerily like charred human arm and leg bones. The thinnest of branches bumped together in the slight breeze. Some of the trees had vines hanging from them, and the vines looked like snakes, their ends like bulbous heads grazing the ground. Other trees were draped in bands of discarded snakeskin.

He could see no birds in the trees, though he spotted a few large parrots flying high overhead, oddly colorful amid all this drabness. There was no evidence of animals, save a few unnaturally large black water snakes coiled at the edge of a stagnant pond.

There were only a scattering of bushes, leafless and looking like collections of blackened finger bones fitted together. A pair of corpses stood out stark white against their surroundings, propped against a tree trunk.

"This place makes my skin crawl," Dhamon said. He breathed as shallowly as possible. The smell of the place made him nauseous. The breeze was laced with sulfur, becoming stronger the farther east they traveled, the acrid scent lodging deep in Dhamon's lungs. He coughed and was rewarded with an even greater concentration of the stuff. He glanced at his companions. Varek looked ill, and Maldred had cupped his hand over his nose and mouth.

"Yes, this is a lovely place," Maldred mused.

"This was your idea," Dhamon growled, "going after Riki. I've only got a knife for a weapon, and Varek dropped his staff in the marsh. This was your idea, your very bad idea, my friend." Dhamon craned his neck around a thick scaly tree and drew his lips into a thin line. "Aye, a truly lovely place we've come to," he added.

An expanse of dark water curved around a marshy island, which was cluttered with more of the serpent-trees. The sky was overcast, and it looked as if it was raining in the distance. Dhamon's keen eyesight managed to pick through the drab darkness. He could see just enough to tell him there were buildings of a sort on the island.

"I think we've found your spawn village," Dhamon said, studying the water. "By the vanished gods, this water smells like a Palanthas sewer." He let out a low whistle. "Check that magical map of yours to be certain this is the place."

He trundled toward the water's edge, sliding down the last of the muddy slope and weaving around the thinning scale-covered trees. Dhamon stopped just short of the bank, noting a profusion of fat-bellied crocodiles and alligators so coated with mud it looked as though they had camouflaged themselves.

"Riki isn't worth this," he whispered. "No one's worth this."

Maldred looked at the map briefly to be sure they'd come to the right place. They walked a half-mile along the curving bank, until they were southeast of the island and had come to a weathered, moss-covered dock that jutted out into the water, one side of it tilting precariously. There was a second dock, across from it, and tied to this was a pair of large rowboats.

"Well and truly wonderful," Dhamon said, as he glanced down at a long yellow-brown crocodile. "Any ideas?"

"Actually, yes," Maldred replied. He knelt on the muddy bank, one eye on the crocodiles which were showing growing interest in the trio. Maldred thrust his fingers into the earth and mumbled something in the ogre tongue.

"What's he doing?" Varek hovered nearby, shifting nervously back and forth on the balls of his feet.

"Magic," Dhamon said flatly. "He's casting a spell."

Varek pointed to the island. "You think Riki's really there?"

Dhamon gave a shrug. "According to Mal's map, Polagnar's there. Supposedly that's where the thieves were taking her. So yeah, I think she's there."

Varek shuddered and dropped his gaze to the tip of his boots.

Dhamon's attention drifted between the increasing number of crocodiles and Maldred. Ripples appeared in the mud, fanning outward from Maldred's fingers and taking on a faint green hue. They raced over the water, making a soft slapping sound. At the same time the crocodiles gave the trio and the magic a wider berth.

"I'm making a bridge," Maldred explained. He groaned, the ground groaning with him and his construct becoming thicker and solid, gleaming wetly in the late-morning sun. "I'm pulling up some of the mud from the bottom, making it solid, so we don't have to risk a swim."

He spouted more Ogrish, and the ripples of mud and water quickened into a dark blur, the green hue fading to reveal a foot-wide earthen path that stretched from their bank to a spot near the rowboats on the other side.

"I'd suggest we hurry," Maldred said, nodding to a particularly large crocodile that had raised its nose against the bridge. There were other forms swimming around it, some vaguely dragonlike, some with six legs, others with two tails. They might have been malformed alligators or breeds of aquatic lizards.

"My bridge won't last long," said Maldred, "and it won't keep our scaly friends at bay. So move."

Dhamon practically ran across the magical bridge, feet spashing and sending a shower of mud behind him. Varek and Maldred followed. The three reached the foliage on the other side only moments before the muddy bridge dissolved.

"How did you . . . ?"

Maldred put a finger to Varek's lips. "I've considerable talent with magic," he said quietly, "and I've no time to explain the mechanics to you."

There was a path ahead, bordered by more of the scale-covered trees. The snakes were too numerous to count, hanging amidst the lianas and filling the air with a loud hissing. The leaves and flowers were black, the sawgrass the color of cold ashes. Nothing was green. Through a gap of midnight-colored elephant-shaped leaves Dhamon caught a glimpse of something angular, the building he'd spotted from the other shore. Closer, nailed to a shaggy-bark and almost obscured by vines, was a moss-covered wooden sign. He brushed the moss away. It read: Polagnar, population 2̶5̶2 50. Beyond that, and through a pair of cypress trunks, he caught sight of another hut.

Dhamon's voice was barely above a whisper. "I'm going for a closer look. Wait here."

Varek shook his head and pointed to a pair of footprints. They were larger than a man's and ended in claws. "These tracks are all over the place."

"Spawn prints," Dhamon stated. "I'll be back soon. Mal, remind our young friend about spawn, will you?" Dhamon darted off the path and into the foliage.

As Dhamon neared the village he slowed his pace to avoid stepping on snakes that writhed everywhere. Peering beyond the trees that ringed Polagnar, he saw a clearing carpeted with snakes, a squirming mass that stretched from one end to the other, without a single patch of open ground.

He saw evidence of fire—the blackened and broken remains of homes and businesses—and of what had once been Polagnar. Primitive huts had been built between the ruins, and these were covered with a mix of thatch and thick patches of snakeskin. Large lizards sunned themselves atop the roofs. Across from the smallest hut was a ring of worked stones and a scorched beam, likely the fragments of a well. There was a massive constrictor wrapped around it.

As he passed behind the largest hut, he spied a live-stock pen. There were at least three dozen elves, half-elves, and dwarves inside of it, as well as a handful of ogres. All of them appeared listless and gaunt. A few shuffled around, but most sat against the railing, not even raising a hand to bat away the clouds of insects that filled the air. Some were talking, but he was too far away to hear the prisoners.

He watched those in the pen for several minutes, noting there were two spawn serving as guards. He decided to move closer to get a better look at the inhabitants, then his attention was drawn to the opposite end of the village, where he spotted a few humans. Crudely dressed, they walked from hut to hut, brushing snakes aside with their feet as they went, and carrying food on large platters. Dhamon watched a young woman holding a shield covered with bread, fruit, and raw meat. She disappeared into one of the farthest huts. There was just enough light through the open doorway for Dhamon to see her give the food to a spawn. She came out carrying the empty shield. The shield was pitted and bore a Solamnic symbol, the Order of the Rose.

Between the spawn and the snakes that were everywhere, it sounded as if a hundred kettles were steaming away. The humans congregated around a pair of large moss-draped lean-tos, which he guessed served as their homes. Twelve snakeskin-covered huts, eighteen spawn that he could see. Bad odds.

Wonderful, Dhamon thought. I have a little knife for a weapon. He circled around so he could more clearly see the pen. The spawn that wandered through the village seemed to take turns keeping their eyes on all the prisoners.

"Wonderful," Dhamon repeated aloud, as he glimpsed something beyond the pen. "A draconian. A sivak." He glided closer, and his mouth opened in surprise.

The creature was easily ten feet tall, with shoulders broader than an ogre's. Dull silver scales covered its torso and arms, becoming a segmented leathery hide along its tail. Its head was wide, set with jet-black eyes separated by a toothlike ridge that ran down its long snout. Spiderweb-fine white hair was scattered along its bottom jaw, matching the color of stubby horns that curved back from the sides of its head. One of the horns was split down the center.

A thick chain was wrapped around its waist, another around its neck. Both chains circled a cypress tree and prevented the creature from moving more than a half-dozen feet in any direction. It had no wings, but its back bore thick scars to show where wings had been.

Dhamon had seen enough battlefield injuries to tell that the wings had been amputated. Of all the draconians, only a sivak could fly, and this creature had been stripped of that ability. But why? Dhamon mouthed. And why was a sivak being held captive?

The ends of the creature's claws had been removed, leaving it with blunt humanlike fingers. Dhamon wondered if the same had been done to its feet. The beast still had teeth, plenty of them, but there was something wrong with the base of its throat, thick scarring and a fresh wound that didn't look as if it had been caused by the chain. A crude attempt had been made to bandage the wound, but the cloth was caught in the chain and seemed only to help the wound fester. There were other scars on the creature's massive body, mostly on its arms.

As he watched, the young human woman with the Solamnic shield reappeared. This time she was carrying strips of meat, which looked as if they came from a large lizard. The sivak backed toward the cypress, and she dumped the meat on the ground, at the very end of where its chain could reach. The creature waited until she left, then moved forward and fell to devouring the food.

Finished, it glanced up and sniffed the air, scarred lip curling upward. It turned and spied Dhamon. The sivak regarded Dhamon for several long minutes, eyes unblinking, nose quivering. It finally looked away, apparently uninterested, and returned to where its food had been placed, searching for a scrap it might have missed.

"They're keeping it like a pet dog," Dhamon whispered. "Why? And where's Riki?" He wanted to find the half-elf quickly and be on his way. "There she is."

He saw her, propped up between an elf and an ogre, looking half-dead. Her clothes were soiled and in tatters, and her hair and face were streaked with mud. She looked exhausted, and her shallow cheeks showed she hadn't been eating. Her eyes were open and unfocused. Though she was in a direct line with Dhamon, she didn't see him.

"We'll get you out of there," he whispered. He edged away and made his way around the rest of the village, cutting back to where he'd left Maldred and Varek. He related everything he'd seen.

"We can rush in," Varek began. "We can—"

Dhamon's stern look stopped him.

"There are at least eighteen spawn, and only three of us. And a sivak that, by a quirk of fate, will probably pose no threat. You've no weapon, and I've a knife. I think our best course is to sneak in at night and come at the pen from behind."

Varek cleared his throat and squared his shoulders. "How about this? The three of us will come at the village from different sides and rush in on my signal, gain a little element of surprise. Confuse the spawn and separate them, shift opponents when necessary, finish it and get Riki and . . ."

". . . commit suicide," Dhamon finished. He let out a deep breath and cupped his forehead with his hand.

"How about I better the odds a bit first? Get rid of a few spawn before you charge in?" Dhamon quickly laid out a plan, then darted toward the spawn's village.

Dhamon closed on the huts, crouching behind a shadblow bush and waiting until a pair of spawn passed by. He scuttled across the few yards of open ground to the back of the closest hut, pressing his ear against the scale-covered reed wall and listening intently. He couldn't hear anything beyond the hissing of the snakes everywhere.

He used his knife to cut through the wall, noting that the snakeskin was thick and fleshy and bled. He persisted, cutting the thatch that lay beneath, fashioning a doorway and slipping inside. He nearly gagged from the smell of sweat, waste, and things he didn't care to try to identify. It took a moment for his eyes to adjust to the darker interior. It took him several moments more to pick through the jumble.

The hut was empty of spawn and humans, but it was crowded with all manner of other things. A thick mat of furs and cloaks made up a bed, the cloak on top bearing a Solamnic symbol from the Order of the Rose. A shield with a rose on it was propped nearby.

Backpacks and satchels were strewn everywhere, most of them shredded and empty. From some objects spilled out. He snatched up a locket. Silver or platinum, it was too dark in here to tell, but it was heavy enough to have value. Dhamon thrust it in his pocket and moved toward the doorway, stepping over the remains of a wild pig that had probably served as a spawn's dinner. Other scraps of spoiled meat and rotten fruit were strewn haphazardly about.

There were crates piled up near the entrance, some labeled in Elvish and some in the common tongue. The latter, which Dhamon could read, proclaimed that at one time they contained wild blackberry wine from Sithelnost in the Silvanesti Forest to the east. Dhamon gently jiggled the crates, surprised to find them nearly full.

He looked at floor around him and considered poking through some of the packs, but noise just outside the entrance he ducked behind the crates.

There was hissing, two or three spawn conversing. The word "elf" surfaced several times, "human" only once, then the sibilant voices moved away. Dhamon felt his legs cramp and was ready to move, but there was more hissing, and a moment later a spawn entered the hut. The creature yawned and stretched as a human would, then eyed the bed and made its way toward it. The spawn paused and sniffed the air. It had started to turn when Dhamon sprang from behind the crates, knife in his hand and aimed at a spot between the creature's wings. The blade sank in easily and found the creature's heart. Before the spawn was able to see who had inflicted the mortal blow, it exploded in a burst of acid that showered Dhamon. The acid ran off his skin, stinging and sizzling, leaving small holes in his trousers.

Dhamon returned to crouch behind the crates, hoping fervently that other spawn hadn't heard their fellow die. For several minutes Dhamon remained still, listening to his own breathing and the sound of a faint breeze rustling the thatch on the roof. Satisfied he'd disposed of the spawn without alerting anyone, he took the tip of the knife and pried at one of the crates, grinning wide when he discovered that indeed bottles of blackberry wine were inside. Dhamon wanted nothing more at the moment than to splash some of the alcohol down his throat, but he only had time to grab an empty backpack and put three bottles inside, padding them with a Solamnic tabard he spotted. Slipping the pack over his shoulders, he headed toward the slit he had cut in the back of the hut.

Just as he pulled the reeds aside and made ready to leave, he heard a soft footfall behind him at the entrance to the hut.

"A man?"

Dhamon released the reeds and whirled to see another spawn, stooped and framed by the entrance. Dhamon dove for the Solamnic shield as the creature stepped inside.

"Man new to village. New man ssshould not have weapon." The spawn held out a clawed hand. "Man give weapon and drop ssshield. Man behave."

"Not this day," Dhamon whispered. He held the shield in front of him and slashed upward, the knife drawing a line of acidic blood across the creature's neck. Its claws shot up to its throat, and it made a gurgling sound, just as Dhamon knelt behind the shield. There was another blast of acid, and Dhamon was alone again.

He quickly returned to the crates and waited several more minutes. When no more spawn entered the hut, he slipped over to the bedding and rearranged it, hiding the cloaks eaten through by acid. He didn't want a creature to come in here after he'd left and discover signs of a fight. Fortunately when spawn died, they left no corpses behind.

He hurried out the rear of the hut, and dashed to the treeline a half-dozen yards away. He dropped his wine-filled pack behind a shadblow bush, then scanned the village again. When he was certain he wouldn't be spotted, he ran to the next hut. He kept the Solamnic shield with him.

There were many hissing voices inside this hut, so Dhamon moved on to another, which sounded empty. He cut through the scales and reeds and made his way inside.

This smelled as bad and looked much the same as the other hut he had visited. A jumble of booty was strewn everywhere: cloaks bearing Solamnic symbols from Knights of the Sword and Knights of the Rose, satchels, bins, scraps of food and bones, a dead snake that had a few bites taken out of it.

Three swords were stuck in the ground next to what passed for a bed. From the center one's pommel hung a palm-sized silver symbol on a chain. It was a bison's head, the horns of which looked to be made of chips of black pearl.

"Kiri-Jolith," Dhamon whispered, as he quickly snatched the chain. The symbol represented the Sword of Justice, Krynn's god of honor and war who at one time was the patron of the Solamnic Order of the Sword. Kiri-Jolith had left years ago with all of Krynn's other gods, and the Solamnic Knights who must have died in this village had no one to hear their prayers. And now Dhamon had an antique that would fetch a fair price, despite its pits and marring. Dhamon rubbed at some dried blood that was along the edge, then put it in his pocket.

He thrust the knife in his waistband and appraised the three swords, selecting the center one, which had the keenest edge. "Finally, a decent weapon," he whispered.

Not far from the makeshift bed was an upended crate on which sat a large, stoppered ceramic pot and a tiny silver box. Inside the pot was a mixture of herbs, all carefully preserved and too bulky for him to manage at the moment. The little silver box was another matter, as it easily fit in his hand. He frowned, for, despite its small size, it had a lock on it. "Later," he mouthed, stuffing it in his pocket and hearing it softly clink against the Kiri-Jolith symbol.

There were many bulging satchels and sacks, and a cursory examination revealed clothes in most and roots and powders in a few others. Dhamon suspected the knights must have had a battlefield medic with them.

Finished with his quick inspection, he crouched to one side of the entrance, waiting and listening. There were no crates in here to conceal him, but the shadows were thick enough to hide in.

A barrel-chested spawn shuffled into the hut, hissing and grumbling to itself. It was the largest of the creatures Dhamon had seen wandering through the village, with a great bull neck. Dhamon picked out the words "snake" and "food" before he decided that the spawn was far enough into the shadowed interior that he might strike at it without being seen. This one took three blows in rapid succession. Dhamon relied on the shield to protect him from the usual acid burst. As before, he did his best to conceal objects that had been damaged by the acid, and moved on, slipping out the back and scurrying onto the third hut.

There were still at least fourteen spawn in the village, and he wanted to take out a few more before they noticed their numbers dwindling.

The next hut held two of the creatures, both sleeping, making a grating and sibilant sound that passed for snoring. He crept toward the largest, moving fluidly, holding the shield in front of him and nearly retching when he got a good whiff of what the spawn was holding in its claw—a partially gutted monkey that was spoiling in the heat. When he was directly over the creature, Dhamon held his breath and rammed the tip of the sword into the beast's heart, then leaped back when the acid burst came. Without pause, he whirled and stepped toward the other one, which was still sound asleep. He slashed at its chest, eliciting a strangled howl. He slashed again and brought the shield up just in time as this creature, too, exploded.

111

The interior of the hut sizzled. The reed and snakeskin walls adjacent to the beds threatened to dissolve and topple at any moment. The twine that held the hut together had disintegrated in places. At a quick glance. Dhamon saw something shiny on the floor and bent to scoop it up: a thin silver bracelet. Rikali might like it, though it wasn't as gaudy as what she usually preferred.

"Nat? Is that you, Nat?"

Dhamon turned to see a young broad-shouldered man at the hut's entrance.

"Sorry. You're not Nat." He had short-cropped hair the color of dry grass. It was uneven and dirty, and though his skin looked reasonably clean, he stank strongly of sweat. "Who are you?"

"I'm a friend of Nat's," Dhamon lied. He motioned the man closer and was surprised when he complied without suspicion. When the young man was an arm's length away, Dhamon shot forward and grabbed him by the shoulder, spun him around, and clamped a hand over his mouth before he could cry out. He eased the struggling man down to the ground, one arm wrapped around him to keep him from breaking free.

"I want some information," Dhamon hissed in his ear. "You supply it, and you'll live. Stay still." He waited for the youth to nod his head, then slowly drew his hand away.

"The spawn in the village. How many all together?"

"Tw-twenty . . . maybe twenty-four," came the stammered reply. "Sometimes more. I don't bother to count them unless it's my turn to fill the plates. They come and go."

"How many today. Now?"

"Less than usual, I think. Some went hunting."

Dhamon drew his lips into a thin line. "They force you to serve them. You are slaves."

The young man shook his head. "No. It's not like that. We're not forced. We—"

"Magic, then. Someone's ensorcelled you." Dhamon growled deeper and clenched his free hand. He turned the youth around so he was facing him, holding the Solamnic sword threateningly to his throat.

"Who? Who is forcing you to serve the spawn?"

The man shook his head. "N-no one, I said. We help them willingly. It's our choice."

"Why? Why do you serve the spawn?"

"It's safe in this village," the man said. "In other spawn villages, too. If we serve the spawn, we don't have to worry about being turned into spawn. Someone has to serve them." He was sweating from the heat but more from fear of Dhamon. He stared at the sword.

Dhamon's eyes narrowed in disbelief.

"It's better than working in the black dragon's silver mines," the man added. "Better than being dead. This is the black dragon's land, and the spawn are her children."

"And you're sheep. Pitiful, weak sheep."

"It's not so bad really. You'll see. The spawn will catch you, and you'll be allowed to serve them."

"Or put in the pen if I refuse."

The man shook his head, dirty hair flying. "No. You're human. They're not caging the humans."

"Why? What are they planning to do with the others?"

The man drew his lips together and folded his arms in front of his chest.

"Why?" Dhamon persisted louder than he had intended. "Why are the other races being sold to the spawn?"

"That is not your concern," the man replied finally. "In fact . . ."

With a move so quick the young man couldn't react, Dhamon raised the sword and brought the pommel down hard against the side of his head, stunning him. "I should've killed you," Dhamon whispered, as he dragged the man to a bed and tied him up, using a piece of fabric.

He stuffed the edge of a cloak in the man's mouth, then slipped out the back.

He had to cross more than thirty feet of open space, stepping on hissing snakes as he went, but he accomplished this without being seen. A second later, and he was inside. He knew he had to work more quickly now, in the event the young man woke up or someone discovered him.

"Should've killed him," Dhamon repeated.

Dhamon managed three more huts, seven in total, slaying ten of the spawn, before starting back toward Maldred and Varek. Finally he heard what might be an alarm. A horn sounded loud and long and thoroughly unmelodious. He glanced behind him, across a dozen open feet that stretched toward the thick foliage of the swamp. He could make it to the trees, hide until he determined what the horn meant. There was a large scaly willow back there. He could wait beneath the veil of leaves and . . . He spied two spawn coming his way, patrolling the perimeter of the village. They didn't seem unduly agitated because of the horn, which sounded once more, then ceased. Another slice with the sword, and Dhamon had cut his way into a small hut. A moment more and he was inside, pushing the flap of snakeskin closed and pressing his ear to the wall, listening. Had the two spawn seen him?

He heard them walk by, hissing and talking, stopping nearby to converse in their odd language in which were interspersed a few human words. He caught several words repeated in the common tongue, ones perhaps that had no equivalent in their own language: "Man," "human," "dwarf," "missstresss," and something, over and over, that had more emphasis. "Nur-" something.

When he was certain the spawn had moved on, he looked at his surroundings.

This hut was the cleanest of those he had visited, and the largest, but it was practically empty. There were a few chests sitting side by side across from a makeshift bed that was much thicker with cloaks and furs than the others. The air in here smelled musky but not unpleasant. There were no scraps of food anywhere. He glided to the doorway, crouching beside it. He heard the horn again, the notes staccato now. A spawn passed by the hut.

Come in here, Dhamon willed the creature. He wanted to take out another two or three if he could. Another spawn passed within his vision, this one followed by three young humans. Come in here, you slimy, damnable . . . .

He gasped and pulled back from the entrance, feeling the tingling against his palm matched by the tingling in his leg. Before he could take another breath, the sensation on his thigh became hot and painful, as if a branding iron had been thrust against his skin. He dropped the shield and grabbed his thigh. Waves of heat raced outward from the scale on his leg, rushing to the ends of his fingers and toes and making it difficult to grasp the sword.

"Who are you?"

Through a haze of pain, he heard the words and faintly registered that a young woman had entered the hut and was speaking to him. She was standing over him, head cocked, long black hair hanging down and tanned hands reaching toward him.

He shook his head and edged backward, keeping his distance and hoping she would follow him into the shadows. He wanted to get her away from the entrance, where she might be seen and where someone might see her talking.

"Who are you?" she repeated. "Are you with Nura Bint-Drax?"

Dhamon cursed as the trembling started, the muscles in his legs and arms jumping, his toes and fingers twitching uncontrollably.

"Are you all right?" The young woman followed him, tentatively. She glanced over her shoulder at the hut's entrance, then looked at Dhamon again. "Who are you? Can you understand me? Are you with Nura Bint-Drax?"

Dhamon fell to his side, legs curling up, chest heaving, fingers still clamped tight around the sword's pommel. He tried to say something, but his throat was instantly dry, and all he could make was a gagging sound. It was hard enough just to breathe and to keep a hold of the sword. She was saying something else to him, but his heart pounded so hard he could barely hear her. She seemed insistent on knowing who he was.

"Are you ill?" She moved closer and brushed her hand against his forehead, pulling it back instantly as if she'd touched a hot coal.

"A bad fever. Who are you? How is it you have a weapon?" he dimly understood. "You're very sick."

From somewhere outside the hut the horn continued to blow, and just beyond the entrance he heard the pounding of feet. The jolts of icy cold started radiating from the scale now, warring with the heat and sending him to the brink of unconsciousness. This time he fought desperately to stay awake.

"What are you doing in here?" the girl persisted. She said something else, but most of it was lost amid the hammering in his head. "You are not with Nura Bint-Drax, are you? You are not supposed to be here." She raised her voice. "Can you hear me? Hear me?"

He opened his mouth, attempting again to speak to her, but only a moan escaped. He shook his head.

"I will get help for you." She was speaking louder still, and indeed he heard her clearly. "I will go to the spawn and . . ."

No! his mind screamed. He couldn't be found out! Not helpless as he was. The spawn would kill him. Dhamon meant to reach out to the girl, grab her arm and pull her close, tell her to stay here and to be quiet, tell her that Maldred would rescue her and the other servants. When the episode with the scale stopped, he would question her. But first she must be quiet and cooperate, and he must gain some relief from the pain. He needed to hold her close and keep her from alerting anyone. He saw a flash of silver. Only a small part of his mind registered that it was his sword and that he was reaching for her with the wrong hand. Stop, he told himself. Too late. The blade had already sliced through the air and plunged into the girl.

A horrified look spread over her face as a line of blood grew across her stomach. She dropped to her knees and opened her mouth to scream. Only a pathetic gurgle and flecks of red came out. She pitched forward, falling across Dhamon. He felt her legs twitch once, then she was still.

Got to get out of here! he told himself. Move! He rolled her off him and found the strength to get to his knees. He tried not to feel pity for her. She was simply a casualty, someone who ventured into the wrong place at the wrong time. She'd only been trying to help. And now her blood coated him.

He crawled to the back of the hut, not feeling his knees move across the earth. The fiery jolts raced through his body, interspersed with jabs of intense cold. Fumbling around the back wall, he tried to find the way out. There!

"There!"

Had he heard something?

"There! A trespasser! A thief!"

The words were in the common tongue, spoken by a human, and Dhamon looked over his shoulder to see a man, hardly more than a boy, standing inside the hut's entrance. He was gesturing madly at Dhamon, then at the

girl's corpse. Behind him towered a spawn, claws outstretched and lips curled back in a snarl.

Dhamon stopped fumbling with the reed flap and
raised the sword. He tried to stand facing the spawn, but
he couldn't get off his knees. He lifted the sword above his
head. The tip struck the wall of the hut behind him and
became ensnared for an instant.

Dhamon's chest grew tighter as the pain increased,
and he fought for air. The spawn took a step closer and
then another.

Swing! Swing at the beast!

His fingers were numb, and his body was so racked with
pain from the scale on his leg that he couldn't obey the
commands of his brain. Claws closed around Dhamon's
hand, tugging the sword from it. The spawn's free claw
grabbed at Dhamon's hair, pulling him forward as if he
weighed no more than a rag doll, dragging him across the
hut floor and out the doorway.

Dhamon registered the sunlight streaming down, the intense afternoon heat of Sable's swamp adding to the
warmth that coursed through him. He felt himself being
pulled across the snakes that carpeted the ground. Several
of them bit him, adding to the heat. After a moment more
all he saw and felt was a cool, welcoming darkness.

Chapter Ten
Nura Bint-Drax

aldred brushed aside a fern leaf, peering into the village. He didn't see Dhamon, but he could tell something was going on. Three spawn stood guard at the pen—-one snarling in its odd language, the other two looking toward a large snakeskin-covered hut outside which a half-dozen human servants were gathered.

"Snakes," he muttered, scanning the village. "The ground is crawling with vipers."

The horn sounded again. It was blown by a tall, reed-thin human who stood on what appeared to be the remains of a well. The peals were not the long, mournful notes Maldred had heard before. These were sharp and short.

Near the pen, Maldred spotted more movement and caught a glimpse of the sivak Dhamon had described as being chained to the tree. Maldred circled until he was practically behind the pen and could get a better look at the draconian. Varek quietly followed him. The draconian was clearly nervous, pawing at the ground and backing toward the trunk.

119

"I see Riki," Varek whispered. "In the pen. She looks terrible. We've got to get her out and—"

Maldred drew a finger to his lips.

The horn stopped, its noise replaced by a cacophony of shouts—words so rushed and overlapping that Maldred couldn't make them out. Added to the human voices were the sibilant utterances of spawn. He reached for the two-handed sword on his back, the blade hissing against its latticed sheath as he drew it.

"I don't see Dhamon," Maldred whispered. "Can't hear anything but the damned shouting."

"Nura Bint-Drax!" someone in the village yelled above the din. "Nura comes! Nura! Nura! Nura!" The odd name was repeated over and over until it became a chant voiced by all the humans and spawn.

The sivak pressed itself against the trunk. At first Maldred thought it was cowering like a frightened animal, but there was something different on its face, an almost-human expression. Contempt? Revulsion?

The chanting continued, growing louder still. Suddenly it was cut through by a high-pitched woman's cry. "Praise Nura! Bow to Nura Bint-Drax!"

"Maldred!" Varek tugged the big thief's tunic.

"Shh!"

"Maldred! Someone's coming behind us. I hear . . ." Varek's words trailed off, and the young man slumped to the ground, a long needlelike barb protruding from his neck.

Maldred whirled in time to spot a spawn with a reed tube in its mouth. Before he could move, a barb struck him, too.

Varek and Maldred woke to find themselves in the pen, hands tightly tied behind their backs. The stench radiating from their gaunt companions, coupled with the odor from the waste on the ground, was nearly overwhelming.

"Pigs, I was hoping you'd come," Rikki exclaimed. "But I wanted you to rescue me, not join me. Where's Dhamon?"

The spawn and human servants were still chanting, softly now, however, like swarms of gnats. The hissing of the thousands of snakes that writhed on the village grounds added to the incessant, enveloping buzz. Suddenly the crowd parted, aligning itself like soldiery and forming two lines facing each other, shoulder to shoulder.

"A corridor of flesh," Maldred observed.

"Nura Bint-Drax comes!" a young human woman shouted.

Immediately the spawn and humans dropped to their knees and hunched their shoulders in submissive fashion. One by one they tipped their chins towards their chests, averting each other's eyes, as a child with copper-colored hair walked between them. Her tiny fingers brushed the tops of spawn and human heads alike, touching each as if blessing them. When she reached the end of the gauntlet, she turned to face them, clapped her hands, and nodded as they rose in unison. All the while, the throng softly chanted: "Nura, Nura, Nura Bint-Drax."

"She's just a babe," Riki whispered.

Maldred growled at the sight of the child. "She is far more than she appears. She is a sorceress," he said in a hush. "One far more powerful than any I've ever laid eyes on."

A barrel-chested spawn easily ten feet tall was walking towards the strange child now, dragging the unconscious body of Dhamon Grimwulf by the hair.

Rikali gasped, and Maldred growled louder. Varek was only half watching the spectacle. He was busy working on the ropes that tied his hands. He had backed up to one of the pen posts and was rubbing furiously.

121

The spawn reverently approached Nura and lifted Dhamon in the air so that his toes dangled just above the ground—a trophy for the child to admire. Dhamon looked dead, but after a moment Maldred could tell that his friend's chest was rising and falling.

The child said something. At least Maldred could see her lips move, but her voice was too soft and his own heart was pounding too loudly, and the damned chanting and hissing continued to fill the air, so he missed the words.

Riki edged forward. "Mal . . . Mal, what do you think she's . . ."

". . . going to do with you?" the child finished, whirling to face the pen. She carefully picked her way through the snake carpet to edge closer to them.

The half-elf's eyes grew wide, astonished that the child had overheard her whispered words.

"It is an interesting question, elf. Just what is Nura Bint-Drax going to do with all of you?"

The child tilted her head and her cherubic face took on an innocent appearance as she neared the pen. The barrel-chested spawn followed, still holding Dhamon. Nura looked over each of the demi-humans and the ogres in the pen, eyeing them up and down like livestock. Then she raised her free hand and pointed to four elves who were clustered together. "Aldor. Them. Now."

The spawn who'd been holding Dhamon unceremoniously dropped him onto a bunch of snakes and stepped forward, separating the elves she had indicated and lifting each out of the pen. She nodded to the creature, and one by one it broke their necks and tossed them in a pile. Snakes swarmed over them, biting at their arms and faces.

"Why? Why did you do that? They did nothing!" Varek shouted. He paused his work on his ropes. "Why?" he repeated.

"They were old," Nura said offhandedly. "They looked too weak for what I have planned."

"Weak only because you aren't feeding us!" an emboldened dwarf shouted. "You're starving us! You had no call to kill them!"

"What about him?" Maldred said, indicating Dhamon.

The child turned to the spawn called Aldor, who again grabbed Dhamon and pulled him up, digging its claws deep in his arm. Nura pointed to Dhamon's leg, where his torn trousers revealed the large scale on his thigh, and the smaller ones rimming it. She stared at Maldred.

"What did you do to him?" Rikali shrieked.

"Pity that this is not my doing," Nura said evenly, turning to Rikki. She studied her reflection in the large scale for several moments and brushed at an errant curl. "The scales make this man unique. A curiosity."

"You're a curiosity, too," Maldred growled. "Just who are you?"

"I am Nura Bint-Drax," she answered. "Aldor, if you would."

The spawn tossed Dhamon into the pen. Maldred quickly moved to his friend's side, gently jostling him with a foot in an effort to wake him up. The big thief said nothing, but his gaze darted between Dhamon and Nura.

The child talked softly to Aldor, then backed away from the pen. The fingers of her free hand twirled in the air like the legs of a spider. A silvery web took shape in her palm, growing larger with each passing moment until it was nearly as big as herself. Tiny black motes appeared and skittered up and down the magical threads, moving faster and faster, becoming a blur.

"Pigs, but I don't like this," Rikali whispered. "I don't like this. Not any of this."

"I'm free," Varek whispered. It was true, Maldred noted with a glance. The young man had managed to cut his ropes.

123

Varek positioned himself amidst the throng of demi-humans so the spawn guards couldn't see his hands, and he began to work on Riki's ropes. Soon she was free, too.

"Varek, I've two small blades," Maldred whispered, "hidden in my belt."

Varek was quick to retrieve them, concealing them in his palms and working on the big man's bonds now. A pair of dwarves pressed close, one mouthing, "Me next." Varek complied, then tugged Riki toward the back of the pen.

Nura continued her enchantment, her voice rising in pitch and taking on a musical quality. Suddenly she extended her hand, and the magical spiderweb she'd been crafting flew at the pen. It billowed and blanketed Dhamon and Maldred, and then the dwarves and the others. They felt as if hundreds of insects were swarming over their skins, robbing them of movement. In the same instant a calmness washed over them. Varek found himself relaxing. All thoughts of escape, his concern for Riki, faded from importance. He dropped the small blades. "Nura. Nura. Nura." He took up the soft chant.

At the front of the pen Dhamon had managed to regain consciousness and now stood at Maldred's side. Both men dully watched Nura, who was in the midst of a second enchantment. One of the human servants bowed to the child and passed her a pale wooden bowl.

The child's voice changed in pitch, and her undecipherable words quickened. The spawn called Aldor brandished a knife and took the bowl from Nura. The bowl was oddly blackened now, as if it had been thrust into a fire. With a low snarl, the big spawn started toward the chained sivak.

"I can't move," Maldred said. "Not an inch."

124

"My feet feel like lead," Dhamon agreed. He kept his eyes on Nura. "They say you create spawn from the blood of true draconians," he mused, "but it takes an elaborate spell. It takes a dragon overlord to cast that spell, to give up a bit of its essence. There isn't a dragon, let alone an overlord, within miles of this village. The scale on my leg would have told me if one was nearby. I don't like the looks of this."

The spawn called Aldor made a deep cut in the sivak's chest, holding the bowl close so blood drained into it. The sivak could do nothing to fight the spawn. When the blood slowed to a trickle and the bowl was full, the spawn returned to Nura's side, brushing aside the vipers as it went.

The child's eyes had rolled back up into her head, showing only whites shaded by rapidly fluttering lids. Her voice was different now, faster, louder, no longer sounding like a child, but like an adult. The tone was seductive.

Everyone seemed enthralled by Nura's voice, most of them chanting her name. Even Maldred was affected. It took all of Dhamon's concentration to blot out the words, and try as he might he couldn't move his feet, could barely twitch his fingers in the child's magical webbing.

"Fight it," Dhamon hissed to Maldred. "We need your magic to get out of here. Don't listen to her, Mal. She might turn the lot of us into spawn."

"Only you, dark-hair," a nearby spawn guard corrected. "Only humans are so blessed that they can be transformed into spawn. They rest will be . . . abominations." The creature locked eyes with Dhamon.

Dhamon watched as Aldor held the bowl out to Nura. Her eyes were wide and dark and flitted back and forth between Dhamon and Maldred. She dipped her fingers into the sivak blood, rapidly stirring it as she continued to recite incomprehensible words. Her voice slowed, and at the same time the sivak became agitated and the muscles in its arms and legs began to jump in time with the child's finger motions.

125

A transparent red mist poured out of the bowl Nura held, flowing to the ground and slowing rolling toward the pen.

The mist thickened and darkened until it was first the shade of blood, then nearly black. Tendrils circled like coiling serpents around the legs of the ogres and Dhamon and Maldred. The mist was cool and damp, easing the heat of the swamp a little but at the same time sapping their strength.

Dhamon felt the fatigue, heavy like a winter cloak. The mist wound tighter around him and seeped beneath his skin. He tried to shake it off and continued to focus his thoughts, thrusting the child out of his mind, imagining himself free.

"I can move," Dhamon finally gasped to Maldred. "A little."

Maldred was looking straight at Nura. "I can barely speak," he croaked.

"Fight it. We've got to get out of here."

"She's stronger than I."

"Fight it. Or we're dead men."

By the time the mist rose to their waists, Maldred had managed to move his hands. He began gesturing with his fingers, working a spell of his own. "Everything is so hard."

"By the power of the First One," Nura stated. "By the will of the Ancient. Give me the force to do your bidding."

The mist around them thickened to the consistency of quicksand. The scale on Dhamon's leg grew warm, but the sensation didn't worsen. Images flashed in Dhamon's head, large yellow eyes surrounded by blackness. A dragon? There was an intelligence in the eyes, and something more that he sensed but couldn't put a word to.

"By the power of the First One," Nura repeated.

Again the dragon eyes flashed in Dhamon's mind, the child's face reflected in them. He blinked furiously, shaking off the image while at the same time trying to banish the sluggishness that threatened to overwhelm him.

Maldred was mumbling softly, his hands working faster. He risked a glance at the back of the pen. He barely made out Rikali and Varek, standing shoulder to shoulder and not moving. His attention was drawn back to Dhamon, who had become completely engulfed by the mist.

Dhamon's throat and chest tightened. It felt as if someone had reached inside him and squeezed his heart. Through the mist he glanced down at his chest. There was a symbol scrawled on it in blood. Funny, but he hadn't felt anything, any wound. Peering about and squinting through the mist, he saw the same symbol on the chests of the elves and dwarves and Maldred. "Mmm. Mmmm." Dhamon was trying to say "Maldred," but all he could get out was a strangled sound.

Dhamon's eyes widened when he spotted one of the symbols on an ogre change its shape. The blood image became a pattern of scales—small black ones that spread outward. Dhamon furiously began brushing at the symbol on his own chest, but the scale shapes were on him, too.

Images again flashed behind his eyes, the dull yellow orbs of a huge black dragon, the child reflected in them, smiling. Through the images and the magical haze he continued to brush at the symbol on his chest, fighting the unnatural fatigue and digging his fingers beneath the scales to frantically rip them out.

I will not become a spawn! He meant to shout the words, but he heard them only in his mind. I will die first!

There was more chanting, soft at first, coming from the far end of the village. Now the servants were repeating

"Nura. Nura. Nura Bint-Drax." The chanting was picked up by most of those in the pen with him.

This can't be happening! It is not possible! Dhamon's mind screamed. Suddenly he found his voice and heard himself screaming. "There is no dragon in this village! Only an overlord can create dragonspawn!"

Through the ever-rising mist and a gap in mutating bodies, Dhamon saw the child smile. She paused in her spell, long enough to lock eyes with him.

"The dragon is everywhere," she said, and he heard her words over the chanting of the villagers and the hissing of the thousands of snakes.

"Nura. Nura. Nura." The chanting grew louder. "Nura Bint-Drax."

"I am a vessel," she continued, speaking only to Dhamon. "One to whom the black dragon grants power."

A vessel, Dhamon thought. He was once a vessel for the red overlord because of the scale on his leg. If the link hadn't been broken, he'd still be Malys's pawn. Now, perhaps, he'd become a pawn for the great black overlord.

"He grants me power to create spawn," she persisted, her voice mocking now, "but I prefer what you call abominations. Singular creations. Interesting. And utterly loyal. Unfortunately you are human, Dhamon Grimwulf, so you will be a spawn and not an abomination."

Dhamon heard Maldred heave in pain behind him.

Around them, some of the ogres were transforming more rapidly than the elves and dwarves. One in particular caught Dhamon's eye, the image filling him with terror. Scales rapidly spread outward from the design on the ogre's chest, running like water down his arms and legs, across a face that was becoming larger and was growing a horselike snout. Twin tails sprouted from his backside, one stubby and thick, the other long like a snake. A viper's mouth snapped and hissed at the end of the snake tail, furiously trying to bite the other mutating creatures around it. Short wings extended from between the ogre's shoulder blades, scalloped like a bat's, but membranous like a dragonfly's. The creature threw back his misshapen head and howled.

A half-elf nearby was growing a second pair of arms, screeching in agony and grabbing at the mist that teased its elongating claws.

The air was filled with hisses, cries of anger and disbelief, a few anguished shouts of Ogrish that Dhamon didn't understand and some that he knew were deeply profane. There were snapping and popping sounds too, coming from limbs that were altering or new ones being birthed, bones that were breaking under stress in bodies that were growing unnaturally large and heavy and distorted.

Maldred voiced a throaty growl, and now Dhamon screamed. There was intense pain in the transformation, worse than he'd ever experienced from the scale on his leg. Where the scales were spreading on his chest, it felt as if his skin had caught fire.

"No!" he shouted, as he threw all his efforts into digging out the scales, moving sluggishly, trying to get out of the mist and away from the child's heinous spell. His legs were rooted to the ground, were difficult to budge. He moved only inches at a time. Out of the corner of his eye he saw Maldred's fingers still twirling, saw the mist thinning around the big thief's hands.

"Wh-what . . ."

Dhamon tried to say more, but found his tongue uncooperative. It felt thick and dry. He glanced down, shuddering when he saw more tiny scales flowing outward from the dragon scale on his leg.

"Dhamon, I am putting our hopes on Riki and Varek," Maldred managed. He balled his fists, which were becoming thicker and black.

For a moment Dhamon thought he saw his old friend's handsome human face, thought he saw him smile. Then the fleshy color was gone, turning blue, his hair becoming a wild white mane as he transformed into the ogre mage he truly was, the only son of Donnag. He towered over everyone in the pen. Black scales spread across him, racing across his chest and up his neck.

His face elongated to form a dragonlike snout, and a thick ridge erupted above his eyes. Maldred grimaced as he took a step forward on legs that were becoming thick as tree trunks, veins wrapped around them like vines. His feet were growing, sprouting claws. Spiny ridges were protruding from his knees and elbows. And his hands, which could no longer maintain fists, were stretching, a double set of talons emerging from what had been his fingers.

"Hope Riki can . . ." No more words came from Maldred's mouth. Instead, a long forked tongue shot out to lick his bulbous lips. He hissed, his arms flailed, knocking over another ogre who was in the midst of growing a third arm. He swung his left arm at Dhamon, striking him hard in the chest and propelling his friend several feet away toward the back of the pen.

Had that been intentional? Dhamon wondered, as he struggled breathlessly to his feet. He could see the rails through gaps in the ever-thickening magical mist.

Have to get out. Move!

Dhamon saw that every ogre, dwarf, and elf was in the process of transforming. None had been spared the child's heinous spell, and none looked the same—none save Riki and Varek, who were cowering at the very back of the pen and so far seemed untouched.

One dwarf was growing a second head atop the first, another was folding in on himself, becoming thick and stunted, his arms turning into another set of legs and forcing him to walk like a dog. The half-elf nearest Dhamon sprouted four eyes. The thinnest ogre was perhaps the most terrifying in appearance, becoming thinner still, looking like scaly hide that had been stretched across a skeleton. Bones threatened to poke through, and a skeletal pair of wings sprouted from his back, flapping and clacking but offering him no chance of flying away.

Dhamon shut his eyes and tried to move faster. He shuffled back a few steps, bumping into something that felt as sturdy as a stone wall—only the wall was breathing and wheezing, another metamorphosing creature. Dhamon's arms and legs ached terribly, and he was certain they were growing or changing.

Got to get away! he told himself, as he blundered blindly. Get away. I cannot serve a dragon again. His thoughts began to muddle, and he sensed that his mind was being displaced. Hungry, he mused. I am hungry. Strong. I am strong. What is your bidding Nura? Look at me, Nura! Nura. Nura. Nura Bint-Drax.

"No!" he howled again, his voice deeper and sounding foreign to him. "By all the vanished gods, no!"

"Varek!" Rikali whispered, furiously blinking. "Varek, I can move." She glanced away from the transforming creatures, unable to stomach what was happening to them.

"So can I," Varek returned in a hush, "but I'm not sure why."

"It was Maldred," Rikali answered, as she moved slowly with Varek through the slats in the back of the pen, hoping the mist would conceal their escape. "I thought I saw him casting a spell. Pigs, but I've seen him do magic enough. It has to be the only reason we're free."

Once outside the pen, Varek tugged loose a slat, shouldering it like a club. He passed to Riki the small blades he had dropped then retrieved, and for a moment considered grabbing the half-elf and running. But Riki was already moving away from him, skirting around the pen, tugging loose slats as she went and stepping through the carpet of snakes as she made her way toward the child.

"Nura!" the half-elf cried. "Stop your spell! Leave these people alone!"

Varek mumbled a prayer to a vanished god and headed after her.

Nura was taken aback. Intent on the abominations she was creating, she hadn't noticed two of her victims escaping.

Some of the transforming creatures spilled from the pen. A few who had just begun to change fled through the broken slats into the jungle. Spawn ran after them, urged on by Aldor. Other spawn tried to herd the transforming creatures within the red mist so the spell could finish changing them.

"The little girl!" Rikali shouted to Varek. "We have to get the little girl! Make her stop!"

"No!" Varek yelled as he shoved past her. "Riki, get out of here. I'll take care of the girl."

The half-elf defiantly shook her head, but she couldn't catch Varek, and a second later she found herself facing a spawn that stepped across her path.

"Pigs, but you're ugly," she spat. She ducked beneath its grasping claws and sliced at its legs with the small blades.

A few yards away, Varek faced Aldor. The large spawn effectively shielded Nura, at the same time spewing a gout of acid at Varek. The creature grinned as Varek cried out in pain. It let out a deep, clipped laugh when Varek crumpled to his knees.

Nura concentrated on her spell. Preoccupied, she did not see Rikali. The half-elf had slain the spawn she'd been fighting and came up behind the girl. Rikali took quick aim with one of the small blades and plunged it downward. The blade sunk into the child's back. She screamed in surprise. The bowl fell from her hands, striking the ground and spraying her legs with sivak blood.

"Fool!" Nura cried as she dropped to the ground, righting the bowl and trying to cup the escaping blood back into it. She ignored the small knife sticking in her shoulder. "You've no idea what you've done! You've ruined my magic. Your life is forfeit! Your life is mine! Aldor!"

Aldor spun away from Varek, claws outstretched and chest expanding as he spat at the half-elf with his poison breath.

At the same time, Varek struggled to his feet and clumsily charged Aldor. Lowering his shoulder and awkwardly barreling into the spawn, he knocked him off balance and threw off his aim. Riki took advantage of the situation and darted in, slashing at Aldor with the remaining blade. Varek swung his makeshift club at the spawn's outstretched arm.

"Varek! Stop the little girl!" she shouted. "I can handle this beastie!"

The child had finished scooping as much of the blood as possible into the bowl and worked feverishly to reinvigorate her spell, ignoring Varek and the half-elf behind her.

"Varek!" Riki shouted. "The little girl!"

Varek reluctantly left the half-elf's side and closed on Nura, swinging the club into the back of girl's head. "Damned child!" he shouted for good measure. "Straight to the Abyss with you!"

Nura was barely fazed by the blow, though plainly angered at this second interruption. The air was filled with noise: the chanting, the screams and cries of the abominations, and the hissing of the snakes that writhed all around them.

"How can you still be standing?" Varek asked. He pulled back on the club again, anchored his feet, and risked a brief glance at the pen as he swung again. The horrifying sight nearly made him lose his grip on the weapon.

A few of the ogres and dwarves had completely transformed. One had six arms and an overlong single wing that flapped madly and threatened to tangle between its ankles. Another had an arm that hung limply from the center of its chest. Others were . . . worse.

"Monsters." Varek shuddered, blindly striking out again and again at the girl, who seemed impervious to his blows.

"I must finish the spell!" she cursed. "They are caught between!"

The grotesqueries lashed out at each other in pain and madness. The skeletal ogre howled as one of his fellows pulled his wings off, blood and acid spraying around them. A creature with two heads snapped at a misshapen beast who was on all fours. A dwarf spotted with scales had buried his head in his hands and was weeping uncontrollably. As Varek watched, this dwarf was skewered on the long talons of one of his fellows.

"They're slaying each other," he said in awe.

"They're caught in the madness!" the child cried. "I must finish the spell. Aldor! Slay the elf! Then stop this flea who pesters me!"

"Ssspawn kill elf," Aldor stated. His eyes glimmered darkly.

"I'm a half-elf," Riki returned defiantly.

As the spawn let loose a breath, Riki ducked, the gout of acid passing over her head and misting behind her. Without pause, she jumped back up and swept her blade in, jamming the tip into Aldor's chest. She pressed her attack, trying to drive the spawn back into Nura, who was busy stirring the draconian blood again, ignoring Varek.

134

The spawn crouched low as Riki lunged, spread its arms wide, and tried to grab her. But the half-elf was fast and sidestepped, bringing the blade up and slashing at its throat. The half-elf slammed her eyes shut and turned her head, and a heartbeat later the big spawn dissolved in a cloud of acid that rained down on her and Varek and Nura.

"No!" Nura howled. The acid mixed with the sivak blood and sizzled in the wooden bowl. "Noooooo!"

Only two of her prized spawn were nearby. The transforming creatures had managed to dispatch several in their maddened fury. Nura gestured to her servants.

"To me!" she cried. "Hurry, my spawn!"

Inside what remained of the pen, only a dozen creatures were standing. Dhamon had managed to pull himself through the railing. He rolled onto his back, coughing, trying to clear his lungs of the last of the red mist. He felt about on his chest, which was marked by raw wounds from where he'd ripped out the scales. His fingers flew over his skin, trying to find more of the scales, digging at a couple near his waist. His strength returning, he lumbered to his feet and backed away, wanting to put a greater distance between himself and the pen. The swamp was so close behind him. It would be easy to lose himself in it. Lose himself. Save himself.

"Maldred." The thought of his friend was the only thing that kept Dhamon from running away. "Got to clear my head," he told himself. "Concentrate." There were still thoughts of power, of hunger, of serving Nura Bint-Drax. "Nura. Nura. Nura," he heard himself say. "No!"

Dhamon focused his thoughts on Maldred and Rikali. He peered at the grotesque fracas, but all he saw were the repulsive and deformed creatures. All he heard were their screams as they fought each other.

He finally spotted Maldred in the center of the mass. Dhamon shuddered. There were traces of his friend that he could recognize, the blue skin and mane of white hair, but patches of black scales covered most of his arms and his chest, and a serpentine tail twitched behind him. His ogre face was distorted and dragonlike, though no scales marred it.

Dhamon turned away and raced toward the closest hut, one in which he remembered seeing weapons. Moments later he emerged, carrying two swords, and he made a dash toward Nura and the two spawn who formed a guard around toward her.

He saw Varek, who was a mass of boils and scars, his clothes and hair melted away. Dhamon shoved one of the swords into his acid-blistered hands.

"The little girl," Varek gasped, as he faced a spawn that had appeared in front of him. "Kill her, Dhamon. Protect Riki."

"I'll kill the little girl all right," Dhamon growled, as he dove at the second spawn and, in two quick slashes, killed it. "I'll send her straight to the Abyss. I'll . . ."

His words died as he saw Nura shimmer, grow, and change. Within the passing of a few heartbeats, the child calling herself Nura Bint-Drax was gone. Something else entirely stood in her place.

"The breath of the world!" Varek gasped. "What is that?"

"I don't care what it is," Dhamon answered. "I just need to know if it can bleed. Because if it can bleed, I'm going to kill the damn thing."

Where Nura had stood now was something that resembled a snake. Only this snake was easily twenty feet long and thick, with alternating bands of black and red scales that sparkled like jewels in the sunlight. The bulk of its body was elevated like a cobra hovering above the ground. Its head was not that of a snake, it was that of the evil child, copper-colored hair fanning away from it like a hood. A small knife still protruded from one side, the one the half-elf had drove into the little girl.

The creature's lidless eyes were eerily fixed on Rikali, as it wove back and forth hypnotically. "You've ruined my plans, elf. Stopped my spell! Destroyed nearly all the precious creatures I was birthing." She swivelled her head toward the pen, to three fully formed abominations that stood apart from the other wretches. "To me, children!"

Dhamon spun to intercept the misshapen abominations that followed Nura's orders, climbing out of the pen. He drew the long sword back. The blade caught the sun, and the edge sparkled so brightly that one of the creatures— one with six arms and two tails—shielded its eyes and hesitated. That was long enough for Dhamon to drive the blade down, cutting deep into the chest of the monstrosity. Like a spawn, it died in a burst of acid.

There were two more abominations. Varek jumped in front of one to keep it from reaching Riki.

Dhamon met the charge of the third abomination, this a creature that looked more like a spawn, save for the third arm dangling uselessly from its chest. This beast also seemed mesmerized by the light playing off the sword. One swing and Dhamon had lopped off the worthless appendage, another swing and he'd managed to cleave the creature's right arm. The abomination yowled, stepping back and looking with uncertainty between Dhamon and Nura.

Dhamon darted forward, the sword held in front of him. It pierced the creature's abdomen, and he was rewarded with a shower of acid that ate at his skin and trousers. Without pause he whirled toward Nura, passing Varek, who was still struggling with his foe.

"Riki, leave the snake-woman to me!"

"I can't seem to hurt her, Dhamon!" Riki was shouting as she slashed with the small blade.

"I can more than hurt you," Nura returned. She opened her mouth, revealing a row of sharply pointed teeth.

Something glistening dripped from them, sizzling when it hit the ground. Lightning fast, the snake struck, her head darting forward, teeth digging into Riki's cheek.

"Pigs!" the half-elf screeched. "That hurt! Like fire!"

In the same instant, Dhamon swung his sword and watched in amazement as it only grazed the snake creature's scaly hide. It would have been a killing blow to a spawn or an abomination.

At least he'd finally drawn blood, he observed, as he swung again and again, aiming at the same spot and finally making a noticeable groove in the thick flesh.

"Riki! Get back!" Dhamon shouted.

"Damn you, Dhamon Grimwulf! You weren't worried about me when you left me all alone in Blöten! Why worry about me now?" The half-elf swiped at the snake creature again and again, nicking it with her little knife. "Bite me, will you, Nura Bint-Drax? I knew you really weren't no little girl."

Nura grinned malevolently and struck again, ignoring Dhamon in favor of the half-elf. This time her teeth sunk into Rikali's arm, and as Nura pulled back, the half-elf crumpled.

"Monster!" Dhamon spat. "Face me!" He put all of his considerable strength into his next swing, and when he connected, blood and scales flew.

Nura raised herself high off the ground, balancing on her snake tail and pivoting to give Dhamon her full attention. "You are strong, human," she hissed, "I truly believe you are the one."

Puzzled by her strange comment, Dhamon didn't allow it to distract him. He lashed out, putting his muscles into each swing, scowling to note how little damage he was inflicting.

"Wh-what is that creature?" This from Varek, who finally had finished off his foe. His clothes were in tatters, his arms and face covered with claw marks. He was still hefting the sword Dhamon had given him as he joined the fight against Nura. "What is it?"

"I am Nura Bint-Drax," the snake-creature hissed. She began weaving hypnotically in an effort to enthrall Varek and Dhamon. "I am the child of the swamp, the daughter of the dragon. I am your every nightmare."

Dhamon struck at her again, this time without as much force or speed. He was slowing, and his mind was clouding. Magic! He knew that the creature had cast a spell at him. Scales danced in the back of his mind.

"Damned beast!" he cursed. Even the words came out slow. He tried to shake his head furiously, but instead he barely moved it from side to side. "Damn you to the darkest corner of the Abyss!" He watched as her head came down, mouth, and corrosive liquid sizzling out to pool on the ground.

"Fight me!" This came from Varek, who'd worked his way around to the creature's side. Though clearly spent, he managed to land a blow where Dhamon had already carved a wound.

"You are an insignificant bug," she hissed to Varek, "not worthy of my attention. Time to end this day's game." Her head bobbed and woved and her form shimmered and shrank. There was a popping sound, and the place where Nura had been erupted in a puff of acrid black smoke. Riki's blade, which had been lodged in the snake, fell uselessly to the ground.

"By the Dark Queen's heads!" Dhamon swore. His gaze shifted between Riki and Varek, who was crawling toward the half-elf.

"What do we do about those?" Varek gestured toward the pen, where a handful of the mutating creatures still thrashed and battled. The things were a mix of scales and flesh, with misshapen limbs and curling

139

claws, flapping wings, hideous heads, serpentine tails, and tangled hair.

"Maldred." Dhamon swallowed hard.

Dhamon rushed toward the pen, stepped through the rails, and passed the first two combatants. See to Maldred, he thought. Deal with the creatures quick, then see to Riki. He thrust his sword into the stomach of a dog-like creature that was lunging for him, slaying and stepping over it.

Another creature moved into Dhamon's path. This one was a terribly thin abomination who'd had its wings plucked off. Its jaw clacked open and shut, a long forked tongue lolling out. It stretched out to grab at him, and he swiftly put it out of its misery. Finally he reached Maldred.

"Mal . . ." he said. "Mal, can you understand me?"

The thing towering above him bore some resemblance to Maldred's ogre form, but it hissed and spat and pawed at the ground like a wild animal.

"Mal!"

The beast's eyes met Dhamon's. There was something pleading in them, and they dropped to the sword in his hand.

"No," Dhamon stated. "I won't kill you. You're as dear as any brother."

The creature howled and reached a claw out to rake Dhamon, but he moved quickly to evade the half-hearted blow.

"You've magic, Mal! Use it! Fight this!"

The Maldred-thing slashed at Dhamon again, attempting to get him to defend himself.

"Don't let Nura—whatever in all the levels of the Abyss she is—win," Dhamon said, still managing to avoid his friend's claws. "Use your magic!"

Maldred threw back his head and roared a string of words in Ogrish. His claws dug at the scales on his chest and neck.

"Concentrate!" Dhamon shouted. He remembered how foggy his mind had been when the red mist circled him. "Fight it!"

Maldred continued to rant in Ogrish. His lips shaped arcane phrases that gave birth to a pale yellow glow encircling Maldred's misshapen form.

"That's it!' Dhamon encouraged, watching as the scales glimmered darkly and then began to melt. "Concentrate!"

"Dhamon! Get over here! Now!"

Dhamon drew his attention away from his friend and glanced at Varek, who was motioning wildly to him.

"Riki needs help!" Varek was sitting awkwardly with the half-elf's head and shoulders resting on his lap.

Dhamon glanced to the far end of the village, where the human servants were nervously gathered, none of them daring to budge. Another look at Maldred, then he was racing toward the half-elf.

"Dhamon! Help Riki!" Varek's acid-scarred face was marked by genuine fear. "I think she's dying, Dhamon. She told me once that you were a battlefield medic. Do something! She's pregnant, Dhamon. Please do something to save my wife and child, or so help me, I'll . . ."

"Don't make a threat you're not able to carry out." The words and Dhamon's withering glance silenced Varek. Dhamon knelt next to Riki and studied her ashen face. Pregnant? It was enough of a surprise that the half-elf was married to this young man. Was she also pregnant? There was a deep bite mark on her cheek and on her arm, and ugly red lines meandered away from the wounds.

"The hut closest to the well," Dhamon said, nodding to Varek. "There's a ceramic pot on a crate inside. It's filled with herbs. There's a few sacks on the ground by it. Bring them all. And hurry."

Dhamon sat, stretching out his legs and gently pulling Rikali away from Varek, who quickly went

141

after the herbs. Dhamon tenderly ran his fingers over the half-elf's wounds. It was a gentleness he hadn't exhibited in quite some time, and his hard expression was gone, too, replaced by something that approached compassion.

"Married and with child," he said to himself. Her loose clothes had well concealed her slightly swelling stomach.

Varek gathered as much as he could carry. He ran back to Dhamon, scowling at a trio of the human servants who were headed in that direction, too.

Dhamon picked through some dried roots in one bag. They were too old, but he managed to find one that had a little sap in it. He rubbed this on the deepest bite wound. Most of the herbs and roots he tossed aside, but there were a few he added to the mixture on Riki's cheek. A fist-sized sack contained a coarse powder, and he stuck this in his pocket, his fingers brushing the small silver box and the medallion of Kiri-Jolith he'd taken earlier. He set aside another sack that contained a gritty blend of moss and shredded roots.

While he worked on the half-elf, the three human servants came close. The eldest appeared to be their spokesman.

"Mistress Sable will be most angry with you," the man stated. "She will hunt you. You are all fools, as Nura Bint-Drax said, and you will all most certainly die!"

"Everybody dies!" Varek shot back. "You're the fools. Serving a dragon and a snake creature. Willingly, it seems! That's all over now. The spawn are all dead. That snake creature, Nura, is gone. That means you're free. If I were you, I'd head straight north, you'll hit the coast in a week or two if you make a good pace, and some ferryman'll pick you up."

The three humans argued softly for a few moments, then the spokesman squared his shoulders and fixed Varek with an icy stare.

"We're staying here," he said. "Polagnar is our home. Nura Bint-Drax will come back. She'll bring more spawn. We'll serve them, and we'll be fed and protected."

"Sheep," Varek muttered. "Pitiful, mindless sheep."

"She'll live," Dhamon said finally, with relief, drawing Varek's attention away from the three men. Rikali was breathing regularly. "She should come to in a little while." He pointed to the largest hut. "There's a bed in there. Let her rest on it. Get her out of this heat. I doubt the snake woman will be back for a while, so we'll stay in that hut and lick our wounds."

"Is there something you can do for that?" Varek nodded at Dhamon's legs.

Dhamon's pants were torn, showing his right thigh completely covered with tiny black scales, all radiating outward from the large dragon scale and shimmering in the sun. Some had traveled down his calf, looking like shiny black beads against his skin, and there were a smattering of scales on his the top of his foot and on his left leg. He didn't answer. Instead, he took the small blade Riki had used on Nura and began furiously cutting at the scales.

"Are you sure you should . . ." Varek began. Dhamon's fierce scowl caused him to swallow the question.

Dhamon cut away at the newer scales, digging out most of them and leaving behind raw wounds. He didn't dare touch the large dragon scale, and his efforts at rooting out the couple of dozen left on his leg were too painful. After several minutes of frustration, he gave up.

He took the gritty mixture he'd found and, grimacing, liberally applied it on his legs. He had to stop every few moments because it stung so badly. There were wounds on his chest, where he'd earlier dug out the scales with his fingers, and he put the mixture on these, too. When he was finished, he glanced back at the pen and Maldred.

The big thief had managed to shake off the remnants of Nura's spell and was leaning against the slats of the pen for support. His muscular form sported a riot of gouges and cuts, and his clothes hung on him in bloodied strips.

Dhamon tossed the bag that contained the last of the gritty mixture to Varek. "You've some deep cuts on your back. Put some of this on them. Should help you heal, reduce the chance of infection. Then get Riki out of the sun."

Dhamon rose and limped over to Maldred. He leaned against the railing next to the big man, staring at all the bodies. Scales and flesh and blood covered every inch of ground. He ground the ball of his foot into the mud. "I should feel sorry for them all," he said, "but I don't. I don't feel anything." He turned from the pen and almost bumped into the village spokesman, who had silently followed him.

"The black dragon will be most angry at what you've done. The black dragon and Nura Bint-Drax will—"

Dhamon slammed his hand into the man's chest, shoving him out of the way. He walked to the hut Riki was in, kicking snakes out of his way as he went. He heard heavy footsteps behind him. Maldred followed him inside.

The acid-scarred Varek was dutifully sitting on the bed next to Rikali, who twitched in her sleep, her thin lips set in an uncharacteristic grimace. Varek's cuts were covered with the gritty mixture.

"You've first watch, Mal," Dhamon said. "All of us need some rest, but we're going to do it in shifts. I don't trust the villagers. Wake me after the sun's down—earlier if there's trouble."

Without another word, Dhamon busied himself ripping up a cloak to fashion bandages for his leg and arms, then settled back against a large crate. Already he felt his wounds closing. His healing ability was another part of the curse, he knew, probably a by-product of the dragonscale on his thigh. Though he was pleased to be mending quickly, he wanted nothing more than to be rid of the accursed scale.

"I need your mysterious healer, Mal," he breathed. He closed his eyes and intended to go straight to sleep, but in his mind he saw Nura Bint-Drax writhing as a snake before him. He opened his eyes quickly.

He listened to Maldred and Varek quietly talking about the half-elf. He heard a few crates being moved, sensed Maldred taking up a spot at the entrance to the hut. He heard movement outside, several yards beyond the hut, and he heard the voices of a pair of villagers. Maldred shooed them away.

Sleep finally claimed Dhamon, his dreams filled with the visages of grotesque abominations and a snake woman with hypnotic eyes who was wrapping herself so tight around him he couldn't breathe. All too soon, Maldred roused him, and it was his turn at watch.

Chapter Eleven
Ragh of Doom

D hamon sat just outside the doorway to the hut, listening to Maldred and Varek snoring. The grating sound was impossible for him to shut out entirely. Riki was slumbering soundly, too, waking only once nearly an hour past. Rising up on her elbows she spotted Dhamon as he glanced over his shoulder, and without a word she lay down again, drifting back to sleep.

He gazed out across the forlorn village, a long sword that once belonged to a Solamnic Knight in his lap. Had the Knight been one of the spawn he killed? Impossible to know.

Several villagers were awake, although it was well past midnight. They'd been taking shifts on watch, too, four of them currently sitting near a small fire they'd built for light only, as the temperature was still dreadfully hot.

They were watching Dhamon intently.

He could hear their wary whispering, making out several of the words—Mistress Sable, Nura Bint-Drax, strangers. He listened more closely and found that he could hear them as clearly as if he were sitting in their midst. The spokesman was debating now what they should do with all of the bodies they had gathered into a pile—drag them into the swamp for the alligators to dispose of, or let them continue to rot here, reeking evidence for Sable to see in the event the overlord deigned to grace the village with her scaly presence? Despite the swarm of insects the corpses had already drawn, most of the villagers seemed to favor the latter option.

Dhamon knew he shouldn't have been able to hear the villagers at all. They were too far away, their voices too low. The fire was crackling, the snakes that carpeted the village were hissing, and his companions only a few feet behind him were snoring. Though part of him marveled at his ability to pick out all these sounds, a greater part of him feared that it was all connected to the large scale on his leg. He wanted nothing more than to be normal again. The pop of something in the fire roused him from his musings. One of the villagers had tossed a too-damp log on the flames, and the wood hissed in protest.

He could hear other things, too, when he concentrated: the gentle rustling of leaves from trees that circled this village; a soft growling noise the sivak draconian made, perhaps its version of snoring, and the coo of a swamp bird.

He felt an insect crawling up his arm. It was a pearl-shaped orange beetle. Brushing it off, Dhamon glanced away from the fire and the villagers, craning his neck and peering south. His eyes probed the darkness, making out rotting corpses and, several yards from them, the sivak. The creature was curled around the base of the tree, as a dog might sleep. Dhamon shouldn't have been able to see it this clearly. There was no moon tonight, and the shadows were thick. But he could even discern that the beast was squirming as if in the depths of a dream. What would it dream about? he wondered. No matter, there would be no more dreams for the sivak—or nightmares for that matter—after this night, once Maldred had his way. Maldred intended to slay it at first light to keep Nura Bint-Drax from using it to create more monstrosities.

Monstrosities like me, Dhamon thought. I feel less human with each passing week.

He removed his bandages and glanced at the wounds on his legs and chest. They were healing exceptionally well. He wasn't tired either, despite only catching a few hours of sleep after the ordeal he'd been through. His limbs no longer ached. He felt good.

His sense of smell was sharper than usual, causing him some discomfort. The cloying bittersweet stench from the rotting corpses mingled with the waste in the pen, the sweat from his companions and the villagers, the pools of dried and drying blood, and the stench of the swamp.

Dhamon stood, careful not to wake the others—not because he was concerned about their well-being and their need for rest, but because he didn't want to deal with them at the moment. Keeping a watchful eye on the villagers by the fire, he strode purposefully toward a hut several yards away, ducking inside and retrieving a crate. As the villagers stared and whispered, he unsheathed his long sword and pried the lid open, selected a bottle, and took a long pull from it. The wine filled his senses, the taste of the blackberries intense.

He steadied himself and listened to the village spokesman protesting to his fellows that Dhamon should be stopped, shouldn't be allowed to take anything from the huts that soon enough would be occupied by spawn, Sable's precious children. Nura Bint-Drax would see that Polagnar was repopulated with the creatures. She would see that the dark-haired defiler and his friends were punished.

To spite the man, Dhamon headed back inside the hut and tugged out several packs. Digging through them in full view of the villagers, he found clothes that would fit, and he changed into trousers and a Solamnic tunic that were worn but well made. The tunic he turned inside-out so the emblem would not show. He stuffed a few changes of clothes into a soft leather pack, including two shirts that looked like they were practically new, and slung the pack over his shoulder, then he headed toward the fire.

In an instant the villagers were on their feet, darting nervous glances. The villagers stopped whispering when Dhamon dropped his free hand to the pommel of his sword.

"You've a fresh water supply here. Somewhere." He was addressing the spokesman, staring ominously into the man's eyes. "There are at least a dozen empty skins back in that hut." He gestured to the building he'd been looting. "I want them all filled with fresh water before dawn. I want two satchels of food. Fruits and nuts preferably, not that snake flesh you seem to be so fond of preparing."

The youngest of the villagers puffed out his chest. "W-we'll do no such thing. W-w-we'll not help the likes of someone who goes against Nura Bint-Drax! Doom to you!"

Dhamon moved his menacing gaze to the man. "You'll attend to it now, boy. Or maybe you'd like to share the fate of those others." He nodded toward the corpses and tapped his thumb against his sword's pommel. "You take care of our supplies, and we'll be on our way soon enough. You'll keep your skins intact, and Polagnar will be yours again. You can tidy up for the next batch of spawn that comes along."

"Nura Bint-Drax will hunt you down," the youngest said softly. His voice trembled, but his eyes showed defiance. "She'll make you pay for what you've done. She'll feed you to the dragon."

"Perhaps I'll hunt Nura Bint-Drax instead," Dhamon returned, as he finished the wine and dropped the empty bottle at their feet. "Dawn's only a few hours away. I'd hurry to those tasks if I were you."

He spun on his heel and searched through the huts he hadn't yet visited, taking his time, and occasionally glancing at the villagers make sure they were indeed gathering the supplies he'd asked for. He found several more Solamnic shields and weapons, as well as tabards and cloaks that had been made into bedding. All bore the emblems of the Order of the Rose and the Order of the Sword. There were only a few pieces of intact armor, and these were leg and arm pieces pitted from the spawns' acid. There were other Solamnic garments riddled with holes and cuts made by claws rather than swords. It was obvious one or two units of Solamnic Knights had fought the spawn. Perhaps any Knights who had survived had been transformed into the foul creatures.

Dhamon shrugged, dismissing it all as beyond his concern and continuing to poke through the Knights' belongings. He discovered a half-dozen more silver medallions of Kiri-Jolith. One with diamonds he decided to keep. There were nearly twenty rings with roses engraved on them, all made of gold. All found their way into his pouches. He tied one pouch to his belt, then stuffed another into his pocket—this one brimming with steel pieces.

He made a return trip to the crates of wine. He carefully padded six bottles in a backpack, and took a seventh with him to his companions' hut. He tugged the cork free with his teeth and took a deep swallow, grateful that it cut the stench of this place. Dhamon suddenly remembered the pack filled with wine that he'd dropped behind the shadblow bush, but he knew there was no reason to retrieve that when he had plenty here.

Maldred and Varek were still snoring. Rikali woke again and watched as Dhamon retrieved a small chest that sat at the foot of her bed. He beckoned her outside, and she followed him, careful not to wake Varek as she went.

The sky was lightening, and the half-elf looked up to see a trio of blue herons fly over the clearing and out of sight. "Daybreak," she whispered. "I think I like this time best. The sky all rosy for a brief time, like a kiss. Then the sky's all blue." She dropped her gaze to Dhamon, who was sitting on the ground and prying at the lock of the chest with a coral-handled dagger.

With little effort he managed to open the lid and began rifling through the gems he found inside. Rikali had taught him how to spot flaws in jewels, and he picked out the most valuable—primarily garnets, sapphires and emeralds. A thumb-sized jacinth caught his eye. He stuffed them into the empty pouch, then tied it on his belt. He filled his other pocket with smaller gems, then snatched up a hammered gold bracer studded with pieces of jade and tourmaline and fitted it on his arm. A thick gold chain quickly found its way around his neck.

"They're pretty." Riki stared at the gems as if she were mesmerized, but she made no move to take anything. "They're not worth much, really," she continued.

Dhamon held up a topaz that was about the size of a plum. "Aye, its pretty, but definitely flawed. Still, you can't have too many gems. And so . . ."

This and several others he added to the second pouch of coins that lay loose at his side. He came across a hammered silver bracelet set with jade chips, and this he tossed to the half-elf.

"No use leaving this here. The villagers don't need it." Or deserve it, he added to himself.

Riki held the bracelet almost reverently, turning it over and over in her acid-scarred fingers before putting it around her wrist. She squeezed it to make it a little tighter so it wouldn't fall off.

"We all could've died here, Dhamon," she said softly. "All of us."

"How old is he, Riki?"

Dhamon's question threw her. "What?"

"How old is Varek?"

"You weren't comin' back for me, Dhamon Grimwulf. I wanted to be with someone. An' he loves me. A lot. Spent every last coin he had on a pretty little ring for me." She waggled her hand at him.

"How old?" he persisted.

"Nineteen."

"He's a boy, Riki. What were you thinking?"

"What was I thinkin'?" She lowered her voice. "I certainly wasn't thinkin' about you anymore, was I? You wouldn't ever have married me, Dhamon Grimwulf."

He didn't catch the twinge of sadness in her voice.

"You wouldn't have even settled down with me for a little while."

"No," he admitted. "I wouldn't have."

"Then why should you care what I do?" The sadness was gone, replaced by controlled anger. "Why should you care how old he is?"

"You're older than me. You're nearly twice his age. Think about it, Riki—pinning him down so young. Not just with a wife, but with a family. It won't last."

She shook her head, her curls catching the light and gleaming. "He's not a boy, Dhamon Grimwulf. He's a young man. A young man who loves me very, very much. Besides, what do you care?"

"I don't." He picked up a cracked jacinth, examined and discarded it. "I really don't, Riki."

The half-elf squatted by Dhamon and stirred the gems with a finger. She stared into the chest, clearly looking at something far beyond the flawed baubles.

"He'll make a good father, don't you think?" She ran her thumb across the face of a chipped piece of jade.

"Riki . . ."

She tipped her head back and put on a face when the breeze shifted and brought the stench from the corpses their way. After a moment she met his stare. "I better go wake him, huh? We'll be headin' out of this ghastly place soon. I heard Mal talkin' about some pirate loot in his sleep. I fancy goin' after some real treasure." She jabbed a finger at the flawed gems. "This stuff isn't worth my time."

She disappeared into the hut, leaving Dhamon to stare at the villagers who were approaching.

The villagers had taken apart one of their lean-tos to build a small litter, atop which rested several satchels filled with food, along with the dozen or so waterskins and Dhamon's backpack filled with the heady elven wine.

He inspected the litter and supplies, only vaguely noting the contents of the satchels. His companions had awakened, and Varek and Maldred and Riki all poked through the Solamnics' clothes to find something to wear.

Maldred snorted and gave a nod of his head toward the sivak, his foot tapping. "Time to take care of that thing." He reached to his back and unsheathed his greatsword, which he'd managed to recover from a hut, the edge catching the dawning sun.

The sivak stood, carefully regarding Maldred and showing no sign of fear as the big man approached. It had made no move to attack them, though its chain clearly would reach far enough. That told Dhamon that it wasn't going to put up a fight.

Dhamon caught the sivak's gaze. "They didn't want you to fly, did they? Afraid you might more easily escape?"

The draconian moved closer to the trunk.

"So they cut off your wings."

Maldred paused. "The thing isn't going to talk to you, Dhamon. Look at that wound on its throat. It probably can't speak and—"

"It was the price I paid for saying no," the sivak answered. There was a whisper wrapped around the edge of the draconian's voice, giving it a soft and unpleasant huskiness.

Coming closer, Dhamon detected a scent he hadn't noticed when he first spied the sivak. It reminded him of hot metal and smoke, a newly forged sword—as if the creature had been birthed in a blacksmith's shop. Did all sivaks smell like this?

"Nura Bint-Drax did this to you?" Dhamon persisted.

A nod. "Because I would not willingly help her."

Maldred took a step around Dhamon, eyes searching the sivak's face. "It doesn't make sense that you wouldn't want to help Nura Bint-Drax. Your kind serve dragons."

The sivak did not reply.

"I suspect it didn't mind serving Sable," Dhamon observed, "and before her, Takhisis. But this Nura . . ."

The creature glanced back and forth between Maldred and Dhamon.

"Sivak, I thought only the dragon overlords could create spawn," Dhamon said.

The sivak fixed his eyes on a spot on the ground.

"Nura Bint-Drax could do it, couldn't she? Make spawn."

"Yes," the creature replied after a moment's hesitation. The draconian canted his head, listening to something beyond the perimeter of the village. He didn't notice Dhamon listening too. He turned slightly and spied through a break in the underbrush a large panther slinking to the north.

"What is she? Just what is Nura Bint-Drax?"

155

The answer was quick this time. "A naga, a being neither snake nor human, but resembling both. I believe Takhisis created them not long after she gave life to us."

"Tell me more."

The draconian shrugged. "I don't know much beyond that. In all the years I served Sable, I saw only two of them—and Nura Bint-Drax was the greater. Even some of Sable's dragons fear her. Nagas are powerful, and Nura Bint-Drax is particularly skilled."

"They can be killed," Dhamon persisted.

The sivak inhaled deeply. "Everything that breathes can be killed. As you will slay me."

"I don't suppose you'd object to that."

Maldred cleared his throat. "It doesn't matter to me if it objects. I revere life, but I don't see that we have a choice here. We can't just let it go. " He addressed only the sivak now. "We'll make it quick, though. You won't feel any-thing." He tightened his grip around the pommel, took a few steps forward, and raised the sword above his head.

"No." Dhamon's hand shot out, preventing Maldred's blow. "We need the sivak, Mal."

"Yes, like we need a—"

"It can help carry our supplies." Dhamon pointed to the litter the villagers had assembled.

Maldred shook his head. "I don't know about this, Dhamon. Even without wings, this thing is dangerous."

Dhamon stared at the draconian. "Not as dangerous as I am." He turned to Maldred and said, "Or you, my friend." He laughed grimly, but a tense moment passed before Maldred responded with a forced chuckle. He lowered his weapon.

"Now, can that map show us the quickest way out of this damned swamp and to your Hollering Hills or Screaming Valley or just whatever it is you called it? There's a pirate's horde to be after, and . . ."

". . . and the healer after that," Maldred finished. He reached into his pocket for the bone tube, carefully extracting the map and holding it open to the sun. Images danced along the surface as he asked the enchanted parchment for a route.

"Find us a place to get some horses and a wagon along the way," Dhamon added. "I'm hoping there's so much treasure we won't be able to carry it ourselves." He stepped close to the sivak, drew his long sword, and used the tip to saw through the chain around his neck.

"Have you got a name?" Dhamon asked the sivak.

"Ragh," he replied. "Ragh of the Lords of Doom."

"Meaning you served Takhisis in the Lords," Dhamon supplied.

A nod.

"Well, Ragh of Doom, you serve me now."

The sivak eyed him coolly but said nothing.

Chapter Twelve
Graelor's End

aldred stood on the bank of a narrow stream, listening to the musical noise the water made as it rushed over the rocks that littered its bed. A few of the larger stones that protruded above the surface gleamed in the early morning sunlight, looking almost like gems. He found himself staring at them for more than a few moments, then he raised his gaze to the horizon, a scowl etched deep on his handsome face.

"What's the matter, Mal?" Rikali sidled up to him and poked him in the arm. "This is lovely. You should be enjoyin' it. No more swamp. No snakes. This all smells so sweet, an' all you can see is tall grass and trees . . . an' that town ahead."

Maldred refused to look at her. Instead his eyes were locked onto what appeared to be the largest collection of buildings and the thin trails of smoke rising around them.

"C'mon, Mal, what's up? Why are we just standin' here rather than goin' into that town? I figure I could buy me a nice, big breakfast—over which you can tell me all about this pirate treasure again. Pigs, but I'm hungry, Mal. An' then I thought . . ." She shook her head when she noticed he was thoroughly ignoring her. "And then I thought I might dance around naked and stick mushrooms in my ears." She snorted when there was still no reaction. "You could at least listen to me, you know."

"I'm listening to you, my love," Varek gently tugged her away from Maldred. He nuzzled her shoulder and twirled his slender fingers in her hair. She relaxed slightly, resting the back of her head against his chest, but she still kept her eyes on Maldred.

"Somethin's botherin' him, Varek," the half-elf persisted.

"Small town. He's concerned there's far too many cook-fires for the size of it."

"Might not mean anything," Dhamon said, as he joined them, "but our course takes us very near that town."

"Through it—our course takes us through that town, if we want to buy a wagon and horses," Maldred said, his gaze unwavering.

The half-elf raised an eyebrow. "Wagon?" she mouthed.

"To haul the pirate treasure in," Dhamon provided. "I'm going in for a closer look." He nodded to Mal and started through the tall grass. "I'll be back soon. Keep an eye on our sivak, won't you?"

The half-elf was quick after him. "I'll come, too."

Varek's hand shot out and firmly closed around her elbow.

"If there's something wrong, Riki," he cautioned, "I don't want you anywhere near the trouble." His glance dropped to her swollen stomach, then he raised his eyes and saw her disappointment. He drew a finger to his lips, silencing any argument, kissed her on the cheek, and started after Dhamon.

Dhamon waited just beyond the edge of the town, called Graelor's End according to the weathered sign . He heard someone coming up behind him and guessed it was Riki, but when he turned he frowned to see it was Varek.

The youth slipped up to Dhamon's shoulder and laid his staff on the ground. "I don't see anyone stirring, do you? Not a single soul out on the streets. But those cook-fires, there's got to be people. Indeed, I—"

Dhamon's narrowed eyes silenced him.

The town had some age to it. The homes spread to the west and were made of field stone mortared together with mud and dung. All the roofs were heavy thatch. There was a scattering of farms to the east. Some of the farmhouses were grand, and Dhamon could see goats and sheep milling about in pens. Two dozen or so businesses and hostels were between the homes and the farms, most of them two- and three-story buildings made of stone and wood.

"Aye, there's people," Dhamon whispered after several minutes. He pointed to the closest house. "Someone walked past a window."

Varek squinted and shook his head, seeing nothing. "Can't see that far."

"There." Dhamon pointed to a business down the middle of a dust-and-gravel street. The street was wide and seemed to be the main thoroughfare through the town. A man and woman were looking out of a bakery window. "But why are they all inside and . . . ?" His voice trailed off when he saw a figure step from a side street onto the main road.

The man was tall and broad-shouldered, with a sweeping black-lined cloak fluttering away from his plate mail-clad form. The armor was distinctive and ornate—a

161

collection of steel plates with chain-mail gussets, more
functional and lightweight than the armor worn by Solamnic Knights or Knights of Neraka.

"A Legion of Steel Knight!"

"A commander, actually. And be quiet," Dhamon sternly
warned. "We can't afford to draw attention to ourselves.
All the townsfolk are avoiding him. We should too. Keep
your head down. We'll watch a few minutes more, then
we'll go back to Mal and Riki and plan a route well away
from here. We'll find somewhere else to buy a wagon."

Varek opened his mouth to protest, but another sharp
look from Dhamon cut him off. Dhamon grasped Varek's
shoulder and pointed. Other figures spilled out of a
business to join the commander—Legion of Steel battlefield medics and sorcerers, judging by the markings on
their tabards. The small group conferred for some time
before the commander clapped his hands twice and
whistled shrilly.

More Knights appeared, drifting out from a few businesses, many from side streets. They formed up, eight
across, all in plate mail, walking stiffly in unison. They
practically filled the main street, as others marched in
from alleys at the edge of Dhamon's and Varek's vision.

"They were camped on the side streets, maybe farther
back on the main street, too, and maybe south of town."
Dhamon whispered. "I used to know commanders who
preferred that to camping in an open field. The buildings
cut the wind, and their presence impresses the locals."
His eyes closed to slits, and the hair stood up on the back
of his neck. "And I know that commander."

Dhamon studied the details of the lead man's weathered face. A steel-gray mustache curled down over lips
that were twisted by a thick, ropy scar that continued
down his chin to his throat. The eyes were an intense
bright blue, and the eyebrows above them bushy white.

"Lawlor," he hissed. "Commander Arun Lawlor."

"Too far away," Varek whispered. "How can you tell who it is?"

Dhamon was so caught up in studying the commander and his men, trying to determine the strength of the unit, that he didn't notice Varek rise, and he didn't see the young man take the first few steps into the town.

"Varek!" Dhamon called quietly when he finally spotted him. "What are you doing? Get back here now!"

Varek glanced over his shoulder and shook his head. "I'm going to talk to them, Dhamon," he said matter-of-factly. "I'm going to ask Commander Arun Lawlor why he has so many Legion of Steel Knights here."

He sprinted forward, staff in one hand and free arm waving to draw the Knights' attention.

Dhamon cursed and wheeled, keeping low and running back toward where he'd left Maldred and Rikali—never once looking over his shoulder to check on Varek. The moment he got there, he grabbed the half-elf by the arm.

"Riki, Mal, let's get out of here. Fast!" He pointed to the southwest, where in the distance there was a small rise and at the top of it the beginnings of a forest. "It looks to be about two miles from here, maybe less. Should be quite a bit of cover there. Run like a hundred Legion of Steel Knights are after you—because that may very well be the case."

"Legion of Steel? Where? Where's Varek?" The half-elf was quick to panic.

"Introducing himself to them."

"Damn fool," Maldred spat. "If he mentions our names . . ." Maldred let the thought trail off and met Dhamon's gaze, then looked at the sivak.

"Ragh, come with me," Dhamon said.

Riki's eyes were wide. "Legion Knights. What about Varek?"

163

"The Knights aren't after Varek," Dhamon snapped.

"Meet us in the woods as soon as you can, my friend," Maldred said. "Be careful. Very." Then he was tugging the half-elf and rushing away.

"Ragh?" Dhamon whirled, and the sivak followed him back toward the town, keeping low in the grass, the two of them practically crawling at times. They circled to the northeast side of the town, between the business district and a farm, lying behind a row of spreading goldenrod bushes where Dhamon could better see the assembled Knights. There had to be at least three hundred, Dhamon guessed, maybe as many as four hundred, an impressive force occupying this small town in the middle of a sprawling plains.

What are they doing here? he thought. What could be going on in the Plains of Dust to interest them? And why in the depths of the Abyss would Varek stroll right in for a chat?

"Why do you fear the Legion Knights?" Ragh's hoarse voice ended Dhamon's musings.

"I don't fear them," Dhamon lied, eyes scanning the throng. "I just . . . what's this?"

He spied Varek, shadowed under a faded awning, face to face with Commander Arun Lawlor. The commander extended his hand, Varek shook it. They talked for several minutes, and Dhamon wondered just what they were discussing and how long they'd been at it before he spotted them. Then Lawlor patted Varek on the back and walked away, inspecting his men as he headed to the front of the column.

"So you're friendly with the Legion of Steel, Varek," Dhamon said quietly. He kept his eyes on the young man, who was leaning against the building now, staff propped next to him, arms folded and face fixed on the assembly.

Dhamon and the sivak crawled toward the east, heading

for a narrow side street extending toward the main road. "Common sense says we should head for the trees, find Maldred and Riki, and give this place a wide berth."

"But Varek . . ."

"Is a fool, Ragh. What are all these Knights doing here?" He sighed and shook his head. "Follow me, and be quiet."

Dhamon led the sivak down the street and into the shadows of a two-story building. Hugging the wall, they inched closer.

The Knights were quiet but alert, eyes forward, looking at Lawlor, whom Dhamon couldn't see at the moment. There was no murmuring among them.

A few steps closer, and he risked a quick glance around the corner. Dhamon was able to get a better look at their numbers. There were at least five hundred Knights, and they stretched south beyond where the main street ended. Dhamon spotted a nervous young woman looking out a second-story window across the street. There were a few other folks watching too, that he could see. On their faces was a mix of indifference, admiration, revulsion, and fear.

There was a wooden wall next to a leather worker's shop, and on it were sheets of parchment. It was too far away for Dhamon to read, though he suspected by the crude drawings on some of the sheets that they advertised things for sale. As he watched, a Legion Knight approached the board, rolled pieces of parchment tucked under his arm. The Knight began tacking the notices up, right in the center of the wall, not caring if he obscured the other postings.

"That's you on the parchment," the sivak whispered.

Dhamon growled from deep in his throat. The sketch on the sheet the Knight was tacking up indeed bore a close resemblance to him. The next one posted looked like Maldred. Two more sheets went up, these sketches of men Dhamon didn't recognize.

"So you have a right to fear the Legion," the sivak continued. "They search for you. What did you do to draw their ire?"

Dhamon didn't answer for several minutes, watching the Knight finish his work, then stroll away to join the column.

"What did—"

The words hissed from his mouth. "I stole from some Legion of Steel Knights who were laid up in a hospital in Khur."

"Khur is a long way from here." The sivak's brow knitted. "For that, an army is looking for you?"

"There was a little more to it than a simple theft," Dhamon admitted. "Mal and Riki were with me. We were finished in that town, had as much coin as we were likely to get from the theft, and we were trying to leave. Unfortunately, more than a few Knights spotted us and gave chase. Some of them were injured, maybe killed. We had to defend ourselves." He paused, watching a few more Knights spill out of businesses and join the ranks. "In our rush to escape we accidentally set the stable on fire. Khur's a dry place. I understand most of the town burned to the ground before they could put it out."

The sivak stonily regarded Dhamon. "For that they might indeed send an army."

Dhamon shook his head. "No one would send that many men after a small band of thieves. I suspect the Legion could care less about a dusty town in Khur. They're just posting notices along their normal route."

The Knights posted notices for the better part of an hour. Dhamon eased farther away from the main street, still staying within earshot and catching bits of Lawlor's orders. The commander was directing the men due east it seemed, naming a small town they would reach at sunset.

166

Truly wonderful, Dhamon mused. How many towns had they already posted the notices in? Travel certainly would be . . . uncomfortable . . . because of it.

Some mention was made of the Silvanesti Forest and the elves, and of the Dark Knights of Neraka. Dhamon, a former Dark Knight himself, wished he could hear more.

Finally the men moved out, and Dhamon sagged against the wall in relief. He waited until the loud and monotonous sound of the Knights' footsteps told him they'd passed beyond the main road and were well into the tall grass north of town, then he edged out onto the street. He intended to pluck the wanted posters from the wall, fetch Varek, and head quickly after Maldred and Rikali, then the pirate treasure. They'd find another, safer town to purchase a wagon in.

"Stay put," he told the sivak. "I'll be back in a moment."

Dhamon had not taken a half-dozen steps when two Knights strolling out of the leather worker's shop crossed his path. Perhaps they wouldn't have given him a second thought, but his usually imperturbable mask melted into an expression of surprise. As well, he was still wearing the inside-out Solamnic Knight tabard.

The tallest Knight inspected Dhamon, taking his measure and clearly not recognizing him—though his sketched image and name in block letters was hanging only a few feet away on the wall. His stockier companion, however, was reaching for his sword.

"Dhamon Grimwulf! Murderer! Thief!" the Knight cried.

The taller Knight drew his sword, too, though by the look on his face he still hadn't made the connection.

"Commander Lawlor will reward me well when I present you to him. You will be strung up and . . ."

The rest of the stocky Knight's words were lost on Dhamon. He spun about and dashed toward the alley where he'd left the sivak. From windows above the street came the shouted questions of townsfolk. "Murderer? Where?" "Thief!" People came out of the shops onto the main street where the dust was still stirring from the Knights' departure.

Dhamon drew his sword as he slipped into the alley. "How many damn Knights are in this town anyway? I thought they all left," he hissed. "And where's the damn sivak?" The draconian was nowhere to be seen.

The two Legion of Steel Knights raced into the alley behind him, and Dhamon parried their first blows.

"I've no burning desire to kill you," he told them, "but I'll not let you take me."

The stockier Knight made no reply, but he had considerable skill with his sword, and Dhamon found himself working to keep the man from skewering him.

The taller Knight was looking for a chance to join the fight, but his companion and Dhamon were moving quickly, circling and dodging and making it difficult for him to get in a solid blow without injuring his fellow Knight.

"I'll summon the others," the taller Knight said finally, withdrawing and heading back toward the street.

"I think not," came a hoarse voice. The sivak stepped from behind a stack of crates, catching the Knight by surprise. Before the man could raise his sword, the sivak had stepped in, grabbed his head, and twisted it, breaking the man's neck. The Knight fell to the ground, and the sivak looked down on the corpse with mild interest. Ragh shoved the body behind the crates, closing his eyes and concentrating. Silver muscles rippled in the shadows, folding in on themselves and changing color. A moment longer the sivak had transformed himself to look like the slain Knight.

"Murderer," the stocky Knight spat at Dhamon. "Thief."

"Aye," Dhamon admitted, as he ducked beneath the swing of the man's sword, leveling his own and slicing forward, finding a gap in the plates of the man's armor. "I am both of those things." The steel hissed against the Knight's ribs, then he pulled the sword free. "Though I hadn't intended to kill you." Another blow and the Legion Knight crumpled. Dhamon bent and wiped his sword on the man's cloak, then rolled the body into the shadows.

Out on the street, Dhamon saw a half-dozen more Legion Knights stirring, obviously responding to the shouts of their comrades. One was striding toward the alley.

"Damn it all," Dhamon cursed. He put his back to the wall and readied his weapon to meet the man, but the sivak—wearing the guise of the tall knight—waved him back. Ragh stepped into the mouth of the alley and drew the approaching Knight's attention.

"I saw the thief," the sivak said. "One of the men on the posters." His hoarse voice drew a puzzled look from the Knight. The disguised sivak gestured down the street. "He was running that way. I'm searching this alley for his companions."

That seemed to satisfy the Knight, and he turned away. Ragh was quick to rejoin Dhamon, who had hid his victim's body behind a crate. Dhamon kept his grip tight on his sword as he glanced out onto the main street.

"So . . . you should kill me here," the draconian stated. "My usefulness has been served. My body will take on your appearance, and the remaining Legion of Steel Knights in this town will think someone killed you. In death I will aid you."

Dhamon inhaled deep and considered doing just that.

"You would wear my guise, revealing your slayer," Dhamon said. "I thought you turned to stone or exploded or something."

"Bozaks."

Dhamon cocked an eyebrow.

"Bozak draconians explode when they are killed. Baaz become petrified like stone."

Dhamon nodded, recalling that the sivak he killed in the mangrove took on his appearance. He hadn't had much experience with draconians.

The sivak glanced away, listening to a Knight passing by on the street. The Knight was talking to himself and shaking his fist in the air. He hadn't noticed them in the shadows, and so the sivak returned its attention to Dhamon.

"You will have little peace in this part of the world if the Knights continue to post signs and seek to—"

"Bring me to justice?" Dhamon gave a clipped laugh. "I haven't known peace for quite a long time."

The sivak took a deep breath. "Peace would be yours if you killed me, if the Knights found your body here in this alley. They would think you dead and end their postings."

A length of silence passed between them, then Dhamon said, "I've got to find Varek, get back to Mal and Riki."

The sivak nodded. "If you are not going to kill me, I will find Varek. It is too risky. It is your turn to . . . stay put."

Several minutes later, the sivak, still looking like the Legion Knight, was leading a surprised Varek into the alley. Dhamon's hand was instantly on the young man's throat, cutting off his words and his breath.

"You pompous young fool," Dhamon snarled through grinding teeth. "You've not got the sense of a pack mule." He relaxed his grip, then dropped his hand to his side. "Do you have any idea what you could have done, Varek, coming into this town with the Legion here? Do you? You walk right in, bold as a rooster, strut right up to the commander. The Legion of Steel Knights—any Knights for that matter—are to be avoided." He glared at Varek for several moments. "C'mon, we've got to find Mal and Riki."

They headed back, circling Graelor's End and aiming toward the rise where Dhamon had sent Maldred and Rikali. As the three jogged toward the forest, Ragh dropped his Knight guise. Varek rambled on about the town, telling Dhamon and the sivak that he learned Graelor's End was named for a wizard of the Red Robes, Cazen Graelor, who more than a hundred years ago died successfully defending the settlement from a force of brigands. Now a dozen Legion Knights were stationed there for defense.

"I could care less what the town's named for," Dhamon said. "I'll not be visiting it again." He picked up the pace.

As he neared the trees, a shrill scream broke the stillness. Dhamon tripped once, on a twisted piece of root hidden by the tall grass, but he picked himself up swiftly and rushed to the top of the rise. A moment more, and he was into the cover of the trees.

The screaming stopped.

CHAPTER THIRTEEN
MAZES AND VEILS

aldred hurried toward the southwest, eyes trained on the forest and hand wrapped tightly around Riki's. "Faster," he told her. "I'd rather face another village of spawn than deal with the Legion of Steel right now."

The half-elf could hardly keep up. "Slow down, Mal," she gasped, attempting to pull her hand away. "I ain't so fast anymore, what with being pregnant. I'm runnin' for two now."

He accommodated her, but only a little.

"Pregnant? Running for two? Well, you'll be dead for two if the Legion catches up with us."

"Pigs, but we shouldn't've stole from them in Khur," she said "Should stick to stealin' from common folks."

"Common folks don't have much worth stealing."

They ran toward the trees, weaving their way around a tangle of bushes and finally reaching the rise. Maldred paused so the half-elf could catch her breath.

"I hope Dhamon finds Varek and don't find no trouble

173

there," Riki said. She was bent over, hands on her knees, sucking in air. "None of us needs more trouble."

Maldred nodded in agreement. "Come. Let's wait in the woods for Dhamon. I'm sure he won't be long, and I'm sure he'll find Varek and keep out of trouble." He was halfway up the rise when he added. "This Varek, Riki. Do you really love him?"

The half-elf pretended to keep her eyes focused on the ground so she wouldn't trip over the myriad of fingerlike roots that seemed to run everywhere. "Yeah, Mal. 'Course I love Varek. I wouldn't've married him otherwise. And I wouldn't be havin' his baby if I didn't care for him."

The trees at the top of the rise were varieties of maples, oaks, and walnuts. Maldred's boots crunched over acorns that had fallen. He put his back to an especially thick oak and looked out toward the town. From here, he could easily see if someone was coming—Dhamon or Legion of Steel Knights.

Riki sagged against a crimson maple. "That map of yours, Mal . . . how much farther past that town is this pirate treasure?"

"Some distance," he answered after a moment.

"Pigs, but I'm tired of walking, Mal. We've got to get us some horses if we're goin' 'some distance.' And I think . . ." She pushed away from the tree and turned to peer deeper into the woods. "Did you hear that, Mal?"

"Hear what?"

"A babe cryin'. I'm sure I heard a babe cryin'." She glided away from Maldred and down a narrow path. "Hear it? So soft. I think it's a babe cryin' for help."

Maldred shook his head. "I don't hear anything, Riki, and I think we should stay here, wait for Dhamon and your Varek. Riki?" He glanced over his shoulder and groaned. She was gone. "Riki." A last look toward the town and he hurried down the path, catching up to her in minutes.

"Hear it, Mal?"

The big man nodded, finally hearing a soft cry. "Might be an animal, though, Riki. Hard to tell."

She shook her head and pressed forward. The woods were darker here, the leaves close and thick overhead and blocking the sun. It was pleasantly cool, and a faint breeze stirred the air.

"It's not an animal, Mal," she said after several more minutes. "I don't see any animals here. Not even a bird."

A shiver danced down his neck. There were insects, as he pointed out to her, beetles in profusion along some of the lowest branches. Spiders the size of walnuts clung to the maple trunks. Large webs hung from some of the trees, and these were dotted with dark green spiders that scurried toward the center of the webs when Maldred and Rikali passed by. The webs were thicker ahead.

The cry persisted.

"We've got to be gettin' closer, Mal."

"Closer to something," he answered.

"Riki?" Dhamon shouted. "Riki!"

Varek pumped his legs harder in an effort to catch up, but he could not muster the same speed. Dhamon raced out of his view, followed by the wingless sivak.

There were no immediate signs of the half-elf or Maldred, but—beyond the screams he had heard—no obvious indication of trouble. A cursory search revealed Maldred's and Riki's footprints headed west toward where the smaller trees gave way to older oaks and maples.

Dhamon followed their trail, listening as he went, moving briskly, then stopping when the sun suddenly disappeared. Foliage had not shut out the light—webs were responsible. A few were artful, huge and beautiful with intricate patterns that shimmered in the diffused light, but most were ugly masses as dense as a dwarf's beard. They stretched between the tallest branches, in several spots reaching the ground.

He pressed forward more cautiously, walking now, keen eyes scanning the ground in search of more of his friends' tracks, glancing at gaps in the webs, where he thought he spied something moving.

What's there? he asked himself. "Who's there?" He stared and saw nothing.

The woods became grayer the deeper into the forest he went—thick with night-dark shadows and with heavier curtains of webs that hung from practically every tree. There were hundreds of spiders everywhere. Some were so small they were barely discernible, black specks jumping from strand to strand. Others were larger, the size and color of steel pieces, and these moved slowly if at all. Dhamon noted a few as large as peaches, shiny black and with eyes that appeared sunken. Others were brown, long-legged varieties, like some he'd seen in the woods near far-away Palanthas.

"By my father!" Dhamon faintly heard a voice up ahead. "Is there no end to these?"

"Mal?" Dhamon called. Louder, "Maldred!"

He heard the half-elf scream again, but faint and muffled this time. In response Dhamon tugged free his long sword. He listened, hearing nothing but the coarse breath of the draconian and footsteps pounding behind him—Varek.

"Where's Riki? Where's my wife? Riki!"

Dhamon tried his best to ignore Varek. He concentrated on Maldred's voice hailing from somewhere to the west.

"Maldred!" Dhamon shouted. "Mal! Keep talking!"

"Here!" came Maldred's reply. "We're in here!" He kept shouting, most of it curses in his ogre tongue directed at something Dhamon couldn't see.

"Here," Dhamon muttered. "Just where is here?" Dhamon headed toward the voice, slicing through veil after veil of gossamer web. Ragh followed, using his claws to tear at the thickest veils. Varek was behind them, constantly calling for the half-elf. Some of the webs were so thin Dhamon simply stepped through them, brushing at his face afterward. He marveled that they felt like pieces of damp fog.

"This is your fault," Varek hissed. "You sent them here, Dhamon. You were so worried over the Legion of Steel Knights. Your damn fault. You—"

"Quiet!" Ragh warned. The sivak and Dhamon brushed aside another curtain of webs and pressed on.

"No, Dhamon. The tracks lead this way! This way!" Varek insisted, pointing at the ground. "Riki! Riki, I'll find you!" Varek was almost screaming, and he had angled to the southwest now, moving away from Dhamon and Ragh.

Dhamon had spotted those tracks, too, but he was instead relying on Maldred's voice to guide him—it hinted at a different direction.

"The boy—" Ragh began.

"Can take care of himself," Dhamon finished. "I just wished he wouldn't bellow. Makes it hard to hear."

"Riki, where are you? Please, Riki!" Varek frantically shouted the half-elf's name.

Dhamon and Ragh slipped behind the web curtain, and then behind another one, and another, moving deeper into the woods. The webs were dampening and distorting everything—sometimes Varek's voice seemed closer and other times it was Maldred.

"A rat in a maze," Dhamon grumbled.

The farther he went, the thicker and even more plentiful the webs became, obscuring most of the trees and effectively forming corridors. He and the sivak followed one twisting path, then paused only a moment when it

177

forked. To the right were elaborate webs with great gaps between the strands, looking like crocheted quilts dotted with beadlike green spiders. "Left," he decided, thinking Maldred's voice was coming from that direction. Another dozen yards and he was staring at a dead-end veil of webs directly in his path. Everything was night-dark. The webs were thick overhead and allowed only the faintest bit of light. He saw the webs move in places from the myriad of spiders crawling over them, not from any wind. He knew there were far more spiders than he could see.

He breathed deep, smelling the damp ground beneath him and an odd muskiness. It left a sour taste in his mouth. He reached to his backpack, finding it covered with webs and spiders. Brushing both away, he tugged free one of the bottles of liquor he'd taken from the spawn village, uncorked it, and took a deep pull.

"Better," he pronounced. He took another sip and held it, then forced himself to recap the bottle and put it back in the pack, offering none to the sivak.

He thought about going back to where the web corridor forked and taking the other path. Indeed, he had turned and started to do that, when, with his acute hearing, he heard Maldred's voice clearer and louder than before. He spun and approached the web wall.

"Your friend sounds close," Ragh observed.

Dhamon nodded. This was all so unnatural. Spiders didn't spin webs like this, at least not that he'd ever heard of. So just what was responsible? Magic? A Legion of Steel sorcerer's spell? Perhaps, he mused, the ghost of Cazen Graelor from Graelor's End was playing tricks. He decided he didn't want to know who or what was responsible. He just wanted to get away. He would find Maldred and Riki before nightfall and get as far away from these woods and Graelor's End as he possibly could.

Whatever would draw Riki and Mal into this . . . mess? he wondered, as he reached out and tentatively touched the dead-end wall. It was spongy but firm, and he couldn't move it aside as he had the others. He knew that despite the half-elf's bravado, she was squeamish and wouldn't traipse into this web maze without a good reason. She had been lured, perhaps by the promise of treasure. Maldred no doubt had followed her.

"Maldred!" Dhamon shouted as he swallowed the wine. It slid pleasantly down his throat and warmed a path to his stomach. "Riki! Maldred!"

He could still hear Varek. The young man had apparently given up on the tracks and was again following him and the sivak.

"Wonderful," Dhamon said aloud. "Ah . . ." He smacked at a spider that had dropped on his sword hand and bit him. A red welt immediately formed. He used his free hand to brush at his arms and neck, knocking more spiders loose—there seemed to be an endless supply of them. He felt something tickling his ankle and kicked out, managing to lodge his foot in a sticky web mass. It took a moment to tug himself free.

The sivak was brushing at some spiders, too. The large ones were able to bite through even his scaly hide.

"This is your fault, Dhamon!" Varek was somewhere close behind, hoarse from all his shouting. "Your fault! You sent Riki here because you were afraid of the Legion of Steel Knights. If she's hurt, you'll wish I would've turned you over to Commander Lawlor. Why, I'll . . ."

Varek stopped short, having finally managed to find Dhamon and Ragh and the dead-end corridor.

"Aye, boy, it's my fault. Everything's my fault. Now, shut up about it, and listen."

Varek cocked his head. "A voice."

Dhamon nodded. "Uh-huh. Maldred is calling to us. He's somewhere on the other side of this wall. I suspect there's a far easier way to get to wherever he is. He certainly didn't come this way."

"How do we get to him and Riki?" A mix of worry and anger playing on his face, Varek slipped past Dhamon. He thrust his staff at the web wall and tried to find a way through it, as he had with other veils. This one defied his best efforts, however. He beat at the wall with the staff.

"I propose we take what I suspect is the shortest route to reach him," Ragh said. The sivak chose a spot near Varek, careful to remain just out of reach of the staff. He sliced his claws into the webs. They were as least as thick as his arms were long, and Dhamon noted that the web wall was home to thousands of tiny dark yellow spiders.

"Maldred!" Dhamon paused and listened again. "Are you truly on the other side of this mess, my friend? Or is sound playing tricks on me?"

He took a deep breath, took a position near the sivak, and sliced into the web wall with the sword again and again. Finally he was able to push himself into the web.

"What in the levels of the Abyss are you two doing?"

Varek stared dumbstruck as he watched Dhamon and the sivak allow themselves to be swallowed by the web. He beat at the wall a few more times, then tried to plunge after Dhamon.

Dhamon could see nothing as he moved slowly through the webs.

Perhaps this isn't real, he thought. None of it. The unpleasant muskiness was real enough, stronger than before, coming from all around him and settling in his mouth, making him gag. He could feel spiders crawling over his face and hands, squirming in his clothes. Some of them bit him. But he couldn't feel the web. He couldn't touch it and tell if it was silky or hard, damp or dry.

There was resistance to his every step, but Dhamon found he could breathe. He could hear—Maldred's voice was still coming from somewhere ahead. He heard Varek behind him making slapping noises. Ragh was just ahead.

Dhamon worked up enough saliva in his throat to spit, trying to get rid of what he was certain were tiny spiders that had wriggled their way inside his mouth. He was able to move faster now, the resistance of the thick webs giving away and the air around him lightening. Dhamon pushed into a clearing, one surrounded by webs but open to the sky in the center. The sivak had emerged a moment before.

Maldred was several yards away, busily cleaving through a spider the size of a large house cat. There were dozens of similarly sized spider carcasses all around him.

"Glad you could finally join us, Dhamon!" he shouted over his shoulder. Maldred's clothes were plastered against him, wet with sweat and the dark blood of the spiders. His legs were coated with webs. "Some help here, please!"

Ragh paused for only a moment before joining Maldred. The sivak clawed at a large brown spider, stomping on several gray ones the size of large rats.

"Keep them off me," Maldred told the sivak. "I can't use my magic and fight them at the same time."

Several yards away, Dhamon spotted the half-elf, hanging suspended from a massive oak. She was wrapped in a web cocoon dangling a dozen feet off the ground. There were several huge spiders on branches near her, one hovering directly over her head. Riki was breathing, though it took him a moment to be sure of that. Her eyes were wide, and her mouth was stuffed with webbing.

"Be careful of those spiders, my friend," Maldred called. "They die easily, but they have a vicious bite."

Dhamon looked for handholds amid the swaths of webbing. He started climbing, keeping his sword out and digging the fingers of his free hand into indentations in the bark while clamping onto the trunk with his boot heels.

"Riki!" Varek had emerged in the clearing. "Oh no!" He dashed toward the tree, dropping his staff and attempting to climb the trunk with Dhamon. The bark was slick with webbing, and Varek slipped to the ground in his panicked rush.

"Riki!" he shouted again.

"Over here, boy!" Maldred shouted. "Ragh and I could use some help. Another wave is coming."

Varek made another failed attempt to scale the tree, eyes locked onto the bundled half-elf.

"Varek! Some help!"

He reluctantly picked up his staff, glanced forlornly at Riki, and opened his mouth to say something to Dhamon.

"Now, boy!" Maldred shouted.

"Hurry!" the sivak urged.

Varek finally turned to see the big man and the sivak covered from head to toe with the great spiders. He stumbled forward, leveled the staff over his shoulder, and brought it down in a sweeping motion, brushing a spider off Maldred's arm. He brushed off another and another, making it easier for the big man to strike at the ones still on his legs. Beneath the spiders, Maldred's bare arms were covered with large purple welts.

Varek turned his attention to the sivak. Most of the spiders Varek knocked off the sivak looked like hairy brown lumps atop jet-black legs. They had fangs—the cause of the stinging welts on Maldred's arms—and eyes that looked as blue as a still, deep lake. A few that were even larger, just now emerging from the webs, were the size of full-grown sheep. They were nut brown with intricate yellow and black patterns on their backs that resembled the visages of dwarves.

Varek brushed a few more of the creatures off Maldred and started clubbing the ones on the ground, grimacing at the sickening popping sound they made when he bashed in their heads. He paused between blows to look over at Riki. Dhamon was cleaving through the spiders around her and edging toward the branch she hung from. The spider that was directly over her was spinning a web to encase her entire head.

"Here come some more, boy! Look lively!"

The sivak moved forward, positioning himself to buy Maldred time to use his magic.

"Help Ragh!" Maldred encouraged.

Varek reluctantly joined the sivak, who had turned to face another swarm coming through the web to the left of them. The pair worked fast, claws rending, staff smashing, feet kicking away spider corpses or tramping across the larger ones that couldn't easily be budged.

Behind them, Maldred was deep into an enchantment, eyes wide, mouth forming words in a silent, arcane language. He thrust his hands above his head, thumbs touching, and concentrated until sweat beaded his brow. His body grew warm as the spell took effect. The heat raced from his chest to his arms and his fingers. Flames arced from his palms up to the webs above in the trees.

There was a great "woooosh!" and a mass of webs caught fire and melted. Twitching, burning spiders fell like rain. Maldred turned to face another section of web and released another jolt of flame. The webs were so dense, and there were so many of them, he could only burn a section at a time.

Varek cried out. He had become distracted by Maldred's magic and found that dozens of the peach-sized spiders had swarmed up his legs. A few purple welts appeared on his arms.

The sivak paused in its slaughter of the rat-sized spiders and brushed the smaller ones off Varek.

Varek crouched and smashed another hairy spider that was advancing, stepping on the body and swatting at another and another. At his side the sivak waded through crowds of the creatures.

The largest spiders had chitinous shells covering their heads, and it took several blows to kill them. Varek was bitten a half-dozen more times before there was a pause between the waves of arachnids. He gagged from the smell of the dead spiders and from the burned corpses.

There was another great roar as Maldred managed to burn away another section of webs. More spiders dropped.

Dhamon had worked his way onto the branch, killing all but one large spider that remained directly above the half-elf. The thing stared at him. Its bulbous black eyes, shiny as mirrors, reflected Dhamon's determined face. Fangs protruded from the bottom of its head, dripping an ooze that smelled strongly of the musk Dhamon loathed.

It made a mewling sound, like a helpless babe, as he raised his sword and cleaved the thing in two, barely slamming his eyes shut in time. Blood sprayed on his face and tunic, and the musky smell soaked his clothes. He wiped at his eyes and carefully approached the web bag, the branch sagging under his weight the farther out he went.

Riki was gagging. The webbing was so tight she could hardly breathe, and Dhamon worried that he might not get to her in time. He sheathed the sword and, warily but quickly, straddled the branch, pulling free a knife he'd taken from the spawn village. He stretched down and with one hand gripped a mass of web at the top of Riki's cocoon and started cutting at the threads that tied it to the branch.

"Be careful!" This came from Varek, who'd left Maldred and the sivak to deal with the last few spiders and was standing below the tree. He shouted the warning louder.

"I can hear you well enough," Dhamon returned grouchily, intent on his task. He'd nearly cut through the strands when he hooked his feet around the branch and leaned precariously forward, his arm reaching down toward the half-elf. He grabbed her shoulder, fingers digging in, as he cut through the last of the strands holding the cocoon. He let the knife fall, as his free hand shot down, grabbing Riki by the other shoulder and pulling her up. The branch bowed perilously under their combined weight. Dhamon hauled her back to the trunk.

He felt around and pulled the webbing away from her nose, paused to catch his breath, then arranged Riki—still inside the web cocoon—over his shoulder and started down the tree. All the while, Varek was calling to her from the ground. Dhamon laid her at the base of the tree and stepped back as Varek frantically pushed him aside. The youth dug the webs out of her mouth and away from her eyes.

"Riki! Talk to me!" Varek gently shook her, as he continued to tug at the webs. The webbing closest to her body was like gray paste.

Dhamon drew his sword again, looking around for more spiders. Seeing none but a pair the sivak was fighting—and none in the webs save those the size of his fist or smaller—he allowed himself to relax a little. Within the span of a few heartbeats, the sivak slew the last of the huge ones and trundled over, his large clawlike hands swiping at the webs that covered him.

Maldred was scanning what remained of the webs, his fingers still working their magic.

"Riki!" Varek had finally managed to free the half-elf's arms and cradled her, rocking back and forth on his haunches, paste and webs covering both of them.

The half-elf was sputtering, spitting webs and spiders out of her mouth.

"Pigs, but that was awful. I thought I was gonna die. All them spiders, crawlin' all over me."

Her voice was hoarse, and Varek fumbled at his waist for a water skin. He let her drink her fill, pouring the rest on her face and hands to clean them, then continued to rock her, unaware that her eyes were on Dhamon the entire time.

"Thanks," she mouthed.

Dhamon looked away, scanning the webs and searching for . . . something . . . anything to give him a clue to this place and what was responsible for the spiders, and if any more might be coming. "Unnatural," he pronounced. Then a shiver crept down his spine.

Had something moved in the webs? He blinked. He'd been staring too hard at a tree trunk. The shadows were playing tricks on him. "No," he whispered. "I did see something." He gestured to get his companions' attention, but Varek was absorbed with the half-elf, and Maldred was looking elsewhere.

The sivak followed his gaze. "By the memory of the Dark Queen," Ragh breathed.

Dhamon crouched. "Spider!"

"There're spiders all over," Maldred said dryly.

"Not like this one," the draconian offered.

What remained of the webs in the clearing wavered, and what Dhamon had believed was a tree trunk moved. It was the leg of a spider—a huge spider. The other "tree trunks" nearby moved also—eight of them—as the monstrosity lumbered forward.

The ground trembled from the thing's weight. Patches of webbing fell like nets to blanket a surprised Riki, Varek, and Maldred. Dhamon and the sivak were barely able to avoid the webbing—at least the first batch.

"In the name of my father!" Maldred exclaimed as he clawed at the webs that covered him.

The spider's body was suspended on legs easily thirty feet long. Its body was black, its charcoal-gray head swivelled to take in its prey below. It had fangs too, and these dripped a caustic liquid that splashed on the ground and sizzled.

As they watched, the giant spider opened its jaws wide, releasing a stench into the air. This was quickly followed by a stream of webbing that struck the ground where Dhamon had stood a heartbeat before.

Dhamon was already on the move, racing forward, sword waving over his head. He let out a cry as he swung the weapon with all his strength, howling as it only managed to graze the thing.

"I-i-i-it's as big as a dragon," Riki stammered. She pulled furiously at the webs that covered her and Varek. Finally they managed to scramble out from beneath the webbing. Riki pulled a dagger.

"Stay behind me, Riki," Varek said.

"You can't protect me from that thing," she returned. "We're all gonna die this time, Varek."

Dhamon attacked the spider leg again and again until his arms felt on fire from the effort. Finally he managed to cleave through one of them, but the creature still trundled forward, ground shaking and trees swaying in its path. Dhamon barely avoided being stepped on. Taking a deep breath, he steadied himself and began hacking at another leg.

In the center of the clearing, Maldred had managed to pull the largest mass of webbing off himself. The spider headed towards him, its great bulk cutting off the sun and plunging the clearing into darkness. Maldred spread his legs to keep his balance and began a spell.

The sivak had also crawled out from beneath the web blankets. He spotted Dhamon swinging at a leg as big around as a healthy birch tree. Snarling, the sivak chose another leg and another tactic. Ragh bunched his leg muscles and sprang up off the ground, claws out-stretched, and grabbed onto the thick, jagged hairs that covered the spider's leg. He began to climb the leg.

In the clearing below, Maldred felt the heat building in his chest, his arcane words speeding the enchantment. The heat was hurtful as it raced down his arms and leaped from his fingers, forming a ball of fire in the air that grew as it raced toward the head of the gigantic spider. The flames cackled like a demon as they cut through the air and splashed against the spider.

The creature screamed, a shrill human sound that in its intensity paralyzed all but the still-climbing sivak. The flames spread across the spider's head, then to its bulbous body, and it screamed louder still. Flames leaped to the webs around it, to the surrounding trees, which were slow to catch fire.

All the while the sivak fought its way higher, clawing at the thing's belly, spider blood covering it.

Below, Maldred focused his mind and coaxed the heat into his body again. He mumbled the words even faster, feeling the burning sensation in his chest and arms as more flames sprang from his hands. Again a ball of flame struck the monster.

The giant spider's scream was long and deafening as it was engulfed in flames. The sivak clawed at it again, then dropped, strong legs absorbing the impact from the fall. He scrambled to get out from beneath the spider, as the creature started gyrating in pain.

Flames spread down its hairy legs. Dhamon avoided a flailing limb and edged back to the trees that ringed the clearing, which, one by one, were catching fire. Every-where webs were melting, and hundreds of spiders of all sizes were falling and burning.

"Let's get out of here!" Dhamon called.

Maldred was ahead of him, tugging Varek and Riki. "We have to be fast," he shouted, pointing to the web maze, which was burning, too. "If we don't move, we're going to be kindling."

The sivak sped by them, pushing Dhamon out of the way of a burning tree limb, then continued on, barreling through a wall of flaming webs.

It took them only moments to find their way clear and reach the rise outside the forest.

Maldred was panting, exhausted. "The fire," he gasped, "will not burn the whole forest. It's too damp."

"It will finish that creature," Dhamon said. "By all the vanished gods I didn't know such a thing could exist."

Ragh was shaking his head and looking at the welts on his scaly arms. "In all my years on Krynn I've never seen such a thing," the sivak said. "Birthed of sorcery, to be certain."

Maldred edged down the rise. "I hope there aren't any more of these spider-woods. We'll be wishing we were back in Blöde." He gave Dhamon an appraising look. "I also hope I don't look as bad as you."

"Worse," Dhamon answered.

There was no part of them that wasn't covered with sweat or webs or spider blood. Purple welts dotted their exposed skin. Varek was carrying Rikali, despite her protests.

"Mal and I were just standin' in them woods," the half-elf explained. "I thought I heard a babe cryin'. Pigs, but it was them spiders. Cryin' like babes, those big ones were. Those horrible, horrible spiders."

Varek hushed her, and when they'd returned to the stream just north of Graelor's End, he fussed over her. He smoothed the rest of the webs away from her as best he could.

"We could all use a bath," Maldred said, sniffing at his tunic and making a face. He studied the welts on his arms and tentatively touched them. They felt warm. "That town you visited . . ." He nodded toward Graelor's End. "If there's not too many Knights there, we could . . ."

Dhamon shook his head. "We're not going into that town. Ever."

Varek gave Dhamon a wry smile. "I talked to Commander Lawlor there. He said more Legion of Steel Knights would be marching in today or tomorrow. Graelor's End is a staging point, it seems. Word is the Dark Knights are out in force."

Maldred raised an eyebrow. "Then we'll keep a good distance from Graelor's End, my friend."

"Aye." Dhamon reached into his backpack and retrieved a bottle, took a few swallows and replaced it. He glanced toward the forest, where a thick plume of smoke was rising.

He did not realize that he was being watched from inside the forest. The child with copper-colored hair was perched in a tall maple tree. She stared out of an elaborate web that shimmered like her diaphanous dress.

"I believe you are the one, Dhamon Grimwulf," the child said.

CHAPTER FOURTEEN
RIVER OF MUD

T he full moon made it easy to see the enchanted map Maldred was unrolling. He laid his great-sword across the northern edge to keep it from curling, and across the southern he placed the Solamnic long sword Dhamon had taken from the spawn village. The Solamnic blade gleamed in the moonlight, revealing a rose that had been deeply engraved in the steel near the hilt and three or four initials that were so scratched as to be illegible.

" 'Tis not so fine a sword as the one you lost to the Ergothian wench," Maldred mused. "This blade is not as strong or straight."

"Ha! The one your father sold me was worthless," Dhamon said with a snort, "and though this one's not magical, it worked well enough to kill abominations and spiders. It will serve until I find something better."

"Perhaps we'll find you a keen-edged cutlass in the pirate horde." Maldred's eyes gleamed in anticipation of the treasure.

191

"Aye," Dhamon agreed quietly, "but I'm hoping we find far more than ancient weapons—else I'll not have enough to pay this mysterious healer of yours. Provided she exists."

Maldred's gaze dropped to Dhamon's thigh, where trousers hid the large dragon scale and the few dozen smaller ones that had sprouted around it. He had tried to ask Dhamon about it on a few occasions since they'd left the spawn village, but the others were too nearby or Dhamon was too distracted or too quick to cut him off. He decided now would be a good time—with Riki and Varek sound asleep several yards away and the sivak resting with his back propped up against a tree.

"Past time indeed to discuss it." He gestured to Dhamon's leg. "Those scales, my friend. Are they . . . ?"

"My concern only," Dhamon answered quickly and a little more brusquely than he had intended. He pointedly avoided meeting his friend's stare, instead making a show of studying the map.

"Dhamon."

"Look, Mal, I hope every last one of the scales'll be a bad memory if this healer exists and—"

"She exists."

"And if this treasure exists so I can pay her."

"I have every confidence it exists."

"I wish I did."

Maldred rubbed at his chin. "The map seems to validate all the tales. I can show you again if—"

"If the map is reliable."

"It led us to Riki in the spawn village."

In an effort to change the subject, Dhamon stabbed a finger at the south section of the map showing an ancient river that emptied into the sea.

"Dhamon, how long have you had them?" Maldred asked. "The scales."

"I said they were my concern." Dhamon's eyes were daggers when he raised them from the parchment, and he waved his hand as if to bat away a bug.

"You can shut everyone else out," Maldred said, his soft voice terse. He glanced over his shoulder to make sure the half-elf and Varek were still sound asleep, then locked eyes with Dhamon. "You can ignore Riki when you want, pretend Varek doesn't exist for whatever reason. I'm not so easy to dismiss."

Dhamon's face became an unreadable mask.

"Dammit! I'm your friend, Dhamon," Maldred persisted. "I feel as close to you as I would to a brother. We've risked death together, saved each other's lives." A sharp intake of breath. "How long have you had all those scales?"

The silence was tense, neither man blinking nor looking away. The breeze brought the scent of the tall grass and damp earth and the blacksmith's odor that surrounded the sivak. From somewhere in the distance an owl hooted softly and repeatedly. Rikali murmured something in her sleep.

"What's happening to you, Dhamon?"

"Nothing, Mal."

"Dhamon."

"By the Dark Queen's heads, Mal, leave it."

The big man shook his head.

"By the Dark Queen's . . . oh damn it all." Finally Dhamon relented with an exasperated sigh. "The scales started growing a month ago, maybe more. Time's been a blur to me. Who knows what they're doing to me?" Killing me, probably, he added to himself.

"Nura Bint-Drax couldn't have—"

"No, it wasn't her doing. Though she gave me a few more to worry over."

"Malys then."

Dhamon shook his head. "The overlord's presence is long gone. I don't know what's causing it." After a moment he added, "I don't care what's causing it. I just want to be rid of the things."

There was another stretch of silence before Maldred said, "Maybe it's a disease. A magical one."

"Maybe, but my dwelling on it—and you talking about it— won't make them disappear." Dhamon shrugged and returned his attention to the map. "Let's just hope this pirate treasure exists and that your healer exists too."

"They do." Maldred's voice seemed more hopeful then certain. "She'll get rid of the scales."

Dhamon let out a grim chuckle. "If not, perhaps you'll have two draconians in your midst. Now, about finding this treasure."

"As I said before, it's supposed to lie just beyond the Screaming Valley." Maldred gave a shudder that Dhamon didn't notice. "The valley is around here." He pointed to a faded swirl of ink at the edge of the ancient river.

The map showed the land centuries ago, before the Cataclysm, when it was a tundra: barren, flat, and cold. There were a scattering of cities and towns indicated, ones Dhamon knew were now long buried and with names lost to history. The ancient Plains of Dust looked smaller than the land was today, perhaps only three or four hundred miles from north to south, and there was no hint of the glacier, only a deep blue sea.

"Tarsis," Dhamon said, eyes locking onto a coastal city.

"Tarsis indeed." Maldred had come up directly behind him. "If I remember my history, Tarsis was quite a port, all big and bustling and with deep water docks to rival any place in this half of the world. Of course, that was many lifetimes ago."

"Aye," Dhamon agreed. Tarsis was now a good distance inland, more than one hundred miles from the sea. The Cataclysm had changed this part of the world considerably.

"Tarsis, before the Cataclysm, was thriving," Maldred said. "That was also before the Kingpriest of Istar tried to become a god. Tales say the gods were angered at his affront and dragged Istar to the bottom of the sea. The world was reshaped over the next few hundred years, and the Plains were caught in that."

"The Shadow Years they were called," Dhamon added, his fingers rubbing at the uneven beard he was growing. "They say mountains fell, new mountains sprang up from flat land, famine and plague swept across the world. A lovely time. Probably just about as lovely as this time we're enjoying with the dragon overlords."

Maldred angled a finger at the sea. "This water receded, leaving Tarsis and other ports inland. Ships were stranded overnight. Terrible quakes rocked the Plains. Cities and ships were swallowed by the earth—ships with bellies brimming with treasure. We'll find them. I have every confidence. Then we'll find your healer." He rocked back on his heels and looked up at the moon. "I read a book once that claimed there were four hundred earthquakes on the Plains during those Shadow Years. The quakes were strongest along the coast, near Tarsis and . . ."

He looked to Dhamon and then nodded toward a trio of small port towns shown in the eastern part of the map. Not even a trace of faded ink hinted at their names. ". . . and were strongest near here. These three towns this old map shows, and the tales, are why I believe my father's map is genuine."

Dhamon raised a skeptical eyebrow.

"It was said that the one town in the center was a pirate port, established by a group of powerful Ergothians who found the pickings better here than around their homeland." Maldred's voice quickened. "It's not listed on most of the old maps you'll find in libraries.

Indeed, I don't think I've ever seen a map this old." His finger drew a line in the air up from the port. "See this faint mark over here? It's a river, one that doesn't exist today. It was just wide and deep enough for the few skilled pirate captains who knew how to navigate it. Legend says those who foolishly chased the pirates up that river ran aground, and the pirates turned back to pillage them, in each case leaving only one survivor to recount the gruesome incident."

Dhamon whistled softly. "It's because of the survivors that people found out about the pirate city and the vanished river?"

Maldred absently nodded. "Some of the pirates would take their ships up the river, well past this port and store their booty in heavily guarded caves, not trusting their fellow pirates back in the city. The caves are, I believe, just beyond the Screaming Valley."

"Map, show us the land as it is now," Dhamon urged.

In the blink of an eye the map changed, mirroring the current geography—much larger and temperate, with grassy plains reaching to a horizon where low rolling hills were dotted with a variety of trees.

Dhamon ran his fingers over the map. He swore he could feel jagged edges of stone where the mountains were sketched to the west. According to this view, the Plains of Dust was nearly three hundred miles across at its widest point, running about two hundred miles from north to south at the center. Only a scattering of towns were marked around the borders of the interior. In the west Tarsis and Rigitt, in the south Zeriak, and in the northwest Dontol, Willik, and Stone Rose. Polagnar was a little to the northeast of Graelor's End. Due north at the edge of the map was the City of Morning Dew, along with a few other smaller places that were named after long-dead explorers.

At the southern edge of the map the Plains were bordered by the inhospitable Icewall Glacier. The map marked it by irregular lines meant to look like mountains, but instead resembling icicles. Dhamon leaned close and felt a chill wind coming up from the parchment.

"Amazing," he breathed.

Though mountains were indicated on the west part of the map—what most considered dwarven lands—overall there were few marks to represent hills. Dhamon knew just by traveling this far that there were plenty of rolling hills and woods. There was no sign of the unnamed ancient river the pirates traveled, just the River Toranth, which originated in Sable's swamp and cut through the Plains' heart, breaking into tributaries and spreading like the fingers of an outstretched hand. There were a few villages along a Toranth tributary to the west, beyond a jagged line that Maldred said was the Screaming Valley.

"We could get a wagon here," Maldred suggested, pointing to a village just north of the valley. "In . . . Wheatland, it's called. A couple of horses. We'll need something to haul all the treasure in."

Dhamon cleared his throat. "Map, are there Legion of Steel Knights in the area? In Wheatland?" Before he could take another breath, glowing motes looking like plump fireflies appeared in various places across the map—including over the town Maldred had pointed to.

"No way to tell how many Knights are in each spot," Dhamon mused. "Maybe one. Maybe one hundred."

Maldred shook his head. "It's not worth taking a chance to find out."

"So we find the treasure first, then we'll worry about a wagon."

"And we've your sivak along, my friend, to carry a good amount."

197

They'd been traveling for nearly three hours, the morning sun climbing well into the sky when the landscape changed dramatically from gently rolling grassy plains to ground so cracked and barren that it looked like the wrinkles on an old sailor's face. For a while they could still see the grassland, to the west and behind them, and they could faintly smell the sweetness of the last of the early fall's wildflowers. But when the plains disappeared entirely from view, the air became acrid and laced with sulphur, as if something was burning nearby. Their eyes stung and watered, but there was no trace of flames or smoke.

Maldred was in the lead, lost in thought and picking his way down a long-dry streambed. The draconian was a few yards behind him at Dhamon's side, eyes darting from left to right and nose constantly quivering.

"What bothers you?" Dhamon asked.

The sivak didn't answer. Instead, he pointed a clawed finger towards the south and narrowed his eyes as if trying to focus on something.

"What, Ragh?" Dhamon persisted. He followed the sivak's gaze, but saw nothing.

"Somethin' there?" This from the half-elf. "All I see is ugly, flat, smelly ground and your wingless back." She padded up behind the draconian, tugging Varek along. "Whaddya see, beastie?"

A growl escaped the sivak's throat. "Nothing," he said after a moment. "I thought I saw movement ahead. Something large. But . . ."

"Mal? You see anything?" Dhamon asked.

Maldred shook his head.

"My imagination," the sivak decided. "My eyes are tired."

"All of me is tired," the half-elf grumbled.

"We'll rest for a few minutes." Maldred stopped and reached for the map. He opened it carefully, studying features he'd already committed to memory. "The valley," he stated. "How far are we from the valley?"

A spot on the parchment glowed softly in response.

"Practically on top of it," he said to himself. He replaced the map and folded his arms across his chest. "We're practically on top of it, but it's nowhere to be seen. I don't understand."

"I do." Dhamon's face took on a troubled look. "We got that map from your . . . from Donnag. Perhaps it's as worthless as the sword."

Maldred frowned and continued to study the landscape. "The map showed us the way to the spawn village, didn't it? Come. We'll find the valley."

After another few miles Maldred stopped again.

"There's still no valley," Dhamon said.

"Nothin' but ugly, flat land," the half-elf added.

"It has to be here." Maldred stepped away from them, consulting the map again, then scanning the horizon. "Somewhere. Where?"

The sivak cocked his head, nose still quivering. He curled his upper lip back in a snarl.

"What, beastie?" Rikali poked Ragh in the arm to get his attention. "You see somethin' again?"

"I hear something," Ragh said.

"Your raspy breathin's all I hear," the half-elf shot back. "In fact—"

Dhamon drew a finger to his lips to silence her. "I hear something, too," he whispered. "Someone crying. Faint. They can't be close."

"Someone screaming," Maldred corrected, "and I think it's very . . ." His words trailed off as the ground beneath him gave way. The big man dropped from sight.

Dhamon raced forward, stopping just short of the hole but not short enough. The ground cracked beneath his feet. "Run!" he shouted to the others. His feet flailed in the air, and he fell.

Riki, Varek, and Ragh fell with him.

The air whipped around them and was filled with a keening wail. The noise only grew louder when they struck bottom nearly fifty feet below, where a river of oozing mud cushioned their fall.

Maldred was the first one out, standing on a rocky bank, hands over his ears, eyes trained on the slowly flowing sludge. Rikali sputtered up next, arms pumping through the muck to pull herself to the opposite bank. She climbed out and lay panting. Varek and Dhamon trailed her—all of them looking like mud men—every inch of them drenched, and all of them holding their ears in an effort to shut out the bone-numbing wail.

They blinked the mud from their eyes, as Varek fussed over Rikali. "The babe?" he shouted over the noise.

She nodded and touched her stomach. "I—I think it's all right. The fall didn't hurt none. Felt like jumpin' into puddin'. Pigs, but I'm covered with this stuff. Get it off me, Varek."

Dhamon tried to scrape the muck from his face, as he held his hands over his ears. He spied Maldred on the other side doing the same.

"The sivak?" Dhamon yelled.

Maldred shook his head—he couldn't hear Dhamon. The screaming grew louder still.

The sound reverberated off cavern walls that rose at straight angles, so steep as to be unclimbable without gear. The noise was high-pitched one moment, then low and moaning the next. It took on the aspect of several voices, a chorus of screams that they could do nothing to shut out.

"We've found your damned valley," Dhamon shouted at Maldred. "Should've found another way around this!"

His eyes were drawn to the mud river, and to a mud-covered hand that shot out of it. A second hand followed, clutching a quarterstaff.

"My staff!" Varek called. "I dropped it in the fall."

Moments later the sivak climbed out on the bank and dropped the weapon at Varek's feet. The creature's face looked pained, his acute hearing pounded by the wailing.

"Let's get out of here!" Dhamon shouted. The sivak saw his gesture and struck out along the bank to the south at Dhamon's shoulder. Neither bothered to see if Varek and Riki were stumbling after them.

On the other side of the river Maldred followed suit. He bumped against the canyon wall, teeth gritted as he shallowly sucked in one breath after the next.

"This is madness," Dhamon said to himself. The wailing seemed to grow in volume, it was digging in like a knife. He gasped as his knees threatened to buckle. The sivak nudged him forward.

The farther they traveled the darker it became, as the light spilling in through the crack in the ground above them angled into a sliver.

Shadows scampered across the rock walls, making it look like the visages of old men staring down at them—mouths open and sightless eyes fixed.

The screams continued, the echoes growing ever-louder. The ground vibrated gently beneath their feet in response to the constant noise, and bits of rock and grit filtered down from high along the walls and from the thin stone ceiling.

They tried to talk to each other but were reduced to gestures and lip-reading. Dhamon strove to quicken the pace, to escape before they succumbed to the hateful sound.

He remembered Maldred telling him weeks ago the valley was dangerous, rumored to drive men mad. They had decided then that the route was worth risking for the treasure and the hope of finding the healer-sage. He hadn't dreamed it would be like this.

Was he going mad? He could have sworn a stony face was watching him, mouth opening and closing, eyes blinking.

"Mal!" he called, but his friend had no hope of hearing. The sound seemed to change in pitch, then, higher, louder, consuming them. Dhamon watched Maldred stumble along the opposite bank, then hesitate as that bank ended where a canyon wall reached into the river.

Maldred looked about, eyes large and white set against his muddy countenance. He caught sight of Dhamon and mouthed something to him, then plunged into the mud-thick water and began to awkwardly lurch his way across.

Dhamon pushed Riki and Varek ahead, gesturing for them to continue. Ragh followed, prodding the couple and looking back over his scaly shoulder to keep an eye on Dhamon.

It was several minutes before Maldred reached Dhamon's side, and minutes more for him to fight his way to his feet, vomiting mud and slamming the heels of his hands against his ears.

"You've got earth magic," Dhamon shouted. "Why not try some?"

Maldred shook his head. "Too loud," he mouthed back. "Can't concentrate."

It might have been hours or minutes they traveled. Time meant nothing amid the agonizing noise. The landscape did not change. The sluggish river of mud went on forever, bordered by walls of marble and limestone stretching above them.

Dhamon stopped, and Maldred nearly slammed into him. "Mad," he mouthed. "I am mad."

Dhamon again saw a huge face high above and across the river, mouth moving, pebbles spewing forth. There were other faces near it.

"I've lost my mind." Dhamon fell to his knees and stared at the faces. They seemed to gaze directly at him.

Maldred watched the faces, too, with a growing realization. He kicked at Dhamon to get his attention. "Move!" he mouthed. Another kick and Dhamon was on his feet. "Hurry!"

They ran again, Dhamon not sure of anything but the noise, which continued to envelop him. It didn't seem painful any longer. It had become comforting in a way, a dear companion.

"Stay," the wail seemed to say. "Stay with us forever."

Once more he stopped and regarded several different visages lining this part of the darkening canyon. Maldred tried to push him along, and this time he resisted.

"Mad," Dhamon mouthed.

Maldred shook his head and shouted something Dhamon couldn't understand. "Move!" he tried. Dhamon refused to budge.

Maldred thrust his fingers in his ears and stumbled to the canyon wall, leaning against it and drawing breath deep into his lungs. He concentrated on his heart, feeling it beating. He desperately searched for the spark within him.

"It's too loud," he told himself. "Can't . . ."

Dhamon was lost to the voices. Riki, Varek, and Ragh had dropped out of sight—lost to the screams, too. Maldred watched as Dhamon shuffled toward the muddy river.

"Stay with us forever," Maldred faintly heard through the wails. "Breathe the river. Stay with us forever."

"No!" Maldred shouted. He threw all his effort into finding the spark, coaxing it to glow. "So hard," he muttered.

"Can't think." Somehow he managed, his mind wrapping around the magical essence inside him, blowing on it as a man would blow on a small flame, pleading with it, willing it to grow. "Must think."

Maldred felt the warmth and focused on it, shoving the screaming to the back of his mind. He thrust his hands at the canyon wall and felt the energy rise from his chest and into his arms, pass down and into his fingers and into the wall. The canyon wall rumbled, and the vibrations increased in the stony ground.

"Stop!" Maldred bellowed. He heard the word above the wails, felt his energy pound into the canyon wall. Cracks appeared around his fingers. He concentrated and forced more energy into the stone. The cracks widened. "Stop! Or I will slay all of you!"

Instantly the wails ceased. The only sound was Maldred's labored breathing and the soft whistling of the wind that whipped across the walls.

"Stop, and allow us to pass."

"What?" Dhamon shook his head, mud flying from his hair. "Madness." He stared across the river to see the faces. All of them now had their mouths closed. Their eyes, narrowed in anger, were dark crevices.

"Not madness," Maldred gasped. "You're not mad, Dhamon. They are."

Dhamon shuffled next to Maldred. The big man's fingers were dug into the stone, and hairline cracks sprouted around them. Dhamon looked up. There were more faces on this side, above him.

"Galeb duhr," Maldred said. "Creatures of stone, as old as Krynn perhaps. They predate the Cataclysm for certain. They're the mad ones."

"They tried to lure me into the river."

Maldred nodded. "Maybe they did the same to Riki and the others. Go back. See to them, I'll follow shortly."

Dhamon didn't hesitate, turning back to look. His head was still muddled, pounding, his ears ringing with the remembered sound of the screams. The canyon curved, and he hurried as fast as he could along the wall, finding the others at the edge of the muddy river.

Varek was in it up to his waist. Rikali was shaking her head, mud flying from her hair, and tugging at Varek. The sivak leaned forward, clawed hands on its knees, great shoulders hunched, head bent into its chest.

"Move!" Dhamon bellowed as he neared. The word sounded like a whisper. He gestured to the far end of the cavern, where he saw an opening.

"Follow him," Ragh gasped. The sivak saw the opening, too, a narrow gap next to a near verticle spire, and followed Dhamon, heavy feet pounding across the stone floor of the Screaming Valley.

It was nearly sunset by the time they found a stream. All of them sank down next to it and cleaned the muck from their aching bodies.

They hadn't talked much since emerging from the valley, mostly because they had a hard time hearing anything. Their ears were still ringing.

"I threatened to bring the valley down," Maldred told Dhamon later that night, "threatened to kill them all. I couldn't have done it, of course."

"They didn't know that," Dhamon supplied.

Maldred nodded. "Fortunately for me they were mad." After a moment, he added: "Pity. Galeb duhr are impressive creatures, and most of them are reasonably benevolent."

"If they're as ancient as you say, my friend, perhaps living through the Cataclysm drove them mad."

Maldred leaned back on his elbows.

205

"Maybe we're mad, too, after all," Dhamon continued. "Slogging through mud rivers to look for long-buried treasure. Me thinking there's a cure for my scales."

"The treasure and the cure exist," Maldred said. He lay on his back and was instantly asleep.

Chapter Fifteen
Broken Nests

orning found them on a sloping field where sheep and a handful of young goats were grazing. Varek pointed to a far rise where a small farmhouse and a precariously tilting old barn sat.

"We're close," Maldred said. "Very close now. The pirate treasure is somewhere beneath us."

"For all the good it'll do us," Varek grumbled. "We've got no shovels, and I dare say borrowing some from that farm would be a bad idea."

"We won't need shovels," Maldred replied. For the rest of the day he lay on his stomach in various areas of the pasture, fingers dug into the earth, jaw working, occasionally humming.

Varek hovered nearby, sometimes fascinated, most of the time bored.

"Beastie, why haven't you run off?" Rikali had settled herself on the ground, an arm's length from the draconian. "I know you can't up and fly away, but you've had chances—ain't none of us been watchin' you close. Dhamon ain't even here now."

The creature let out a deep breath, hissing like a snake. "Beastie?"

"My name is Ragh." The whispery voice sent a shiver down the half-elf's spine. "Perhaps I've nothing better to do. Perhaps I simply find your little band . . . interesting."

The half-elf raised an eyebrow. "Or perhaps you want some of the pirate loot. And that ain't gonna happen."

The sivak closed his eyes. "Coins and baubles mean nothing to me."

"Then what? What . . . ?" The half-elf's eyes widened as she leaned closer. "Beastie . . . Ragh . . . are you here 'cause you think you owe us some kind of debt? 'Cause we rescued you from that village?"

The sivak glanced at her, then looked away.

"An honorable draconian?" she pressed. "That's it, isn't it? Well, don't you worry. I'll keep your little secret. Everyone's got a secret, don't they?"

◊ ◊ ◊ ◊ ◊ ◊ ◊

Dhamon made himself scarce, using the excuse he was scouting the area to make sure there were no Legion of Steel Knights around. He knew there was nothing he could do to help Maldred, as the big man was using magic, and magic took its own time. He used the time to run.

His strides were long and easy, and he concentrated on his pacing and speed. The exercise kept his mind off everything but the act of motion. At times he would study the landscape in front of him, then close his eyes and run blindly from memory, letting the air wash over his face. When he opened his eyes he would pick up the tempo, feet pounding against the earth, legs pumping until he couldn't go any faster. He kept the pace up for some time, feeling his heart thundering wildly in his chest and sweat beading on his skin, then reluctantly slowed to a quick walk, dragging great gulps of air into his lungs before starting to run again. The exertion felt good, and rather than tire him, it seemed to give him more energy.

He covered considerable ground, noting the remains of a tiny village that had been beset by fire long months ago and a single standing farmhouse with a large field. The far quarter of the field was filled with corn and showed some evidence of being harvested. He saw thin, twisting roads in the distance, which he suspected led to a few of the small towns he'd noted on the map, and he saw great expanses of grass, dead from the lack of rain.

Wild animals were few in the open. He spooked a grazing deer, and a dog spotted him at the end of a small ravine and gave a merry chase, but it had no hope of catching him. At the edge of a large pond, he spied wolf tracks, but they were not particularly fresh. He stared at his reflection in the water.

His face was shallow, his eyes sunken, and his scraggly beard and tangled hair helped to complete his haggard appearance. He sat on the bank and fished about in his pocket for a small knife. Sharpening it on a stone, he shaved himself. Next he cut away at the knots in his hair. A quick plunge in the pond to refresh himself, and he counted the small scales on his leg.

"Twenty-nine," he said. "Twenty-damn-nine."

He rose and ran again. After another hour Dhamon glimpsed three riders to the east—the first people he'd caught sight of all day. From their angular outlines he felt certain they were armored. Perhaps they were more Legion of Steel Knights. He tried to circle behind them, but they were moving quickly and took a road to the southeast. Dhamon had no intention of traveling that far away from his companions.

Dhamon returned to the vale at mid-afternoon, finding Maldred still talking to the earth. He headed out again, running for a few more hours until his boots had rubbed his heels raw, and he finally felt a hint of fatigue. It was sunset when he finally came back. Varek and Rikali were sitting next to a small fire, roasting something that suspiciously looked like lamb. Maldred was on his back, snoring loudly, the draconian standing over him.

"I can't pretend to understand what he was trying to do with his magic," Varek said, indicating Maldred. "Whatever it was, it didn't work."

Rikali nudged her husband. "Mal says this just isn't the right spot. Said we'll go a little farther south tomorrow and he'll try again." She fell to devouring a hunk of meat Varek had passed her, not coming up for air until all that was left was a bone.

Dhamon ate very little and found himself wishing for some alcohol to wash the food down and relax him. It was hours before he could fall asleep.

By mid-afternoon the next day, Maldred had directed them to another likely place, but this, too, proved unrewarding. For three more days they wandered the countryside, passing a village and a cluster of sheepherders' homes, crossing a prairie, and coming to a narrow strip of woods that looked as though loggers had worked it over in the spring.

Again Maldred stretched out on the ground, and again Dhamon took to running, gone from sight in minutes. The big man's fingers sifted through the grass, which was brittle and yellow.

"Fall's taking a strong hold here," Maldred said. "The weather will start getting cool very soon." Within moments he was humming and thrusting his fingertips into the ground. Minutes later he rose and moved west, stretching out again and repeating the process.

Magic had come so much easier to Maldred when he was young. Now it was work, even the simplest of enchantments. Sweat soaked his clothes and ran from his forehead, though the day was not especially hot. His throat was dry and his tongue swollen. He asked Rikali for water before he moved onto another spot, and then another and another. He was about to ask her for water again when his mind finally touched something wooden beneath the branches of a locust tree. It wasn't roots, and the wood was not alive—it was rotting and speckled with nails.

"Where's Dhamon?" Maldred managed to gasp.

Varek and Rikali shrugged in unison.

"Running," the sivak said. "Watching for Knights."

"Find him for me, would you?" Maldred asked Varek.

The young man twisted his lips into a crooked frown and shook his head. However, Rikali gave her husband a pleading smile, and he grudgingly acquiesced, trotting off to pursue Dhamon's tracks. The half-elf watched him go, then turned her attention back to Maldred.

"What did you find, Mal? You can trust me."

He didn't answer. He was humming once more, digging until his hands were covered with dirt, pulling them free, edging forward a few feet, and digging all over again. The half-elf followed him, persisting with her questions, and Ragh kept nearby as well, intently watching the big man.

Before the hour was out Maldred was exhausted, after having put so much energy into his spell, but he refused to quit. He dug into the earth in a half-dozen more places before moving to the top of a scrub-covered bank, where he rolled over onto his back and gasped.

"Mal? Mal!"

"I'm all right, Riki," he said after a moment. "Just let me rest for half a minute."

Without his asking, she fetched another skin of water, cupped the back of his head and poured practically all of it down his throat. Her hands brushed the sweat off his brow.

"Learning to be motherly, Riki?" he asked, after he had caught his breath. He saw her pinched expression. "Hey, I didn't mean anything by it."

Her face relaxed only slightly, and he rolled over onto his stomach and started humming again, thrusting his fingers into the soil.

"There is something here," he said after a few minutes, his voice raspy despite all the water he'd drank. "Big, broken." Maldred rested his face against the earth, concentrating on the feel of the dry grass and the dirt against his skin, working to send his senses even deeper into the ground.

The magic let his mind travel. Burrowing like a mole, his mind went past the remnants of roots from a tree that used to be here, past rocks and dried husks of bugs, past the skeleton of a small animal. There was a thin sheet of slate, then he was traveling through more dirt, more rocks, past large chunks of stone that appeared to have been worked—perhaps remnants of a building. There were pieces of wood, thin and polished and somehow preserved despite, or perhaps because of, the weight of the earth.

"Table legs," he whispered. "A cooking pot." There was more worked stone, roughly uniform. Probably they were the bricks of a house or a well. And so he rose and moved on another hundred yards, then a hundred more.

"Iron," he whispered. "More iron. No wood this time." He sagged in disappointment and was about to give up for the day, but his mind was still restless, still roved and touched object after object.

"Iron," he repeated. His eyes flew open wide. "Iron? An anchor!" Maldred refused to let himself become too excited. That would break his concentration on the finding spell—and threaten the enchantment that cloaked his ogre body.

He delved deeper, searching in concentric circles away from the anchor. How large was the anchor? His magical senses couldn't tell him that. Was it from a fishing boat? How old was it? Was it from a ship on that river he'd noted on the old map? His spell could answer none of those questions, and he didn't want to stop to consult the enchanted map.

"Ah, finally. Wood. Curved timbers. Broken timbers." He spoke in Ogrish, his native tongue coming easier to him. Riki tapped her foot in frustration. His mind floated over sections of wood that were little more than mulch piles, then pieces that had been better protected by slabs of slate that covered them. He discovered something he couldn't put a word to, and for several minutes his mind caressed it as he might run his fingers over a lover's back.

A sail, or what's left of it, he finally decided, attached to a shattered spar. Another anchor. Bones—lots of bones. A ruined sea chest.

"Where's Dhamon?" he finally croaked.

The half-elf shrugged, even though she knew he couldn't see her with his face pressed against the ground.

"Go get Dhamon!" His fingers stopped working, and his eyes closed.

"Mal?" Rikali knelt by him. "Asleep," she said after a moment. Sighing, she sat next to the sivak. There was little she could do except wait for Varek and Dhamon to return.

Varek came back in the mid-afternoon, shaking his head and muttering that he'd tracked Dhamon at least four miles before giving up. He hadn't wanted to stay away from her any longer, and if Maldred wanted Dhamon so badly, he could go search for the man himself. Riki didn't argue, but she put a finger to her lips and nodded toward the big man, who was still soundly sleeping. Varek sagged next to her and closed his eyes.

Dhamon arrived shortly before sunset.

The half-elf was on her feet, intercepting him before

213

he reached Maldred. She wrinkled her nose, sniffing. "Town nearby?"

"About eight, nine miles. It's small. You'd be hard-pressed to even call it a village."

He knew why she'd asked. The half-elf could be perceptive when she wanted to, and he knew she smelled alcohol on him. Dhamon had wandered into the village after spotting its only business, an inn with inviting smells coming from it.

Dhamon reached into his pocket, pulled out a handkerchief, and passed it to her.

"Venison," she said approvingly. "It's spiced." She gobbled the dried strips without a thought of sharing.

Behind the half-elf, Dhamon saw Varek's eyes narrow. Is the young husband jealous? he wondered. Or am I? Dhamon brushed aside thoughts of Rikali and went over to Maldred. He knelt by the big man and prodded him awake.

"I found something," Maldred said, as he pushed himself to his knees. "Something right here." He thrust a finger at the ground in front of him and grinned lopsidedly. "I'm not sure just what it is, but I think we should take a peek."

"You still look tired," Dhamon observed.

"Magic does that to you." Maldred leaned over the spot he'd indicated and pressed the heels of his hands into the earth. He closed his eyes and started humming.

Dhamon was quick to interrupt him. "You sure you're up to this? Whatever's down there has probably been down there more than three hundred years. I'd say it could wait another day."

"I appreciate your concern, my friend," Maldred replied, "but I'm not that tired. Not when there's pirate treasure to be had." He resumed his humming, and Dhamon sat back. Varek and Riki approached quietly.

Maldred's tune was different this time, deeper and throatier, louder and without much fluctuation—like a bass horn sounding one long, constant note, then sliding down a measure as its player runs out of breath. He kept up the monotonous tune, snatching a breath here and there, letting his humming become softer yet at the same time more intense. Suddenly the sound wavered.

Dhamon was on his feet, motioning Riki and Varek to back up. The ground trembled gently at first, then shook, pebbles bouncing as the big man hummed louder. Maldred moved too, crawling backward on his hands and knees without stopping his spell. The ground split in his wake.

"By all the vanished gods!" Varek cried. His face was filled with astonishment, and his feet were frozen to the spot. The half-elf yanked him back. The sivak approached cautiously, clearly awed.

Where Maldred had knelt was a gaping hole, sides irregular and looking like the open mouth of a hungry beast. The vibrations continued, and the companions— save the sivak—stepped back, though the hole didn't widen. Rather it deepened, as if Maldred's magic were a giant drill that was excavating far into the earth.

Dhamon tested the ground near the edge. The earth fell away into a black nothingness far below. There was a rumbling, followed by a tremor. The shaking continued for several minutes more, then finally quieted.

"Pigs, but I thought you were makin' an earthquake, Mal. I thought it was gonna be like that Vale of Chaos all over again." The half-elf shook a finger at the big man, then crept forward, leaning dangerously over the edge despite Varek's attempt to hold her back. "Can't see much," she announced. "It's a long way down there and there ain't much light. Just some dirt and rocks and wood."

"Wood," Maldred said grinning. "Worked wood where

215

there shouldn't be any."

"Lots of wood," Ragh added.

Dhamon was leaning far over, his keen eyes picking through the shadows. "Oh, there's more than wood down there," he said, breaking into a rare grin. "I see a ship's mast, my friend, and part of a sail. And there are a few broken crows' nests."

Chapter Sixteen
Abraim's Tempest

F oolish thing to do at night," the half-elf grumbled. "Gettin' dark up here, sun settin' an' all. Darker down there. We ain't got a lantern. And we ain't got a rope. Never mind that we can't see the treasure. How we gonna get to it?"

"Gotta be a twenty-foot drop to down there," Varek judged.

The sivak shook its head. "Thirty."

Rikali tapped her foot. "Pigs, some thieves you are, Dhamon, Mal, comin' on a treasure hunt an' not coming prepared. How'm I gonna get down there?" She anxiously paced around the hole. "Not even a torch."

"I can see well enough," the sivak pronounced after a moment. "I do not require a lantern."

"But you can't fly down there, Ragh," the half-elf continued. "Neither can we."

I can see well enough, too, Dhamon thought. He could make out the forms of five ships, none of them wholly intact. There were other shapes farther back, perhaps

217

rocks or more ships. He heard something down there, too, a sound faint and hard to discern over his companions' talk. Sand falling from the cavern ceiling, pebbles bouncing off the ships, he decided after a moment. A stone shifting—all from the aftereffects of Maldred's spell.

Rikali stopped pacing and glanced at Maldred. "Can you make some steps with your magic? We could walk right down an' . . ."

Maldred shook his head. "You know my magic is not that precise, especially with . . . dirt."

"How about some light?"

"That I can do," he said, "though it won't last long."

"Right—clothes will help." Dhamon slipped away toward their meager supplies, pulling spare trousers and shirts from their satchels, a long dress from Riki's sack. Despite Varek's and the half-elf's protests he began ripping the clothes into thick strips and tying them together. He wound a small strip around a dry branch he picked up. "It's not a proper torch," he told Maldred, handing it to him. "It won't last long, but it'll have to do."

They had one blanket among them, which Varek had taken from the spawn village for Riki. This, too, Dhamon tore into strips, adding the length to his rope. When he was finished, he looped one end around a rock a few feet away and tested its strength. "Should work," he said.

Maldred was holding the makeshift torch close to his chest, caressing it, mumbling to it. For a brief moment heat pulsed in his chest, then his arm. The cloth around the end of the branch caught fire.

Dhamon glanced at the sivak. "You're the heaviest, so you're last. But you are coming." So we can keep an eye on you, he added silently.

"I'm light. I'll go first," Varek volunteered.

Maldred made a move to stop him, but Dhamon put a hand on his friend's shoulder.

With a nod to Riki, Varek grabbed the torch and was quick over the side.

"Your magic loosened the earth, Mal," Dhamon said in a hushed voice. "Nothing wrong with our over-anxious young man being the one to test just how sturdy the ground is below." He watched as Varek reached the end of the cloth rope, then jumped the remaining ten feet. Varek walked in a tight circle before motioning for the others to follow.

"Can't see much!" He yelled. "Maybe one of these ships has a lantern!"

The half-elf made a grab for the cloth rope. "Ladies next," she said.

"No. You're staying up here," Dhamon told her, taking the rope out of her hands. "Someone needs to keep an eye out for any Legion of Steel Knights, maybe for the farmer who owns this land."

The half-elf slammed her foot against the ground. "There's been nobody come by the whole time we've been here—not that you'd know that with all of your gallivantin', Dhamon. You just don't want me to see what's down there, do you? Don't want me to have a proper share of the treasure. I want what's due me, Dhamon Grimwulf. You ain't leavin' me behind again an'—"

He put a calloused finger to her lips. "I don't want anything happening to you, Riki. See Varek down there? The rope didn't reach all the way. He had to jump." He dropped his finger to her rounded stomach. "You're not in any shape to be doing this."

"Don't want anything happenin' to me," she repeated softly. "Then why'd you leave me stranded in Blöten?"

"Riki, I . . ."

"I didn't know you cared, Dhamon Grimwulf." Her tone was skeptical. "Didn't know you cared about anyone 'cept yourself."

He opened his mouth to reply, then thought better of it. A moment later he had disappeared into the hole.

"Pigs, but I was in good enough shape to save you and Mal from them thieves," Rikali fumed. "Saved your worthless life. I'm pregnant. I ain't an invalid. I can jump, Dhamon Grimwulf, an' I can—"

"You'll get more than your fair share of any treasure we find, Riki," Maldred said. "If there's any treasure to be had." He made sure Dhamon was off the rope before he started down, frowning as he saw the makeshift torch had been tossed on the ground and was burning out. "We won't cut you out. I promise. Now, keep an eye out."

She watched Maldred scramble down the rope, her anger building, then watched the sivak climb awkwardly after him, the rope of cloth strips straining and threatening to tear.

"I don't want to be left behind again," she said too softly for the men below to hear. "I don't ever want to be left behind again."

They were moving away from the opening, as the torch burned itself out. She couldn't see them any longer, and the light from the setting sun was waning.

"Ever, ever again." She took a deep breath, waited a few moments, then followed them.

◇ ◇ ◇ ◇ ◇ ◇ ◇

"By my father," Maldred gasped. He'd fashioned another torch and lit it, the feeble light revealing that the three men and the sivak stood in a cavern so large that they couldn't see it all.

"It stretches a few hundred yards in that direction," Ragh informed them.

As they moved forward, their light caused shadows to dance across stone and earthen walls and over the ancient wooden hulls.

"Ships," Varek said, his voice cracking with awe. "I can see a dozen of them, I think. It could take days to search all of them." He was standing motionless, transfixed by the sight of so many ancient ships. He didn't hear the half-elf jump to the cavern floor and pad up to his shoulder, didn't hear her gasp of amazement.

Rikali's eyes were wide, her mouth gaping. She struggled to absorb it all, her mind filling with possibilities when Maldred dropped this torch and watched it burn out.

"Pigs but I can't see nothin' now," she said. Her hand flailed about until she touched skin. A moment more and her fingers had fluttered down to grasp a hand. "Dhamon?"

He made no move to release her hand. "I told you to stay up top."

She tugged free and groped until she found Varek.

"Ragh?" Dhamon peered through the darkness.

Maldred was on his hands and knees, feeling about for a dry piece of wood. The sivak was moving away from them, toward the closest ship.

"Ragh!"

Within a heartbeat it had disappeared inside the hull.

"Damn draconian."

A few moments more and Maldred had a piece of wood burning merrily. "This isn't going to work, Dhamon," he said. A flash, and the wood became a long, glowing ember. "Wood's so dry down here it goes up like kindling. We'll have to backtrack, go to Wheatland and get some torches, lanterns. Might as well get that wagon while we're at it, and . . ."

His words and the last of the light died.

"Pigs but I don't like all of this dark. It's creepy. And it's so cold."

The half-elf was right, Dhamon realized. He'd been so caught up in the discovery of the ships that he hadn't

221

paid attention to anything else. The cavern was notice-
ably colder than the land above. The air was downright
chill, raising goosebumps on his exposed skin. His
senses acute, he felt the hair on his arms teased by a
faint breeze—as if the cavern were breathing. It was an
unnerving sensation, made more so because of the
darkness. After a moment he realized what was causing
it—the warmer air from above seeping in and displac-
ing some of the colder air. In a way, he mused, the cave
was breathing.

"Pigs, but I don't like this," the half-elf hissed.

"Then you should have stayed above." This stern
response came from Maldred, who a heartbeat later had
coaxed a long plank into flames.

The draconian was back, carrying a rusty but merrily
burning lantern in one claw. The handles of three unlit
lanterns were looped over his other arm.

"A handy beastie you have, Dhamon," the half-elf said.
She was quick to take one of the lanterns from the sivak.
"Pigs but this is filthy."

"There are a few small barrels of oil in the hold of that
ship," Ragh told Dhamon. He handed Dhamon an unlit
lantern, then passed the others to Maldred and Varek.
"There was not much else of value that I could see."

Rikali held her lantern high and sucked in her breath.
"Look at all of this. I'll have somethin' wonderful to tell
my baby," she whispered in awe. "All these ships, so far
beneath the earth and so very far away from the sea. This
is . . . well it's . . . unbelievable. She glided forward, one
hand outstretched. "Such a tale I will tell you, baby, 'specially if we find treasure on each and every one of these
ships. Gems and strings of pearls. You'll grow up in a very,
very fine house."

"Riki," Maldred cautioned. "Wait for us. There's no
telling how stable the ground is."

To the south was a squat-looking ship, one that appeared nearly as wide as it was long. It was a cog with a largely intact main mast. The topmost part had snapped off, and the hold was buried deep in sand and dirt.

"This way," Dhamon said as he moved toward the cog.

The sivak narrowed its eyes. "I said there was nothing of value on that ship."

Dhamon didn't reply for a moment. Instead, he gestured to Maldred. "No harm in all of us looking," he finally told the sivak. "Besides, I could use some oil in this lantern." He hurried ahead of all of them. He didn't want them to see the uncharacteristic wide smile painted on his face and the excitement that had been so long absent from his eyes.

The cracked beams at the stern made the ship easy climbing, and within moments he was standing on a deck that creaked with each step he took. The wood was so old and weak, the planks bowed under him, and Dhamon knew he might crash through to the decks below at any moment.

He spotted the hatch to the cargo bay, which was partially covered by a thoroughly yellowed square sail. He crept toward it, moving the rotting fabric and ropes aside so it would be easier going. He noted claw marks on the door and handle, the sivak's work. The sivak had been here first.

A ladder descended into darkness, and Dhamon held his breath and gingerly started down, counting on his luck to keep the rungs from breaking. "If they held for the draconian," he said to himself, "then they'll . . ."

Above him the deck creaked ominously, signaling the arrival of his companions, the heavy tromping coming from the sivak. "In here!" he called to them as he continued down. "Watch your step!"

"The search might take days, Varek?" Maldred laughed as he headed toward the ladder. "Indeed, I hope it takes

223

many days. Weeks!" A grin was splayed across his tanned face, as his dark eyes danced merrily. "And if there's any treasure to be had here—oh, and there certainly must be treasure—-may there be so much of it we never have to steal again, not once in the rest of our hopefully long lives."

They searched the hold for nearly an hour, finding several more lanterns and the oil the sivak told them about. They filled all the ones they carried, but decided to light only one at a time—to preserve the oil as best they could.

There was nothing else of value on the cog, and Ragh gave Dhamon an I-told-you-so look. There were plenty of bones, and barrels that contained foodstuff so petrified they looked like odd-colored rocks. There must have been two hundred skeletons in the deep-bellied ship, Dhamon guessed by eyeballing the skulls, and all of them in pieces next to ankle chains affixed to beams and columns.

"A slave ship for certain," Dhamon said with a grim shake of his head. "I didn't know pirates trafficked in human cargo."

"At least their slavers died with them," Ragh said.

Dhamon and the others were quick to explore the ship's other two decks, finding a dozen more skeletons. There were only a few trinkets worth taking, a gold chain here, a jeweled brooch, a few buttons and belt buckles. Perhaps the cog's wealth had been the slaves, and the captain didn't have time to sell them before the Cataclysm struck. Or perhaps someone had already found their way down here, decades ago, and looted everything.

The only sounds were the ones they themselves made, moving crates and chests, clinking metal objects against each other, wood snapping here and there beneath their weight, their muted conversations. When they stopped and stood still, the eeriness of the place settled in.

Quiet as a tomb, Dhamon thought. Indeed it was one, one vast tomb. It felt surprisingly dry, though the air had a strong staleness to it. Until they got used to breathing the underground air, they all returned to stand beneath the hole and gulp in the warmer fresh air that slowly spilled in.

Maldred selected the next craft to explore, this one a three-masted sohar with a hint of once-sleek lines, despite the broken timbers that were jutting away from it. The ship was nearly ninety feet long, and the sides had been painted green, but only chips of the color remained, giving the hull the appearance of dried fish scales. There was a gaping hole near the bow, where something had struck her.

"Bring the light, Riki," Maldred called. "I can hardly see anything." He made sure everyone was following before he slipped inside the rent in the hold.

It took more than a day to thoroughly search the first few ships, and Dhamon guessed the sun was rising again, judging by the light filtering in from the hole above. They had been moderately successful in his search of the sohar and of one caravel, finding a small but heavy chest filled with gold coins—-not the steel pieces that had been used as currency in most of Ansalon for at least the past two dozen decades. These were thin and round, with holes in the center. On one side were raised stalks of wheat, on the other was writing none of them could decipher.

"Very old," Maldred simply pronounced. "Valuable for their age if not for their metal."

Too, there was a cask filled with rare spices that had somehow weathered the passage of time. The big thief claimed this—he intended to hire a cook who would use it to expertly prepare his meals.

Varek and Rikali found a small hammered silver box filled with tiny emeralds, and Dhamon suspected the half-elf had found more and had filled her pockets with other things. Varek gathered quite a few old maps that had been rendered on cloth, certain that a collector would pay good coin for the antiquities.

Ragh dutifully followed them everywhere, lifting things that were pointed to or thrust upon him and gathering all of the recovered goods in a pile. They didn't intend to take everything up to the surface, just the choicest items, and the most valuable. Maldred said he could seal the entrance and they could always come back for more.

There were delicate ceramic rose vases that had been protected in a thickly padded crate, some of them practically as thin as parchment. The half-elf had pronounced them "sellable." There were miniature game pieces carved of jade, depicting dragons and knights, a sextant inlaid with pearls, ivory belt buckles, vials of perfume, a few captain's logs that Maldred favored, a pair of bejeweled tankards, daggers with jade handles, and more.

By now two dozen lanterns illuminated the growing treasure, lit from flasks and small barrels of oil they'd found on another cog. From the looks of it they wouldn't have to worry about not having enough light to search by. The problem would be how to haul their find.

It was midway through the fourth day when Dhamon disappeared into the sohar's hold on the pretense of looking for a crate. Maldred followed to find his friend curled up in the dark, teeth bared and hand pressed against his thigh.

Maldred said nothing, standing watch until the episode passed. "The map led us to Riki and to this treasure. It will lead us to the healer," he reassured his friend.

Dhamon's hair was plastered against the sides of his head from sweat, and his fingers fumbled as he tried to count the growing number of smaller scales on his leg. "You said she was expensive, Mal."

"The emeralds should please her."

"Maybe."

The big thief extended a hand to help Dhamon up. "There's still a good bit of cavern to search and a ship we've not explored."

"Aye, perhaps we'll find something grand yet."

When they emerged from the ship they saw Varek and Rikali curled up on a bed of the blankets. The sivak was sleeping soundly nearby. They hadn't ever seen him sleep much, but they'd been working him hard these past few days.

"Surprised he's still with us," Maldred mused. He yawned and looked for an inviting stretch of dirt to lay on.

"He probably has nothing better to do," Dhamon said. "Get some sleep, Mal. You need it."

"And you? I don't think you've slept in two days."

"I'm not tired. See that small cargo ship? The one we haven't touched?" Dhamon pointed to the back of the cavern. "I'll rest when I'm done there. There's a tunnel back there, too. Perhaps it leads to something." Maybe to something more than we've found, Dhamon added to himself.

Maldred looked as if he intended to argue with Dhamon, but he thought better of it and settled down on his back. He was sound asleep before Dhamon was halfway to the ship.

Dhamon wasn't tired, despite not sleeping much in the past few days. He actually felt invigorated, though he told himself this was nervous energy over their find. He made his way toward the back of the cavern, then climbed onto the cargo ship's deck. Letters on the bow were so faded he had to concentrate to read them. ABR___'S T__MP__ST, was all he was able to make out. He quicky headed toward an open hatch and found his way down to the crew's quarters.

The galley was filled with skeletons and a petrified banquet scattered across the table and the floor—made eerie by the soft lantern light that played across the scene. It was as if the men had gathered for one last meal and hadn't been able to finish before all hell broke loose—and the gods taking revenge on the Kingpriest. Plates and goblets were strewn everywhere, benches were overturned, but there was a great silver platter still in the middle of the table. Some of the skeletons had rings and neck-chains amidst their bones, and Dhamon passed over these, perhaps not wanting to disturb any spirits who clung to the dead. Probably Riki would snap up the trinkets tomorrow anyway.

He moved toward a cargo hold only half-full, and this with crated bolts of silk that were too riddled with insect holes to be of any value. At one time, they would have fetched a high price in practically any port town in Ansalon. Now they shredded like cobwebs when he touched them. He spent longer than he intended in the crew quarters, searching through rotted sea chests that contained clothes, jugs, personal mementos, and a few musical instruments. He left all of these behind and found his way to the captain's cabin.

It was impressively furnished, with a bed of polished mahogany and a tall-backed chair artfully carved and inlaid on the arms with brass. Despite the condition of the rest of the ship—-and of the other ships Dhamon had visited—this room looked as though it had been frozen in time. There was a writing desk, bolted to the floor, and a stool tipped over. There wasn't a hint of dust anywhere, and the polished wood floor he walked across was strong and didn't creak.

Dhamon set the lantern on the desk and righted the stool, sitting and shuffling through papers that he had expected to crumble at his touch. They felt crisp, as if new. There was journal in a niche, and he gently tugged this out. Why it interested him he wasn't certain—he'd paid little enough attention to any other papers and maps he'd come across. Nevertheless, he hefted it, then traced words on the cover that had been rendered in gold leaf.

The Journal of Abraim's Tempest, Dhamon read. He opened the book to the middle, where a wine-red ribbon marked the page. Placing his finger to the first line, he began to read, stopping but a second later when he heard the cry of a sea bird. He swivelled to stare out a brass-rimmed porthole—-which was open—showing a bright blue sky. There were gulls dancing low across the waves, and their cries sounded musical.

He sputtered and rose, walked over to the porthole, and shook his head when the vision disappeared. The silence of the cavern and the ship closed around him, and he smelled the staleness of the air again.

Had he only imagined the birds and the smell of salt-water?

"I am tired," he told himself. Still, he returned to the stool and the book, again glancing at the page and finding that the ship seemed to once more move beneath him, as if it was riding waves in a wind-tossed sea. "Impossible," he said.

The ship's timbers softly creaked with each swell, and a lamp that hung from the ceiling suddenly lit and swayed with each rise and fall of the bow. Dhamon slammed the book shut, and the room returned to its ancient emptiness.

"Abraim's *Tempest*," he repeated. The book's title would match the letters on the bow. Was Abraim the captain of this ship? Was he a sorcerer? Or had he merely acquired a grand magical book? Once again Dhamon returned to the journal, this time starting at the beginning of the pages. Immediately he heard the snap of billowing sails from the deck above.

"The book relives the ship's journey," he said in a whisper. "Remarkable."

He settled on the bed, finding the light from the lantern above more than sufficient to read by and the mattress comfortable.

The sound of the gulls grew louder, the creaking of the timbers and the snap of the sails joining in. There were footsteps on the deck. A bark of orders: "Trim the mainsail! We're running fast, boys!" and later, "Tack, mates! Head her into the wind to change course."

Dhamon lost himself in *Tempest*'s exploits, feeling as if he were part of the crew—boarding merchant ships with bellies so heavy they rode low in the water, hauling the cargo into the pirate's hold, finding pleasure in the arms of one wench after another, standing on the bow and turning his face to catch the splash of seawater.

Hours passed, and still he kept reading, skipping pages here and there, vowing to go back and read them all later. A magical book such as this should fetch an incredible price.

"A singular book," he murmured. This is what he would give to the healer, and it should be sufficient to meet her price for curing him.

But first he would read just a bit more, savoring it. "Only one more page," he told himself, but there was another and another. With the next entry he felt as if he'd been tossed into the Abyss.

He found himself staring into the face of Abraim, a tall hook-nosed man harshly weathered by the sea and the sun. Abraim was frantically waving, calling for the men to lower the sails, to tie down the water barrels. The wind had picked up without warning as they made their way down the river to the pirate port.

"So you were a pirate, Abraim," Dhamon said softly, "and this book is your greatest treasure."

The men were worried they'd run aground, but Abraim took the wheel and threw his strength into keeping the ship on course. His lips began to move, and Dhamon recognized a spell. The sorcerer-captain was trying to calm the wind about the ship. For several minutes it seemed as if he'd accomplished that, and the crew on deck relaxed.

The wind kicked up with an even greater velocity.

"Reverse course, Captain?"

Abraim shook his head and continued his magic, one hand on the king's spoke, the other gesturing to the sky. Again the wind calmed, but not for long.

The wind came at the *Tempest* with gale force now. Too late the captain realized he should have reversed the course and headed out to sea. Dhamon felt the man's fear rising into his own throat, felt his temples pounding, hands gripping the spokes tighter.

"My magic can't counter this! Below decks!" the captain barked to his crew.

The brutal weather was caused by angry gods, and no man—no matter how much magic he commanded—could stand up to it. When the earthquakes started and the river bucked like a maddened thing, when the squall chased them up the river, the captain gave up. He turned and saw a wall of water rising high above and behind *Tempest*.

Dhamon heard the thunderous roar of the water and the faint screams of the men washed overboard. He heard wood splintering as the mainmast snapped, heard a great rumbling from the land on either side of the river.

He heard and saw only water above him and earth below where the river parted, felt a great force pushing against his chest, plunging him into eternal darkness. Dhamon gasped and shook his head.

There were a few more pages in the book, but they were blank. The story ended with the death of Abraim and *Tempest*. The cabin had grown dark again, save the lantern that glowed only faintly on the desk, the oil all but consumed. Dhamon rose from the bed and steadied himself, gingerly tucking the book under his arm, and left to rejoin his companions. This book will more than pay the healer, he thought.

He and Mal could leave in the morning to find the healer. A smile tugged at the corner of his lips, and he patted the book. To be free of the damned scale. Rikali and Varek—and the sivak for that matter—could stay and explore the rest of this place for as long as they liked.

He climbed down from the *Tempest* and peered toward the back wall of the cavern, to the narrow tunnel he and Maldred had first noticed two few days ago. He and Maldred could leave in the morning . . . but they might take a quick look down there first.

CHAPTER SEVENTEEN
SWEET MAGIC

hey could see their breath in the narrow passage, the limestone walls cold to the touch. Dhamon led the way, Maldred holding the lantern high behind him, and Rikali and Varek following.

The sivak paused for a moment, watching them go, then out of a mix of duty and curiosity followed. He found the passage a tight fit. There were only inches to spare on either side of his broad shoulders, and the jagged shards of crystals that crunched beneath the boots of the others dug into his feet. He paused again a few dozen yards later, clawed hands running over knobby clusters of coral and pieces of shells embedded here and there in the wall. He traced the fossil of a crab.

Farther along the passage widened and the ceiling that had been only a few feet above their heads disappeared in the darkness.

After the better part of an hour, Dhamon stopped and turned to Maldred. "Time to go back," he said. "Head out to the healer. There's nothing here."

233

Maldred nodded and made a move to retreat, but a moment later Dhamon's hand shot out.

"Wait. I hear something." He turned again and followed the passage for several more minutes. "The wind, I think, Mal." Disappointment was clear in his voice. "I admit, it was my idea to come in here. My idea to waste our time." The stony corridor had opened into a small circular cavern, nearly the entire floor of which was taken up by a pool of water.

Both men glanced up. Dhamon spotted a thin crevice high overhead through which rain could have entered to create the pool.

He shook his head. "I thought I heard music. I still hear it." Softer, he added, "It might be the wind." Again he was just about to retrace his steps, when he spotted a crevice across the cavern—another tunnel, this one narrower than the one they had just traversed.

"Pigs, but I ain't squeezing through that," Rikali said. She sagged against the wall, her fingers brushing her stomach. " 'Sides, I'm not feelin' too well this mornin'. This bein' pregnant ain't fun."

Dhamon was working his way around the pool of water, Maldred following. Varek stood next to Riki and coaxed a light from the lantern he'd been carrying.

"Then we'll stay here and wait for them together, my love."

Riki frowned. "What if they find somethin'? We don't want them cuttin' us out of anythin' valuable. They would, you know."

He hesitated.

"I will stay with her," Ragh said.

"Now I know I'm not going with them, Riki."

The half-elf gave him a lopsided grin. "I'll be just fine with this beastie, Varek. He ain't gonna hurt me."

Ragh unceremoniously sat near the pool, clawed feet dangling just above the water. Varek glanced at Riki, who gestured for him to hurry. A few minutes later he disappeared into the crevice after Maldred and Dhamon.

"Your big shoulders and all, you wouldn't have fit in there," she told the sivak.

"I wouldn't have wanted to."

The thin tunnel curved back on itself and the ceiling dropped so that Dhamon, Maldred and Varek were almost crawling. Varek had to leave his staff behind. Somehow Maldred managed with his greatsword.

At one point Dhamon thought the tunnel dead-ended, but as he approached what seemed to be a stone wall, he discovered a mesh of tree roots that had penetrated this far down through the rocks. It was from a tree, long dead, but the thick taproots formed a dense mat. He broke through and continued on.

"I hear something too, now," Maldred said after a while, "but I don't think it's music."

"Crystals teased by the wind," Dhamon said. "Sounds a little like music." The tunnel opened onto a wider crevice, the depth of which was impossible even for Dhamon's keen eyesight to gauge. Spanning it was a narrow bridge of rock, which led to another crevice on the other side. Crystals were embedded in the walls, and stalactites hung from the ceiling, some of them solid crystal.

"Your music," Maldred said.

"We've gone too far now to turn back," Dhamon said, as he headed across the bridge. Maldred was slower, constantly looking around, and glancing up repeatedly at the stalactites as he walked across. Varek waited until both men were on the other side before he risked it.

The next crevice was not so long or so cramped, and at the other end Dhamon poked his head out to find a cavern

235

nearly as large as the one they first explored. There was a noticeable breeze in here, coming from a trio of narrow rents in the rocky ceiling above, a mist of rain water seeping in.

"More ships," Dhamon said. "Caravels and cogs."

These ships were in slightly better shape than the others, though there were not so many of them as in the other cavern. And there were plenty of splintered boards to suggest docks to which the ships had been moored in ages past.

Dhamon moved forward, Maldred behind him, raising the lantern high in the process. The light bounced off a myriad of crystals that dotted fingerlike stalactites hanging from the ceiling.

The crystals fairly glowed, and the added light helped to illuminate crumbling stone buildings wedged into the southern wall past the ships.

"We've found one of the ancient pirate ports." Maldred beamed. "Ha! We might find a true fortune here."

Even Varek was excited, slipping by them and to a caravel with intact masts.

They set about searching the ships first, finding exotic silks and foodstuffs, wines that had turned to vinegar a hundred years ago. Insects had invaded many of the holds, ruining wood carvings and paintings.

There were gems to be had, small urns brimming with pearls, elegant boxes filled with diamond necklaces, ruby pins, a small collection of brass-inlaid peg-legs, and more. One exceptional piece of jewelry caught Dhamon's eye. It was a necklace, fashioned of rare black pearls and highly polished volcanic glass beads. That something so dark could have so much fire and color impressed him. He passed the piece to Maldred, who agreed it was one of the most valuable things they'd come across.

236

"We could give it to Riki," Maldred suggested.

Dhamon shrugged and resumed his search.

Varek discovered a cache of objects that were probably enchanted—a small glass globe that alternately glowed green, then orange; a dagger that gave off a faint blue light, which he was quick to thrust in his belt; a palm-sized onyx wolf, that, when its side was rubbed, played an old tune; and a silver goblet that continually filled itself with cool water.

"For the healer if your book isn't sufficient," Maldred said, gesturing to the magical treasures they'd gathered into a sack from one of the ships. Dhamon set a bronze circlet with this collection, swearing he heard voices in his head when he put it on.

As they moved deeper into the cavern, they discovered more remains of buildings, mostly consisting of a few stone foundations. These were far east and south of one row of ships, probably marking what had been the bank of the east side of the ancient river. There were dozens of skeletons amid the debris, all picked clean with scraps of cloth laying around them. Varek tossed an old sail over three small skeletons, which he suspected from their wide feet were kender rather than human children.

"Dhamon, after we're done, finished plundering all of this . . ."

"We find the healer, Mal."

"Yes," Maldred agreed, "but after we're finished with that business, we have to tell someone where all of this is. A historian, I think. Give him a map and let him come here."

"Not our enchanted map."

"Never."

"After we've taken what we want." This came from Varek. "Everything we want."

Maldred nodded. "But this is history, something remaining from before the Cataclysm, and it should be shared and recorded. Dhamon, we must tell my father. He'd be pleased to know his map took us to a true treasure."

"You'll be the one to tell your father," Dhamon chuckled as he examined a stone door on the most intact building in the cavern. All the windows had been covered by sheets of slate, which were uncomfortably cold to the touch. "You'll not catch me in Blöten ever again, my friend."

"Fair enough. It's not so bad a city," Maldred said. "Fine places to eat. Grim Kedar's to visit, but I've no desire to stay there either. Too much of the world to see. Maybe we should buy a ship, Dhamon, sail to lands we've only heard about."

Dhamon offered him a half-smile. "After the healer."

"Maybe follow another one of my father's treasure maps."

Varek cleared his throat. "Riki and I won't be going with the two of you on any more treasure hunts. We'll take our share from this and be done with you." The young man helped Dhamon pry at a piece of slate.

"Buy a nice house somewhere?" Maldred posed, a gleam in his eye. "Settle down and forget the adventuring life? Raise a big family and plant your roots deep? Riki'd like that just fine." The last he said with a touch of sarcasm, which was lost on the busy Varek.

Dhamon stepped back and resumed examining the building, though his mind was on the half-elf now, of her settling down to a mundane and safe life with a young man Dhamon didn't care for—too young, too impetuous. Am I jealous? he wondered.

He admitted that it had bothered him every night seeing Varek sleeping with his arm protectively around Riki. Dhamon tried to tell himself that it didn't matter, that he didn't love the half-elf, that he'd only kept company with her because she was pretty—and convenient at the time. I don't love her, he thought. I never did. But did the half-elf love the boy? Riki didn't smother the young man with affection, didn't hang on him the way she used to cling to Dhamon. She looked different, too, than when she'd been with Dhamon. She no longer painted her face and didn't dress in garish, tight clothes. She cursed less frequently and often seemed softly feminine.

"I'm better off without love," he whispered. "I don't want it, don't need it. I'm better off alone." He tried prying at a different piece of slate and discovered that like the one Varek still worked on, it had been fused to the window—perhaps some act from the Cataclysm or perhaps a sorcerer's spell, the latter something Maldred might be capable of.

"I don't need love," he repeated.

He turned and gestured to Maldred. "Over here. I want to get a look inside this building. Could be some treasure vault the way it's all sealed up. I think we're going to need your magic to get inside."

"What are you lookin' at, Ragh?"

Rikali eased herself down at the sivak's side and leaned close to get a look at what was in his palm.

"It's only sand and silt," the draconian told her. His words themselves sounded like sand blowing across stone, raspy and soft from his scarred throat. "And ash, I think."

"Ash?"

"From a volcano." Ragh pointed a claw toward a spot high on the wall and moved the lantern. "See?"

"All I see is rock."

"Different kinds of rock," he said, his grating voice slow and even, as a teacher might speak when lecturing. "They've been melted together—chert and granite and sand, shells, some fossils probably. A solid piece. The floor we sit on. Beneath this . . ." The sivak brushed aside some sand. "It's indurated, soil and rock all fused together."

She raised an eyebrow. "How could that happen?"

"Time could do it, enough pressure on the ground. So could a volcano, the heat melting everything together. It would explain the ash and maybe explain the tunnels and this chamber. They might have been formed by a lava flow."

The half-elf shivered. "I've been through an earthquake. Pigs, when Mal an' Dhamon an' me were in the Vale of Chaos. . . . The vale, it's a . . ."

"I know what and where it is."

The half-elf traced a design in a patch of sand.

"I am old, Rikali. I have seen much of Krynn."

"Smart, too," she said. "You seem to know a lot. Smarts don't come with age."

The sivak let out a long breath, which sounded like a strained whistle. "I learned a lot about Krynn out of necessity. A spy for Takhisis, then for Sable, I would slay men and take their places for as long as I could hold their forms—explorers, politicians, ambassadors, dwarves. From the dwarves I learned a lot about caverns and stone."

Rikali shivered at the thought. "How many did you kill?"

"More than I can remember." Ragh tipped his head back to study the ceiling. "But all of that ended when Sable gave me to Nura Bint-Drax."

"Like them thieves sold me and other folks to her." Rikali shivered again. "I could've been turned into a spawn."

"An abomination," Ragh corrected her, a clawed finger drifting up to touch the scars on his chest where he had been bled to create the creatures.

"I hope they won't be too much longer," she said as a way of changing the subject. "Ain't comfortable to sit here."

◇ ◇ ◇ ◇ ◇ ◇ ◇

"Magic," Maldred said. "It fused the slate on the windows and sealed the door. I'd say the resident was a wizard who thought barricading himself inside might save him from the Cataclysm."

Varek continued to struggle at a window. "Then maybe he might have saved all his magical trinkets." He huffed and tugged a moment more, then shook his head. His chest heaved from the effort he'd put into it. In frustration, he kicked at the door. "Can you get us in there?"

Maldred grinned and splayed his fingers wide, chest high on the door. "Shouldn't be too difficult, I'd wager." He started humming a tune Dhamon had not heard before. Interspersed in the melody were Ogrish words, a monotonous chant.

Varek glanced around the cavern. "Maybe there are some more chambers. That old map showed the river going farther south, another pirate port maybe."

"Don't you think we're rich enough?" Dhamon asked. He knew that if he had not wanted to find the healer, he'd be exploring farther. It was his greed that sent him down the crevice to this place anyway. In the back of his mind he was considering a return trip. Maldred could seal the hole that brought them underground, and he could come back after he'd been cured of the spreading scales.

"What's rich enough?" Varek rubbed the ball of his foot against the stone floor. "I want to buy Riki a real nice house. Buy her anything she needs."

"Almost have it!" Maldred's shoulders were straining the seams of his tunic, and the outline of his muscles shown through the fabric. He was using more than just his magic to get through the door.

"Though if this place weren't so old . . . and if the door was set in here any better . . . . There! Hmmm, what's this?"

241

Strips of green wax fell away as he began to push the door inward. The big man put his shoulder to it and pushed harder, grinning when the door moved a few more inches. "Some help, here, Dhamon."

Dhamon was quick to join him, the hair prickling on the back of his neck when the door moved a few more inches and part of the rocky ceiling came down. A fist-size chunk of stone hit him on the arm, and he muttered a curse.

"It's nothing," Maldred said. "It seems you heal easy enough anymore. Come."

One more push, and the door swung wide. Maldred jumped away from it and grabbed up the lantern. He was back and through the opening before Dhamon had moved. The air felt dead, still, cold, and heavy with the scent of decay, and Dhamon fought to keep from gagging. Maldred was affected too, but his senses were not as keen. He plunged ahead.

"You stay out of here, Varek!" he warned.

The young man shook his head and followed. "You're not cutting Riki and I out of anything."

"Doesn't look like any sorcerer's house," Dhamon stated. "Varek, why don't you wait outside?"

There were eight large chests spaced evenly in the center of a rough-hewn square room—four on each side, separated by wooden pillars that looked as if they might collapse at any moment.

Varek brushed by Dhamon and Maldred and moved to the first chest, noting more of the green wax around the edges.

Dhamon felt the air chill.

"Varek, I don't think this has anything to do with pirates or sorcerers."

Varek tried to lift the lid. "Some pirate who didn't trust his fellows in the port put his wealth in here."

"Let me give you a hand with that." Maldred thrust his fingers under the lid and pulled up.

"Mal . . ." The air was getting colder still. "I don't think this room was buried in the Cataclysm. Look. Magic or no, none of the walls are cracked. The chests don't look as old as the wood on the ships or from the other chests we found. I think this was put here well after the Cataclysm. See. . . ."

Dhamon pointed to the far end of the room, where three stone steps led to a wall sealed with more of the green wax. "I think we should leave here. You ought to—"

"There!" Maldred exclaimed. "There hasn't been the lock or door made that could defeat me!" He and Varek stepped back and flipped open the chest, coughing when a swirl of dust erupted.

On the heels of the dust cloud came a diaphanous figure with glowing red eyes.

"Undead!" Dhamon snapped, drawing his sword and lunging forward. "Well and truly wonderful."

The creature was vaguely man-shaped, but as it moved, it grew and separated, becoming two.

The first floated toward Maldred, wispy arms outstretched, mouth forming and cackling. The second sped toward another chest, thrusting insubstantial arms inside, solidifying, then breaking the wood. Another creature came out.

Dhamon raced toward this second chest, sword sweeping in front of him and passing through the again-transparent creature. His sword continued its path, striking instead one of the wood columns and cleaving it in two. Rocks rained down from the ceiling, stinging his arms and head and doing nothing to the creatures.

"By the vanished gods!" Varek cried. "What are these things?"

"Wraiths," Dhamon shot back as he swung again.

243

"Your death," one of the creatures answered, its haunting voice echoing off the stone walls.

There were four of the undead creatures now, the newly freed one dividing also.

"We are free," one of them whispered. "Bound no longer, we will join our brethren."

"Yes," another joined in. "Free, we must go."

Maldred swung at one directly in front of him, snarling as the blade passed through it, inflicting little, if any, damage.

"Why don't you just die?"

"Free," they repeated as one.

"We are at last freed from our prison," said the one nearest Dhamon.

Dhamon raced to another chest that one of the wraiths was attempting to open. It glared balefully at him and solidified an arm to take a swipe at him, but Dhamon was faster, bringing up his sword at the last moment and meeting something solid. The wraith howled.

Its eyes glowed brightly and seemed to burn into him. "We could not answer the summons, trapped. Free, we can answer now!" It floated to another chest and thrust an arm inside. In a moment, another creature was free.

"Free!" It became a hissing chant, and through it Dhamon heard Maldred gasp as he continued to spar with one of the creatures. Varek muttered curses at one hovering near him, jabbing at it with the glowing dagger he'd taken.

"Brothers, this one stings!" the wraith howled, as Varek's blade burned the thing's insubstantial form. "This one must die first."

"Sweet death," they chanted. "Death to the man who stings."

Dhamon heard a splintering, popping sound cut through the chanting. "No!" he shouted. "Mal! Varek! Look out!"

One of the wraiths had solidified adjacent to a wooden column and tugged at it, laughing manically when it broke and brought down part of the ceiling with it. Big chunks of rock fell on another chest, splitting it open and releasing more undead.

"We are free!"

"We are summoned! Called to join our brethren!" another cried. "I feel the pull!"

"Let it pull you out of here," Dhamon shouted. "Leave us!"

Some of the creatures were indeed slipping from the chamber, a cloud of death gliding into the cavern beyond. Others were working on the pillars to bring the building down.

"Maldred, Varek, get out of here!" Dhamon barked. He realized that the undead were going to break open the rest of the chests and free the rest of their macabre comrades, using the rocks falling from the ceiling. The weight of the rocks couldn't hurt something that was already dead.

"We are called!"

"Magic!" one of them wailed. "I smell magic."

"It is in the man's blade. It stings us."

"Magic!" became the chant as three of the wraiths descended on Varek. One stretched out a diaphanous hand and wrapped it around the glowing blade.

"It stings me!" the wraith cried, but it refused to let go of the weapon. "Magic! I will drink the magic!"

"Dhamon! Help!" Varek tried to pull the dagger from the creature's grasp, but its two companions had solidified and were holding him in place.

"Sweet magic," the wraith cooed. Finally it released the weapon, but the blade no longer glowed.

"Sweet magic," its companions echoed as they hurled Varek against the stone wall, so hard that they momentarily stunned him.

245

They turned as one to Maldred. "Magic!" they cried.

Dhamon frantically tried to push the wraiths away from the pillars, at the same time trying to make his way around the shattered chests to reach Maldred, now surrounded by the ghostly images.

"There is magic in this man!" one cried. Its eyes glowed white hot in anticipation.

"Sweet sorcerer," the wraiths chanted. "Sweet death for the sweet sorcerer."

"Fight me!" Dhamon howled, but the wraiths seemed interested only in Maldred. One of the undead solidified in front of Dhamon to block him.

"The sorcerer's blade!" the creature cried. "It was forged in magic. Drink the magic!"

"Sweet magic."

"The man!" another keened shrilly. "He holds far more magic than his weapon. Drink the magic! Drink his life!"

"Sweet magic."

"Varek!" Dhamon shouted as he swung at the wraith before him. It reached a clawed hand out and scratched at Dhamon's face, the nails like icicles digging into his skin. "Varek! Get to Maldred!"

Varek shook his head and pushed away from the wall. The ghosts smashed another pillar, and a great chunk of the ceiling fell, burying Varek. From beneath the rubble the young man groaned, and Dhamon saw that rocks were pinning the big man, too.

"You say you're been summoned, you filthy thing!" Dhamon spat at the wraith, blocking him. He rained a series of blows against the creature, all of them ineffectual. "Leave! Go to whoever's calling you."

"Sweet magic!" came a cry from the chamber beyond the building.

Dhamon realized the creatures had discovered the sack containing the magical trinkets.

"Drink the magic!"

"Sweet magic," cooed the one in front of Dhamon. In a breath it became insubstantial and drifted to join its feasting brothers.

Dhamon hurried toward Maldred, slipping around rocks that barred his way, around a chest where more undead were surging forth.

"Drink the magic!"

"Sweet magic!"

"We are summoned! Called, we must answer!"

"Dhamon!" Maldred's bellow was filled with pain. A quartet of the undead remained around the big man, and Dhamon watched in horror as one reached ghostly hands inside of Maldred's chest, the arms solidifying. The big thief screamed.

"Sweet magic!" the four undead cried as they thrust their claws into Maldred's body and feasted.

Dhamon tried to pull them off, but his hands closed on nothing but bone-numbing cold air. He gasped and redoubled his efforts.

"Can't hurt these things," he grunted. "Can't do a damn thing to them!"

"Summoned, we must answer!" one cried from the cavern beyond.

"Sweet magic," the four in the room repeated. "Sweet magic gone." As one, they glided to the door and beyond, into the cavern where a cloud of the creatures hovered like fog above the stone floor. Swiftly the cloud lifted. The wraiths faded from view.

"Maldred!"

Dhamon felt about on his friend's chest, finding nothing broken. Mal's face was ashen. "Be alive, Mal. Be . . . ah!"

Maldred sucked in a breath and began shivering uncontrollably. The temperature had plummeted so quickly from the presence of the undead that frost coated everything.

Maldred was changing. His form expanded, his skin turned pale blue, his hair grew long and turned white before Dhamon's eyes. His human form melted, replaced in an eyeblink by his true self——a hulking ogre mage.

Dhamon gritted his teeth and pulled at the rocks that pinned his friend. He shouldn't have been able to move the chunks of stone, he knew. They were too big, too heavy for one man to manage—but he was stronger than a normal man.

What's happening to me? Dhamon thought as he picked up the largest stone and threw it aside. He worked his way behind Maldred and grabbed him beneath the armpits, dragging him from the room.

Maldred's limbs and mouth quivered. It was several minutes before he opened his eyes. "Dhamon?"

"Aye, I'm here."

"They were—"

"Undead. Yes, I know. Without an enchanted blade I could do nothing against them."

"My sword . . ."

"Probably isn't enchanted any longer. It seems they robbed you of your magic. They were drinking it like a mob dying from thirst."

"No. My magic." Maldred propped himself up on his elbows. He closed his eyes and his brow wrinkled in concentration. "The spark. There has always been this spark inside of me, a fire that I called on to cast spells. It's gone, Dhamon. I can't even cast the simplest of enchantments. The one that lets me look human—that magic is gone."

Dhamon had gone back inside the building and was moving the rocks that pinned Varek. He thought he'd find the young man dead or his ribs crushed, but Varek was breathing regularly, though unconscious. A deep gash across his forehead had been caused by a rock. Dhamon checked his eyes.

"You'll live," he said.

The heaviest of the rocks had fallen on Varek's legs, and when Dhamon moved the last of the rubble aside, he grimaced.

"Maybe better that you had died," he said. One of Varek's legs was crushed. From the knee down it was a pulpy mass of blood and tissue. "Maybe I should let you bleed to death. Your spirit might thank me for it."

For a moment Dhamon considered doing just that, then closed his eyes, let out a deep breath, and carried the unconscious Varek out into the cavern.

Maldred had managed to sit up. His hands were balled into fists, and he was pressing them against his chest.

"Gone," he repeated. "All of it." His expression changed from pity for himself to concern for Varek.

"By my father!"

"That leg has to go," Dhamon said matter-of-factly. "Part of it anyway. If not he'll bleed to death, or his body will become so badly infected he'll die that way."

Dhamon stepped away from the young man and walked to the nearest ship, tugging free a few dry pieces of railing.

"We'll need a fire," he explained as he worked, "so we can cauterize it when I'm done. I'll use your sword, if you don't mind."

Maldred was pushing himself to his feet. "I'll do my part. They took my magic, but not my strength. Where's my sword?"

Dhamon nodded toward the building. "Now, Varek, if you'll only stay asleep until this is all over it will go much . . . wonderful."

Varek's eyes fluttered opened, and his face twisted in pain. He started shaking, and Dhamon put his hands on the youth's shoulders.

"You're hurt," Dhamon said.

249

"C-c-c-cold," Varek stammered. "I feel so cold." Beads of sweat dotted his face and arms, and he felt clammy to Dhamon's touch.

"You're in shock," Dhamon told him. "You've lost a good bit of blood. We'll take care of you, but you need to—"

Varek screamed. "Monster! Dhamon there's a . . ."

Dhamon glanced over his shoulder to see Maldred coming out of the building, greatsword in hand. His clothes were in tatters, hanging on his giant frame.

"He's not a monster, Varek," Dhamon said. He positioned his face over Varek's to help blot out the sight of Maldred's ogre body. "It's Maldred. We'll tell you all about it later. Just close your eyes."

Varek refused and, tossing his head from side to side, tried to rise. He screamed again, this time in excruciating pain. "My leg, I . . ."

Dhamon kept one hand on a shoulder, relying on his strength to hold Varek down. The other drifted to the knife in his belt, the pommel of which he thrust between Varek's teeth to quiet him. "Now, Mal! Just above the knee."

Maldred raised his greatsword above Varek. The young man's eyes went wide with fear. He saw the blade descending and felt it sunder his limb. Varek's teeth clamped down on the knife pommel, and darkness claimed him.

Dhamon thrust the Solamnic long sword in the fire, and when the steel was hot he applied it to the end of Varek's leg.

"You've done this before," Maldred stated.

A nod. "When I was with the Dark Knights." Dhamon added, "Most of the men didn't make it. They'd lost too much blood or had other injuries. I think Varek will live through it."

"He's young." Maldred shook his head. "My loss of magic seems inconsequential next to that."

"We'll stay here until he comes to again and get him drunk on that wine we saw. Got to be enough alcohol left to put him in a haze. Then we'll drag him out of here."

"Riki . . ." Maldred sighed.

"She'll handle this," Dhamon said. "She's tough. Now, let's find something reasonably clean and make a bandage. After that, we'll see what's worth hauling out of here with him."

"I'm going to bring something along I think Varek will need," Maldred said. His hulking blue body disappeared into the gaping hole of a caravel's hull.

Rikali screamed and jumped to her feet, waving her arm at the blue-skinned ogre who had barely managed to scrape his way through the crevice, dragging a big canvas bag behind him and holding a lantern high in one meaty hand.

Ragh was up in a second, claws flashing, trying to put the half-elf behind him.

"M-m-monster," Rikali cried, hand flying to the dagger on her waist, pulling it free. She spun from behind the sivak and crouched, ready to meet the creature. Her eyes narrowed when she spotted Maldred's greatsword strapped to the ogre-mage's back.

Dhamon emerged from the crevice, tugging a still-unconscious Varek.

Rikali screamed again at the sight of her battered husband.

It took the better part of an hour to calm her down and to explain what had happened to Varek and to Maldred and to tell her who and what Maldred was. All the while her fingers stroked Varek's too-pale face.

"This is my fault," she moaned, "I told you to follow them. It's my fault. Oh, Varek, your leg."

Dhamon didn't say anything, knowing his words of sympathy would ring hollow. Without a word, the sivak shouldered the canvas bag, picked up one of the lanterns, and started down the corridor.

"Wait for me," Maldred said, following the sivak.

"Monster," Riki said, as she watched Maldred head down the corridor.

"Dhamon." Tears streamed from the half-elf's face. "Varek is . . ."

"Going to live at least," he said.

"He's maimed," she sobbed, "and Maldred's a . . . a monster. Should've never saved you from them thieves, Dhamon. I should've never talked Varek into coming after you and Mal. Should've let them women kill you."

She brushed at the tears, streaking dirt across her face. "My husband's maimed for life!"

"Riki, be grateful he's alive." Dhamon looked down the corridor, seeing the light from the sivak's lantern fading. He picked up the remaining lantern and gestured for her to go first. "Be grateful you still have a husband for your baby."

She seethed. "It's my fault. I sent him after you and Mal. It's my fault I made him fall in love with me, marry me." She choked back a sob. "The baby's not his, you know. Not that you or I will ever tell him the truth."

Dhamon's eyes were saucers.

"It's yours, you fool. You left me pregnant and alone in Blöten, Dhamon Grimwulf."

She slid by him and hurried down the corridor.

Dhamon stood stunned for several minutes before he slowly picked his way after her.

When Varek finally came to, Dhamon had to explain all over again about Maldred being an ogre mage. The young man took the news better than Riki had, perhaps because he was preoccupied with dealing with his leg.

"You'll be able to walk on your own again," Maldred said reassuringly. Fishing about in the canvas sack they'd brought back, he pulled out a mahogany peg-leg inlaid with bronze and silver. "There's two more in the bag. You can take your pick."

Varek groaned and lay back on Rikali's lap.

The half-elf watched Maldred and the sivak gather up the treasure and place it beneath the hole. Dhamon hovered near them, though most of the time he watched Riki. She stared at him impassively and stroked Varek's face.

"You climb up first, Dhamon," Maldred suggested, "We'll tie some of these bundles to the rope and you can pull them up. We'll take these." The ogre mage gestured at the choicest assortment. "Between us, we can manage this. I'll follow you. Ragh can bring Varek and—"

"Seal up the hole," Dhamon said numbly.

"Yes, and we come back for the rest later. With a wagon."

"My book?"

"It's here." Maldred pointed to a satchel.

"Not so fast," Riki said, easing Varek's head onto the floor. "I'm going first. Ragh'll bring Varek, and then we'll pull the treasure up. I'm not taking the chance you'll leave us here."

Dhamon didn't argue. Instead, he picked her up and held her so she could grab the rope. A moment later she was out of view, tugging the rope after her and tying Dhamon's sail to it. It was several minutes before it dropped back down.

"She wanted us to stew a bit," Maldred said.

Dhamon nodded to the sivak. Varek had his arms locked around Ragh's neck as the creature started up.

"Hope they're not too heavy," Maldred mused. "I wouldn't want to be trapped down here."

The bags of loot came next, save for the satchel containing Abraim's magical book, which Dhamon strapped to his back.

"You first, my friend," Maldred said.

Dhamon complied.

Yet when the ogre mage emerged from the hole a few minutes later, he was greeted by an unexpected sight.

Three dozen Legion of Steel Knights stood at attention. Another half-dozen had Dhamon and the sivak in custody, with thick ropes wrapped around them. A commander held Rikali's wrists with one hand. The other hand held a dagger at her throat.

"Should we just kill the draconian?" one of the Knights called.

The commander shook his head. "Commander Lawlor's in Wheatland. He'll want to question the creature first. It might have some valuable information about the dragons around here." After a moment, he added, "Tie the ogre up, too. Lawlor can decide what to do with it."

A dozen Knights came forward to handle this task.

"Put the lot of them on that wagon," the commander growled

There were two wagons. The other held the loot that Dhamon and the others had gathered.

"A fine treasure," the Knight commander beamed.

"I'll wager there's a lot more treasure down in that hole." The voice was smooth and feminine and came from a slim Ergothian, who stepped out from behind a line of Knights.

"Satin," Dhamon said.

The dark-skinned woman was still wearing Dhamon's tunic, and Wyrmsbane, his magical long sword, was scabbarded on her hip. She smiled slyly at him.

Three more familiar forms joined her: the other thieves who had stolen from them and nearly killed them in Blöde.

"Should be more than enough treasure to feed and house an army of your Knights, Commander," said Satin. "For a long while."

The commander nodded. "My thanks, lady, for telling us where to find these thieves. The reward for Dhamon Grimwulf is substantial."

Satin chuckled. "I'll just take this if you've no objection," she said, fishing about in a small bag on the wagon and tugging free a handful of baubles, including the necklace made of black pearls and volcanic glass beads. "More than enough." She waved to the other women. "C'mon girls. We can settle down with this."

Rikali was unceremoniously shoved onto the wagon bench, a Knight pressing a dagger to her side to make sure Dhamon and Maldred, who were relegated to the back of the wagon, caused no trouble. Varek was stretched out between the two men.

The commander waved a sheet of parchment. It was a wanted poster, like the ones tacked on the wall in Graelor's End.

"It's about time someone caught you," he said. "Well past time you paid for your crimes."

Chapter Eighteen
Ropes and Good-byes

D hamon had the largest cell to himself. Despite the thickness of the iron bars, the newness of lock, despite a guard with a drawn sword stationed only a few feet away in the hall, the Legion of Steel Knights had seen the need to put him in heavy chains. They took no chances. His cell was clean and tidy, not what he'd expect of a prison. There was a flask of water and a bowl filled with spiced oatmeal on the floor, and there were heavy blankets on a cot that had been neatly made, but there was a thin film of dust on the top blanket and on practically everything else. Dhamon decided the jail wasn't used often. Perhaps Wheatland was a law-abiding place.

There were four other cells in the jail, three of these occupied by his companions. Maldred, in chains modified to fit his larger wrists and ankles, lay in a heap on the floor with what had once passed for a cot crushed beneath him. He was sound asleep, drugged by some vile concoction the Knights forced down his throat before carrying him

257

into his cell. The sivak in the cell across from Maldred's was likewise drugged, though unchained, only because the blacksmith had not yet finished making large enough manacles. They would be coming soon, Dhamon had heard the guard say.

"Dhamon, what're they gonna do to us?"

He made no reply.

"Dhamon, I'm talkin' to you!" Rikali was in the cell directly opposite Dhamon's. The half-elf sat on the cot, leg tucked up under her awkwardly because of her ankle chains—they'd not chained her wrists—with Varek's head cradled in her lap. She was stroking his sweat-slicked brow and fussing over him.

Varek's stump had been freshly bandaged by the Knights. Dhamon had cauterized the wound well, but he knew Varek was feverish and still in the throes of shock from having half his leg removed.

"Keep him warm, Riki," Dhamon told her. "Use the blanket under you. Can you reach into Ragh's cell and get that one, too?"

The half-elf eased herself out from under her young husband and wrapped first one blanket around him, then the other. When she was finished, she grabbed the bars and glared at Dhamon.

"What're they gonna do to us?" she repeated.

"Hang us probably," came Dhamon's cold reply. He turned away from her and went to the back of his small cell, chains clanking and stirring the dirt on the floor. There was a window high on the wall, and Dhamon managed to pull himself up by the bars to look out. The window was too small to fit through. He had already considered that, but it afforded him a view. There was a massive oak with thick, wide limbs. A platform was being erected beneath the biggest branch.

"Yeah, they're going to hang us, Riki."

"Don't we get us a trial, Dhamon?" Her voice wavered with fear. "Knights are supposed to be fair and chivalrous and all."

He gave her a curt laugh and watched the Legion Knights hammer away. "Would a trial help? We did steal from the Knights in the Khur hospital, after all."

"*You* stole!" she said. "You're the one who had to steal from the hospital, Dhamon Grimwulf. I didn't steal from that hospital. I probably didn't even get my fair share."

"We fought our way out of town . . . ."

"So a few Knights got hurt," she said. "Hurt. We was defending ourselves."

"A few might have been killed, Riki," Dhamon admitted.

"Self-defense, I say."

He shrugged. "We burned down most of the town."

"An accident. Fetch started the fire when we was all tryin' to escape."

Dhamon gave another laugh. "Fetch is dead, so he can't take responsibility for it, now, can he? Besides, I doubt the Legion of Steel would believe a kobold." He heard her shuffle away to settle on the edge of the cot.

"I'm too young to die, Dhamon Grimwulf," she said in a hushed voice.

"Everybody dies, Riki."

"Everybody lies," she shot back. "You and Mal lied to me, damn you. Made me think Mal was my friend, was a man and not some . . . some blue-skinned monster."

"An ogre."

"Monster." She let out a breath, the air whistling between her teeth, stirring the curls that fell across her forehead. "You lied to me, lettin' me think you loved me."

"Maybe that wasn't a complete lie," he said so softly she barely heard him.

"You left me all alone in Blöten, no intention of ever comin' back for me. All of them ugly ogres everywhere.

259

An' that's not the worst of it, Dhamon. Look at what happened to my Varek—an' all 'cause he followed you into that cavern."

She wiped the sweat away from Varek's face and smooth the strands of hair away from his eyes. "And now we're all gonna hang. 'Cause of you."

It was an hour or longer before Dhamon heard the front door to the jail open and heavy footsteps clomp toward the cells. The approaching Legion of Steel Knight was rumpled, dirt staining his tabard and streaking his face.

"Commander Lawlor has just returned to town," the Knight announced.

The Knights who carted Dhamon and the others to this jail had been surprised to find Lawlor and several of his men missing from Wheatland. They were out on patrol, someone had mentioned, trying to track down a lead on fleeing Sylvanesti elves.

"He will pass sentence on the sorry lot of you soon," the Knight added, pivoting on his dirt-caked leather heels and striding from the prison.

"We're all going to hang," Dhamon said.

It was nearly sunset before Lawlor visited the jail, after first inspecting the gallows, which seemed to be finished to his satisfaction. Dhamon watched him and his men from the window in the cell.

"Dhamon Grimwulf," Commander Lawlor said, stroking his mustache and slowly studying Dhamon from head to toe. Lawlor was holding one of the wanted posters that bore Dhamon's likeness.

Dhamon glowered at him.

"You must die," the commander said calmly. "Before morning, for all your crimes against my Knighthood."

"All of us?" This came quietly from the half-elf.

"I only have a notice on Mister Grimwulf," the commander replied, not taking his eyes from Dhamon's, "but I understand you are all his followers." He waved Maldred's poster in front of Dhamon. "Where is this man, your confederate?"

Dhamon shrugged. "I haven't seen him for quite some time."

Lawlor interrogated him about the hospital robbery and the burning of the Khur town, about a variety of thefts in which he had been—falsely—implicated. Lawlor asked repeatedly concerning the whereabouts of Maldred. Finally he tossed Dhamon the wanted posters and turned to Varek. The young man was sitting up on the cot, Rikali at his side, holding his hand. The half-elf was gazing intently at something on the floor, not raising her eyes to meet the Knight Commander's.

"Varek."

"Yes, sir."

"I'm not sure how a respectable young man like you fell in with this pack of thieves."

Varek made a move to answer, but Lawlor cut him off with a wave of his hand.

"I'm not sure that I want to know." Lawlor moved closer to the cell door. "Varek, your father and I are good friends, and it would crush him to know about the company you've been keeping. Give me some additional information about this group, some evidence that I can use against Dhamon Grimwulf, some idea of where I can find this other man, and I'll let you go. You need healing, young man, and if you cooperate I will gladly let you go."

Varek shook his head.

"I don't think you understand, son. Though I won't see you hanged, I'll see you languish in jail—just for consorting with this man. Give me some evidence."

261

Varek's lips formed a defiant line.

"Loyal, like your father."

Varek remained silent for a moment, squeezing Riki's hand.

"Everything will be all right," he whispered to her. We won't be hung. We won't even be kept in jail for very long—especially not with you being pregnant."

"But I'm not so loyal," she said gently, edging away from Varek and raising her face, shuffling forward, close to Commander Lawlor. "I've no reason to be loyal any longer to Dhamon Grimwulf. I'll give you whatever evidence you want against him. Things nobody but me knows."

"Riki, no!" Varek practically shouted. He tried to stand, but only toppled facedown onto the dirt-covered floor. "You don't have to say anything on my behalf." Varek squirmed over to the cot and began to pull himself up. "Please Riki. We'll get out of this somehow. My father has influence."

"I'll tell you about every robbery Dhamon Grimwulf's ever done, every man I've seen him kill. Every little dark secret in his hard dark heart. I'll tell you all about Maldred, too, the man on that other poster you had." Her fingers moved in the direction of the second parchment on the floor. "See that blue-skinned monster over there? Believe it or not, that's Maldred."

"Riki . . ." Varek was still pleading.

"He's an ogre mage, able to use magic to make himself look like a big handsome man. Probably likes bein' a human better'n his ugly, monstrous self."

Lawlor smiled grimly as Rikali prattled on, as Varek's protests finally died, as Dhamon stared in disbelief.

"An' that beastie," she concluded, nodding her head toward Ragh, who was clearly unconscious. "He's the only one who ain't done nothin' wrong. Sure he's a beastie, but he don't deserve to be hanged. Not like Dhamon an' Maldred."

Lawlor glanced at the draconian. "If the creature comes to, we'll question him. I cannot let him go, though. He's a draconian. My men will make quick, merciful work of him."

Riki returned to Varek's side with a defiant expression. "Varek and me are married, Commander Lawlor, an' we're gonna have us a baby." She smoothed the tunic over her stomach. "An' I don't want my baby born in no jail."

"He won't be," Lawlor reassured her.

"And I don't want my husband spending any more time in this awful, awful place."

"The two of you will be released immediately." He spun about and took a few steps, stopping abruptly and looking back to catch Varek's gaze. "You've a good woman, son. Take care of her. I'll arrange for a wagon and a horse. And I'll leave you with some small bit of the treasure we confiscated to help you on your way. A sack of coins—" he paused—"and a peg leg or two." The commander gestured at Varek's stump. "You'll be able to use them when the swelling goes down. I trust you'll use the wagon to take yourself and your, er, wife back to your father's estate."

Silence filled the jail after the last of Commander Lawlor's footfalls faded.

Varek and Riki left without another word. For a long, long time Dhamon continued to stare at their empty cell.

"At least she's safe and away from here." This came from Maldred, who'd managed to shake off enough of the drug so he could stand up and lean against the bars. He tried to budge them. "These could hold an elephant."

Dhamon shook his head.

"You wouldn't have wanted her to die with us, would you?" Maldred said. He kept his eyes closed.

263

"No, I wouldn't have wanted that."

"With luck, we won't die either." Maldred eased himself down on the floor again, shoulder leaning against the bars, fingers splayed in the dirt.

"You've got some magic left?"

Maldred looked up to be sure there wasn't a guard within sight. "A little, I think. I felt it returning before they made me drink that . . . concoction." He closed his eyes and bent his head forward, his mane of white hair falling across his face. Then he softly hummed.

Long minutes later, the manacles fell from Maldred's wrists and ankles, too large for his human body. Maldred moved the chains away and rubbed at his ankles. Then he took a deep breath and returned his hands to the floor. He dug his fingertips into the earth and began chanting.

Maldred had managed to create a hole almost big enough for him to squeeze through when Commander Lawlor returned with a quartet of Legion Knights.

"Time to die," Lawlor announced, his eyes gleaming with pleasure when he saw that Maldred had shed his ogre-form.

Dhamon and Maldred were roughly ushered from their cells and down the hall, out to where a small crowd of Knights and townsfolk had gathered around the gallows.

Back in the jail, Ragh finally groaned and opened his eyes, looking around to wonder where Maldred and Dhamon were.

"Dhamon Grimwulf," Commander Lawlor began. "You have been sentenced to die for the burning of an entire town, for theft and mayhem in a hospital, for crimes committed against the Legion of Steel, and for various offenses committed against residents of Khur and no doubt other places."

"May his soul rot in the Abyss!" a townsman cried as Dhamon was ushered up on the platform and the noose fitted around his neck.

"Burn them!" another shouted. "Hanging is too kind for thieves!"

"Maldred the ogre," Lawlor continued, speaking over the jeers of the crowd, "for those crimes which I have listed, you also will share blame and hang."

Suddenly a Legion Knight ran toward the gallows, shouting, trying to force his way through the crowd.

"Wait!" the Knight cried. "Stop!"

The Knight executioner paid no heed. At a nod from Lawlor, he pulled a lever. The floor of the gallows dropped from beneath Maldred's and Dhamon's feet.

In the next instant several things happened.

Maldred released the enchantment that gave him his human form. His larger, and much heavier ogre body, was too much for the rope, and it broke, spilling him to the ground.

Dhamon began to suffocate. He flailed about like a desperate man, then decided that he should accept his fate of execution. It would end his misery from the scale. He relaxed and felt the rope tighten.

The shouting Knight finally made his way through the crowd and jumped on the platform. He raised his sword and sliced at Dhamon's rope. "Stop this!" he yelled in a hoarse voice.

Knight Commander Lawlor had been enjoying the execution and didn't appreciate the interruption. He fumbled angrily at his waist for his sword. He sputtered at the Knight who had released Dhamon and who was now helping him up onto the platform.

"You, stop!" a red-faced Lawlor bellowed. "Insubordination!" He turned to a group of Knights behind him. "Get them! Get all three!"

The men rushed forward, freezing when they heard a shrill scream behind them. Wheeling as one, they saw the thatched roof of the jail burst into flames.

Lawlor directed a few of his men to the jail to put out the fire, while the rest he ordered in pursuit of Maldred and Dhamon and the strange Knight, who were running pell-mell away from the gallows. With a loud roar the gallows burst into flames, forcing the crowd and the Legion Knights back. Another roar and Wheatland's stables also burned merrily.

"Stop them!" Lawlor screamed, as he, too, tried to gave chase.

Maldred chanted as he ran, pulling all the magic from his body he could collect, directing that energy in the form of fire at building after building, burning Wheatland as they had burned the town in Khur some months ago. He chuckled deeply.

"Like old times, my friend," he shouted to Dhamon, who was running next to him.

Dhamon did not reply. In amazement he watched the running Knight at their side transform into the sivak Ragh.

"Just like old times," Maldred repeated.

It was an hour before they could pause to catch their breath, hiding in an earthen cave Maldred had created with his magic. He left an opening so they could watch the dozen Knights searching the area.

Dawn painted the sky pink before Maldred had regained enough strength to cast another spell. "Like the good, old times," he said. He hummed, fingers twirling in the air as he adopted his human guise once again.

"Aye," Dhamon said. "Old times, but not good ones. Running from Legion of Steel Knights."

"Running and thieving." The sivak tossed Dhamon a coin purse that had been on the guard he'd killed, whose form he had assumed. He threw the sword to the ground. "Your lives are . . . interesting," Ragh said.

Dhamon brushed the dirt from his tattered clothes, feeling the scales on his leg. "And hopeless. We've no enchanted map and no chance of finding the healer now."

Maldred stretched and arched his back, turning first one way and then the next. "There's always hope, Dhamon. I swore I'd help you find a cure. You're as dear as any brother, and I won't let you down. We don't need the map any longer. I think I know where we need to go."

He studied the horizon to the east. "I don't think we should risk staying around here. I'll wager they'll be putting up more and bigger posters soon—maybe sending out an army."

Dhamon smiled sadly at that thought.

"Shall we?" Maldred pointed northwest, then struck out in that direction at a brisk pace. He glanced over his shoulder to make sure Dhamon was coming.

"Very interesting," Ragh repeated, following a few yards behind.

Chapter Nineteen
Hidden Strengths

The town that spread out below them was a scabrous ruin. Most of the buildings had collapsed. The few that were relatively intact were stunted stone towers—the sides of which had been blackened as if by some great fire. These were spaced along what passed for the main street. Rocky spires rose amid piles of rubble, like jagged teeth aimed menacingly at the sky. Marble statues looked as though they were broken and melted, more resembling monsters than the men who long ago had been important to this place.

Shapes flew about the spires, and Dhamon realized they were black dragonspawn. A few were perched on the sides of the tallest buildings, while some walked through the littered streets, shoving people out of their way. A streak of silver moved among the highest-flying spawn: a sivak. Dhamon noticed that Ragh watched it with envy.

Tents were scattered in the shadows of the buildings. A row of lean-tos stretched across the western edge of the

269

town. People huddled under them seeking respite from the rain that pounded down on everything.

"If we had the map, we could be sure this was the right town," Dhamon said. He stood on a rise that circled the town, which rested in the middle of a bowl-shaped depression. Cypress trees grew in profusion along the rise and half-way down it, vines and snakes draping thickly from their branches.

Maldred rubbed thoughtfully at his chin. "It's the town, all right. I memorized as much of the magical map as I could. This is the only town it could be."

Dhamon inhaled sharply. "I hope you're right, my friend, but your map implied this healer was in the Plains of Dust. We're clearly back in Sable's swamp."

They stood silent for several minutes, watching the rain beat down, turning the streets into rivers of mud, painting everything ever more dismal looking.

Ragh cleared his throat. "This town was in the Plains of Dust until some time earlier this year."

Dhamon gave the sivak a puzzled stare.

"Sable's swamp has been growing. Common news, I know, but most don't realize just how fast it's growing," the sivak continued. "I believe the dragon will soon claim all of the Plains."

"She did this to the town?" Dhamon asked, gesturing at the rubble.

The sivak shrugged. "Her. Her allies. The swamp. It doesn't matter, does it?"

"No, it doesn't." I just want to be free of the damn scale, then be free of this land, Dhamon told himself. He started down the rise, angling toward the line of tents, intending to talk to the people there. He hadn't taken more than a few dozen steps when the sivak caught up with him, stopping him with a clawed hand on his shoulder.

"What you're looking for, you won't find there," Ragh said.

"I'm just looking for information, to see if anyone here's heard of the healer."

Ragh shook his scaly head. "They're not going to talk to you." He pointed a claw at Dhamon's attire and then at Maldred's. "You look like escaped slaves or deserters from some army. Certainly people to be avoided."

He directed his next words at Dhamon. "You, they might think, are some sort of dragonspawn."

Dhamon still wore the Solamnic tunic. It was muddy, sweat-caked, and ripped in several places. His trousers were torn, revealing the scales on his leg. There were more than three dozen of the smaller scales now, covering his thigh and creeping down his calf.

Though Maldred was still maintaining his human form, his clothes were in tatters, barely hanging on him, and his chest was criss-crossed with welts from a briar bush he'd walked through.

"I don't care what we look like," Maldred said. "We'll make them talk to us."

The sivak made a hoarse sound. "Come with me." Ragh picked his way down the opposite side of the rise.

Dhamon opened his mouth to argue but decided to follow the sivak. Only a few of the people they passed gave them a second look as they edged into the town. Most of the humans who walked about were dressed poorly, though not as raggedly as Dhamon and Maldred. A handful had rusted chains about their ankles, while others carried heavy sacks for spawn that walked in front of them, leading them as though they were pack animals. Most of the people seemed to be laborers. One group worked hard to reinforce what appeared to be the largest still-standing building. A handful of men and women were dressed in clean clothes that were in good repair.

These people gave the workers as well as Dhamon and Maldred a wide birth.

"Information brokers," Ragh said of the better-garbed individuals. "They come here from throughout Sable's realm and the Plains and from as far away as New Ports and Khuri-Khan. They sell news of happenings in Ansalon to the dragon's allies. They are paid very well, depending on the usefulness of their information. Some sell creatures. Sable has quite a menagerie in towns throughout the swamp. She pays small fortunes to those who can bring her unique animals."

"These slaves . . . ?" Dhamon pointed to a trio in chains.

"Some sell people here, but for these she does not pay nearly as much as for information or unusual creatures."

They took what appeared to be the widest, most-traveled street, and as they made their way along it and deeper into the town Dhamon noticed a number of small, one-room buildings constructed of weathered wood planks and draped with lizardskin or oiled-canvas roofs. Ragh stepped toward one, pointing to a crudely painted sign that said it was a tailor's.

"You have coins from the Legion Knights," Ragh stated.

Dhamon felt in his pocket for the coin purse. He squared his shoulders and disappeared through the doorway, Maldred following after and making sure the sivak would guard the entrance.

They emerged from the shop several minutes later, Dhamon dressed in a shadow-gray tunic and black leggings. There was a belt-pouch strapped around his waist, and in this he hid his dozen remaining coins. Maldred wore drab garb as well, a shirt and trousers of faded dirt-brown.

They made another stop, this one at a market run by the only dwarf they'd seen. Dhamon was hungry and tossed the proprietor a few coins for a flask of liquor and three-dozen thick strips of dried boar meat. Some he passed to the sivak. He took a few for himself and gave the rest to Maldred.

"T'ain't seen you here 'fore," the dwarf stated, eyeing Dhamon and Maldred with narrow eyes.

"Because you haven't looked," Dhamon lied. "Though I'll admit I'm not one to frequent this town."

The dwarf stuffed the coins in his pocket and waved a stubby arm at other jars containing more meats and pickled fish. "Interest you in anything else?" the dwarf asked.

Dhamon shook his head.

"I'm interested in old and unusual things," Maldred interjected.

"Lots o' old things 'round here," the dwarf said. He glanced around Dhamon to see the sivak in the doorway, scowling and shaking his head at the creature. "Old creatures, draconians . . ."

"People," Maldred said. "Very old people."

The dwarf stroked his beard.

"Ever hear of a sage," Dhamon asked, "an old woman who—"

The gravelly laugh filled the small shop. "Sage? There's one on every street corner."

Maldred drummed his fingers on the dwarf's counter. "An old woman. Very old. A sorceress and a healer."

"Said to predate the Cataclysm," Dhamon added.

The dwarf's eyes fairly twinkled. "That would be Maab. Mad Maab's what some call her. She used to be a Black Robe sorceress. Before the Chaos War. Before the gods fled. Before the black dragon came and swallowed this town up into the swamp. Some say she was born long before the Cataclysm, but that would be impossible, wouldn't it?"

"You've seen her?" Dhamon couldn't keep his eagerness in check.

273

"No. Never. Though I've friends who claim to have seen her decades back. No one's admitted to seeing her for years."

"Dead?" Dhamon asked.

"Might be dead. Probably is dead. Word was she tried to keep the swamp from takin' this place."

"And . . . ?" Maldred pressed.

"Well, the swamp's all around us, ain't it? This place is all but fallen down."

"Where is her tower?" Maldred's fingers clutched the edge of the countertop, the knuckles turning white. "She was supposed to live in a tower."

"Oh, it's still here, so to speak. A tower with the mouth of a dragon." The dwarf gave them directions.

Dhamon and Maldred hurried down the street, Ragh following them at a respectable distance. They didn't stop until they reached the marketplace. Dozens of sights, sounds, and smells assaulted them—none of them pleasant.

Despite the rain, there was a crowd standing before a series of stone and steel cages that rimmed a bog that likely once had been a park. There were children at the front of the crowd, and they were ooohing and aahing at the creatures inside the cages.

"New acquisitions," Ragh said. "Sable's agents have not yet looked them over. The choicest will be taken directly to the dragon in Shrentak. Others will go to an arena deep in the swamp. A few will be kept on display here for the people to enjoy."

"How . . . ?" Dhamon let the question hang.

"Trappers bring them here. It is a lucrative way to earn a living."

Dhamon stared at some of the better dressed men toward the front of the crowd. They were muscular and armed with swords and spears. He suspected they were the trappers who captured the beasts. One of them was using a spear to poke a mud-brown lizard the size of a cow. It had a dozen legs ending in cloven hooves and a wide body that could easily swallow an alligator. The man was trying to get it to perform for the audience. Finally it began to roar and hiss, sending a gob of spit between the bars and into the face of a wide-eyed girl. She shrieked and scurried away.

Another creature looked like a big, black bear, but its head was that of an eagle, with white and sand-colored feathers that fanned back from a massive beak and fluttered about its broad shoulders. It looked sad, sitting in its cage, staring back at the people. Next to it was a huge owl, a magnificent animal nearly twenty feet from its claws to the top of its head. It was crowded in the cage, not able to stand fully upright, and one of its wings was injured. The feathers were crusted with dried blood. With unblinking eyes it took in the audience.

"A darken owl," the sivak pronounced. "Many years ago I flew with them in the Qualinesti Forest. Keenly intelligent, they are. The men who captured this must have been very skilled. They will be well rewarded by Sable's agents."

The other cages contained even more fantastic beasts. There was a thanoi, a walrus-man from far to the south. He was a stocky brute with long tusks and a mix of thick skin and fur that made him unbearably hot in this climate. A young man near the front was wagering with a girl that the beast was so uncomfortable it would die before nightfall.

There was a bulky, round-shouldered hairy creature that looked like a cross between a man and an ape. It smelled like a mix of dung and rotting wood. Near it were three man-sized frogs that stood on their hind legs and chattered in a strange, throaty language. One balled its fist and shook it at a passing spawn.

Dhamon stopped near an especially large cage, and shouldered his way to the front. The two creatures crammed inside were easily the size of small dragons.

"Manticores," Maldred breathed.

"Aye. I wonder how trappers managed to catch them?"

"It was tough," said a barrel-chested man an arm's length away. "Our gamble nearly cost us our lives." There was considerable pride on his face as he gestured at the manticores. "Me and my mates caught their cubs, probably while they were off hunting. This pair didn't put up much fight when they came back and we threatened to kill the cubs. In the end they practically let us drug 'em with the last of Reng's magic powder."

"Where are the cubs?" Maldred asked.

He shrugged his broad shoulders. "Sold 'em this morning for a very good turn o' coin. Ain't gonna be able to sell these adults for a good price until they heal up some. Time's on our side, though. Word is Sable's agents aren't here right now. We're gonna clean up on these beauties."

The manticores would have been impressive were it not for the great chains around their legs and the myriad of wounds in their sides. Their bodies were that of huge lions, though they were easily the size of bull elephants. From their wide shoulders sprouted massive leathery wings shaped like a bat's. The cage confined them, however, and their wings were crushed against their sides. Foot-long spikes ran in a ridge from their shoulderblades to the tip of their long tails. Most amazing were their heads, vaguely human in shape but with thick manes of hair and wild-looking beards. Their eyes looked overly small for their features and rolled this way and that, staring at the crowd.

The smaller one made a mewling sound. Dhamon met its gaze. The creature repeated the sound, and Dhamon heard the very human word "please" in it.

"I've seen enough," Dhamon said, edging away from the audience and heading along a side street filled with mud puddles. Maldred and the sivak lagged a few yards behind. "I kept company once with a Kagonesti who would have paled at that sight," Dhamon muttered. "She would have vowed to free every one of those creatures and punish the men who collected them. No doubt the black dragon, too."

"Fortunately she is not here with us," the sivak said. "She would die trying."

Dhamon didn't reply.

The dwarf's directions to the old woman's tower yielded nothing. They found a street with tents and poorly built wooden homes. After another hour of searching Dhamon considered giving up, but Maldred was determined to look longer.

The rain had become a drizzle by noon, everything so thoroughly soaked that there was a sameness to each turn of the muddy walkway. Dark, ramshackle buildings sheltered tents on the verge of collapsing from the water. The ways were thronged by downtrodden slaves and optimistic "information brokers."

"Perhaps this is the one." Maldred nodded to one of the more-intact towers around which a trio of sivak draconians and a dozen spawn clustered. But after two hours, there was no sign of any other activity, and not a soul entered the place, and so they moved on.

"This could take days, you realize," Ragh offered. "Weeks. If this healer truly exits."

"No," Dhamon said. "I'm not going to spend that long here. I hate this place."

"Perhaps the healer hated the place, too, and left," Ragh ventured.

By late afternoon the rain had stopped, just about the time they discovered a building that met the dwarf's description of the mad sage's home. It was several streets back from where he said it would be and shielded by piles of rubble heaped up high on either side of it. They were certain they must have passed by it several times earlier. Perhaps they had not noticed it because of the rain and gloom and because it didn't look like a tower.

The structure was, at best, three stories tall. It was blackened like the other structures around it, but in places the trim gleamed silver and bronze. There was a great gaping doorway with stony fingers pointing down from the arch, looking like an open jaws of a massive, toothy beast. It was dark beyond the arched entrance, save for a sporadic flickering of what might have been firelight.

"Perhaps this is the one," the sivak tried. "The dwarf said it had the mouth of a dragon."

"Perhaps it is." Dhamon and Maldred stepped into the shadows of a spire across the street. Maldred yawned, and Dhamon noticed the ash-gray circles beneath his eyes.

"You're tired."

"Very." The big man yawned wider. He glanced down the street to his right at what was obviously an inn. A large wagon pulled by a pair of sorry-looking and over-taxed mules was out in front, and huge barrels were being unloaded from the wagon. The man who had driven it up was trying to repair a wheel that was cracking. Maldred watched him.

"I really don't want to spend the night in this town, Dhamon. I don't think I would get any sleep. But we could get a room there. Better than being out on the street in this gods-forsaken hole, I suspect. Or better than curling up in a tree in the swamp. Sun's setting, and . . ."

278

"We've stayed in worse," Dhamon agreed, looking at the ramshackle inn, then at the tower. "This healer, if she's alive, might not see me this late."

"I suppose, but . . . hey!" Maldred was out of the shadows in an instant and starting toward the wagon.

With a loud crack, one of the rear wheels had fallen off, tipping the wagon and spilling a few of the barrels. The man who'd been unloading them was trapped beneath three of the barrels, and his partner who'd been attempting to fix the wheel was pinned under the wagon.

A few passersby were watching, but only one of them attempted to help. This was an old fellow who couldn't budge even one of the big barrels. The man beneath the barrels groaned loudly for help, while his partner pinned beneath the wagon offered only a whimper.

The moment he reached the wagon, Maldred put his back to the task, straining his muscles in an attempt to lift it. Too many barrels remained on the wagonbed, weighing it down.

"We'll have to offload some of these barrels first," he grunted to Dhamon, who had materialized at his side. "We'll have to lighten the load before we can hope to lift the wagon. The barrels must be filled with bricks."

Maldred turned to help the man caught under the barrels and picked up the first one. "This feels like a ton of bricks," he said, as he moved it aside and reached for the second.

Dhamon was already working on the wagon. Bracing his legs, he hooked his fingers under the wood where the broken wheel canted. Looking down at the trapped man, he saw the pain in his eyes and the trickle of blood spilling out of his mouth. "Not good," he muttered. Dhamon took a deep breath and bunched his muscles, bent at the knees and slowly raised the wagon.

"Mal . . . Pull the man out."

Maldred had just taken the last barrel off the man. He set it down and whirled on Dhamon. "By my father," he started, "how could you have . . ."

279

"The man," Dhamon said. "Pull the man out. Please."

Maldred did just that, and the previously-inert citizens fell to helping the two wounded men inside the ramshackle inn. Dhamon set the wagon on the ground, brushed off his hands, and headed back down the street toward the shadows of the spire.

"Wait a minute, Dhamon." Maldred followed him, and despite his longer strides was not quite able to keep up.

Dhamon walked faster, ignoring Maldred. He was surprised to find the sivak still in the shadows across from the old sage's tower. The wingless draconian could have taken the opportunity to part company with them.

"What?" Dhamon turned to his large friend.

"Dhamon, how did you do that? Lift the wagon?" Maldred's eyes were daggers. "I couldn't lift the wagon and I'm an—"

"Ogre," Dhamon finished. His face showed anger, though it wasn't directed at his friend. "I don't know. I don't know how I did it. I don't know how I'm able to do a lot of things—run for hours without getting tired, sleep little and hear so well. I don't know."

"In that village, Polagnar," Maldred cut in, "you stopped me from killing the sivak. With one hand you stopped my blow. That's been bothering me. In the caverns with the ships, when the rocks held my legs. I should've known something was wrong, when you so easily moved those rocks."

"I wasn't as strong then as I am now." Dhamon could have added that he didn't like feeling this strong, didn't like it one bit. "I think it's the scale."

"Scale? Scales, Dhamon. Spreading like a rash on your leg. You kept that and your strength from me."

"You made me believe you were human. Everyone has secrets, Mal."

"It might not be the scale," Maldred offered. "Maybe it's—"

"I know of no other explanation."

There were several minutes of silence as the threesome stood in the growing shadow of the spire and watched the doorway across the street.

"No. I suppose you're right," Maldred said after a time. "I suppose it would be the scale." The big man let out a deep breath, and his shoulders slumped. "We'd better hope that sage is alive and in there," he said, "before you burn out like candle."

"Aye, I hope she is in there, but I want to watch the place a bit longer first. We've seen no movement yet."

They watched the building for another hour, until twilight overtook the town. Just as Dhamon decided to approach it, two spawn flanking a draconian came out. Three human slaves shuffled behind them, dragging bloodied canvas sacks that from the shape of them probably contained bodies. The draconian was a bozak, birthed from the corrupted egg of a bronze dragon. The creature wasn't quite as tall as Dhamon, but it was much broader in the chest and wore a mix of boiled leather armor and chain. Its wings were folded tight against its back, and in its hands was a wickedly barbed spear festooned with black ribbons.

Ragh grumbled a word that Dhamon couldn't make out. "One of Sable's agents," he whispered. "I remember him from my time with the dragon."

"And the spawn? Are they familiar, too?"

The sivak shook its head. "I refuse to pay attention to their kind. They are not worthy of my interest."

"If this sage exists. If she's alive," Dhamon said, "she might be allied with the dragon, too."

Maldred shifted back and forth on the balls of his feet and yawned again. "All right, Dhamon. I'm going to get us a room at that inn." He gestured down the street. A quartet of burly men were working on the wagon that was still out front. Someone had taken the two mules away. "Then I'm going back to the marketplace and visit a tavern or two." He looked at the sivak. "Dhamon, keep Ragh with you. When you're done here—whether or not you decide to approach this sage tonight—meet me later at the inn."

"Aye," Dhamon acknowledged, not taking his eyes off the old building's front door.

He and Ragh waited across the street for nearly another hour, watching only three more spawn leave the building in that time. The flickering started again.

They finished the rest of the dried boar. Dhamon washed it down with some liquor, which he did not share. He was finally ready to head toward the building, despite the number of people strolling nearby—apparently headed toward a tavern at the end of the street—when a sound drew his attention.

A trio of ragged young boys were running south, mindless of the dark and the puddles, shouting. Others were moving in that direction, too, and within minutes the street was cleared.

"Now," Dhamon said. He strode purposefully toward the building, eyes trained on the entrance and picking through the darkness. The flickering was a torch well back from the doorway. The air was fusty under the arch, smelling of dampness and of the rancid fat the torch had been liberally soaked in. There was no door, just steps that led up and inside the place. Dhamon took them two at a time. Within moments he was standing in a spacious, round alcove.

The walls here were black, too, though not because of a fire. They were covered with mosaics made of onyx and chert chips, and, looking close, Dhamon could make out the images of men in slate-colored robes.

"A place of Black Robe sorcerers," he whispered, pointing at the figures. "Look here." His finger reached higher along the wall to an orb made of black pearl chips. "Nuitari. Their moon of magic."

The sivak watched out of politeness. The mosaic meant nothing to him. He glanced away toward where a stairway led down off the circular alcove. Nearby was a hallway. Ragh waited patiently until Dhamon was done studying the wall.

Then Dhamon pointed to the alcove floor. It, too, was covered with mosaics and made in the image of Nuitari. He saw the stairs that led down, but he looked to the hallway and took it instead.

The hallway was curving and rounded. "Like the inside of a snake," he whispered. He was struck with the thought that the building was swallowing him and the sivak. He shuddered and turned back, deciding to take the stairs down, instead.

"What . . . ?"

Beyond the stairs in the opposite direction was a hallway he hadn't noticed before. "That wasn't there a moment ago," he said. It, too, was rounded and curved. "Let's go down," he told Ragh.

The stairs were made of slate, smooth and concave from the number of feet that had traveled them and worn them down through the decades. Dhamon moved quietly and gracefully, fingers flitting to the pommel of the Solamnic long sword from time to time.

He listened intently. From below was the sound of dripping water from today's constant rains. From deeper still was the whisper of feet against stone, and voices, one human-sounding, the other sibilant. The voices were growing steadily. Two individuals were coming up the stairs.

Dhamon leaned against the stairwell wall. The sivak copied him, head cocking and obviously hearing what Dhamon had picked up. A few heartbeats later a well-dressed half-elven male appeared, long blue cloak sweeping on the steps behind him. A spawn trundled after him, hissing that the elf would have to come back tomorrow to be paid.

"Who are you?" the half-elf paused and sniffed, wrinkling his nose at Dhamon and the sivak.

"We are none of your concern," Ragh returned.

"You're missing your wings," the half-elf purred. He glanced at Dhamon. "And you are missing your manners. I asked your names."

"None of your concern," Dhamon parroted. He'd begun to sweat, though not from nerves. He was feeling the heat of the scale on his leg, catching images of black scales and yellow eyes from the spawn and feeling the familiar uncomfortable warmth pulsing through his body. He knew the intense cold would start soon and incapacitate him.

"What is your business here?" the spawn asked.

"We bring information," the sivak quickly said.

The spawn prodded the half-elf up the steps. "Thissss information," the spawn prompted. "You can tell it to me. I will sssee that it gets delivered and that you get paid—if it is worth it. Tomorrow you will get paid."

Dhamon shook his head. The fingers of his left hand found a niche in the wall to grab onto. His right hand squeezed the pommel of the sword, as if those gestures might help diminish the pain. "This is important information. Too important to give to you."

The spawn shoved the half-elf along now, growling at him. "I am listening, human. Tell me thisss information. Mistressss Sable's agent is not here. Nura Bint-Drax will not be here until tomorrow or the day after that. It is she who will pay you."

Dhamon shuddered at the name, recalling the naga from the spawn village. "Nura Bint-Drax . . ."

". . . is Sable'sss chief agent here," the spawn finished.

"Our information can't wait," Dhamon began, thinking quickly. "We know of a scheme . . ." He gulped in air, feeling an icy jolt shoot through him. It was followed by intense heat, as if he'd been branded. He forced himself to concentrate.

The spawn tapped its clawed foot against the stairwell. "Give me thisss important information."

"That is not for your ears," Ragh cut in.

The spawn hissed, acid pooling over its lip and trailing down to strike the step. It moved close to the sivak. "I decide what isss for my ears. I—"

Dhamon stepped back just in time to avoid the cloud of acid that showered the stairway and the sivak. He'd skewered the spawn in the back with the Solamnic long sword, instantly slaying it. "There are more of them," he gasped, nodding down the stairwell. "Spawn or draconians. I hear them hissing." He sagged uselessly on the steps, still holding onto his weapon.

Ragh was hurt from the acid, especially where it struck the area along his neck where the scales had worn away. Despite the pain, he rushed by Dhamon, claws reaching into the darkness beyond to meet spawn flesh. Dhamon heard another splash of acid, signifying the death of another of Sable's minions, then felt the sword tugged from his fingers. Ragh had taken it and was using it against another advancing spawn.

Chapter Twenty
Reflections of Madness

Black scales formed a curtain so wide Dhamon couldn't see around it. After a few moments, there was a break in the darkness—immense yellow eyes that glowed dully, cut by black-slitted pupils that stared straight ahead.

The eyes closed and there was only the black wall of scales again.

Dhamon shook his head, banishing the dream and waking in darkness with a pounding head. He leaned against a paneled wall covered with mildew. The air was still and musty, carrying with it the strong scent of decay and a softer odor hinting of a blacksmith's shop. The sivak was nearby.

After a few moments his keen eyes perceived shades of black and gray, and something paler that was evidently giving off heat.

"Ragh?" he whispered. He could hear the draconian breathing. Concentrating, he swore he could also hear its heartbeat, much slower than a human's. "Ragh."

The draconian made a sound.

Dhamon brushed his sweat-damp hair away from his eyes and pressed his ear against the wall. There were at least two spawn talking beyond the wall, arguing softly in their odd, sibilant language, which featured a smattering of human words. It seemed they were discussing something about an elven trapper who had caught a most unusual lizard. They talked for several minutes, then moved away. Dhamon reached a hand to his waist, discovering that the sivak had returned his sword.

Dhamon's legs were cramped, and he tried to straighten them but only managed to kick the sivak. He had little room to move. "Where are we?" he whispered.

"A house box," Ragh returned.

"A what?"

"A house box." The draconian paused. "I believe you humans call it a . . . closet."

Wonderful, Dhamon thought.

"After I killed the spawn, I had to find some spot to put you, somewhere that spawn or draconians wouldn't think to go. You were . . ." the sivak searched for the words.

"Unconscious. Delirious. I know." Dhamon almost thanked Ragh, but caught himself. He could not bring himself to acknowledge that he owed the draconian anything. Again he wondered why the sivak hadn't left him or turned him over to some authority in this place. He knew if Ragh hadn't found somewhere to hide him, he would probably have been discovered and captured, possibly killed. He made a move to stand, bumping his head on a shelf, softly swearing. There were garments hanging in here, rotting ones that felt small, as if they belonged to an elf or to a child.

"This isn't the home of a healer or sage," Dhamon said, careful to keep his voice to a whisper. "Maybe at one time, but not now. Let's go find Maldred."

Finally he maneuvered himself around until he was standing straight and feeling about for a latch. Pressing his ear to the door to make sure no creatures were beyond, and keeping his hand on the pommel of the long sword, he eased outside.

The sivak followed him into a narrow, torch-lit, curving hallway. Dhamon caught himself staring at Ragh. The draconian wore the form of a spawn, black as pitch, with wings that swept gracefully down to the back of his thighs. There was no trace of the scars that had riddled his silver body.

"I forgot," Dhamon said quietly, "that you take on the form of what you kill."

"Can take on the form," the draconian corrected. "If I choose too." He pointed to his right, where the hallway curved and the torchlight barely reached. "There is another staircase," he indicated. "It goes up and smells unused. There are several other halls and rooms here, two smelling of recent death. I was about to leave you in the closet to investigate, but more spawn came along, and I decided to avoid them."

"And I woke up." Dhamon looked down the hallway in the other direction. "Do you know how to get out of here?"

A nod.

"Let's . . ." He stared past the sivak. The hair prickled at the back of his neck. "Let's investigate just a bit more." He found himself thinking of Palin Majere. It was many long months since the two of them had worked against the great dragons. He remembered that Palin favored the higher levels of the Tower of Wayreth.

"Sorcerers build towers, I think, because they put themselves above the common man. They look down on the world from the top. The sage was a Black Robe sorcerer, so she might be found as high as she could climb."

289

Dhamon hurried toward the staircase, Ragh following him, quietly objecting. "You said the healer could not possibly be here."

The stairs were confining, the slate steps worn. Dhamon had to tuck his shoulders in and put his head down to make his way up them. Ragh had much more difficulty, with his nine-foot frame. He scraped his scaly skin against the stone and left a stripe of blood on each side of the stairwell.

The steps wound upwards for more than thirty feet, emerging onto to a small landing made of chips of volcanic glass, and branching into an equally narrow corridor with a high ceiling. Straight ahead was a thin wooden door, its black paint chipped and faded.

"At least we will not have to worry about spawn up here," Ragh said. His shoulders were bleeding from rubbing against the stone. "The stairwell was made for imps and faeries."

"And sorcerers," Dhamon said. Sorcerers tended to be on the slight side, he thought with grim amusement.

The sivak stared down both directions of the hallway, which, though high-ceilinged, was practically as narrow as the stairwell. "Smells like nothing has been up here for years. Maybe a child could traverse these halls."

Dhamon shut out the sivak's comments and strained his ears, listening. The only sound he heard was a steady drip-drip, this coming from where the roof was leaking. Water had pooled on the floor, making it look even more shiny, a black mirror in which he could see his haggard reflection.

There were no torches, yet there was light. Dhamon noticed a trio of thick black candles set in a sconce several yards down on the wall on either side. The wicks burned steadily, yet there was no smoke and no trace of wax running.

"Magic," he said in a hushed voice.

There were no windows, nor had he noted any when he viewed the building from the outside, but the air here smelled fresh, it must be flowing in from somewhere. He glanced up at the ceiling and guessed it to be twenty feet high. There were marks in the center of the ceiling, perhaps what was left of a painting or mosaic. Dhamon could make out a few images of men in dark robes, but the paint was so faded he could not tell what the figures were supposed to be doing.

"What do we want with this place?" the sivak asked. "Your healer can't be—"

"I don't know what I want," Dhamon told him. "We're here, so we'll look around. I've a feeling there's something to this place." He drew his sword as a precaution and headed down the hall to his right. The sivak pressed itself against the wall as Dhamon squeezed past.

Dhamon passed by a narrow wooden door and continued to follow the hallway. He passed two more doors, both oddly narrow, both dangling from their rusted hinges. He swore he'd seen the end of the hallway from the landing, but when he reached that spot, the hall snaked abruptly to his left and turned sharply again as if doubling back on itself.

Finally Dhamon came to an impressive bronze and ebonwood door, the trim of which gleamed in the light of more black candles. He reached for the latch but stopped himself, turning and sidling toward a narrow door with cracked paint that looked like patches of black scales.

"Someone is in here," he whispered. "I can smell them."

Dhamon reached for the latch, his fingers trembling slightly. Nerves. Behind him, Ragh flexed his claws. The two stood for several moments, both of them listening and hearing only the sounds of each other breathing.

After several moments, Dhamon tightened his hand on the latch and swung it open. He raised the long sword high and was greeted with a blackness as intense as a starless sky. Even his acute vision could discern nothing. He heard Ragh back away, spawn claws clicking softly against the floor. A moment later the sivak returned with one of the candles and passed it to Dhamon.

It cut the darkness only a little. Dhamon stepped inside. The sivak stood in the doorway, alternately glancing down the hall and into the room.

It felt colder than in the hall, and the air was fresher still, carrying with it the scent of spring wildflowers. There were other odors, too, a mustiness of old clothes, human waste, and the unmistakable smell of strong spirits. Dhamon sniffed. Animals too? Mice or rats, he decided.

"Do not be shy, young man. Come in. Come in. My sister and I have not had visitors in quite some time. Certainly not since . . . was it yesterday?"

The voice startled Dhamon. It was velvety and rich, as though the speaker was exotic or a little inebriated, or perhaps both.

"Who are you?" Dhamon ventured. He wanted to add and what and where are you?

"Not your enemy."

Dhamon sheathed the sword. At the same time he took a few steps forward. "I can't see . . ." he began.

He heard flint struck. A moment later an oil lamp glowed on a small pedestal and chased away the shadows.

"Is that better?"

Dhamon nodded.

The woman was tiny, a wizened old thing with rounded shoulders, head thrust forward, looking like a turtle because of the moth-eaten cloak that swelled away from her back. She was seated on a wooden stool, which made her look smaller still. Diminutive slippered feet hung several inches above the floor. Dhamon guessed she was little more than four feet tall. The myriad of deep creases across her face suggested great age. Her ice-blue eyes hinted she might be even older.

The room seemed large because of its sparse furnishings. There was a bed with several chamber pots beneath it, the pedestal with the lamp at her side, a bench that contained a half dozen jugs of the alcohol Dhamon smelled, and a large cage full of mice. The walls were covered with mosaics made of black and gray stone, except for one spot where a thin beveled mirror hung, reflecting the old woman.

Dhamon tried to blow out his candle, but the light refused to even flicker. The woman cackled and gestured with her fingers to douse it.

"My sister and I wonder, what brings you to our castle? The servants didn't announce you. Perhaps it is late, and they are in bed. Or perhaps they are lazy, and we will need to replace them. Again." She glanced at the mirror and nodded. "What's that you say, sister? Oh, sorry. She tells me I have forgotten my manners."

The old woman extended a crooked hand to Dhamon. It was skeletal, skin stretched tight over bones, so pale and thin that the blue veins stood out beneath it. The joints were knobby, especially at her wrist. He spotted a curving black tattoo beginning just past her wrist and extending up her sleeve, but he couldn't see enough of it to deter-mine what it was. This close to her, he could smell the alcohol heavy on her breath. Her hand was cold, and he held it for only a moment.

"My sister points out that I have been rude again. She is right. She always is. My name is Maab." She added another cackle and a smile, her eyes shining. There were no whites to her eyes, and no pupils that Dhamon could see, just solid ice-blue. She made an attempt to straighten her back.

293

"I am Lady Maab of High Elkhorn, mistress of this castle. And you are . . . ?"

"Dhamon Grimwulf," he answered, bowing his head. "My companion is called Ragh."

"Ragh." The old woman nodded as well and spoke again to her reflection in the mirror. "No, sister, I didn't know those spawn creatures had names either."

She looked back at Dhamon. "You make sure your beast stays outside. I've never cared for those sorts of things— smelly and boorish they are. If it comes in, I will be forced to slay it."

The sivak held his place in the doorway, looking between Dhamon and the woman, then glancing down the hall to make sure no one was coming. He tapped his foot, showing Dhamon he was perturbed and didn't want to linger here.

Dhamon stared at the old woman, wanting to ask her a dozen questions. Maab. That was the name the dwarf shopkeep gave to the sage. He looked past her to the mosaics. Perhaps some of his answers were on the walls.

"My sister wonders if you are thirsty? Our servants brought us some jugs of ale last week." Maab gestured to the bench. Dhamon sniffed at each container.

"Ale," he said, "and bitter rum. That's all they bring you?"

"We ask for water and wine, but it seems they cannot find any. We make our own water from time to time, causing it to rain in the town so the leaky ceiling will bring some in here. But it also makes the floor slippery, and I am afraid I will fall. Hungry?" She gestured to the cage filled with mice. "My sister and I have plenty to share."

Dhamon gritted his teeth. "Your servants bring you mice to eat and spirits to drink?"

294

She nodded, softly sighing. "We are not very satisfied with our help. We slay some of them from time to time, but the ones who eventually replace them are just as bad, if not worse."

"Your servants. Are they humans?"

"Mmmm."

Dhamon took that as a yes.

"They did not come to attend me for quite a while this summer," she added. "We think they got angry at my sister and me and were trying to starve us so they could inherit this castle and our fortune. We think they were trying to kill us."

"Kill you?" This sarcastic jab came from the sivak. "Why would they want to inherit this place?"

Maab scowled. "Oh, we did not let them starve us. We cast a spell, a nasty one, that turned the air beyond this room most foul and unpalatable. We were fed shortly after that." A pause, and then she added, "Fed by the ones left alive."

Dhamon swallowed hard.   "You are a sorceress?" he asked hesitantly.

She cackled madly. "My sister and I are most powerful ones," she returned.

"Of the Black Robes."

"Of course." She smiled slyly, revealing a row of broken, yellowed teeth. Some were missing on the bottom. "We are, perhaps, the most powerful Black Robe sorceresses remaining on this desperate world. The most powerful sorceresses of any color."

Dhamon looked at the mirror, then at the woman. "Your sister . . ."

"Her name is Maab, too. She doesn't speak."

"She's probably as mad as you," Dhamon muttered to himself.

"My sister? Ha! No, she's not mad. She's never been angry a day in her life."

"Are you . . . a healer?"

"I used to be." With some effort she got off the stool and brushed by Dhamon, careful to stay within sight of her reflection in the mirror. She reached for one of the jugs, uncorked it, and took a sip. She offered it to him, but he declined. Though he was certain strong drink would sit well with him right now, he didn't trust what was in the jug.

"Why, you need healing?"

"I . . ." Dhamon looked at her as he searched for the right words. "What I need is . . ."

"Help obviously," she finished, "else you wouldn't have found your way into our castle." She returned to the stool, huffing and wheezing and managing to climb atop it. "What is it Maab and her sister can do for you? Have you a palsy or a curse? A gaping wound we can't see?"

Ragh cleared his throat. "He has a dragon scale affixed to his leg. From an overlord. The thing is poison to him. More are growing."

"And they are slowly killing me."

She wrinkled her nose. "My sister and I do not pay attention to such creatures as dragons. Not any more. They are bad-tempered and irrational. We do not like them." She fixed Dhamon with a baleful stare. "We do not like dragons at all. We never did."

Dhamon clenched his jaw, his breath hissing out between his teeth. "I would pay you," he began.

"Pay me with what? You haven't a coin in your pocket."

"I would find a way to pay you." Dhamon was impressed that she could see past the fabric and leather. Or perhaps she was looking into his mind. He balled his fists in frustration. Physically, the sorceress would be no match for him, but she obviously commanded magic.

"Still," she mused, "although we have no need of money, and we don't need more magical trinkets, a dragon scale on a human is interesting." She closed her eyes in thought for a moment, then opened them. "I think it was days past—or was it decades—my sister and I studied dragons. Never ever liked them, I tell you, but they were worth studying. In fact, studying them consumed us for a while. We thought of nothing else, explored no other magic. Red dragons in particular. In fact we—"

"In fact it is a red dragon's scale." He tugged up the leg of his pants, fingers fumbling excitedly. The smattering of small scales and the bottom of the single large scale showed and gleamed in the lamp light.

"No, no," she clucked. "That is clearly from a black dragon."

Dhamon explained to her about the overlord Malys and how the scale was thrust on him by a Knight of Takhisis, and how, some time after that, a shadow dragon and a silver dragon broke the connection between him and the Red.

"The scale turned black in the process," he said.

"Touched, he is," Maab told her reflection in the mirror. "The young man is mad, I think. Ill in the head. Don't you agree? Color-blind, too." She waited, cocked her head and listened. "Very well. Perhaps we can help him anyway. Just because he was nice enough to come and visit us." She returned her gaze to Dhamon, eyes narrowing. The wrinkles on her face seemed even more pronounced in the uncertain light.

"You might not have a single coin, but there is a price for our magic."

"This is foolishness," the sivak grumbled. "She is the mad one. We should leave here."

"Name it," Dhamon snapped. "Name your price and I'll find a way to pay it."

She twisted her head to look in the mirror again and twirled her fingers. "We will think of something, my sister and I. Something we would like you to get for us. But it will be expensive. Very."

The sivak groaned. "You can't be serious to consider this, Dhamon. She cannot help you. We are wasting our time." Ragh tapped his clawed foot faster. "Besides, Dhamon, I cannot hold . . ."

Dhamon turned, watching with wide eyes as the image of the spawn shimmered. In the passing of a few moments the black spawn guise melted away and the scarred, wing-less draconian stood in its place.

" . . . the form very long."

"So I see."

"Interesting," Maab said. "Keep your odd pet outside my room, please."

"The scale on my leg . . ." Dhamon prompted, returning his attention to the old woman. "I was told if I removed it, I would die."

"Probably," she said, "but it would be another matter entirely if my sister and I were to remove it. We under-stand dragon magic. Of course, we would need my tools. My books. There are some powders that would be handy." She looked at the mirror. "Oh, yes. We would need that, too, dear sister. That precious little trinket Raistlin gave us. When we are done, and he is rid of all those black scales, we will establish a price for our services."

Dhamon looked around the room again. He saw none of the tools she mentioned. "Where are these powders and books?"

With considerable effort she eased herself off the stool again. "Downstairs." She padded toward the doorway, waving a gnarled hand at the sivak, as if dismissing him. "Deep downstairs. My sister knows the way." She turned, not able to see herself in the mirror, looking panicked and clutching her hands to her chest, then shuffled back to where she could see the mirror. She relaxed.

"So sorry. We cannot help you after all, young man. My sister doesn't want to leave our room today. She is not feeling so well. Come back tomorrow and see if she feels better."

Dhamon growled. "You don't have a sister, old woman."

She looked hurt and her shoulders folded inward even more. "You insult us."

"It's a mirror," he said. "It's nothing but a damn mirror, and you're looking at your reflection. You're all alone here. You have no sister." And you are no sorceress or healer and this was all a wasted trip, he added to himself.

She shook her head. "Young man, I feel sorry for you. To have walked so few years on this world and to be plunged so far into madness as you are! How can you enjoy life in your state? Indeed, I believe you have entirely lost your mind." She raised a bony finger and shook it at him. "My sister and I can cure your scale and your insanity—a simple matter for us, though admittedly the madness is a tougher feat to purge. We might not be able to cure you of that."

She crossed her arms, keeping her eyes on her reflection. "But we cannot help you today if my sister refuses to budge from the room. She is quite stubborn. Always has been. Worse now that she is older. Come back tomorrow or the day after. Perhaps she will be persuaded to leave this room then."

Dhamon closed his eyes and let out a deep breath. He took a step toward the mirror and raised his fist to smash it but found he couldn't move.

"Don't you dare threaten my sister," Maab warned. "I would be forced to slay you. That would end your problem with the black dragon scale, wouldn't it?"

His chest felt tight, as if all the air had been sucked from the room. A wave of dizziness struck him like a hammer.

After a moment, he was released from the spell. He dropped his hand to rub at his throat, taking in great gulps of the fetid air.

"There, that's better," she said. "As I said, come back tomorrow, and we'll see if my sister feels like traveling."

"No." Dhamon moved to stand in front of the old woman. "I will not come back tomorrow. I need your help now."

She shook her head. "So sorry."

He felt the air growing thin.

The sivak tapped at the door frame. "We should leave, Dhamon."

What am I doing here? Dhamon thought, feeling dizzy again.

"My sister is not so powerful as I, but she is handy in the laboratory," Maab continued. "I cannot help you without her. Besides, you are rude, and perhaps I should not help at all."

Dhamon ran his fingers through his hair. What if she really is powerful enough to help?

"Let me see if I can get your sister to come along with us. I can be quite persuasive."

He walked to the mirror slowly so Maab wouldn't think him a threat. His fingers quickly worked at the fastenings that held the mirror in place. After a moment, he carefully tugged the mirror off the wall. He held it in front of him so Maab could see her reflection. As she moved toward the door this time, Dhamon walked alongside her.

"Dear sister, too bad this mad young man hasn't come by before to coax you from our room. I would've liked to have taken a stroll before now."

They worked their way back along the twisting corridor, the sivak leading the way and Dhamon, holding the mirror, walking just ahead of Maab.

"I hope this isn't a fine dose of foolishness," Dhamon whispered, grateful that Maab seemed to be hard of hearing. "I hope she really is my cure."

Several minutes later they found themselves at the bottom of the narrow stairway. The draconian's arms and shoulders had fresh wounds from scraping against the walls.

"My sister thinks you should have that looked to," Maab told Ragh. "Not that we would help." She turned up her nose. "We will not treat your kind."

"What I would love is to kill Nura Bint-Drax when she arrives in this town," the sivak hissed.

"We do not like your pet, young man," Maab scolded. "My sister thinks you should keep it outside where it will not soil the floor."

They passed by the closet where Dhamon and the sivak had hid, and Maab insisted on stopping to get a warmer cloak. "It is cold and damp very far downstairs," she said.

Dhamon managed to open the door while still keeping the mirror trained on the old woman. The grumbling sivak pulled down one rotting cloak after the next until Maab was satisfied with one made of black wool.

Dhamon tried to pass the mirror to the draconian, but Ragh, eyes filled with venom, refused to carry it. However, the draconian was quick to tug the long sword from Dhamon's sheeth.

"I know how to use blades well," the sivak stated, "and they have a longer reach than what are left of my claws."

Dhamon returned the draconian's narrow stare, but made no move to protest. He knew he couldn't hold the mirror and the sword.

Again the sivak took the lead, slaying a spawn that was trundling up the stairs and again taking on the sleek black form.

"It is a most amazing pet you have," Maab observed. "Reminds my sister and me of Takhisis's children, the sivak draconians. They are able to do such deadly and wondrous things. They have beautiful forms, and they have beautiful wings and can fly."

The sivak hissed, gesturing down the staircase. "Is this the way to your books, old woman?"

She shook her head, looking at her reflection in the mirror. She shuffled to the wall opposite the stairway. She poked one stone after the next until a section of the wall spun around, revealing a staircase nearly as narrow as the one that had led to her room.

"Too dark," she complained. A twirl of her fingers, however, remedied that. A globe of pale rose-colored light appeared in the palm of her hand.

Dhamon stared. He remembered Palin Majere casting a similar spell when they were in the great blue dragon's desert.

"My sister knows the way better than I. She says follow these stairs to the very bottom."

Ragh paused, rubbing a clawed hand across its chin and looking decidedly unhappy about scraping his shoulders raw again. "Does your sister know anything of Nura Bint-Drax, the naga who is coming here in the next few days?"

Maab shook her head. "Of course not. My sister hates the hideous creatures and pays them no heed."

The sivak sighed and started down the tight stairwell.

"However, I know a little of Nura Bint-Drax and where she travels," Maab added. "While my sister is not so interested in such creatures, I make it my business to know what slithers across every inch of this town."

"Tell me about her," Ragh said, his voice echoing softly. "Where does she travel?"

302 "If you are polite to us. After we are done helping your master."

Dhamon steadied himself against the stairwell, with considerable effort walking sideways, going slowly, matching the old woman's pace, while holding the mirror so she could watch it. He risked a glance down at the sivak, catching a glint of the sword the creature held high.

Chapter Twenty-One
Raistlin's Gift

N ow where do we go, old woman?" The draconian stood at the bottom of the staircase. Three narrow, circular tunnels led away from him. Each was lit by flickering, smokeless torches. They caused shadows to dance so wildly across the stonework that it looked as if the tunnels writhed like serpents.

"Which of these paths do we follow?"

Maab tossed her globe of light into the air and blew it out as one might extinguish a candle. "Oh yes, dear sister. I know it was the dwarves," she stated smugly. "Very able dwarves." Staring at the mirror that Dhamon held, she put her ear a few inches from it. "What's that you say? Yes. Yes. I know that, too. The dwarves built this castle and the rooms beneath it. More below ground than above. Good dwarven masonry. The best we could buy!" She snickered. "Yes, dear sister, I remember that it was your idea. They built these secret tunnels too. These that our new friends see—and more they can't and never will."

"Why?" Dhamon found himself asking.

"Why all the tunnels?" She cocked her head.

Dhamon meant why such an inordinate amount of space. He suspected this place was as large or larger than the Tower of Wayreth, in which Palin Majere sometimes resided. But he nodded yes to her question.

"We wanted the tunnels in the event our enemies came to our castle and took it over. Centuries past . . ."

Centuries! Dhamon thought. Perhaps she was as old as Maldred's tales hinted.

". . . long centuries past, perhaps still today, there are those who hate us Black Robes. Hate us because of our power. It's envy, really. No sorcerers are as powerful as the Black Robes. My sister and I wanted the tunnels so we could move about undiscovered. Watching the trespassers, striking when we wanted. Escaping if we had to. One of the tunnels, I won't tell you which one, extends well beyond this town. Miles."

The sivak let out an exasperated sigh. "Your enemies have taken over your castle, old woman. There are spawn everywhere. Draconians, too. Sometimes the black dragon's agents crawl through this city."

She waggled a bony finger at him, dropping her voice to a whisper. "I know precisely what is in my castle, you insolent creature. I can scry every inch of it when I've a mind to, every inch of this rotting town for that matter. That is exactly my point. Our enemies do not know about all of these tunnels and cannot find us here. No one alive knows about all of these tunnels."

Dhamon chuckled. "Dwarves live a long time, Maab. The ones who built this place might still remember where all the tunnels are. You forget about them."

She gave him a malevolent smile. "Not the ones who built this castle. They didn't live a long time. My dear sister killed every last one of those handy dwarves so they would not tell others the secrets of our home."

"What about us then?" A shiver ran down Dhamon's spine. He started to say something else, but the sivak was faster.

"I am losing my patience," Ragh said. "I want the naga more than Dhamon wants his cure. If the cure you claim you can deliver is not fast in coming, I'll leave the two of you and wait above for her arrival."

"Three of us," Maab huffed. "Testy beast."

"Which way do I go?" Ragh repeated. "Which way to your books and powders and this nonsense of a cure Dhamon is driven to pursue?"

She waggled her finger again. "To the left. Our laboratory is at the very end of the tunnel. Now move, creature. It is damp down here, and that is bad on these old bones. Besides, my sister misses our cozy chamber far above. She is hungry for a plump rat."

The sivak made a grumbling sound, taking the passage Maab had indicated, moving sideways at times when it narrowed. After several hundred yards—well beyond the boundaries of the building above—the tunnel widened, but the ceiling lowered and he had to crouch to keep moving. The air was fresh here, as it had been in Maab's room, and the hint of spring wildflowers was present. Dhamon wondered if the old woman brought the air and the smell with her, not wanting to breathe the stale stuff that would otherwise fill this dank place.

He followed close behind Ragh, mirror tilted for Maab's benefit. He noted that the tunnels were lit by the smokeless torches, which gave off no smell and no indication that the fire was consuming the wood. He moved faster, bumping into Ragh's leathery spawn wings.

"Hurry," he told the draconian. The scale on his leg was warming again, and he knew that soon the painful sensations would become insufferable.

307

Ragh growled and increased his pace, still keeping a grip on Dhamon's sword. "Old woman," he said as he neared the end of the tunnel and passed by a torch that was held in the top of a wolf's snout. "If you and your sister are such powerful sorceresses—"

"We are among the most powerful of the few Black Robes still alive in Ansalon. My sister claims we are the most powerful. She says that not even Dalamar or—"

"Why didn't you simply snap your fingers and banish all of these spawn and draconians from your castle? From this town? Then we wouldn't have to squeeze ourselves through these damn tunnels."

She giggled. "Creature, we are old, my dear sister and I. Wisely, we have no desire to leave our home. These . . . spawn . . . as you call them, give us something interesting to watch. The smallest of them catch juicy mice that our servants bring to us. My sister likes to listen to the screams of the prisoners they sometimes torture in the other chambers beneath our home. The screams are music to her. She especially likes it when the creatures make . . . more spawn . . . of some of the men. The sounds that come to us then are . . ." She paused until she'd decided on the words. "They are unsettling and most pleasant. Interesting."

The sivak sadly shook his head.

"Besides, they have left us alone. I slew the handful who bothered me, and the rest keep their distance."

"This tunnel is a dead end," Ragh snapped. "We will have to turn around and try another way."

"Creature, you are blind."

Maab squeezed by Dhamon, who pivoted so she could still glance into the mirror if she wanted. His fingers clenched the beveled edges, steeling himself against the pain that he was certain would get worse. A stab of icy cold shot upward from the scale and into his chest. It had been a long time since the scale had pained him twice in a single day.

"Why now?" he hissed.

She touched something on the wall and shuffled toward the sivak. Ragh pressed his back against the wall and snarled as she squeezed by. She prodded the stones at the end of the tunnel until she found one that was softer and pressed on it. A thin section of the wall swung open, and she walked through, drawing her moth-eaten cloak tight around her, calling for her sister to come along.

The room beyond was filled with shadows that fled to the far corners when Maab coaxed another ball of light into her palm. The place was cavernous, but so cluttered that it looked cramped. Shelves upon shelves lined every inch of wall. Resting on them were crumbling books, bone tubes that protected scrolls, and stacks of parchment that looked so fragile they would dissolve if they were touched. Skulls, some of them human, served as bookends. The skull of what must have been a large and impressive minotaur rested on a pedestal toward the center of the room.

Preserved animals were posed on other pedestals and scattered on the top shelves. A raven with its decaying wings spread wide stood poised as if to take flight. Lizards, squirrels, and several large rats were caught in time as if they were forever running. A small lynx held a ragged rabbit in its frozen jaws.

Spider webs hung from everything.

The scent of fresh air and wildflowers that seemed to follow the old woman warred with the myriad of odors that lay thick in this room—the rotting animals, mixtures neither Dhamon nor the draconian could put a name too, dried blood, and rotting wood. Moss grew on some of the table legs and on a few of the bookcases. There were patches of slime on the floor, and along a section of the ceiling an ugly gray-green vine tenuously clung.

As the light globe brightened and grew larger, Maab tossed it toward the ceiling, where it hovered and illuminated more of the place. The ceiling, and the patches of the walls that were visible, were filled with the mosaics depicting Black Robe sorcerers in various activities. Directly overhead, a trio of the sorcerers were shown summoning a many-tentacled beast that was partially obscured by the ugly vine.

Tables stood end to end in the middle of the room. Most had beakers and vials and odd-shaped bowls on them, all covered with a thick layer of dust. Others held big jars in which floated brains and various other organs. One held the preserved form of a five-legged piglet, another the head of a young female kender. Beneath some of the tables were large sea chests, blanketed by webs and dust. Shields were propped up against some of the tables. One bore the emblem of the Legion of Steel, two had once belonged to Dark Knights, a fourth had no markings, no trace of dust on it.

"It's been far too long since we've been down here, dear sister," Maab clucked. "I so miss this place and all of our wondrous things. Perhaps it was good you came along after all, Dhamon. Now, about that cure."

She shuffled toward the nearest shelves, so caught up in looking through the books that she did not notice Dhamon was not following her closely with the mirror. She plucked one book after another from the shelves as high as she could reach, returning to a slate-topped table and reverently placing them on it. There were some books she couldn't reach. For these she snapped her bony fingers and beckoned the sivak to retrieve them for her.

"The red one," she told him. "Not that red one. The one with a spine the color of fresh blood. Yes, that's it. The color of a red dragon. The three black ones at the top. Precious books. Mind your claws don't scratch the bindings."

Rolling his eyes, Ragh did as he was bid. A few of the books were bound in what appeared to be dragonhide. One was covered with charred and preserved human flesh.

"Put them on the table. Now, be a good creature and see that my sister comes over here."

The draconian growled and headed toward Dhamon.

"Ragh, I . . ." Dhamon's voice caught in his throat.

"You can have your sword back," the sivak told him. "After you set that damned mirror down over by a bookcase so she can see herself." The draconian gave Dhamon only a passing glance. He was too absorbed in the contents of the room: a pedestal holding a section of a silver dragon's egg, a rack at the far end of the room over which was draped part of the skin of a red dragon. He walked past Dhamon and toward a curio cabinet that displayed claws and eyeballs.

"Ragh."

There was a crash, and the sivak and Maab whirled to see Dhamon lying amid the shattered mirror. He was twitching, his face and hands cut from the glass, his skin pink and feverish.

"No!" Maab wailed. "My sister! He's chased away my dear sister!"

The old woman fell to her knees and howled. The sound grew so loud and shrill that glass vials shook in their holders. The sivak dropped Dhamon's sword and threw his hands over his ears, looking behind him for the doorway they had entered through. All he saw were shelves upon shelves of books and artifacts.

The globe of light brightened and changed hue from yellow to orange and now to a red that painted everything with an abyssal glow. The spawn form melted from the sivak, as he could no longer concentrate on retaining it.

The air grew hot and dry, and breathing became very difficult.

"My sister!" Maab screeched. "I am all alone without my sister! You chased her away! Now you'll die!"

Ragh's keen hearing picked up other noises, a scrabble of feet above. No doubt whatever was on the street above or in other buildings had overheard the woman's wail and was moving away from the ominous noise. He heard a vial shatter behind him, then another and another. There was a soft patter of mosaic tiles from the ceiling hitting the shaking floor.

Dhamon moaned.

"The shield," Dhamon managed. "Show her the shield, Ragh."

It took a minute for Ragh to realize what Dhamon was talking about and another few minutes for him reach beneath the table and grab the unmarked shield.

Maab's cloak billowed away from her in a blistering hot wind that had arisen from nowhere. Spiderweb-fine white hair stood away from a wrinkled face etched in fury. Her eyes were wide and red now, no longer covered with the blue film, and her wail had changed to an indecipherable string of words. Bony fingers twirled madly in the air, illuminated and distorted by the blood-red orb that was still growing against the ceiling.

Ragh fought his way toward her, struggling through air that had become palpable, so thick he felt as if he were being smothered and baked by it.

"Your sister!" the sivak shouted, his hoarse voice somehow reaching the old woman. "I've found your sister! Look here!"

Instantly the air thinned and the red globe faded to yellow, then to white again and shrank. The old woman was still shaking, fingers smoothing at her thinning hair, as her ice-blue eyes locked onto the mirror-finish shield that Ragh held in front of him.

"My sister," she said, breathing with relief. She struggled to her feet and touched the edges of the shield, moving her face this way and that so she could see her reflection more clearly. She pressed her ear close. "What's that you say, Maab? Oh, you were here all along, I just lost sight of you. Yes, I was wrong to panic. Look at this mess I've made. All this glass to clean up. What? Of course we will tend to that young man's cure first. Come along now."

The old woman shuffled toward Dhamon, who lay so still he might have been dead.

"Can't see him breathe," she muttered. "This trip down here was maybe for nothing."

"Dhamon is breathing," the sivak told her. "Barely."

She waggled her fingers at Ragh and pointed to the table with the slate top. "Put him on that. Mind yourself that you don't get cut on all that glass."

The sivak slipped the shield on his right arm and balanced Dhamon over the other shoulder.

She kept an eye on her reflection for a moment more, then scurried away, plucking down a few more books and searching through the bone tubes until she found an especially thick one that was blackened on one end.

"Raistlin's gift to me and my dear sister," she whispered.

She hurried back to the table, which was long enough that Dhamon was laid out straight on it, her books arranged in a semicircle around his head. As she thumbed through them, the pages flaked at the edges. The thinnest volume, one bound in green dragonskin, was plagued by wormholes.

"The bugs ate too many of the good words," she said, discarding the book and reaching for another. "Ah, this one should do."

The sivak looked over her shoulder. Despite all his years on Krynn, Ragh had never learned to read, but he was curious about what she was doing. She elbowed him away, making sure she could still see her reflection.

"You must help Dhamon," Ragh entreated.

"Compassion for a human. Odd in your kind."

"I don't care a wit for him," the sivak shot back. "I just want him cured. I am certain he will help me slay the naga. Nura Bint-Drax. You will tell me about her after you are finished, yes?"

"And if for some reason I can't help your friend?" Maab wondered aloud.

"I will take his sword and find her, fight her alone. Maybe that is what I should be doing now anyway. Tell me what you know about Nura Bint-Drax."

She shook her head. Her hair floated like a halo. "One creature against the naga that slithers through the dragon's swamp? You haven't a prayer, beast. No. I'll not tell you now. Maybe I won't tell you ever. You have nothing to pay us."

The sivak propped the shield against a bookcase, angled toward the old woman so she could glance at it.

"Then I'll die trying to find and slay her."

"You exist for revenge," she cackled lightly. "My sister says life has little meaning to a sivak without wings. Is she right?"

For the next few hours Ragh dozed lightly as Maab continued to page through the books, making notes in the air with her fingers and mumbling softly in an odd language. When he woke she was standing on one of the old sea chests, though she shouldn't have been able to tug it from beneath the table given her size and age. Several small ceramic bowls were lined up by Dhamon's side, each filled with a different colored powder. One was filled with what looked on first inspection, to be beads but that revealed themselves to the sivak as tiny lizard eyes. There was a small jar filled with a viscous green liquid and near it the curled foot of a raven. The draconian shook his head. Long ago he had decided that the trappings of a wizard were unfathomable.

He watched her arrange the materials, consult a few pages that had fallen out of a book, then look over her shoulder at the shield.

"We are ready, sister." To the draconian, she added, "You'll have to rip his leggings for me. I don't have much strength in my hands any more."

The sivak did not reply but slid a talon along the fabric and tore it from ankle to hip, revealing Dhamon's scales.

"Looks black to me," Maab said. She was looking at her reflection in the scales. "From a black dragon."

"It was from a red dragon."

"I heard you—and him—the first time," she said. "Mad, the both of you are. Still, it doesn't matter what color the dragon was. This should do it." She let out a deep sigh, like fall leaves chasing each other across the dry ground.

"Magic was so easy before. You could so easily see the energy in the air, in the ground, feel it wrap around you like a blanket at night. Not much left anymore, my dear sister, but with Raistlin's gift we might find just enough to help this young man. Mind, we will charge him exorbitantly for our services."

The sivak stepped back, watching as she poured one powder after the next over Dhamon's leg, mumbling the entire time. She paused, took a handful of the lizard eyes, and popped them in her mouth before continuing with her ritual until not an inch of skin or scale could be seen beneath the colorful mixture.

"Exorbitantly," she cackled, as she reached for the pages and began reading, the paper magically dissolving as she went. When there was nothing left of it, she snatched up the bone tube and thumbed the end off, tilting it so something slid into her palm.

The sivak stared at it. The thing was a hunk of jade the size of a large plum, carved in the shape of a frog. Its eyes were holes through which a leather thong was strung. She put it over her head, and it dangled down almost to her waist. The sivak moved around to the other side of the table for a better look.

Maab was talking again, rapidly, only a few words of which were discernible: Lunitari, Solinari, Nuitari, the moons no longer present in Krynn's skies; Black Robes; Malys; Sable; and names that meant nothing to the sivak. As she continued to prattle, the frog on her neck pulsed as if it was breathing. As the sivak stared, he saw its legs move, its head swivel. The jade carving's mouth opened and bit through Maab's robe until it had made a hole. It burrowed through it and into her skin, disappearing inside of her, leaving behind only the dangling leather thong. Within seconds, the wound made by the object healed over and the fabric magically mended itself.

"I feel the magic deep in my belly," she murmured. "It moves to my heart."

Beneath the old woman's hands, Dhamon began to stir.

"I feel power in Raistlin's gift. Already some of the dragon-poison is leaving your friend, moving far away."

Dhamon's body was on the table, but his mind was far away from this underground wizard's laboratory and far from this town. He saw himself in a forest south of Palanthas, fighting a Knight of Takhisis—and he was winning. Several Knights lay around him, slain by him and his companions. One man was the only enemy remaining. Dhamon's heart pumped with the exhilaration of battle, and his swings were precise, honed from years in the Dark Knights and then under the tutelage of an old Solamnic who had saved his life. A few strokes more and he severely wounded the man. A minute later and he knelt at the dying man's side. Dhamon held his enemy's hand and offered comfort during those last breaths of life. He was rewarded when his enemy tugged a blood-red dragon scale from his chest and thrust it on Dhamon's thigh.

The pain overwhelmed him, while at the same time a dragon filled his vision, red and so powerful that she took control of his mind and body. She let him think he had beaten her for a time, holding herself in the back of his mind, waiting for the right opportunity to reassert herself. That time came when he was in Goldmoon's presence and the Red ordered him to slay the famed healer. Dhamon almost succeeded, but Rig and Jasper, Feril and others did their best to try to stop him—and succeeded.

Other dragons flitted across his feverish mind—a mysterious shadow dragon who pinned Dhamon beneath an immense claw, and a silver dragon. Both worked to break the Red's control. His mind drifted back to the laboratory, seeming to perch on the ceiling and survey all that was below, including himself.

He watched the mad old woman hover over his body, drawing designs in the powders she had spread on his leg. It was an odd sensation, watching the woman, glancing across this old laboratory, spying the sivak. Dhamon felt pain, not from what she was doing, but from the alternating jolts of hot and cold that speared him. Other images superimposed themselves over Maab—the Knight of Takhisis who cursed him with the scale, Malys, and the shadow dragon, who grew larger and darker. Its body became black, its eyes a dull, glowing yellow.

His chest felt tight, as if he were being squeezed in a vise, and his breathing became ragged. He heard a voice intrude on his pain, a hoarse whisper. The sivak.

"Will he live? Will he be cured?"

"Too early to tell," Maab said. "My spell is not complete, and it has not yet broken through the magic that curses him. See, some of the smaller scales have vanished. Let us hope my sister and I are successful. Let the spell continue. We have decided on a price for our assistance."

The visions of the shadow dragon and the Red faded, the lab turned to darkness, and Dhamon felt his mind sucked back into a feverish body that could not move. All he saw through closed eyelids was a muted light from the glowing orb on the ceiling. All he heard was his heart pounding in his ears.

Maab sat on the old sea chest next to Dhamon's table. She stared at the draconian, who sat on the floor and stared back. The frog had returned to its place on the leather thong. Ragh held the sword in front of him, the pommel a little too small to fit comfortably in his hand. He dropped his gaze to the blade and saw part of his visage reflected back at him. "The naga, old woman," he said. "Nura Bint-Drax. What do you know of her? Do you know where I can find her?"

Several minutes passed before the old woman broke the silence. "I know Nura Bint-Drax. I met the naga years ago, when my sister did not insist that I stay at her side. I found her rude. Too bad that she is expected in town tomorrow. I am certain she is still . . . bad-mannered."

"Nura Bint-Drax," the sivak pressed. "Where can I find her when she returns?"

When Maab would not answer, the sivak made a move toward the wall, selecting a spot between two book cases, Maab sliding off the chest and shuffling after him.

"This is where we came in. I know it."

"Creature, you are not going anywhere. Your human companion—"

"Yes, I will wait for him," Ragh said. "Hurry and finish your spell. I grow tired of this. I want his help in slaying the naga. He is surprisingly formidable for a human."

He felt about on the wall. "Finish the spell, will you?"

"It is almost finished. A few minutes more, and he will be free of all of the scales—even the large one. For sorceresses of my sister's and my ability, the dragon-magic was not so difficult to counter after all."

"You can send him out into the hall when it is through." The draconian's fingers found a seam.

"I said you're not going anywhere, beast."

The sivak turned. Maab was only a few feet away, one bony hand set against her hip, the other gesturing in the air. The nails of two of her fingers glowed a pale green.

"I've decided on a price for curing the human—and that price is you. Creature, you'll make a fine servant. Better than the ones who scurry around my castle. Strong. Smart, judging by the way you talk. The human must relinquish his well-trained pet. My sister likes you—she just told me so. We've decided that you are my price for curing Dhamon."

The glow spread to her other fingers, then her entire hand picked up a sickly green hue that edged up her arm and disappeared into her sleeve.

"I'll be no one's slave ever again," the sivak hissed.

"Sorry, creature. You'll be mine. It will not be so bad. You can catch my sister big, plump rats."

Ragh moved so quickly he caught the sorceress off guard, bringing the sword up and around with all of his strength behind it. The sword bit into her neck at the same time the green glow spread from her fingers and toward the sivak. Ragh dropped to a crouch, the blade slicing all the way through and lopping her head from her shoulders. A green haze hung suspended just above his own head and he crawled out from under it.

"I hate sorcerers," he muttered, as he wiped the blade off on her moth-eaten cloak. "So much so that I won't take on your form, old woman. Old dead woman. You were not so powerful after all. Just mad."

The sivak moved to the sea chest and opened it, finding it empty. He stuffed the body and head inside and put the jade frog around his own neck. Hurriedly he cleaned up the blood, then remembered the shield.

"Dear sister, you might as well keep her company."

319

He laid the shield on top of the body and slid the chest beneath Dhamon's table, then returned to the wall. He was careful not to touch the green haze but tried to find the mechanism that might open the hidden door.

"It feels as if an elephant stepped on my head."

Ragh whirled to see Dhamon sitting up on the table, clothes and skin streaked with a rainbow of colors from Maab's mixtures. His face was flushed and shiny, a reminder of his fever, and he looked gaunt from his ordeal. He took a few deep breaths and shook his head, his tangled hair flying away from his face.

"How are you feeling?"

"Like that same elephant also sat on my chest. I'd feel better if you returned my sword."

He gingerly swung his legs over the edge of the table, knocking a few of Maab's bowls off and wincing as they crashed loudly on the stone floor. "Still hear better than I should," he mumbled. "About the scale . . ."

Dhamon closed his eyes and let out a deep breath. When he opened them he looked at his leg and began brushing at the colorful powders and sand. They were wet and gritty, and it took some work to remove them.

There was one large scale beneath. The smattering of smaller scales were gone.

Dhamon stared at his skin and choked back a sob. "I should have known there is no cure," he said. "I should have known."

"That is why she left . . . with her sister," the sivak said. "She feared you would be angry that she could not help you. She said she was hungry for her rats."

Dhamon prodded his leg. It was tender where the smaller scales had been. "At least she managed something," he muttered. His breath caught in his throat, and he tipped his head back. "I should have known not to have hoped. This was all wasted. I should have—"

"I am still hoping," the sivak interrupted, "that as long as we are here in town, we can find and slay Nura Bint-Drax."

Dhamon slid off the table and strode toward the sivak, hand outstretched. "I want her dead as much as you, but I'm not going after her. I need to find Mal. First we both need to get out of here."

It was with some reluctance that Ragh relinquished the sword. Dhamon was quick to sheathe it.

"Let's see if we can find our way up to the street. I wonder how late it is?"

Dhamon looked around the room, noting a fading green haze and the globe of light on the ceiling that was becoming dimmer and freeing the shadows from their corners.

Dhamon walked past the sivak and to a gap between bookcases. His fingers prodded the bricks until he found one that moved. The wall swung open, and he stepped into the narrow corridor beyond. He glanced back at Ragh. "Coming?"

CHAPTER TWENTY-TWO
TWISTS AND TURNS

hamon stared down the corridor. It looked different somehow than when they'd followed it to the laboratory, not curved, but angular and narrower in places. The air smelled different, too. There was no trace of the wildflowers as there had been when the old woman was present. Instead, the air was heavy and damp.

Perhaps they'd exited through a different spot than they'd entered the laboratory. He turned to find the wall had closed shut behind him. Fingers working across the stone, neither he nor the sivak could locate a way to reopen the section.

"You should have made the sorceress wait until I woke up," he told the sivak.

"She would not listen to me," the sivak said sullenly.

Dhamon let out a deep sigh and started down the corridor. They passed torch after torch, each held by a different wall-sculpture: one an elephant, the torch serving as a trunk, another a baboon. There were several creatures to which they could not put names. They walked for several hundred yards without speaking a word. Dhamon briefly wondered if each sconce was linked to a secret door that led to chambers filled with Maab's treasures or Sable's minions. In another lifetime he might have wanted to explore, especially if Mal had been with him. Now all he wanted was to find a way out.

"Should've had Mal come in here with us," he said to the sivak.

They traveled, Dhamon suspected, half a mile, but did not come to any other corridor. Nor did they find a stairway that would take them back into Maab's tower. Dhamon's ire at the situation was growing, but he did his best to keep it in check—it wasn't the sivak's fault they were lost or that the old, mad woman had disappeared.

"Here," the sivak stated several minutes later. He stopped in front of a sconce that looked like the head of a snub-nosed alligator. "I feel air coming from a crack here."

Dhamon stared at the sculpture, then at the wall on either side of it. He spotted cracks around two of the bricks, flaws he wouldn't have noticed before his senses became unnaturally acute. Concentrating, he felt the play of air across his skin. The scent was still oppressive but different. He picked up a faint odor of blood and of human waste. They'd not smelled this on their way down.

"We can't still be under her tower," Dhamon mused to himself.

"No," the sivak answered. "We've traveled too far. In what direction?" He shrugged his wide shoulders.

"West, I think," Dhamon said, stepping forward and pressing on the bricks, watching as a narrow section of wall slid away to reveal a corridor partially filled with stagnant water. "Let's just get out of here."

There were no torches in this corridor, though Dhamon suspected that at one time there had been. Elaborate sconces lined the wall, all bearing the visages of dwarves of various nationalities. He tugged the torch out of the alligator's snout and curiously passed his hand near the flame. As he suspected, it did not give off heat. He brushed by the draconian and edged his foot forward. There were stairs beneath the water. He followed them until he found the corridor floor, the cool, foul water rising to his waist.

They moved quietly, traveling for a few hundred yards before the tunnel branched to the right and left. Dhamon looked over his shoulder. There was a word scrawled in black on the brickwork to the right. "Sorrows" it read. The "s" curved round to make an arrow.

"To the right then," Dhamon said without hesitation. He could smell the cloying sweet odor of death in that direction, and he could smell nothing but the heavy dampness in the other. Dhamon followed this course only a short way before he climbed more submerged steps that took him into another winding corridor, this one relatively dry. Unfortunately, it dead-ended after another hundred yards.

"Wonderful," he growled. "We're a pair of rats in a maze." He made a move to retrace his steps, then thought better of it. The smell of death hung heavy here, and it had to be coming from somewhere. He passed the torch to Ragh. There were more tiny cracks around two bricks, and he could hear faint hissing voices on the other side of the wall. It sounded like a pair of spawn in the middle of a heated discussion. He drew his sword and pressed on the bricks. The wall pivoted, and he stepped through, coming face to snout with a surprised spawn. Without hesitation, Dhamon drove his sword forward and was greeted with a splash of acid that burned at his clothes and skin. The other speaker, a slightly smaller spawn, retreated down the corridor.

"Oh no," Dhamon warned. "You're not going to get help or sound an alarm." He sped behind it, feet slapping against the damp stone floor, then he thrust out the sword, skewering the spawn in the back where its wings joined. The creature cried out, turned and lunged, but Dhamon was faster, dropping beneath its outstretched claws and bringing the sword up to slice deep into its abdomen. The spawn shuddered and then dissolved in a burst of acid, just as Dhamon leaped back.

The sivak edged into the next corridor behind Dhamon, holding the torch out. There were other torches here, guttering fat-soaked ones hanging from iron holders spaced evenly along the walls. These torches gave off scent and heat and illuminated a ghastly site. Dhamon had entered a hallway lined with cells that were crowded with both emaciated prisoners and rotting corpses.

"By the Dark Queen's heads, where are we?" Dhamon breathed.

The sivak cautiously moved up. "Dungeons are found throughout Sable's swamps. Some are Sable's. Some belong to humans who believe they hold some measure of power here. Though horrid, these cells offer us good news—surely we will find stairs and a way to the surface now."

Dhamon sheathed his sword and tested the bars of the closest cell, finding them too sturdy for even his considerable strength.

"You can't think to free these people. Look at them."

Indeed, Dhamon looked closer. None of those in the first several cells would live beyond the next few days. They'd been either starved nearly to death or beaten so severely that moving them would only hasten their demise. Despite that, he tried the bars one more time.

"You're no hero," the draconian told him. "Why are you bothering?"

I used to be, Dhamon thought. I used to be Goldmoon's champion, and I used to care about things beyond myself.

Aloud, he said. "What could they possibly have done to deserve this?"

The sivak offered no answer.

Dhamon hesitated for a moment, deciding whether to retreat back through the hidden passage and take the other fork, the one where he could smell nothing. A trace of a familiar voice stopped him. He hurried farther down the corridor, again drawing the sword.

"Dhamon? Dhamon Grimwulf?"

"Aye," he said, standing in front of another cell and peering between the bars. "Why does my life seem so intertwined with yours?"

Beyond were a dozen more prisoners and an equal number of dead. Among the prisoners were Rig and Fiona.

"Aye, Rig. It's me."

They looked beaten, and not just physically. There was no life left in their eyes. Fiona's skin looked as pale as parchment. Rig had lost a considerable amount of weight, and his clothes hung on him.

"You've got a sivak . . . !"

"Time for answers later," Dhamon said, as he passed the sword to the sivak. He braced himself, gripped the bars of the door, and pulled. Despite his strength, the bars did not budge. He tried to bend the most rusted bars, throwing all his effort into it, muscles bunching, jaw clenching. The veins on his neck and arms stood out like thick cords. When the bars did not yield to his first attempt, Dhamon strained harder. Finally he was rewarded with the groan of metal.

"Dhamon," growled the sivak. "you are not a hero. Think of yourself."

"Maybe I've been doing a little too much of that lately."

"Listen," Ragh continued. "Do you hear—"

"Aye, I can hear them. More spawn're coming," Dhamon returned.

"Or draconians," the sivak said. "You'd best hurry. Free them quickly or let's move on."

Dhamon took a deep breath and forced the bars again. The effort caused motes of white to dance behind his closed eyes. The metal moved just enough. Prisoners slipped through into the corridor. Dhamon spun on the draconian and grabbed his sword, looking past the people and down both ways of the corridor.

"Hurry," Dhamon urged them. "We're going to have company very soon."

Rig helped Fiona out. She was so weak he half-carried her.

"Thanks," Rig muttered. "I never thought I'd be so glad to see you again. I thought we were going to die in there."

"We still might die," the sivak shot back. "Look." He gestured with a claw down the corridor, then brushed by the mariner and Fiona to stand shoulder to shoulder with Dhamon.

"You might want to be a hero," Ragh told Dhamon through clenched teeth. "All I want is the naga. I don't want this."

A particularly large spawn had spotted the entourage and was charging down the corridor, webbed feet slapping against the damp stone. Holding his sword like a lance, Dhamon rushed to meet the spawn. Carried forward by its momentum and stupidity, it was unable to stop in time and impaled itself. Dhamon backed up quickly, bumping into Fiona and Rig and avoiding the burst of acid.

"I didn't think I ever wanted to see you again," the Solamnic Knight said to Dhamon, "but somehow I knew you'd come here to help us." She gave him a slight smile.

There was the sound of a rainwater barrel crashing over and another burst of acid, signaling another dead spawn, courtesy of Ragh.

"Dhamon, how did you find us?" Rig asked. "How did you know we'd been captured?" The mariner's overly large clothes were in tatters, torn by what were probably the claws of the spawn. His skin bubbled from acid scars. He had a deep gash on his forearm, and on his neck was a thick ropey scar that glistened pink in the torchlight. Fiona seemed wan and small without her plate mail. Her face was scarred on the left side. Both of them were breathing raggedly. "How'd you even know we were here?" the mariner persisted.

"I wasn't looking for you," Dhamon said finally. "I didn't know you'd been captured. Frankly, I don't care how you came here. I was here looking for . . . something." He waved them along the corridor, eyes flitting down alcoves hoping to find stairs. They passed into a large open area. There were no torches here, though there were elaborate empty sconces.

"Rig, grab a torch from back in the hall, will you?"

The mariner was quick to comply and passed out a few more torches to the freed prisoners. "Looking for what?"

A narrowed look told the mariner not to ask again.

"Trappers caught us," Fiona said. "We saw their campfire after we'd left you and Maldred at the silver mine. It looked like they were only trapping animals."

"The four-legged kind," Rig interjected.

"We relaxed our guard, and they took us. They captured others on the way here. I think we've been down here for . . . I don't know how long. Weeks. A month or more. We had no idea what they were going to do to us. If you hadn't come along and . . ."

"They would have let you die, from the looks of it," the draconian said, eyeing the pair of them and the other freed prisoners who were scrambling alongside them. "Or turned you into spawn when your wills were completely broken."

Rig worked to keep up with Dhamon. "There are prisoners everywhere down here. You and I, we can free them and—"

329

"You and I," Dhamon said tersely, "can get out of here with our skins intact. We can't free the town, Rig. You're loose only because I'd lost my way down here. Maldred's somewhere in the city above. I've got to reach him, and then he and I will be leaving this place very far behind."

The mariner's eyes grew wide. "All these people, Dhamon."

"I sympathize," Dhamon said. "I feel for them. I'm not so entirely heartless that I'm not affected by this." He sped up his pace, the others behind him hurrying to keep up. "But I won't risk my life saving theirs."

"The draconian," Rig said after another hundred yards had passed. "What's that about?"

"Revenge," Dhamon replied. "Ragh is about revenge."

They fell silent as they made their way down one corridor and up the next, sometimes passing cages that contained prisoners, and sometimes passing by cages that contained rotting corpses and skeletons that had been picked clean by rats. At one cell the bars were so rusted that Dhamon gave them a quick yank, and they broke, spilling forth a half-dozen men who could barely walk. They clung to each other and to the walls for support, mumbling their disbelieving thanks.

"What about the others?" one man demanded. "The other cells."

"Fiona and I will be back for them," Rig said. "When we've weapons and armor and Solamnic Knights."

Dhamon passed by two other cells, the bars of which were more rust than iron. These, too, he tugged open, then continued on his way without a word.

The freed prisoners, nearly thirty now, were a diverse lot. Some were obviously knights—of Solamnia and the Legion of Steel by the ragged tabards they wore. Others, by their sun-weathered skin and calloused hands, looked like farmers or fishermen. They ranged in age from men barely out of boyhood to in their late fifties. The youngest and fittest said they had been told they were to be made into spawn soon. They stank of sweat and urine, and many had festering sores that were in need of attention. A couple of men, who looked so fit it was obvious they had not been held long, carried an injured comrade between them.

Equal numbers of men were left behind because they were dying or too injured to walk or because Dhamon made no effort to tug at the bars. Rig made it clear as he passed that he would do all in his power to come back for as many as he could.

The odors were intense, especially to Dhamon's acute senses, and he fought to keep from retching.

"Move faster," he said to no one in particular. "Move or be left behind to rot here."

They reached a corridor that dead-ended, and Rig was about to motion the entourage to turn around when Dhamon stopped him.

"There's an air current here."

Dhamon felt the bricks. He pressed two of them, and the wall swung open. He and Ragh quickly slipped into the corridor beyond, the others following.

"We're going to have company again," Dhamon told the sivak. His sharp hearing told him so. Up ahead were the faint sibilant hisses of spawn. There were only two, and in a few moments they were puddles of acid on the floor.

The next tunnel they took was dry and musty. The ceiling was filled with spider webs that were brushed aside by the sivak's head. They followed it for the better part of an hour as it wove and doubled back. They passed countless magical torches set in sculpted sconces.

"I can't be sure of the direction any longer," Dhamon told the sivak, "but it feels as if we're traveling north.

And . . ." There was a hint of fresh air reaching Dhamon. It was coming from a crevice in the wall. He quickly squeezed through, motioning the others to follow.

Several minutes later, they entered a moss-lined cave. The few torches the men carried didn't shed enough light to reach to all the walls, but the light one man held showed another crevice, this one wider and filled with steps going up. Without a word, Dhamon led them, listening closely, hoping to hear what might lie ahead and instead picking up only the slapping of feet against the steps behind him.

Dhamon found a lone spawn at the top. He rushed forward, swinging before it could react. Two quick blows finished it, acid spraying into a cell full of corpses. Now they entered another corridor, this one easily twenty feet across. More cells opened off it, though all but the one filled with corpses were empty.

"Move."

Dhamon headed past the cells and through a door he spotted at the end, rushing up another flight of the steps, pausing only long enough to make sure the others were following. He came to another dead end, but the cracks in the bricks were easy to spot, now that he knew what to look for. He listened before pressing them, hearing nothing beyond. The wall swivelled open onto another twisting passage, one barely three feet wide. He rushed through, calling for the others to keep up.

They continued to travel the tunnels for nearly an hour before they found themselves in a corridor covered with small glossy black scales—just like the trees had been in the spawn's village. Dhamon reached a hand up to touch them. They felt sleek, as if they belonged to something alive.

"In the name of the Maelstrom," Rig whispered.

Dhamon increased his pace. The tunnel rose and doubled back, dipped sharply, then rose again.

"Stairs," he said, letting out a breath of relief. These were wooden and stretched up to reveal the night sky. "We're out."

The freed prisoners gained energy with his words, and within minutes they were all up the stairs and standing in the ruins of what might have been a temple in decades past. Stars winked down.

"Ragh, just where in this damned city are we?"

The sivak poked his head out from behind a crumbling column to get his bearings. "Not far from the market. I suspect we've been going in circles."

"So tired," Fiona whispered to Rig. "My legs." She was leaning against him, hair plastered from sweat against the sides of her face.

Dhamon stepped out onto the street. The city looked different at night, when the darkness hid much of its ugliness. He saw no one out and guessed by the position of the stars it was well past midnight. Dawn was only a few hours away. He crossed the road and started down a wood sidewalk, stopping when he spotted something familiar—the dwarven merchant's. The marketplace was only a few blocks away, and near it the inn where he could find Maldred.

He hurried back to the sivak and the others, and, rubbing his hands on his pants, he addressed the freed prisoners.

"I can't tell you what to do," he began. "We're near the center of town. I suggest all of you leave, climb the rise, and keep going until you run out of swamp."

"I know the safest way out." This from a grizzled, middle-aged man. "I was a guard here, before I fell out of favor. To the east is a path no one watches."

Dhamon nodded.

"Take it, them, and everyone else with you. Rig, Fiona, you go, too. You're not in any condition to follow me. I've Maldred to find, and then I'm leaving, too."

"Even if saving us was an accident, I'm grateful for it." The mariner extended his hand, and Dhamon shook it.

Dhamon moved away, the sivak on his heels, running where the shadows were thickest, heading toward the ramshackle inn past the marketplace. The freed prisoners mirrored their course, though not moving as quickly and taking the other side of the street. Dhamon watched the grizzled man lead them.

Just as the marketplace came into view, Dhamon saw the man lead them down a side street to the east. Overhead Dhamon heard the flap of wings, and glanced up to see a spawn flying overhead. Against the stars he saw other shapes, spawn or draconians patrolling the city.

"The inn," Ragh announced, stopping at the end of the sidewalk and pointing beyond the market's collection of cages. A few lights burned in the lowest windows. There were a few lights elsewhere, too, but not near the number Dhamon expected for a town of this size.

He started toward the inn but stopped at the line of cages. The hair prickled on the back of his neck.

"Something's not right," Dhamon whispered.

"In this town," the sivak whispered back, "nothing is right."

"No. There's more to it than that." Dhamon scanned the cages. A few of the creatures were sleeping, curled tightly in their close confines. Some were awake. The gold-flecked eyes of the huge owl were wide and watchful. The manticores were awake, too, the larger looking Dhamon's way. Two spawn patrolled the market—on this side. Dhamon suspected there were more.

"Something. Maybe something is watching us, maybe . . ."

His words trailed off when he heard a high-pitched wail. It was coming from the direction the freed prisoners had gone.

A glance skyward. The spawn and draconians were out of sight. He still heard the flap of wings, however, and the sound of pounding feet and desperate shouts.

"The men you freed have been discovered," the sivak said. "We had best hide or we will be hunted, too."

Dhamon didn't budge, still watching the sidestreet the slaves had slipped down. He caught a glimpse of a skinny, barely dressed man, one of the last he'd released from the cells. Rig and Fiona were just in front of him, the mariner shouting for everyone to stay together. Fiona called to them to look about for anything they could use as weapons. Though there was only little light from the stars and from a few windows, Dhamon could see the panic on Fiona's face.

"We have to hide," the sivak said louder. He gave Dhamon a poke with a claw for emphasis.

Behind and above the freed men were a dozen spawn and sivak draconians.

"They'll be butchered," Dhamon breathed.

"Yes, and we will too, if we don't—"

Dhamon unsheathed his sword. Rather than running toward Rig and Fiona, he hurried to the marketplace cages, meeting the charge of the two spawn guards he'd seen. The sivak follwed several paces behind him, demanding he come to his senses.

"You're no good to me dead!" Ragh snapped. "You can't help me against Nura Bint-Drax if they catch you."

Dhamon threw his strength behind a sideways sweep of his blade, practically cutting the first spawn in half. He continued on to the second target as the first dissolved in a burst of acid. Two swings this time before the spawn went down, neither creature quick enough to land a blow against Dhamon.

He rushed to the pens, raising the sword high over his head and bringing it down on the chain that held the nearest door closed. The metal link parted from the blow, and Dhamon sheathed the sword, fingers fumbling to tug the chain free, then arms bunching to tug open the massive door. A second later, an angry six-legged lizard the size of an elephant trundled out.

It was followed by other grotesqueries that Dhamon freed, using his strength to pull at the cage doors now, rather than risk breaking his only weapon.

"What are you doing?" the sivak cried. "Have you gone mad?"

"Guards!" someone shouted. "The menagerie is getting loose! Guards!"

Overhead the flurry of wings increased. From all directions came shouted orders—the voices of spawn and of men who'd thrown their lot in with the dragon and her allies. From well beyond the marketplace came the pounding of feet—other guards Dhamon suspected.

"What are you doing, Dhamon?"

"I'm providing a distraction, Ragh, giving the spawn something to worry about other than a few dozen escaped prisoners. Maybe some of them, maybe Rig and Fiona, can get free of this Abyss."

The sivak fell to helping Dhamon with the cages, muttering all the while this would be the death of them.

"Keep this up," Dhamon told him. "You're strong, pull the bars open. I'm going to find Mal, then we're going to get out of here."

"Nura . . ." the spawn croaked.

"Nura Bint-Drax isn't my worry, but you're welcome to stay until she shows up. I'm not going to help you with her, Ragh."

Dhamon rushed toward the inn, barreling his way through the door. He woke the proprietor, who'd been sleeping in a straight-backed wooden chair behind a stained and pitted desk.

"Maldred. A big man named Maldred got a room here this afternoon." Dhamon paused to catch his breath.

The proprietor stared at him, eyeing him up and down.

Dhamon's clothes and hair were slick against him from sweat, and he was riddled with acid burns. He stank of the corridors below, and his features were streaked with dirt.

"A man named Maldred," Dhamon repeated with urgency. "A big man. What room?"

The innkeeper shook his head. "No one with that name. No one who looks like that is here."

"Earlier today," Dhamon's words came faster, and he glanced toward the street. The sounds of chaos were growing louder.

The innkeeper heard the ruckus, too, and pushed himself to stand, craning his neck and looking out the open door. "I'd know if a man like that had checked in. Been here all day. I'm always here all day."

He lumbered away from the desk and to the door so he could get a better look.

Dhamon ran to the stairway and shouted. "Mal!" he roared, loud enough to rouse the people on the floor above. "Maldred!"

There was no response.

With a growl, he hurried by the innkeeper back out to the street. Madness greeted him. Spawn and draconians were on the ground, trying to contain both the creatures escaping from the pens and the prisoners, whom the spawn had inadvertently herded to the marketplace. Rig and Fiona were using slats of woods for weapons, trying to defend the weakest of the weaponless men. He didn't see Ragh, though that didn't surprise him. He suspected the wingless draconian slipped away and would hide until he found Nura Bint-Drax.

Dhamon raced toward the menagerie cages. A few were still closed. These contained the beast that looked like a horrid cross between an eagle and a bear. Another held the massive manticores. The latter creatures were alternately watching him and watching the battle. Dhamon raised his sword as he neared the cage, brought the blade down hard on the chain, and prayed the sword wouldn't break.

"I'll free you!" he shouted, "and you can fly away from this hell. But you'll fly me with you, understand? And as many men there as you can carry."

"Please," the larger repeated, "free."

"You'll take us out of here with you?"

The creatures nodded. Three more blows before a link was severed. A heartbeat later and he had the chain off, opening the cage door and motioning the creatures out.

They spread their wings and beat them, a keening sound grew louder, almost painful. The spawn covered their ears, quickly followed by the freed men. Dhamon clamped his teeth together. The noise was agonizing.

Free from the confines of their cages, the manticores joined in the fray. Leaning forward on their front paws, they launched a volley of spikes from their long tails. The barbs found their marks in more than one draconian target.

"Rig!" Dhamon shouted when he again spotted his old comrade. He waved wildly to get the mariner's attention. "Grab Fiona! Now! We're leaving!"

He glanced about, hoping to spot Maldred. He could not see through the press of bodies and creatures, and he could not hear over the keening sound of the manticore's wings.

"Can't see."

But from a higher vantage point he might.

In a heartbeat he was at the larger manticore's side, grabbing onto its hide and pulling himself up. Careful not to skewer himself on the spikes that ran along its back, he stood on the creature's shoulderblades and looked out over the jumble of creatures and men.

Nearly half of the men Dhamon had freed were dead to the spawn and draconians. Rig and Fiona were fighting their way toward the manticores, bringing some of the survivors with them.

A pair of bozak draconians wrestled with the six-legged lizard, which had its tongue snaked like a lasso about the waist of a spawn. Lights were being lit in windows, and Dhamon saw shapes appear in them, none of them broad-shouldered enough to be Maldred.

"Had he been captured? Killed looking for Nura Bint-Drax?" Dhamon spoke the question aloud, though he hadn't meant to.

"Probably he has," said a spawn that was climbing onto the back of the other manticore. From his voice, Dhamon recognized him as Ragh. The sivak had obviously killed a black spawn and assumed its shape.

"A hand, Dhamon." Dhamon barely heard the words amid the cacophy. It was Rig, passing up an emaciated young man. Dhamon grabbed the man's wrists and pulled him up, settled him between two of the manticore's back spikes, and told him to hang on.

"You're next!" Dhamon yelled to Rig. "More guards are coming—human and otherwise. We've got to get out of here."

"Fiona first!" Rig grabbed her about the waist, and she dropped the bloodied plank she'd been wielding. "Take her!"

Dhamon leaned over and scooped her up beneath her arms. She was so light, and her skin was clammy. He settled her right behind him, then motioned Rig to the other manticore. "That's Ragh," he called, "the sivak."

The mariner shook his head but ushered two more men in front of him to the other manticore. He was helping the first up, Ragh assisting, when the second wave of Sable's minions arrived. These were a mix of spawn and men, the latter wielding swords and spears and hurling daggers at anything that looked like it was trying to escape—the freed men and the bizarre creatures particularly.

"Hurry!" Dhamon shouted. He settled himself in front of Fiona, between a pair of spikes, and grabbed two handfuls of manticore hide. "Rig, move! Maldred! Maalllldred!"

The mariner boosted another man up onto the other manticore, which was beating its wings faster now. Rig was nearly knocked off his feet by the force of the wind. He grabbed the manticore and climbed. He had nearly reached the top of the beast's back when a spear found him.

Through the din, Dhamon heard the mariner cry out. He saw a second spear plunge into Rig's back, saw the mariner fall like a broken doll, blood trickling from his mouth, his neck twisted from the fall.

"Rig!"

Fiona looked on in disbelief. "Dhamon?"

"Rig!" Dhamon shouted again, but the mariner didn't move. Dhamon knew he would not move again. He swallowed hard and dug his knees into the manticore's back.

"Fly!" he shouted. "Get us out of here!"

The beasts were quick to comply, each carrying three riders. Fiona tried to scramble off, however, reaching futilely toward Rig. Dhamon had to twist about to grab her and keep her in place.

"Rig," she said, her face ashen, eyes filled with tears. "Rig's down there. I've got to go to Rig."

Dhamon managed to pull her in front of him, holding her tight even as she tried to fight him.

"I've got to go to him," she sobbed. "I love him Dhamon. I have to tell him that I love him." She buried her head in Dhamon's chest as the manticore rose higher. "We're to be married."

"He's gone, Fiona." Dhamon found his own eyes filling with tears. "Rig's gone." He peered one last time over the manticore's side, catching a last glimpse at the mariner's body. He saw spawn swarming around the remaining men, and he saw the bizarre creatures of the menagerie being shoved back into their cages. The curious residents were coming out onto the street now that things seemed a little safer.

Dhamon did not see a young girl standing behind a spire on a nearby roof. She was no more than five or six, with copper-colored hair that fluttered about her shoulders in the breeze.

Nor did Dhamon see another familiar figure, this one stepping from a night-dark doorway only a few dozen yards away from where the fight had broke out. Maldred had watched the scene from the beginning—Dhamon bringing freed men to the surface, helping them by unleashing chaos in the marketplace as a distraction, tugging the Solamnic Knight up onto the back of the manticore. Rig dying. Dhamon now flying away.

He'd watched everything and kept his distance. Done nothing.

He balled his fists, turned back to the doorway, and entered the night-dark room beyond.

Above, a dozen spawn tried to follow the manticores, but the great creatures were too fast and quickly left the swamp-held town behind. Dhamon hugged Fiona with his right arm, and with his left he leaned forward and managed to grab a handful of mane. He tugged on it to get the manticore's attention.

"We need to land," he said, practically shouting. "I need to see to these men here." He did his best to find a clearing that was far enough from the town to suit him.

341

CHAPTER TWENTY-THREE
BETRAYAL

It took Dhamon nearly an hour to bind the wounds on the three men they'd brought with them, using what he could salvage from their clothes and his tunic. Even Ragh helped. They would live, though they needed rest and food. Dhamon vowed to make sure the manticores deposited them somewhere reasonably safe and beyond the swamp. That task handled, he turned to the Solamnic Knight.

Fiona's eyes were dull, emotionless. "Rig," Dhamon began. "I'm sorry about Rig, about him dying. I didn't always get along with him, but he was a good man, Fiona, and—"

"Rig?" She looked up to meet his sad gaze, illuminated by the stars that so faintly winked down in a lightening sky. "We'll see Rig again very soon, Dhamon. We're to be married next month. You'll have to come to the wedding. It will be grand. I'm sure Rig will want you to be there."

Dhamon stared deeper into her eyes and saw madness there.

343

"Rig's dead," Dhamon said patiently.

She laughed eerily. "Don't be silly. Rig's waiting for me, Dhamon. In New Ports, at the harbor. He's going to captain a ferry there. We'll live along the bluff where we have a nice view of the sea. The wedding will be on the shore, I think. Rig will like that. You'll see how good everything will be for us."

Dhamon guided her to the larger manticore, helped her up, then helped up the three men up on the other manticore—he'd never bothered to ask their names. He walked around to the front of the creatures, staring up into its too-human eyes.

"I've another request of you," he said. "Another place to take us. You'll be truly free after that. Though I suppose you can refuse this."

The smaller beast bent its head down to better regard Dhamon.

"Where?" was all it said.

"These men need to be taken to Schallsea Island. There's a community of mystics there who won't turn them away."

Dhamon climbed up behind Fiona on the larger manticore.

"There's a Solamnic fortress in Southern Ergoth," he said, as he grabbed a handful of the creature's mane. "It's very far from here, but it's where Fiona's from. I want to take her there. The other Knights will help her, take care of her. The people there can get word out for me. About Rig's death. Palin Majere should be told, and some others. Will you do this?"

Almost in unison, the great creatures flapped their wings, making the hurtful keening sound again. As one they rose from the clearing and headed west.

 I will return here, Dhamon vowed to himself. I left Maldred somewhere in that foul town. My closest and dearest friend. I will come back for him.

◇ ◇ ◇ ◇ ◇ ◇ ◇

Not far to the east of the town was a massive cave. The darkness inside it was an almost palpable blanket that comfortably cloaked the creature that laired within. Only its breath gave the creature's presence away. Its breath was raspy and uneven and echoed against the stone walls. The breeze teased the copper curls of the child who stood just inside the entrance.

Nura Bint-Drax appeared as a cherubic girl of no more than five or six, clothed in a diaphanous dress that shimmered as though it was made of magic.

"Master?" she said in her child-voice as she came forward. She knew this cave by heart. As she walked her form changed, becoming that of a young Ergothian woman with close-cropped hair. She was clad in a black leather tunic now, one that had once belonged to Dhamon Grimwulf. "Master."

Twin globes of dull yellow appeared in the midst of the blackness, casting just enough light to reveal the creature's massive snout and the dark-skinned woman who was dwarfed by its size. The creature's eyes were larger around than wagon wheels and laced with murky catlike slits. The thick film on them hinted at the beast's age.

"I have finished testing Dhamon Grimwulf," she announced proudly in her temptress voice. "He survived my tests, survived my forces in the town nearby. He is the one. As I am your chosen. Your favorite."

"One of my chosen." The creature corrected, its words interminably long and drawn out, words so loud the ground rumbled with each syllable. "The other arrived just before you."

A sun-bronzed human stepped away from the cave wall, coming close enough so the light from the creature's eyes could reveal him.

345

"Maldred," Nura Bint-Drax hissed.

The ogre mage wearing the guise of a human nodded to her, then turned to face the creature.

"Dragon," Maldred said. "I, too, have tested Dhamon Grimwulf. I agree that he is the one."

"He is the one." The heavy words sent the floor to shaking. "But will he cooperate?" the dragon wondered. It secretly noted with pleasure that Nura and Maldred glared at each other, the hate between them thick and sweet in the air. "Will he do what I require?"

Nura opened her mouth, but Maldred spoke first. "Oh, he'll cooperate," he said evenly. "I can manipulate him into following your plan. I've manipulated him well enough thus far. Like a blind fool, he trusts me. He believes I am his closest friend and ally. He'll be coming back soon to find me. What he has left of his honor demands that."

Satisfied, the dragon closed its eyes, plunging the cave into absolute darkness. Maldred and Nura Bint-Drax waited until the sound of its slumber sent a wave of gentle tremors through the ground, then they left the cave and headed out into the swamp beyond.